Also by T. M. Brown

Sanctuary: A Legacy of Memories, T. M. Brown
Purgatory: A Progeny's Quest, T. M. Brown

TESTAMENT

Share Your Thoughts

Want to help make *Testament* a bestselling novel? Consider leaving an honest review of this book on Goodreads, on your personal author website or blog, and anywhere else readers go for recommendations. It's our priority at SFK Press to publish books for readers to enjoy, and our authors appreciate and value your feedback.

Our Southern Fried Guarantee

If you wouldn't enthusiastically recommend one of our books with a 4- or 5-star rating to a friend, then the next story is on us. We believe that much in the stories we're telling. Simply email us at pr@sfkmultimedia.com.

TESTAMENT
An Unexpected Return

T. M. BROWN

In Irish folklore, a Banshee is a female spirit recognized by a red or green hooded cloak who heralds the impending death of a family member . . .

CHAPTER ONE

"THEO, WAKE UP! MARY'S HERE." LIDDY JOSTLED MY HAMMOCK, DISRUPTING my mid-summer siesta.

Pressed by Cornerstone Publishing, my former employer until eight months ago, the final draft of my expanded manuscript of Jessie's Story rested in the gifted hands of Mary Scribner. Over the past four months, I had holed myself up for hours on end leaving no stone unturned as I combed through dog-eared files and scrawled notes used in writing the articles first published in the Sentinel last December, retelling Jessie Masterson's story.

As Mary exited her sky blue hatchback, I swung my legs onto the floor and stepped beside Liddy at the foot of the steps.

Liddy tendered an approving smile as she smoothed the back of my hair. "That's better," she whispered as she squeezed my waist and added, "Mary's Cheshire Cat smile must be a good sign."

"Theo, I think you'll be happy. Jessie's Story is ready to earn Cornerstone's editorial final blessing. Your rewrites provided the conclusion the entire town will be proud to read." Mary extended the swollen envelope she'd been cradling.

"Thanks, Mary. I couldn't have done this without you." I slid the immaculate manuscript from the envelope.

Liddy chuckled. "Mary, this most certainly looks a far sight better than all those raggedy, yellow legal pads filled with his chicken scratch."

Mary's eyes danced between Liddy and me. "Oh, it wasn't that bad Miss Liddy," she managed to say stifling her giggles.

"Mary, truth told, you don't know how much I've admired your uncanny knack of deciphering and transcribing the maestro's handwritten drafts." Liddy eyed my laughable expression of faked innocence.

Mary attempted to hide her growing smile with her hand. "Miss Liddy, it was my pleasure. Besides, whenever he took exception to any suggestions I offered, he never said anything I hadn't heard my dad spout at work. I enjoyed working with the maestro on this project." She removed her hand, unveiling an amiable grin.

Mary eyed my appreciative stare before she added, "I gotta confess, though, I'm still amazed that you donated all your royalties to support Sanctuary. I just know the pre-Thanksgiving book launch right here in Shiloh will be nothing short of a huge success."

Liddy grabbed Mary's and my elbows and prompted us up the porch steps. Storm clouds overhead infused a whiff of dampness within the increasing Gulf breeze. Liddy excused herself to fetch some sweet tea while Mary and I sat in our porch rockers.

"As good as some rain will feel," Mary said looking skyward, "I sure hope it passes through tonight. When I stopped by Priestly Park to take some photos for the paper, city employees scurried about, sprucing up the grounds and erecting the stage for tomorrow's ceremonies. I even managed a candid shot of Harold Archer surveying the work while sitting behind the wheel of his big old black truck."

I walked up to the porch rail. "Looks to me as though this should blow over pretty quick, and bring temperate breezes from the Gulf tomorrow." I turned and leaned back against the rail scratching my chin. "So you saw Harold behind the wheel of his truck? I haven't seen him out and about much since Hal became mayor. It'll be good to catch up with him tomorrow."

A silly grin rose on my face moments before I noticed Mary in deep thought. "Hey kiddo, having second thoughts about your visit to Cornerstone?"

Mary vacated her mesmerized stare. "Oh, no. Mom's already agreed to cover for me at the office."

"You've earned this trip. And don't forget, Barry and Agnes expect you for lunch, so you best leave first thing Monday morning. They're anxious about your visit and plan to provide you with the nickel tour of the facilities and to introduce you to the staff right after lunch." I paused until she looked up and made eye contact. "If you're still dead set on exploring your career options in Atlanta, this trip might present you with a good beginning. But you know, I still hope a rewarding opportunity manifests right here. Shiloh needs talented, homegrown go-getters like you. And I think your dad needs you too."

Liddy stepped onto the porch juggling our drinks. "Mary, you still contemplating leaving Shiloh?"

"Oh, Miss Liddy, I'm merely considering my options." She reached for a glass and took a sip. "Anyways, this decision isn't as simple as I had figured a few months ago."

Liddy handed me a glass and sat on the other side of Mary. "Is everything okay with your dad and mom?"

Mary navigated the rim of her glass with her index finger. "They're fine. I'm just cogitating over everything. That's why this trip means so much to me."

I glanced beyond Mary toward Liddy and cleared my throat. "Looks like we're in for a good soaking rain this afternoon."

Liddy shifted her attention from Mary still rimming her glass and searched the gray clouds. "Yep, think you're right." Liddy wore a silly smirk as she winked.

The unfamiliar rumble of a truck approaching broke Mary's fixation upon her glass. She peered at Liddy and then me before she left her rocker and approached the porch rail. A moment later, the three of us watched Pete run his fingers through his curly red hair and smooth the tuck of his shirt before he quickstepped up the walkway.

"Hope I'm not disturbing y'all. Mary's mom said she'd likely be here." Pete looked at Mary with puppy dog eyes and a crooked smile before turning his ruddier-than-usual, chiseled face toward Liddy and me. "I've got some news for y'all too." His eyes begged our approving response.

Liddy stood with extended arms prompting Pete to stomp his dirty boots at the foot of the steps. In the midst of Liddy's welcoming embrace, she asked, "What kind of news?"

"Andy's getting back from Waycross tomorrow morning, and he's bringing Megan with him. They particularly inquired if the two of you would be at the Jubilee tomorrow."

"What'd you tell them?" Liddy's emerald eyes prodded Pete's stuttered response.

"I told them as far as I knew you planned on attending. And, before you ask, neither said anything else." Pete shrugged his shoulders and turned his attention to Mary. "Mare, I couldn't wait to show you how my truck turned out." He reached his hand out.

Mary beamed. "Will you excuse us for a minute?"

I chuckled. "Sure, go right ahead."

Pete looked back with a sheepish grin. "Y'all coming? I'd sure like your opinion too." Mary grasped Pete's calloused hand, and we followed them back down the walkway.

I had gotten wind that Pete had been working on his truck the last couple of weeks, and his arrival a few minutes earlier came without the usual clickety-clack and rattling that previously advertised his truck's comings and goings. At the curb, I hardly recognized it with the shiny cherry-red exterior and glistening chrome grill and bumpers. Pete had transformed his former rust bucket into a showroom-ready, classy pickup.

Pete beamed as he opened the passenger door and pointed to the new black leather seat covers and matching vinyl floorboard. A stark contrast to the torn and tattered seats and mud-caked, bare-metal floors that used to haunt his thirty-year-old pickup truck.

Mary and Liddy stood speechless, shaking their heads, until Liddy busted out and said, "Pete, this just cain't be the same ol' beater we've gotten used to you driving around town."

Pete's face dropped. "Miss Liddy, don't you like it?"

"Of course I do. I've just never considered what it'd look like all fixed and gussied up." Liddy spun in my direction with a wrinkled nose and half-grin.

"If you ask me, there's only one rational explanation why a young man, like Pete, would invest all this money and effort to spruce up his prized runabout truck." With my arms crossed and a half-cocked stare, I measured Pete and then Mary.

Mary's cheeks matched Pete's by the time he cleared his throat and said in a fluster, "Mary, you just never mind that ol' coot. What matters to me is what you think?"

Mary sat in the passenger seat and ran her hands across the metal dashboard before grinning at Pete's nervous stare. "I'll let you know after you take me for a spin and promise to drive me to the Jubilee tomorrow."

Liddy poked my side. "Y'all better hurry to take your test drive. These clouds are about to let loose. In fact, this ol' coot and I are headed straight to the porch."

Mary jumped out of the truck. "The dedication ceremony begins at eleven. Come hungry. There will be lots of food followed by all sorts of games and activities throughout the day."

"We'll see you there." I smiled and waved before taking Liddy's hand.

Mary hollered at Pete, "Meet me at my house!"

The first raindrops dotted the street and sidewalks as we stood arm in arm on the porch and watched Pete's and Mary's vehicles disappear.

CHAPTER TWO

THE STORM FRONT BLEW OVER AS PREDICTED, ALLOWING THE SUNSHINE TO break through partly cloudy skies by the time we arrived at Priestly Park. "God Bless the USA" blared over the public address system as we snaked through the growing crowd in search of our friends.

Bob "Bubba" Patterson and Cecil Chambers, owners of Bubba's BBQ, along with Silas Thrope from the Butcher Shoppe, tended twin smokers that filled the air with the mouthwatering aroma of roasted pork. Beneath a red, white and blue canopy, Barbara Patterson, Cora Chambers, and Bernie Thrope readied themselves to sell their husbands' highly anticipated, finger-licking fare.

I surveyed the sea of people until I locked onto Larry Scribner waving his arms. A minute later we set up our chairs between Larry, his wife Martha, and Sam and Susanna Simmons.

Martha snickered. "Would have thought Mary warned you to get here early. The whole town has been abuzz for weeks since the city formally announced the Jubilee's new venue, especially after news got out about the park's dedication ceremony."

Liddy peered at me with a told-you-so sneer followed by a playful punch to my arm when I said to Martha, "Don't blame her. I just didn't expect this kind of turnout, but I'm glad to see it for Harold's sake."

Sam added, "Give poor Theo a break. This crowd is the biggest I recall ever attending a Jubilee. No doubt Harold's vision for Priestly Park intended to give Shiloh's annual Jubilee a shot in the arm." He pointed at the building under construction with its steel skeleton cordoned off by yellow caution tape and bright orange plastic barrels. "Can't wait to see the new community center when it finally opens."

Liddy asked, "Has anyone seen Arnie and Judy? What about Zeb, Marie, and John?"

"Preacher's over behind the grandstand with Judy waiting for the ceremony to get underway," Martha groaned, craning her neck, half-raised from her chair. "And there's Zeb behind the pavilion leaning against his truck shooting the breeze with John and Marie."

"Susanna, where's Andy and Megan?" Liddy asked, scanning the crowd.

Susanna shrugged her shoulders. "Not sure, but they promised they'd be here."

Liddy nudged closer to me and whispered, "Hal just pulled behind the grandstand driving Harold's dually with Harold in the passenger seat and parked beside Phillip's red Wrangler."

Sam jumped from his chair and whistled above the clamor of the crowd. Susanna stood as Andy and Megan appeared making their way around the throng of blankets and chairs.

Megan's relaxed smile, ponytail, and makeup-free, suntanned cheeks presented a welcome contrast to the pretentious, prim and proper young woman we encountered only a few months ago. In place of high heels and glamor, she clung to Andy's elbow wearing green and gold GCU warm-ups and a white cotton tank top. After we all exchanged hugs, Andy and Megan sat down beside Susanna and Sam.

Moments later, the shrill piping of a fife and a rhythmic drum cadence quieted the crowd before a voice barked, "For-ard harch!" Pete, Jay, and Jim marched abreast in step to the lead of the teenage fifer and drummer, all wearing Minutemen costumes. Jay and Jim held shouldered muskets on either side of Pete, who carried the American flag with both hands. The crowd came to its feet as the color guard approached the makeshift stage until Jay shouted, "Color guard, halt!"

Hal Archer stepped to the podium and invited Miss Phoebe Thatcher, the high school's music director, onto the stage to sing the Star Spangled Banner. Arnie Wright followed with a prayer of thanks for our nation, community, and today's Jubilee. Hal then welcomed everyone to Shiloh's one-hundred-and-fifteenth Independence Day Jubilee and added, "Before we enjoy all this scrumptious food and the activities planned this afternoon, I'd like to introduce my father, our Mayor Emeritus, the Honorable Harold Archer."

Harold rose from his seat and gripped the podium to steady himself. His baggy shirt and slacks affirmed rumors of his declining health. His voice cracked as he spoke. "Friends, fellow citizens of Shiloh, first of all, I want to thank you for allowing me the joy of witnessing my son serving as your new mayor. He represents the third generation of Archers to be so honored. But, that'll be enough of that. There's a far better reason I am here today. Would John Priestly and Marie Masterson join me?"

John escorted his cousin Marie onto the stage before Harold continued.

"Last December, I promised the citizens of Shiloh that I would build this park for our city right here on this picturesque site next to Shiloh Creek. I humbly stand before you, proud we're celebrating this year's Independence Day Jubilee on this property my family deeded to the city."

Harold looked back toward the unfinished steel framework and pointed. "And, my son Phillip assured me that the new community center will be open before summer ends." Harold smiled at Phillip who stood beside Jeannie Simmons in front of the stage. "With that assurance," Harold eyed John and Marie by his side, "I now and forever more declare that Priestly Park shall henceforth commemorate the Priestly family's contribution in making Shiloh a better place for our families to prosper."

Harold picked up a plaque off the podium and paused as he cleared his throat. John stepped closer and patted Harold on his back. Harold took a deep breath and slowly exhaled before he continued. "I asked Missus Masterson and Coach Priestly as members of the Priestly family to accept our city's small token of appreciation for all that their family has meant to our community throughout the years." He handed the framed pewter plaque to John. "A larger duplicate of this plaque will be mounted beside the entrance to the Betty Priestly Community Center when it opens in the coming weeks."

Hal returned to the microphone as Harold escorted John and Marie off the stage. He raised his arms to quiet the crowd's applause. "I've been advised that the roasted pigs are about to be carved. Don't forget to check the pavilion bulletin board for times and locations of this afternoon's activities. Otherwise, please enjoy the day at Priestly Park and remember the fireworks will begin right after sunset." Patriotic music returned to the public address speakers as Hal exited the stage.

Pete, still wearing his 1776 Minuteman outfit, appeared moments later with Mary and invited all of us to an area they had staked off near Zeb's truck behind the pavilion. We gathered our chairs and found John and Marie already chatting with Zeb's sons, Jim and Jay. Zeb sat on his tailgate and offered everyone a cold drink from the ice chest in the bed of his truck.

LONG AFTER I confessed to eating way too much, I found myself surrounded by empty chairs. The grunts and moans of the more athletic, younger members of our group drew my attention to their heated volleyball game. Zeb and Sam refereed the match, standing on opposite ends of the net. Liddy and Marie had disappeared earlier to sign up for the annual egg toss, thanks in large part to the persistent goading of Megan and Jeannie. Although Judy, Martha, and Susanna urged me to watch, I opted to catch up with Arnie meandering toward the creek.

"You know we're both missing out on the celebrated egg toss." I leaned down and flung a couple of pebbles into Shiloh Creek. Arnie chuckled and skipped a stone across the surface.

"Hey Arnie, you're closer to Harold. You've known him as his pastor for a long time. Is he going to be okay?"

Arnie reached for another stone and juggled the smooth tawny pebble between his fingers. "Not sure, Theo. Just because I'm his pastor doesn't mean I'm privy to know everything. I know, like you, that second trip to the hospital in January sucked the wind right out of his sails."

"But is it just physical? I've hardly seen him around town since."

"I'm not a doctor, but I believe a broken spirit can be as lethal as any heart attack. And, in Harold's case, he's experienced both. Since his release from the hospital, he's spent every day cooped up in his study. He hardly drives anywhere anymore. In fact, last month when I visited Hank at the county jail I learned Harold hadn't visited him since Hank and Megan's divorce finalized in May." With an extended sigh, Arnie chucked the stone skyward and watched it disturb the water's calm surface.

"He sure looked washed out as he shuffled on and off the stage. I know he's holed himself up in recent months, but I had hoped he'd get better, not worse. I've not reached out to him as I probably should've, but I'm glad you've talked with him."

Arnie gazed at the expanding ripples on the glistening creek's surface. "Theo, I fear Harold's never gonna get better. Even the doctors warned him that his tired ticker needs lots of rest and less stress. But what I am afraid of the most is that he's convinced he failed Hank when he needed him most."

The stone I fumbled with slid through my fingers and fell into the wet sand at my feet. "What can we do to help? He's not been to church since he got out of the hospital either. Maybe Liddy and I should've made a better effort to visit him."

"I'm not sure you and Liddy can do anything more except keep him in your prayers right now. Hal and Phillip keep a close eye on him and . . ." Arnie looked up with a partial smile. "You and I also know Maddie's using her, well, her mother hen instincts to indulge Harold's needs."

I chuckled as I pictured the look on Maddie's face sharing her hard-love quips meant to snap Harold out of his woebegone moods. "If Maddie's struggling to nurse Harold back to health, how much good can we offer?"

"Of course, Harold did agree to take part today. Maybe getting around the town's people and laughing again will help. I also think him seeing how Priestly Park turned out has helped too. Perhaps this Jubilee outing will galvanize his mental and physical recovery. If not . . ." Arnie went silent as he squatted at the water's edge and stared at the far side of the sun-drenched creek. I crouched down alongside and tossed another pebble to break his locked gaze.

Arnie flinched and looked at me. "I was thinking back on what you said about Harold's sluggish appearance today. It made me wonder about his state of mind. When Hal and I first persuaded him to come, he seemed chipper enough and much more upbeat than he appeared today."

"Do you think something happened in the last couple of days?"

"I don't know Theo, but it wouldn't hurt checking up on Harold before Hal or Phillip takes him home."

"Before who's going home?" A familiar deep voice reverberated behind us.

Arnie and I stood and stared at Harold's weak smile directed at us.

Arnie stammered, "Didn't hear you walk up, but we're sure glad you decided to join us." Arnie picked up a stone and flipped it toward Harold who instinctively snatched it out of the air.

I said as Harold matter-of-factly let the stone fall and brushed his hands off, "You sure must be proud of how the park turned out."

Harold offered a tired grin. "Hal and Phillip made me feel very proud today. I just wish the community center could've been ready." Harold paused. "So tell me, how have you been Theo? Haven't seen hide nor hair of you lately."

"Guess that's my fault." I concentrated on his face though his eyes focused on the ground. "I've not seen you around town either, but I should've visited you long ago."

Harold mustered a forced grin, but his hesitant look revealed the truth. "Not a problem Theo. I haven't felt too sociable lately either. How's that book working out?"

"Mary's delivering the manuscript to Cornerstone Monday. Barring any unforeseen issues, books should be off the presses and arrive well in advance of Larry's advertised book launch shindig before Thanksgiving. I reckon you'd like to know how it turned out?"

Harold nodded with a curious shrug.

"I chose not to dodge the truth about Hank's mistakes, but in the epilog, I added how our country has failed to adequately care for our veterans, especially those coping with underlying mental health symptoms of PTSD."

Arnie added. "Theo's done a masterful job based on what little he's allowed me to read. He treated all the victims in Jessie's Story with the greatest respect."

Harold's dark eyes looked up. "I've got no doubt, Arnie." He rested his right hand on my shoulder but turned toward Arnie. "Preacher, do you know what a banshee is?"

Arnie stared back, speechless.

Harold squeezed my shoulder as he asked me, "Do you?"

"Some kinda witch, I think, or something ominous like that," I replied with one brow arched.

"I dreamt, or at least believe I dreamt, that a banshee visited me last night. She wore a dark, hooded cloak that covered her face and wailed three times from the foot of my bed, 'Death awaits. Get ready.'" Harold looked right through me as he spoke. "It brought back memories of my grandpa's tales about a banshee's visit days before his father passed. Though my father dispelled my grandpa's tale as hogwash, I can assure you that I awoke in a cold sweat this morning."

Arnie asked, "Could you make out the face beneath the hood of the cape?"

"Not really, but she, and it was a woman, seemed familiar, but she never answered when I asked."

"Did she say or do anything more in your dream?" I asked.

"No, but she pointed directly at me before she spoke her final warning and disappeared."

"Harold, this sounds like nothing more than a nightmare," I said as I patted his hand still clenching my shoulder moments before I sensed a slight wobble in his stance.

Harold wrinkled his face. "I just can't shake the chill it gave me."

"Let's head back up before someone wonders what happened to us," Arnie suggested as he took a position on the other side of Harold. We walked together back to the pavilion ready to steady Harold if needed.

Hal met us near the pavilion. "Dad, you feeling okay?"

Arnie laughed. "Hal, I think your dad's just a bit tuckered out. You might want to run him home."

Phillip ran up as Hal drove off with Harold in the passenger's seat. "What's up? Is dad okay?"

"He's just tired," I answered. "By the way, did he share with you anything about a dream he had last night?"

Phillip's head swayed with a puzzled look. "No, but he seemed lost in deep thought during breakfast. What dream?"

"Just a dumb dream that caused him to lose some sleep. He'll be fine after he gets some rest. I think today took a lot out of him."

"You're right, I'm sure." Phillip laughed. "You missed the tug-of-war and egg toss. Zeb, Bubba, and Silas got Mister Simmons and Mister Scribner to join Hal's team to take on my team with Pete, Jay, Jim, and Coach Priestly. I couldn't believe it. Those old men whooped us! More importantly, you better find Miss Liddy and Miss Marie. They won the egg toss."

———

WE FOUND MARIE and Liddy laughing with blue ribbons pinned to their shirts. Judy, Martha, and Susanna huddled around them while Megan and Jeannie walked from Zeb's truck sporting glum faces.

Liddy broke from her shared laughter. "There you guys are. You'll never guess!"

"Let me see. You and Marie won the egg toss."

Liddy raised an eyebrow as she chuckled, "Silly me. Forgot I had this still pinned to my shirt."

Marie giggled pointing to Megan's egg-stained pants stretched out across Zeb's truck. "Megan and Jeannie came in second."

Megan, now wearing athletic shorts, stood beside her chair and flashed her red ribbon with a conciliatory grin. "If Jeannie hadn't taunted your wife and Miss Marie, we would've won!" Megan glanced at Jeannie curled up in her chair trying to suppress her laughter.

Marie said, "Liddy and I won fair and square. Sorry, you missed it, Theo."

Andy joined Megan. "Since we finally have everyone here, we'd like to make a couple of announcements."

Megan wrapped her arm around Andy. Both shared a coy smile.

Zeb barked, "You two have our attention, what's the news?"

Andy paused, looked down at Megan, and then whispered in her ear. She raced over to her warm-up pants and returned wearing a diamond ring on her finger. With deep-set dimples turning redder by the minute, Andy stammered as he looked at Susanna and Sam, "We've been dying to tell y'all the whole day."

Susanna squeezed her cheeks. Her eyes popped at the news. Sam's face broke into an ear-to-ear smile as his head swayed.

Pete roared, "Guess I don't have to keep y'all's secret no more!"

Mary elbowed Pete. "You knew about this and didn't even confide in me? What's up with that?" Pete shrugged his shoulders and gave a sheepish smirk.

Zeb asked, "So when's the big day?"

Megan looked at Andy and muttered with some reservation, "The second of August."

Zeb edged a step closer to the newly engaged couple. "You mean like next month or next summer?"

Andy said, "Well, to answer that, let me tell y'all the second bit of news we'd like to share. As of yesterday, I accepted an offer to join the GCU coaching staff. Megan and I already signed a lease to move into married housing as of next month."

Arnie slapped Andy on the back of his shoulder. "So I imagine the three of us need to get together right after church Sunday to work out the details for this wedding." Arnie looked over his shoulder at Judy. "Better get that on the church calendar first thing in the morning."

Andy squeezed Megan's hand. "Yes, sir. Sounds like a good idea. By the way, Pete's gonna serve as my best man, and Jeannie's gonna be Megan's maid of honor." He looked at Pete. "Thanks for keeping this a secret. I know how difficult that must've been for you."

Pete said to Sam. "Sorry Pop, I couldn't tell you, but John and I figured there's not as much need for me out on Marie's farm anymore, so I plan on stepping up and filling in for Andy with the family business now that Coach Simmons is heading to Waycross."

Sam nodded as he smiled at Andy. "Now see what you've gone and done?" Sam embraced both Andy and Megan. "We're so proud of y'all. Our loss will be GCU's gain. Welcome to the family, young lady."

John winked at Pete and gave Andy and Megan a nonchalant thumbs up.

———

AT SUNSET, WE turned our chairs toward Shiloh Creek. We all shared "oohs and aahs" watching the choreographed pyrotechnic display that lit up the sky. When the finale's last burst faded, the crowd dispersed, ending our first Independence Day Jubilee in Shiloh.

On our way home, Liddy told me that Megan asked her, Marie and Mary to be bridesmaids. Liddy's eyes sparkled as she rambled on and on about their wedding plans until I flicked out the porch light, and we climbed into bed.

CHAPTER THREE

ARNIE DRAPED HIS NAVY BLAZER ACROSS THE CHAIR BEHIND THE PULPIT, rolled-up his sleeves and loosened his red, white and blue tie. Undaunted by the church's aging air conditioner, he plunged into the sermon. Twenty minutes in, Arnie paused and took stock of the sanctuary aflutter with bulletins flapping. He motioned for Mary to ready herself at the piano.

Arnie sipped from his water bottle, yanked a monogrammed handkerchief from his hip pocket and dabbed the nape of his neck and forehead. He closed his black leather Bible and stepped to the edge of the platform.

"As much as I'd like to complete my holiday homily, I'll conclude early today." He slid his finger from holding his place in the Bible as he gazed upon our relieved faces.

Arnie took another long swig of water and cleared his throat. "My dear friends and church family, we have enjoyed a wonderful Independence Day weekend. But lest we forget, even in our beloved Shiloh we cannot escape the mounting crisis America faces. Our country and community are being yanked and pulled in a tug-of-war not much different from what we witnessed at the Jubilee, except on a grander scale with far-reaching significance. On one end, staunch traditionalists clinging to the past stubbornly hunker down straining against the opposing end of the rope gripped by determined progressive visionaries pursuing changes for a brighter future. How can such a struggle be good for all of our people? Without God's indubitable blessing, the America we know and love, and the Shiloh we likewise know and love, will surely stumble and succumb to the infighting."

Arnie lifted his Bible over his head. "Our future rests in God's hands alone. Each day, God proves that we can hold fast to our past while envisioning a better tomorrow. God uses our tug-of-war battles to safeguard the quantity and velocity of the inevitable changes. Thankfully, God has twisted the strands of the tug-of-war rope to withstand the back and forth strain of our fickleness."

Arnie waved his Bible from side to side. "Regardless of which side you choose to stand on, rest assured our struggles are for the good of all who love and trust God. May all of us embrace the struggles caused by our differences as God's way of making us stronger for the challenges that lie ahead for our country and community."

Modest relief arrived as we entered the main foyer. The wide-open doors at each end provided a slight breeze as we mingled among the few people not ready to venture into the sunshine.

Stationed at the main entrance, Arnie clutched his handkerchief in one hand and greeted members as they filed past with the other. Judy stood beside him in a blue and yellow, sleeveless summer dress and showed little ill effects from the uncomfortable, humid conditions. She kept the line moving, smiling and whispering to each person as they exited and sometimes used a slight, gentle nudge to prevent anyone from lingering too long.

As I appreciated the teamwork of my pastor and his wife, Martha grabbed my elbow and looked at Liddy. "How about y'all meet us at Bubba's? Sam and Susanna are going. We're about to invite Arnie and Judy as well." Martha then eyed me. "I know you're game. What do you say?"

I nodded as Liddy chimed our approval. "We're game, but what about Arnie's meeting with Andy and Megan?"

"Mary told me that Arnie met them for breakfast this morning. Oh, and did you hear? Marie offered to host the wedding and reception."

"No, but sounds like a splendid idea," Liddy responded. "Megan mentioned she and Andy wanted a low-key, private affair. How about we meet you in thirty minutes at Bubba's? We need to change into more comfortable clothes. Oh, what about Zeb?"

"He'll be there. Sam already invited him," Larry said. He stood beside his wife and appeared out of character with his hair all mussed, vest unbuttoned, and tie ends dangling from his open shirt collar. Caught in a wistful stare, he futilely fanned his red cheeks with his crumpled bulletin.

I patted Larry on his shoulder and said, "Bet Bubba's AC is working just fine."

Larry managed a wrinkled grin. "I'm counting on it. As soon as we give Mary a heads up, we're out of here."

"Why don't you and Martha get going? Liddy and I'll get with Arnie and Judy, and we'll tell Mary too. I'm sure she'll be along any minute." I smiled as I noticed Pete standing at the entrance to the sanctuary.

———

CECIL LOOKED UP from the counter with his usual tooth-filled grin as we entered Bubba's with Arnie and Judy who we'd met in the parking lot. "Good afternoon, Preacher. Glad to see you and the missus on this beautiful Sunday afternoon. Some of your flock leaked the good news of how you let 'em out early today. Miss Liddy, how are you and Mister Phillips?"

"We're famished but good otherwise. Thanks for asking."

Cecil looked toward the fire pit. "Bob! Say hey to the preacher and his wife and Mister and Missus Phillips."

Bubba set aside his long wood-handled, basting brush, wiped his hands on the terry towel draped over his shoulder and stepped from behind the counter. "Hey, folks, glad to see y'all!" He double-checked his hands before extending one to Arnie and then me. "I've got another batch of ribs about to come off the pit. Hope you're hungry."

I looked at Arnie, and we both laughed. I said, "I think both of us have recovered from the pig roast at the Jubilee. Your mouthwatering ribs sound fine to me."

Cecil reached across the counter and tugged Bubba's arm. "Bob, the pit's flaming up!" Bubba excused himself and scurried back to tend the racks of basted meat nestled in the open flames.

Cecil pointed to the back of the restaurant. "You folks go on back. They're waitin' on y'all, and Mister Zeb looks mighty hungry to me."

Cora stood over Zeb's shoulder as we found our seats and asked, "Y'all ready?"

No one needed to check the menu, and a moment later without jotting down our orders, Cora yelled to Cecil as she grabbed two large pitchers of sweet tea, "Old man, we need five full and four half platters." She filled everyone's mason jars and placed the half-full pitchers on our table before disappearing.

After a few minutes of idle chatter about the morning service, Larry leaned forward, raised his voice and said, "Now that everyone's here, I'd like to get all y'all's opinion." He eyed each of us and then gave me an inauspicious wink.

Zeb set his sweet tea down and stared at Larry. "Okay, whatcha got? We're all ears."

"As of tomorrow, Theo will be freed up again to tackle another special interest project for the Sentinel." Larry looked in my direction. "So, although I haven't discussed the specifics with him yet, I'd like to toss an idea out to all of you."

I stared at Larry who glanced back with a sly grin and another quick wink. Chuckles and giggles filled the table. Even Liddy enjoyed my wide-eyed stare.

Larry raised both his hands. "Hey guys, I'm serious. My gut tells me the whole town is anxious for more of Theo's articles. What do you think about him writing about Coach Priestly's return to the sidelines? A lot has happened since John's unfortunate hiatus. Now that he's back in the saddle, the team's all fired up and ready to put the last three losing seasons under three different coaches behind them."

Arnie sat back and crossed his arms. "Larry, sounds interesting, but are you expecting too much from him? Have you talked to John about this?"

Sam spoke up. "Arnie, I understand your concerns, but Pete tells me the players are working harder than ever getting ready."

Larry smiled. "John and I have spoken, and he's agreed under one condition."

Arnie asked, "What condition?"

"Theo meets with him, and they agree about the scope and content."

Liddy nudged me and whispered, "You already talked about doing this." Her scrunched nose and curled lips encouraged me to speak up.

I cleared my throat, prompting everyone's gaze. "Larry, I've been thinking this over the last couple of weeks, but I've got a condition too."

Larry's grin disappeared. "What condition?"

"I'm not a sports reporter and certainly don't want this assignment to place any undue pressure on the players or John during his first season back." I focused on Larry's raised brows. "Will you trust me as you did on the Jessie and John articles last winter?"

Larry sank back into his seat and scratched his chin. He surveyed the heads nodding in approval. "Why not? I imagine you'll handle this with your unique flair and perspective, but will you at least keep me in the loop once in a while?"

As we shook hands in agreement, Cora appeared balancing platters in her arms. "Am I interrupting y'all folks?"

Zeb looked over his shoulder. "Miss Cora, set one of those right here."

As we began enjoying our dinners, Judy got everyone's attention. "Arnie and I have something to share with you too. Hillary's coming home."

Susanna looked at Judy and set her fork on her plate. "What do you mean coming home? Are she and her husband visiting?"

Judy peeked at Arnie before answering. "Hillary and Mark are getting divorced. We haven't said anything to y'all before this, but now that she wants to come home to get her bearings, I believe she needs your support, and right now, we need it too. Divorces are such a touchy subject around the church, especially when it impacts the pastor's family."

Liddy glanced at Susanna and Martha and then offered Judy a reassuring smile. "I think you can count on us. When's she coming home?"

Arnie said, "In two weeks."

"Is she going to be staying with you?" Susanna asked.

Judy nodded. "For the time being, but she wants to find a place of her own if she decides to stay in Shiloh. She doesn't think a thirty-three old woman needs to live with her parents."

"Well, you can count on us. How about we all get together this week and talk some more? I think Liddy would like to know more about Hillary," Susanna said.

———

As WE PULLED into the driveway, Liddy asked, "Do you know what Cora asked me while you and Larry talked with Arnie?"

"No. What?"

"She wanted to know what a banshee was?"

I turned off the engine and stared at Liddy. "Why did she ask such a question?"

"She said Maddie told her about a nightmare Harold experienced the other night. Neither of them understood what Harold got so upset about."

"What'd you tell her?"

"I told her I'd check into it but not to lose any sleep fretting about it."

"Remind me to tell you what Harold said about his weird dream. Mary's due to stop by shortly, and I need to call John Priestly about getting together."

Another round of late afternoon thunderstorms threatened but brought a break from the sweltering humidity. The first raindrops fell about the same time Mary pulled up. I greeted her at the door, and we went inside to find Liddy who walked out of the kitchen into the living room just as we sat down.

"Would you like a drink, Mary?" Liddy asked.

"No, ma'am. I can't stay. I haven't packed yet. Just need to pick up the manuscript." Mary looked at me. "Mom said you agreed to write about Coach Priestly and the upcoming football season."

"Your dad sure is a wily old dog. He knew I'd be intrigued about writing a follow-up on John Priestly after those articles on his exoneration and return to Shiloh."

"You know, he referred to you the same way." Mary shared a giggle with Liddy at my expense.

"So, you two think I'm a wily old dog?" I jested as I reached into my attaché case for the manuscript. Both women burst into boisterous laughter. "All right. At least I don't snarl or bite. Here's the manuscript with some brief notes."

Mary opened the envelope and peeked inside.

"Don't look so apprehensive. Here're some directions, but I reckon you'll use your fancy phone to guide you. Just promise you'll call after you arrive."

"I promise."

Liddy stood with Mary. "This is an off-the-wall question, but do you know what a banshee is?"

Mary raised an eyebrow. "No. Never heard of a banshee. Why?"

Before Liddy replied, I butted in. "Oh, don't bother about that. It's just something that came up when we were talking earlier."

Liddy shot a quick look at me but said nothing.

Mary said, "In that case, I gotta run. I promise I'll call. Thanks again for letting me have this opportunity."

"Enjoy yourself. Now scoot. It looks like the rain almost stopped."

Mary tucked the envelope under her arm and walked briskly to her car.

After she drove away, I looked at Liddy. "Hun, I gotta call John. Would you like to come with me when I visit him?"

"Sure. Neither of us has seen John's new place since he moved in. Besides, I'd like to spend some time with Marie while you're hashing things out with John. Megan and Andy went out there this afternoon to talk about their wedding."

I reached John at Marie's. He confirmed Megan and Andy, along with our other young friends, were enjoying hamburgers and reminiscing.

"John, I'd like to stop by to discuss Larry's idea about another series of articles for the Sentinel."

"Tomorrow afternoon will work for me if it suits you. Why not bring Liddy too? I'd appreciate her opinion about my new place. Besides, I've got a new roommate to introduce to the two of you."

"Liddy's already nodding. Tomorrow about three then?"

I hung up the phone, and Liddy blurted, "A roommate?"

I shrugged. "We'll find out tomorrow."

We sat on the porch as darkness enveloped our neighborhood, and I shared what Harold revealed to Arnie and me. "Sorry about being so evasive on the matter, but I felt Harold's dream didn't need to wind up in the town's gossip mill."

Our conversation soon turned to sharing how Harold's deteriorating health coupled with his nightmare revelation appeared to have impacted him beyond losing a little sleep.

CHAPTER FOUR

MONDAY'S RAINBOW DAWN DISTRACTED ME FROM JOTTING FURTHER THOUGHTS about the weekend into my daily journal. Instead, I set it aside and rocked on my porch listening for the familiar yips and howls throughout the neighborhood heralding our punctual paperboy's arrival. His uncanny accuracy had long convinced me Coach Priestly likely already had intentions of recruiting him for the high school team as soon as he was old enough. However, on this particular morning, instead of the usual flop of the paper at the foot of my porch steps, I heard the distinct snap of his kickstand.

"Good morning Mister Phillips," Timmy said with a broad, freckled smile. He unfolded a morning paper as he marched up the walkway.

"Why thank you, Timmy, but you didn't have to interrupt your busy delivery schedule on my account."

"No biggie, Mister Phillips. Thought you'd like to see the front page."

I took the paper from Timmy and pointed to the rocker beside me. Beneath a picture of me standing with John Priestly at the Jubilee, Larry's article detailed the latest news regarding my book, including the Sentinel's planned book launch the weekend before Thanksgiving.

"Mister Phillips, both my mom and dad sure are excited. They can't wait to get their hands on a copy of your book."

"I'll be sure they get one. By the way, how's your summer been going?"

"Pretty busy lately. Coach Priestly asked me to be the team's equipment manager. I've been helping Coach almost every day get ready for the upcoming season." Timmy puffed his chest out.

"That's great, Timmy. Coach sure could use your help. How's the team look?"

Timmy stroked his scrunched chin. "There's only a handful of returning players on the team, but Coach is rallying them to believe we can win again."

"Glad to hear it. I'll be sure to check out a couple of practices before the season begins."

Timmy checked his watch. "Oops! Gotta run. Nice talking with you Mister Phillips. Have a great day, and say hey to Missus Phillips for me." His last words arrived on the fly as he hopped onto his bike and rode away.

NOT LONG AFTER breakfast, I left the house headed toward Larry's office, but at the corner of Main and Broad, I stopped by the Butcher Shoppe to purchase a cup of Bernie's Mediterranean brew to go. Though I bore little reservation about our move from Atlanta to Shiloh, The Butcher Shoppe's Greek fare satisfied my lingering cosmopolitan cravings.

"Good morning, Mistor Theo," Bernie said as I entered.

I pointed to the odd-looking copper coffee pot on the stove. "Good morning to you, Bernie. Where's Silas and Alex?"

Bernie filled a paper cup with the frothy, aromatic brew. "Alex is visiting family in Atlanta. As for his good-for-nothing father, most likely losing at checkers again, wagging his tongue with Bubba and Zeb as usual."

"When's Alex getting back?"

"End of the month. He heard about Andy and Megan's engagement and promised to be back for the wedding. Miss Megan stopped by this weekend and asked us to cater the reception."

"Megan did well asking you. Have you worked out a menu?"

Bernie swapped my buck for the tasty coffee. "No, not yet," she said a bit flustered.

I savored a quick sip. "Thanks, Bernie. I'm sure whatever you come up with, Megan and Andy will be pleased."

Next door, I noticed Jeannie Simmons at her desk inside Arians Realty and Property Management. The bell above the door announced my impromptu visit.

"Theo, what a pleasant surprise. What's up?"

"I'm working my way to the Sentinel. Did Nick and Joe get back yet from Saint Simons?"

"They should be back next weekend."

"You must be doing too good of a job holding down the fort for Nick. How was your cookout at Marie's?"

Jeannie tilted her head. "How'd you know?"

"Coach and I talked last night."

A relaxed grin replaced her inquisitive stare.

"I won't keep you. Tell Nick I stopped by and would like to catch up with him when he gets back."

Five minutes later, I tossed my empty paper cup in Martha's trash can after she pointed to Larry's office. "Sorry, I've got my hands full, but Larry's back there."

"Have you heard from her?"

"Nope, not since she left bright and early this morning." Martha swept stray hairs off her forehead and returned her attention to her desktop.

I rapped on the doorframe, walked straight in, and scooted my usual seat closer to the front of his desk before I sat down.

Larry closed the folder on his desk and leaned back in his executive chair. "Well, good morning. Mary tells me we share similar opinions about each other."

"Guess that means we're both wily, old dogs."

Larry chuckled. "What's the latest? Have you talked to John yet?"

"Headed over there this afternoon."

"Look, Theo, about this assignment. I'm sorry if I put you on the spot yesterday. But to be honest, I felt sure you'd be interested."

"You did catch me a little off guard, but your instincts didn't fail you."

"Fine. Now, if you don't mind, I gotta tackle the layout for tomorrow's edition. Someone, who shall go unnamed, sent my talented assistant out of town." A theatrical, gritted-teeth growl ensued.

"Quit your fussing. Mary oughta get back soon enough. Talk to you in a couple of days."

I DECIDED TO swing by City Hall before heading home for lunch, and in short order walked across the polished lobby of the Masterson Administration Building and entered the city's administration office. The desk in front of the mayor's private office remained unoccupied. All the phone lines were unlit, but I heard a file drawer open and then slide shut beyond the mayor's closed door.

As soon as I knocked, Hal snarled from the other side, "Come in!"

Hal took a double take when I stepped into his office. "Sorry, I thought you were the clerk I expected an hour ago for her interview. What's up Mister Phillips?" His mussed hair and untucked shirttail caused me to gawk before I answered.

"Sorry to barge in unannounced. I've been running errands and thought I'd check with you about your dad. How's he doing?"

Hal leaned against the front edge of his desk. "Better, but that's not saying much. Maddie's keeping a close eye on him."

"By any chance did he talk to you about his recent dream? He seemed rattled when he spoke with Arnie and me at the park."

"For some reason, he won't discuss it with Phillip or me. Since that night, Maddie told me he spends his days in his study thumbing through old papers and reminiscing over old family photo albums. Frankly, I'm concerned."

"Hal, your old man is a tough son of a gun. Maybe a little rest and some of Maddie's cooking will cure what's ailing him."

"I hope so," Hal muttered, staring at Harold's picture on the wall of his dad's former office.

"Have you spoken about any of this with Hank?"

Hal took a step towards the window, and sank both hands into his pants pockets. "I'm ashamed to admit I've not spoken to him, much less visited him since . . ." Hal swept his hand across his face. "Since the day dad got him to confess to framing John Priestly."

"He's still your brother. Aren't you the least interested in how he's doing?"

"I've caught a glimpse of him working on his tan around town on prison work details. In spite of a little embarrassment, maybe he'll get discharged from jail a changed man. At least I'd like to think so, but I'm not convinced that'll happen." Hal stared at me and added, "Doesn't matter. I'm not sure I'll ever be able to forgive him for what he did to Megan, John and me, say nothing about dad and Phillip."

"I can only imagine how tough this has been." I paused when Hal looked away. "On a whole other topic, Arnie and Judy announced yesterday that their daughter Hillary's coming back to town."

"Really? Why? What happened?"

"Arnie only shared that Hillary and Mark couldn't make their marriage work. Mark's job took him on the road every week. Hillary's career kept her too busy to recognize the problems in their marriage until it was too late. Once she accepted Mark's affections had traveled with his work, she kicked him out and filed for a divorce."

"That's so sad. Hillary and I grew up together. If there's a silver lining, they never had kids as far as I know."

"That's the only consolation from what I can see. As you well know, divorce always impacts so many others beyond the husband and wife."

"Is she planning on staying in Shiloh?"

"Arnie thinks so if she can land a job and find a place of her own. Evidently she doesn't relish the notion of living with her parents."

"I think I'll talk to Arnie. I can't seem to find a suitable replacement to fill Megan's old position, at least not one with the right experience."

"Won't hurt to ask. Look, I know you're busy. Please keep me abreast of your dad's condition."

As soon as Hal pulled the door open, a wild-eyed, young girl stood up from the chair beside the desk. "Mister Mayor, I'm . . . I'm here to interview for the position you advertised."

Hal waved her inside and gave me a smirk that morphed straight into a grimace before he pivoted back into his office. He left the door open and said, "Thanks for stopping by."

CHAPTER FIVE

JUST BEFORE THREE, I TURNED ONTO THE GRAVEL ROAD MARKED BY MARIE'S green, rural mailbox, now accompanied by a run-of-the-mill, black mailbox. The narrow road wound across Shiloh Creek and beyond the woods that hid Marie's farm and surrounding fenced meadows.

The first sign of John's expanding presence on Marie's farmstead appeared beyond the main entrance. The new gate at the head of the pasture fence and tire tracks indicated the direction of John's new home, but we continued on the gravel road to Marie's place.

As we drove up, Marie and John, along with Phoebe Thatcher, walked from the shadows of the barn and waved. Marie gave Liddy a warm embrace while John and I exchanged a hearty handshake.

"Theo and Liddy Phillips, I don't believe anyone has properly introduced y'all to Miss Phoebe Thatcher. We work together at the high school," John said as Marie nudged Phoebe.

Liddy offered her hand. "I've been dying to meet you, Miss Thatcher. You have such a beautiful voice."

"Please call me Phoebe."

"What brought you out here today?" Liddy asked with an eager grin.

"John mentioned you were coming, and I wanted to meet you."

Liddy squinted at John.

Phoebe's growing smile recaptured Liddy's attention. "Missus Abernathy told me all about you and asked me to reach out to you and answer any remaining questions you might have. She's eager to hear from you about the art teaching position. Besides, if you accept, our classrooms will be across from one another."

Liddy dipped her head to hide a blush-dimpled grin. "You came out here just to meet me?"

"That plus Marie promised a delicious chicken finger lunch," Phoebe confessed with equally reddened cheeks and a sheepish grin. "While John and your husband talk, I thought you'd join Marie and me. Maybe the two of us can sweet talk you into joining us at Shiloh High."

Marie grabbed Liddy's arm and motioned for Phoebe to lead the way inside the house. John pointed to his truck, and we drove along the gravel road to the far side of the fenced meadow where John's rustic cabin sat nestled amongst a mature pecan grove. As I exited his truck, I noticed another fence gate matching the one we saw when we drove to Marie's.

John chuckled. "I see you're admiring my private gated access. I installed the gates, so I won't disturb Marie whenever I come and go at odd hours." He opened the front door to his cabin. "Come on in."

John excused himself, washed his hands at the kitchen sink, and grabbed a couple of soda cans from his fridge, extending one out for me.

The cabin had a simple, great room layout. At one end, a stone fireplace served as the centerpiece of a sitting area that included a leather sofa and two armchairs, replete with rustic end tables and a cluttered coffee table ladened with magazines and file folders. At the opposite end of the great room, a short hallway led to John's bedroom and bathroom. A crude ladder provided access to the guest loft.

While I wandered about, John said, "Every board and timber came from Jay and Jim Adams' Shiloh Creek Lumber Mill, which struck an exclusive deal to harvest Harold Archer's pine timber."

"I remember walking with Harold through his groves of loblolly pines. Sounds like a win-win deal and also good for the town with the old eyesore operational again. Zeb told me the old mill has a long history in Shiloh."

We ventured onto the porch, and John said as we sat down, "Oh yeah, I'd like to introduce you to my new roommate." He slipped two fingers into his mouth and whistled. A moment later, a black and brown dappled hound scampered from the side of the cabin. John stroked his ears. "Good boy. Did ya miss me?"

"And who's this fella?" I snapped my fingers, and the dog flashed a curious look as his ears raised, but John held his collar.

"Theo, this is Ringo. After Zeb introduced us, it was love at first sight for both of us." John let go of Ringo's collar, and the dog strolled over and sniffed my hand.

"Why'd you name him Ringo?" I asked, scratching his ears.

John laughed. "Scratch his belly."

I leaned forward, ran my fingers along his side and watched his hind leg begin to twitch. When my fingers scratched his underside, the twitch evolved into a pronounced thumping. I looked at John and laughed.

While still chuckling, John said, "What better name fits such a natural drummer?"

Ringo rested at our feet while we discussed the football program's upcoming season. Our conversation soon turned toward my writing about John for the Sentinel. He initially bucked at the idea of focusing on the challenges he's had to overcome since his return but nodded his approval as soon as I suggested I highlight his players and their stories since John returned as their coach.

Although we agreed that subsequent articles during the season remained a possibility, I reiterated that I neither wanted to be a sports-writer nor a distraction for John's first season back on the sidelines. Our discussion ended talking about Timmy's visit. John hinted that Timmy's story might be well-suited for my articles. He then suggested I hold off until the first official practices begin next month.

John added as he rocked back with a broad grin, "Champions have big hearts, not big heads. I need a few more days to whip the boys into shape and prepare them mentally before exposing them to any of your inquiries and the notoriety that will undoubtedly follow."

"John, now that that's settled, what do you think about Andy and Megan?"

"What do ya mean?" John's eyes examined mine.

"Did Andy's acceptance of GCU's coaching offer spur their marriage plans along?"

John sank into his chair and smiled. "Well, I hope so. We spoke a couple of months ago about how serious his feelings had grown for her."

"Was he unsure or afraid of how he felt?"

"Andy feared Megan's feelings for him might be more of a rebound thing after her divorce from Hank. I merely suggested that he follow his heart, not hers. He also expressed concern that he'd interfere with Megan's dream of completing her teaching degree. That's when he brought up the idea of leaving Shiloh to move near her."

"What'd you tell him?"

His wry smile grew wider as he rocked back with his feet propped against the porch rail. "Let's just say God provided a clear pathway for Andy to make up his mind about him and Megan. Of course, mind you, a timely phone call to Coach Dean at GCU didn't hurt either."

I propped my feet up and stared at the lush grass in the pasture, mulling over what John said. No doubt God used John once again to steer the hearts of those who trust him.

John interrupted my thoughts. "Theo, by the way, I saw Hank on a work detail at the stadium."

"Did you say anything to him?"

"Naw, not a word. Figured if I walked up to the sheriff's deputy and asked to talk to him, Hank would balk anyway, so I watched from the end zone for a short while. Don't know if he saw me or not. Leastwise, he didn't make any indication one way or the other."

"Hope for his sake and his family's sake that he realizes what you did for him."

"I just hope he can move forward when he gets out in December."

"Hey, we need to head back and see what the women are up to."

John pointed to the truck and whistled. Ringo stirred, wagged his tail and bounded onto the tailgate. Before John turned over the ignition, he asked, "Do you think Liddy will accept the teaching offer?"

"Guess we'll both find out in a few minutes."

At Marie's house, Ringo jumped from the truck bed and stood wagging his tail beside John. I looked at Liddy and said, "Liddy, this is Ringo, John's new roommate."

Marie smiled at both Phoebe and Liddy. "Well, not to be outdone with introductions, let me introduce you to Shiloh's new art teacher."

John walked up to Liddy and raised her off her feet with a bear hug.

"Put me down you big galoot," Liddy managed to say, giggling nonstop.

I smiled at Liddy as she straightened her blouse. "Phew, glad this decision is over. You can tell me all about your conversation on the way home."

We waved goodbye and followed Phoebe in her European mini-wagon all the way back to the center of town. She turned into the alley between Mister Edwards' barber shop and the Methodist Church. Liddy pointed to the second floor. "I believe that's where Phoebe said she lives. I think I'm going to enjoy working with her."

Liddy cleared the breakfast table and phoned Missus Abernathy while I finished my coffee and the morning paper. The inflection of Liddy's voice went from exuberant to reserved as the conversation progressed.

She hung up the phone but kept her grip on it, though it rested in its cradle. She blurted, "Missus Abernathy told me how tickled pink she felt about my decision, but it'll be another couple weeks before I can get started."

Liddy slid her fingers from the phone and sat down across from me at the kitchen table. "She apologized but said the janitors don't want anyone traipsing about the halls while they finish stripping and buffing the floors. But she told me not to fret. There's plenty of time to get the paperwork taken care of before teacher orientation begins on the twenty-eighth. She also said Phoebe volunteered to help get me settled."

"Maybe having to wait a few days is a good thing. John asked me to chill for a couple more weeks too." I placed my hands on hers and stared into her dark eyes. "Let's call the boys and take advantage of the time spoiling some grandkids. What do ya think?"

Liddy's eyes came to life. "I believe there's absolutely nothing going on for the next couple of weeks that can't wait. I'm sure they'll welcome a visit."

———

LATE FRIDAY MORNING, I zipped the last of our bags just as the phone rang. Liddy hollered from the living room, "It's Mary. She just got back."

I reached for the phone. Liddy kept her hand covering the phone and whispered. "Sounds like something's wrong."

"Hello Mary, glad you called. Liddy and I decided to visit family for a few days but hoped to hear from you before we left."

Mary sounded drained. "The drive back gave me plenty of time to think. Gotta say, Cornerstone would certainly be a fantastic place to work, and, well, last night Barry broached that exact subject at dinner."

"What did Mister gung-ho have to say?" I liked Barry's confident, proactive nature when he worked for me. In this instance, though, I remembered how persuasive and charming he could be as well.

"He spelled out what they would expect of me if I accepted the position in the new creative graphic design department. I felt a bit intimidated, but the possibilities of working with the latest technology sounded exciting."

"Did you accept his offer?" I hoped I already knew the answer.

"Told him he painted a convincing package but said I'd need a few days before deciding. I used Megan and Andy's wedding to buy some time. Barry said the job is mine if I want it, and after meeting me, coupled with your high recommendation, he said Cornerstone could afford to wait a few days. He also respects how significant the change would be for me transitioning from Shiloh to bustling Atlanta."

"Sounds like Barry. Look, we'll be back in ten days. Call me if you want to talk. I recognize how challenging this decision is for you."

"I promise. Gotta run. Dad's yelling my name. Enjoy some well-deserved time with your family and say hey for me."

I hung up the phone and met Liddy's stare. "She got an impressive offer from Barry but asked to have until the end of the month to decide."

"What do you think she'll do?"

"I think we just need to trust that Mary's a smart, level-headed young woman. She'll make the best decision for her. How about a sandwich before we load up and leave?"

———

THE HORIZON OFFERED up its last glimmer of light by the time we pulled into our driveway, concluding our nine-day family visit.

Though fast asleep in her seat as I shut down the engine and removed the key, Liddy held onto a Mud Lick State Park brochure, a memento from the day the entire family spent together on Lake Guntersville. Liddy, Stacey, and Kari had whipped up a special picnic reminiscent of our family picnic last October in Peachtree before we moved.

"Liddy . . . Hey, Hun. We're home." I gently tapped her shoulder.

She stirred and wiped her eyes. "Sorry I fell asleep on ya."

"At least you waited until we got through Albany before you dozed off. Why don't you go on inside? I'll get our stuff."

Liddy squeezed my hand and managed a partial smile as she unbuckled and headed into the house.

I had just put down the last of our bags when Liddy replayed an answering machine message from Judy. "Hope y'all had a great time with your family. We missed you both at church this morning. Liddy, I'd like to invite you to have lunch with me and my daughter Hillary. I'd love for you to meet her. Please call me in the morning."

"Judy's likely to be home by now. Go ahead and call her."

"I'll wait until the morning. Besides, I want to speak with Missus Abernathy first. Right now I'd rather fix us something to eat and take a shower before I call it an early night."

CHAPTER SIX

THE TANTALIZING SMELL OF BACON SIZZLING AND BISCUITS BAKING LURED ME out of my deep sleep. I instinctively grabbed my robe and headed into the kitchen but stopped dead in the doorway. Liddy, her back to me, fiddled with bacon in one skillet and scrambled eggs in another. Without uttering a word, I admired the sway of her hips as she hummed along with Neil Diamond singing, "Monday, Monday" on the radio.

In a fluster, her cheeks reddened as she fumbled for the volume button as soon as she noticed me out of the corner of her eye. She faced me with her hand over her racing heart. "Theo Phillips! You scared the bejesus out of me."

"Why'd you stop?" I asked with a half-sincere chuckle. "You and Neil sounded good together. Besides, I loved the way you swayed to the beat." She just gestured with the tongs toward the table where the morning paper waited beside my empty coffee mug.

Liddy had regained her composure by the time she poured coffee. "By the way, Timmy said hello and asked me to tell you he looks forward to seeing you at practice next week." She returned the coffee pot to the burner and paused before she glanced back with one of her impish, playful grins. "Are you gonna wear shorts and tote a whistle out there?"

"That's not even remotely funny. When I do go, it'll be as an interested observer, nothing more."

Liddy snickered. "I'm sorry but I pictured you in those old gray coach's shorts that you used to wear back when you helped coach our boys."

I changed the subject. "Don't forget to call Judy right after you speak with Missus Abernathy. I'm curious about their daughter. I think Hal's hoping she might be interested in Megan's old position."

Liddy placed breakfast on the table. "I'll call Missus Abernathy while you eat your bacon and eggs."

A couple of minutes later, Liddy hung up the phone. "Do you mind if I take the car? Missus Abernathy, I mean Kay, asked me to stop by this morning to start my paperwork."

"I can walk into town later and check in on Mary."

"Think she'll stay or choose Atlanta?"

"Not sure if I should answer that. I'm trying to stay neutral. No doubt Larry's spinning his version of a guilt trip on her to stay."

"Good luck remaining neutral." Liddy reached for the phone again and walked into the living room.

I opened the paper and found a photo of John amidst his players going through drills. Even the recap of last evening's Braves game got buried beneath Larry's piece plugging my upcoming articles on Coach Priestly's return as head football coach of the Shiloh Saints. Nothing like a little pressure for a supposedly retired, part-time freelance journalist.

Liddy hung up the phone and placed her hand on my shoulder. "Hillary sounds charming. I look forward to meeting her tomorrow."

"I gather you got to speak to her?"

"Judy already left for the church, but Hillary confirmed our lunch date and said Susanna might join us if Joe lets her break away in time."

Liddy smooched my cheek and bolted down the hall. "I've gotta get ready to meet Kay. Do you mind cleaning up the dishes?"

———

ON MY STROLL through town, "Monday, Monday" played in my head until the morning sun reminded me I forgot to heed Liddy's plea to put sunscreen on before I left. I took some consolation as I adjusted my new Georgia Bulldog safari hat and picked up my pace.

A burst of cold air welcomed me as I stepped inside the Sentinel. Martha approached her desk sipping a cup of coffee. "Good morn, stranger. Just made a fresh pot. Would you like some?"

"Think I'll pass. Thanks all the same. Maybe I'll grab a Coke instead."

"Hey Theo, let me get one with you." Mary sprang from behind the two large computer monitors atop her desk.

Martha smiled when I eyed Larry's corner office. "He's back there and mighty eager to see you too. Go on back once you and Mary get your drinks." Her smile turned into a mischievous look as I walked past her desk.

Mary opened the break room fridge and retrieved two Cokes. "Got a sec?" Mary asked as she placed my soda can on the lunch table.

"Sure, your dad can wait. Besides, the walk over here made me pretty thirsty. Today's going to be another scorcher." I tore off a paper towel and wiped my forehead after dropping my hat on the bench beside me. I then popped open my can and enjoyed a refreshing swig of coke.

Mary stared at the unopened can she clutched with both hands. "Theo, I want you to know how much I appreciate all you did for me. Cornerstone's offer has been on my mind since I got back." A pregnant pause followed as she fiddled with the condensation that coated her iconic red soda can.

"Mary, what are you trying to tell me? Have you decided to accept their offer?"

Mary lifted her eyes and sighed, "Oh, Mister Phillips. I don't want you to think —"

"Think what Mary? Whatever you decide, I'm fine with it as long as it's what you want. You're talented enough that any number of places would gladly jump at the opportunity to welcome you on board."

She reached her hand across the table and put it on mine. "I appreciate that, but I've already made up my mind. Please don't be upset with me."

"Why would I be upset? Congratulations young lady. Whatever decision you've made, I have no doubt it's the best one for you. So who hooked you?"

Mary bit her bottom lip before she spat out, "My dad."

An ear-to-ear grin rose across my face. "Your dad? Tell me about his irresistible offer."

Her flushed cheeks framed a cautious grin. "You're not disappointed after arranging everything for me at Cornerstone?"

"Of course not."

"That's certainly a relief." She slid both hands around her Coke can again. "After you and Liddy left town, dad and I talked about the trip and Barry's offer. When I asked his advice, at first he appeared disappointed, but the longer we talked the more I realized how hard it'd be leaving this sleepy old town, my family and all my friends. Then dad pulled an envelope from his desk drawer and handed it to me. He said he and mom wanted to provide me with their counteroffer to mull over. He admitted they suspected my trip to Cornerstone might result in a job offer."

"If you don't mind sharing, what'd they offer you?"

"Invested interest in the Sentinel and a new title. Dad offered to make me Managing Editor. He said it was time for him to slow down, and fulfilling his duties as Publisher would keep him plenty occupied."

"Fantastic! I guess that makes you my new boss too."

Mary blushed. "I kinda think dad might have something to say about that." We exchanged laughs, oblivious to Larry's arrival.

"Theo, are you buttering up our new editor hoping to wrangle yourself some undeserved favoritism?"

"Oh, Daddy!" Mary stifled her laughter.

"Larry, you don't know how good I feel about your daughter's decision."

The gleam in Larry's eyes shone on Mary. "Theo, you don't know how good I feel that she accepted my offer over Cornerstone's most generous offer, thanks to you." He did not attempt to hide his sarcasm.

Mary tilted her head back and gulped the last of her Coke. "Now that I've managed to thrill both of you, can we get back to work? We've got another edition to get ready before we go home tonight."

"Don't blame me for holding you two up. Let me have five minutes with your dad, and I'll skedaddle. I learned long ago to avoid at all costs ticking off the editor when there's a deadline."

Larry smiled as Mary returned to her desk. "Thanks, Theo. You're a good friend and a pretty wily, old dog too."

"What do you mean?"

"Tell me you didn't know all along that her trip to Cornerstone would wind up with Martha and me making sure she stays right here where she belongs."

"Let's just say I prayed hard she'd discover for herself why she should stay right here in Shiloh. The town needs more people like her to make the same decision." I grabbed my safari hat and adjusted it on my head. "Besides, I would've hated to see that outstanding University of Georgia education you and Martha paid for go to waste. When I look back, there were plenty of times I wished I'd stayed with my father's small town paper too rather than chase the big-city corporate dream."

Larry slapped my shoulder. "Let's not forget that your corporate dream is publishing your book and giving sleepy old Shiloh a little notoriety."

"Guess that's putting a shine on it. I better run. I found out what I intended to find out."

Larry shook my hand and turned toward his office but froze in his tracks. "Hold up a sec Theo. I almost forgot. Sam stopped by this morning and asked if I'd talk to you about coming to a bachelor shindig planned for Andy."

"Gosh, I haven't been to a bachelor party since Tommy's wedding twelve years ago. When is it?"

"Friday, the night before the wedding, at the Shiloh Creek Lumber warehouse."

"I'll be there."

———

I TILTED THE brim of my hat to better shade my eyes from the bright sunshine as I returned to the sidewalk. When I reached the town square, I decided to stop by Hal's office before venturing to Zeb's store. The soles of my shoes squeaked as I wandered across the lobby headed to the mayor's office. Hal's door opened as I prepared to knock.

Hal stammered as he glanced at his watch. "Sorry Mister Phillips. I'm headed across the street for a lunch date with Nick."

"Don't intend to hold you up. I'm headed to see Zeb myself but wanted to drop by to give you a heads up that might prove beneficial."

"What's that?"

I pointed to Megan's old desk. "Looks like you've still not hired an assistant?"

Hal's frustration surfaced in his drawn out, "Nooo."

"What if I told you Liddy's having lunch tomorrow with Judy and Hillary?"

"Oh really? I didn't realize that Hilly, I mean Hillary, had gotten into town yet."

"It might be a good idea for you to have lunch at the Butcher Shoppe tomorrow too." I cleared my throat. "You know, for an impromptu, chance encounter." A sly wink followed.

"Sounds worth considering. Thanks, Theo. Oh, if you haven't heard, Jay and Jim are hosting a bachelor party for Andy."

"Just got the news from Larry. You going?"

"Phillip and I wouldn't miss it." He glanced again at his watch. "Hey, I gotta go. Thanks for the tip. I owe ya."

Hal walked across the marble-floored rotunda and headed out the front door while I turned the opposite direction toward the rear exit. My thoughts turned to the prospect of some friendly banter, a game of checkers, peanuts and another refreshing cold drink at Adam's Feed and Hardware. I had learned that investing a portion of a lazy day at Zeb's place offered the best latest scuttlebutt about my new hometown.

———

THE SIGHT AND smell of freshly mowed grass provided a fleeting sense of satisfaction that my lush, green lawn matched the meticulously manicured lawns of my neighbors. Showered and pleased with my sweat-filled morning behind me, I chomped into a Dagwood sandwich and gulped sweet tea from the comfort of my hammock on the front porch. The ceiling fan deflected the muggy air, which grew more humid by the minute as temperatures soared into the nineties. I monitored the advancing cloud banks as the sun wrestled to hold its oppressive grip for yet another July Tuesday in South Georgia.

The remains of my double-decker sandwich soon rested beside my nearly empty glass on the porch rail. The hammock's gentle sway and the fan's cool breeze lulled me into a quick snooze before Liddy returned from her lunch with Judy and Hillary.

"Theo. Hey, you awake?"

Arnie's voice interrupted my siesta. "I am now." I rubbed my eyes and turned my head toward Arnie perched in one of our rockers. "What time is it? How long have you been here?"

Arnie smiled. "I reckon about fifteen minutes. I tried to wake you earlier, but you just grunted and drifted back off."

My feet landed on our battleship gray porch deck. "It's after two. Have you heard from Judy?"

"She called me right after you decided to catch another round of your catnap."

"Guess they're enjoying their lunch date." I moved to a rocker beside Arnie.

"Judy wanted to let me know they'd be a little longer than planned. Something about stopping by City Hall, but they said they'd meet us here."

"What do you think they're up to?" I wondered if Hal had visited during lunch.

"Haven't a clue but looks like we'll know soon enough." Arnie pointed to our Expedition pulling into the driveway with a white Camry right behind.

Liddy waited for Judy and Hillary before all three walked toward the porch chatting and laughing all the way. Arnie greeted them at the top of the steps while I stood beside my rocker. "Theo, I'd like to you to meet Hillary, our oldest daughter."

Aside from her darker brown hair, Hillary left no doubt she was Judy's daughter. I stepped beside Liddy. "Hillary, this is Theo."

"Pleasure to finally meet you. Mom and dad have spoken so much about you," Hillary said as we exchanged perfunctory grins.

"Pleasure's all mine. I guess welcome home is in order." I stumbled for the right words, uncertain how she felt about her circumstances.

Liddy rescued me. "I'd suggest we sit out here, but it looks like those clouds are about to bust. Let's go on inside."

Arnie and I followed the women into the living room. Liddy took drink requests and returned minutes later with refreshments. Arnie sat on our raised hearth, allowing Judy and Hillary opposite ends of the sofa. Liddy and I sat across from them in our chairs.

Liddy looked at Hillary and then Arnie. "Go ahead, Hillary. Tell your dad the good news."

Hillary offered Arnie a reluctant look and giggled.

Judy nudged her. "Go on, silly. Don't act so shy about it. I know you're dying to tell him."

Arnie suspiciously eyed Judy and Hillary.

"I've found a place of my own."

Arnie's wrinkled brow relaxed. "That's great news, I think. How'd you manage that so fast?"

"At lunch, mom introduced me to Missus Thrope. She asked me if I planned on staying in Shiloh. When I told her only if I could land a suitable job and a place to live . . ." Hillary put her hand on her father's knee. "You know I love you and mom, and there's a host of fond memories in that old house, but I'm just not the innocent, young girl you sent off to school anymore. Let's face it. Neither of us wants to cramp each other's lifestyles. Right?"

Arnie grinned and nodded. "Sounds fair." He peeked at Judy's hidden smirk. "So what happened?"

"Well, Miss Bernie grabbed my arm, laughed and said. 'Follow me. I want to show you something upstairs.' We went through a door in the back of the restaurant that led upstairs. They have a musty but quiet, cozy four-room apartment up there. Bernie said they lived in it until Alex turned twelve, and they decided to buy a bigger house in town. Dad, it's perfect, and Miss Bernie said I don't need to pay rent until I get a job. She even promised to remove their restaurant stuff out of there by this weekend, so I can start to fix it up as it suits me."

Arnie eyed Hillary and Judy. "What will you need? Does everything still work okay?"

Judy and Hillary giggled as they glanced at each other.

"Dad, it comes with the cutest old refrigerator and stove, and Bernie offered to leave the kitchen table and chairs. All I'll need is some living room and bedroom things." Hillary's puppy eyes almost won Arnie.

"But what about getting a job?" Arnie snapped back.

"I landed a job too. Can you believe it?"

Liddy and Judy unsuccessfully stifled their giddiness as they stared at Arnie's shocked face. "You got a job this afternoon too?" Arnie saw me shrug my shoulders, though I guessed who likely hired Hillary.

Hillary giggled. "When we got back downstairs, Hal Archer and Nick Arians had arrived and pulled their chairs over for a few minutes. Before they left, Hal asked if I'd consider a job opening in City Hall and invited me to stop by his office. He showed me the empty desk in front of his office and briefly described what he expected from an administrative assistant. The pay certainly falls short of my old job but would suit my financial needs here in Shiloh."

Arnie's growing smile reflected his approval. "So when do you start?"

"Hal asked if I could stop by in the morning but said if I needed a couple of days to get settled into my new place he'd understand and even offered to lend a hand moving."

I slapped my knees and stood. "Congratulations, Hillary. I guess that means you'll be staying right here in Shiloh."

"Looks that way Mister Phillips, I mean Theo."

Rain slapped the windows as cracks of thunder rumbled. Liddy laughed. "Guess we can talk about what Hillary needs for her new place while this blows over."

By the time the rain stopped, Liddy and I learned far more about Hillary's formative years in Shiloh before she scampered off to college in North Carolina and landed a sociology degree and a husband. Hillary explained how she and her husband Mark drifted apart physically and emotionally after a miscarriage. On the lighter side, Hillary, or Hilly as her family and close friends know her, talked about her teenage friendships with Hal and Nick's wife Tammy. Hillary's eyes misted as she reflected upon Tammy's funeral after her car wreck out on River Road seven years ago.

CHAPTER SEVEN

LIDDY BEGAN SCOOTING OUT THE DOOR BRIGHT AND EARLY EACH MORNING to spend most of her days at school before lending Judy a hand to get Hillary's new apartment ready. I took advantage and shifted my focus to writing about Coach Priestly.

My previous research into John Priestly involved gathering details and background material pertaining almost exclusively to his unfortunate incarceration, which manifested after I had dug into his cousin's untimely, tragic death. I now needed to delve deeper and decided to once again dive into the Sentinel's grungy archives, nicknamed "the morgue." There, Shiloh's distant past resided in dust-laden, musty storage boxes above the file cabinets I had ransacked months earlier.

I already knew John orchestrated Shiloh's gradual gridiron success not long after he arrived sixteen years ago, but I hoped to uncover a few new nuggets that might serve as backdrop material. The morgue's dankness stirred a fit of sneezes and sniffles before I adjusted and first assessed the paraphernalia stuffed in the file cabinets. I sorted through each drawer looking for photos and notes having to do with Coach Priestly and the Shiloh Saints football team during John's previous twelve seasons. In short order, I discovered that John graduated from Valdosta College and remained as a graduate assistant coach while he earned a Masters degree before returning to his alma mater.

After two days rummaging the morgue, I harvested two bulging folders chock-full of discolored, dated photos, scribbled notes, and clipped articles. Each added another mosaic tidbit depicting John's time before false accusations and a rush to judgment exiled him to prison four years ago. Though the truth exonerated John several months ago, I only knew of his earlier years through the wild and legendary tales shared by Pete, Andy, Jay, and Jim about the back-to-back glory-filled, State Championship seasons they experienced under Coach Priestly a decade ago.

———

SUNDAY MORNING LIDDY and I stood at the foot of the church steps as Hal maneuvered his father's black dually into their usual parking spot across the street. Phillip jumped out of the rear seat and opened the front passenger door. He offered his hand as Harold stepped out onto the street. Harold brushed Phillip's hand aside and adjusted his tie as he surveyed the church before he made his way across the street and greeted Liddy and me.

When Harold first introduced himself eight months ago, his auspicious comportment demanded center stage, but his once loud and proud persona had since eroded. No longer able to stand tall and proud, he worked his way through the church foyer with head and shoulders hunched. Though his former magnetic charm eluded him, he still managed to acknowledge everyone who addressed him with his inexorable smile and wave but avoided voicing more than a perfunctory pleasantry with anyone. Phillip and Hal then escorted him to his usual seat along the center aisle near the front of the sanctuary.

Liddy and I caught up with our usual clique near the back row of pews. I joined Zeb, Sam and Larry huddled together while Liddy engaged Susanna and Martha standing not far from Jeannie, Pete, Jay and Jim, deep into conversations of their own.

Moments later, Mary's piano solo silenced the usual pre-service chatter that percolated throughout the sanctuary. Arnie's smile broadened as Melissa Arians and Hillary entered and settled into their seats beside us.

Melissa whispered with blush cheeks, "We lost track of time after I dropped the twins off in the children's department." Hillary tried to hide a growing grin as she and Missy exchanged glances.

The organist joined Mary moments before Marie Masterson led the choir down the center aisle and up into the choir loft. Nick and Joe Arians took their customary seats beside John along the back row.

Once the music stopped, Arnie rose sporting a grand smile. "Doesn't our new air conditioning feel a whole lot better?" Applause erupted while heads bobbed up and down with an occasional resounding "Amen!" tossed in until Arnie thrust his hands high into the air. "Let us give thanks to God who graciously provided us with a benefactor after our old system just couldn't combat the sweltering summertime heat any longer. Their generosity made it once again possible to enjoy our time together in spite of the summer heat or winter chill for many years to come."

Arnie's message, ironically, rested upon the passage about the widow's offering in Luke's gospel. "It's not the size of the gift but the sincerity and generosity of the heart that measures the value of our offerings," Arnie concluded.

While we waited to file into the foyer, Zeb tapped my shoulder. "Hey, how 'bout you and the missus come over for a little cookout?" Martha nudged Liddy and told her they planned to go.

Liddy squeezed my hand and asked Zeb, "Would you like us to bring anything?"

Zeb grinned as he shook his head. "But I would suggest you wear comfortable clothes. If the weather cooperates, we'll be out back."

Melissa and Hillary had disappeared to fetch the twins by the time we exited our pew. Larry, Martha, and Zeb chatted with the Simmons.

In the foyer, Liddy and I found Harold, Hal, and Phillip off by themselves. "Good to see you out and about Harold," I said.

Harold patted my shoulder. "Why thank you, Theo. I'm feeling much better. Must be Maddie's cookin' and mother-hen attention."

Liddy wagged her finger at Harold. "You best keep minding Miss Maddie, ya hear? She'll fatten you right up again. You'll be good as new in no time."

"Pop's been doing much better as a matter of fact," Hal said before he caught Phillip's attention. "Phil, stay with Pop. I'll be right back."

Harold said, "Well Theo, I read that Larry's got you writing a couple more articles."

"You read right. I've been prepping to spend two or three evenings a week at the stadium to gain some insight on Coach Priestly's magic touch from his players' perspective. I suspect more than a few folks in Shiloh are curious to see if he still has that magic touch and if the Saints can get back to winning again."

Harold managed a hint of his former exuberant laughter. "I sure hope so. That big stadium hasn't been more than half full the last couple of seasons. I remember when we increased the seating capacity because of all the standing room only crowds we used to contend with." A pause followed by a distant stare took over.

"Liddy and I are looking forward to seeing the Saints in action for ourselves this year. A few wins, and I'm sure the crowds will return."

Harold refocused but appeared flustered. "Oh, um, yes, Theo. Let's hope John can manage one or two unexpected victories this season."

Hal returned. "Hey, Zeb's having a cookout. Y'all goin'?"

Liddy beamed. "We are. Are all of you going?" She glanced at Harold.

Phillip peered over at Hal. "Yes, little brother, all of us are going." Harold eyed Hal. "Pop, Zeb specifically asked if I'd bring you. Besides, you need to get out, and Maddie deserves a break."

Harold surrendered with a half-hearted nod. "I reckon I can find a shady spot and make the best of an afternoon away from the house."

Nick's voice rose above the few remaining voices in the foyer. "Hal, y'all coming?"

Hal waved. "We'll be there. Theo and Liddy will be there too."

"Great, see all y'all in a bit." Nick caught up with Joe, Missy, and their twins and filed past Arnie along with the last of the congregation.

Harold, Hal, and Phillip opted to exit the side door, while Liddy and I stopped to say hello to Judy and Arnie now that we found ourselves the last to leave.

Arnie shared a sly grin as we shook hands. "See you two at Zeb's later?"

"Right after we change clothes, we'll head that way."

"We're going to help Hillary with the last of her things, and then we'll stop by for a bit. She's itching to sleep in her new place tonight."

"How's she enjoying working with Hal?" Liddy asked.

Judy said, "You can ask her yourself this afternoon, but sure sounds like she's enjoying the challenge of keeping the Mayor's office running without a hitch. At least I think that's how Hilly described it."

Liddy shared Judy's laugh.

———

By the time we pulled into Zeb's long driveway, more than a handful of vehicles already cluttered his front yard. Anticipating the arrival of more guests, I maneuvered closer to the road before I parked to avoid getting blocked in whenever we decided to leave.

Country music blared from Zeb's back porch, and aromatic smoke drifted across the yard as Jay and Jim tended the smoker and a charcoal grill. Two large trash barrels guarded each end of a folding table ladened with jugs of tea and lemonade.

Liddy found Martha, Marie, and Susanna and left me standing in line to get some sweet tea. Zeb appeared wearing a white t-shirt, overalls and a wide brimmed straw hat covering his scraggly, mostly gray hair. "Glad you made it. Where's Liddy?"

I greeted Zeb and pointed to the gaggle of women swelled by the arrival of Judy, Hillary and Melissa. The men huddled close to where Jim and Jay were cooking. "So this is your idea of having a few friends over?"

"I don't have as many folks over like I used to, but maybe you'll get the chance to put some names with the less than familiar faces before this shindig breaks up this afternoon." Zeb gestured toward Sam and Larry who waved and motioned us to join them. "Them two know almost everyone that'll be here."

"Thanks, Zeb. I'll let you mingle with your guests. Catch you later."

Carrying my glass of tea, I joined some of the men in time to hear the tail end of Arnie's digested update on Hillary's apartment before he added a couple of humorous stories about her first few days finding her way around Shiloh's administration building.

Nick added between bursts of laughter, "Sounds as though Hilly's sure to be running city hall before long."

The Archers arrived just in time to hear Jay and Jim scream, "Come and get it!" Harold found a vacant chair in the shade beside Zeb while Phillip got drinks. Hal appeared headed toward us but waved with a smile as he walked past us, stopping briefly where some of the women had gathered before retrieving dinner for himself and his father.

Liddy and I filled our plates with pulled pork, beans and slaw before we claimed a shady spot behind one of Zeb's sheds.

"Sorry I've been ignoring you," Liddy confessed between bites.

"Figured you were enjoying yourself."

"I was, but you gotta promise not to tell."

"Tell what?"

"Theo Phillips, you gotta promise me."

"Okay, I promise not to say anything about whatever you're about to tell me." I crossed my heart and raised a Boy Scout salute.

"Since Andy's getting a bachelor party next Friday, we figured Megan deserved a bachelorette bash too. She didn't enjoy a fancy wedding or any of the fun stuff before."

"Sounds like a marvelous idea."

"Marie already talked with Bernie and Silas. They will have closed up by the time we plan to start. We'll have the restaurant to ourselves. We were also discussing ideas to entertain ourselves for a couple of hours. Hey, you wouldn't know any Chippendale dancers?"

My jaw dropped.

Liddy's cheeks glowed red. "That was one of Hillary's suggestions."

"Well, since the preacher's daughter suggested it, I'll see if I can find a pair of leather chaps and a cowboy hat."

"Over my dead body! Seriously, we need to come up with a couple of silly games. We already discussed each of us bringing gag gifts to embarrass Megan."

After we dumped our plates, Liddy grabbed my hand and pulled me toward Kay Abernathy. I recognized her husband from my visits to the post office though we had never really talked. He stood at least two inches taller than Zeb or his boys. Not only had Ray Abernathy been Shiloh's Postmaster for the last twenty years, but I learned he had also played defensive end at Georgia under Coach Dooley not long after Liddy and I graduated. We shared much of the remaining afternoon reminiscing. Ray provided his perspective on being in the second wave of recruits who broke the color barrier in Athens. The Abernathys' past and present reminded me how far towns like Shiloh had traveled from the not-so-distant days of segregation in South Georgia.

The skies had turned a darkened reddish-orange by the time we excused ourselves and climbed into our Expedition. Liddy exhaled and said, "Ol' Zeb sure draws a crowd to his little get-togethers. I'm bushed and couldn't eat another bite. What about you?"

I started the engine as I glanced over at Liddy. "I call first dibs on the shower if you don't mind."

Just as my foot slid off the brake, a loud smack on the back window caused me to hit the brake. John's silly grin appeared in my side-view mirror as I lowered my window.

"Sorry if I startled you. Just wanted to remind you that we start practices Friday morning. I've given the boys a couple of days off before we get into full pads. I wanted to ask you, if ya don't mind, to be there for our first team meeting before practice starts Friday."

I gave Liddy a quick glance and said to John, "Sure. What time?"

"How 'bout seven? I'll make sure there's plenty of coffee and donuts."

Liddy grinned. "I'll drop him off before I head to my classroom. Kay said we'd be busy getting ready for the first day of school on Monday."

John stepped back and nodded. "Y'all get some rest. See ya Friday, Theo."

CHAPTER EIGHT

"I'll be ready in ten minutes. Lunch is in the fridge. And for goodness sakes, please don't forget your sunscreen."

"Yes, dear. I'm nearly ready."

After stashing my lunch and composition notebook inside my knapsack, my face and exposed fair-skinned appendages received a quick layer of the SPF70 Liddy left out on the counter.

"Ready? We gotta run," Liddy said as she pulled two bottles of water from the fridge. "Here. Make sure you drink plenty of water today."

"Yes, ma'am." I grabbed my hat after sliding a water bottle into the side pocket of my knapsack. "Those dark clouds tell me we'll be lucky if John gets his practice in before it pours."

Liddy glimpsed out the window. "You might be right. Better grab your rain parka just in case."

———

Thunder interrupted John's spirited talk to his players at the end of their abbreviated practice. The team broke ranks and raced for the locker room before John could lower his whistle. By the time John and I jogged in out of the pouring rain, the clanging of metal lockers and the clamor of back-and-forth banter greeted us as we headed into his office. I pulled off my drenched parka and grabbed a towel as John's whistle blast silenced the locker room.

"Coaches, I want every one of 'em outta here in ten minutes, or I'll change my mind about no practice tomorrow. If you need to make a call to your parents, see Coach Simmons or Adams." John postured himself just beyond his office door, arms crossed.

Jay's gruff voice followed. "You heard Coach. I don't care if you have to finish getting dressed in the rain. You got nine minutes to vamoose!"

In short order, the sound of slamming lockers and feet scurrying out the locker room door died. John maintained his formidable pose until Pete appeared beside him. "If you don't need Jay and me anymore, we'll see you tonight." Pete saw me in the office. "You too, Mister P."

I nodded as John barked, "Go on and git. I'll lock up. Thanks for a good first practice in spite of the rain. We'll see you guys tonight." A partial grin creased John's gritty appearance as he toweled his wet hair and plopped behind his desk. "Heck of an introduction to your first practice. What'd ya think?"

"The boys sure busted their butts. Gotta hand it to you. They've got plenty of spunk and speed but not much size."

John rocked back and clutched the ends of the towel draped around his neck. "This is a young group, mostly inexperienced underclassmen. I'm praying for some growth spurts before the season ends. In the meantime, they'll just have to make up for their overall lack of size with bulldog tenacity. There's not a quitter in this bunch. The loafers and slackers cut themselves during summer workouts."

John jostled a side drawer in his rickety wooden desk and pulled out a brown sack lunch while I reached for mine. "Let's thank God for holding off the weather and for our sandwiches. My stomach's growling."

A knock interrupted us a moment before Timmy poked his head around the door. "Sorry, Coach. I'm all done, and all the equipment is either put away or set out to dry."

John looked my way. "You know Mister Phillips, don't ya?"

"Of course, sir." Timmy smiled and waved. "Hello, Mister Phillips. What do ya think about the team?"

"Pretty impressed. I believe you and Coach Priestly might wrangle a few surprise wins this season."

John grinned. "Good job today. Now git outta here. Enjoy your weekend, and don't forget to stop by my office Monday morning. I'll arrange to get you dismissed early with your last period teacher. Do you need a ride home?"

"No, sir. Momma's outside." Timmy said with a tooth-filled, freckled grin as he pulled the door shut behind him.

"If I had a team full of Timmy's, we'd win another state championship," John said as he reached into his sack lunch. "He already can throw better than anybody I got right now, and he knows most all our offensive plays."

"I noted how the players responded to his hustle and encouragement too. You better hope his mom and dad don't move out of Shiloh."

John shook his head in the middle of biting into his sandwich and mumbled before swallowing, "Over my dead body."

We continued chatting about various players and how Jay, Jim, and Pete juggled their schedules to tag-team as assistants.

When the rain stopped, John checked his watch. "We gotta head over to the school. I promised Kay I'd stop by her office before I left. Besides, don't you want to check out Liddy's classroom?"

"It's all I've heard about for the past week."

During our walk across campus, I asked, "How well do you know Ray Abernathy?"

"Kay's husband? Beyond an occasional school function or bumping into him around town, not well. Why?"

"We met at Zeb's cookout and talked quite a bit. We had another chance to talk today during practice while we sat together in the bleachers."

John tendered a curious grin. "As long as I've coached here, he's been a fixture at practices. He pretty much sits by himself, though, except when Kay wanders by to watch."

"Did you know Vince Dooley recruited him to play at Georgia?"

John stopped dead in his tracks. "I know he and Kay graduated from Athens, but he never said anything about playing football."

"He told me he graduated in 1980, which got me thinking. Liddy and I both remember the introduction of the first black football players in '71. When I asked him about his best memories as a Georgia Bulldog, he said, 'Meeting Kay and getting his degree.' When I inquired about his playing days, he pulled up his pant leg and pointed to scars up and down both sides of his right knee. He told me when Georgia won the national championship his final year, he and Kay watched the Sugar Bowl on the television in their apartment."

John offered a blank stare. "Theo, I feel awful. I never knew that about Mister Abernathy. I need to make it my business to get to know him better."

"I would if I were you. Besides, I've decided to see if Ray will allow me to mention a little about his football past in one of my articles. You oughta know, he confessed that you're the best football coach he's witnessed. He said, Coach Dooley might've recruited stars as his players, but you coach players to become stars."

Across the hall from Liddy's art room, we heard Liddy and Phoebe singing to Aretha Franklin's "You Make Me Feel Like A Natural Woman." John and I slipped into the back of Phoebe's music room. When their giggles announced the end of their song, we applauded and shouted, "Bravo. Bravo!" Liddy and Phoebe turned with startled, red faces.

Liddy chimed, "Enough with you John Priestly. We were just having fun before we went looking for you guys."

"How about showing me your art room?" I grabbed Liddy's hand. "Please excuse us for a couple of minutes."

When we got back, John sat perched on one end of Phoebe's desk while she occupied her chair. John said, "We were just talking about Andy and Megan's wedding tomorrow. Y'all cutting out?"

"The sky looks ready to dump again. Think we'll go ahead and head out. See you tonight John?"

"Most certainly. Wouldn't want to miss the fun."

———

ARNIE CALLED DURING dinner. We arranged that he would ride with me to Andy's bachelor party, and Judy would take Liddy with her to the Butcher Shoppe to help Susanna and Jeannie decorate before the others showed for Megan's bachelorette soirée, as Judy called it.

Dark clouds chased the sun into an early retreat, leaving behind a fading deep orange horizon as we drove across town. Arnie and I pulled through the open gates of Shiloh Creek Lumber Mill just as Nick and Joe arrived. They followed us to where we found Pete's red truck, Phillip's Wrangler, and Zeb's Bronco parked outside the warehouse entrance. Pete, Jay, and Jim leaned against a bundle of lumber while Phillip sorted through a collection of CDs. As we entered, Phillip shouted to no one in particular, "Hey guys, how about some Rascal Flatts?"

Zeb cringed from his perch on a crate across the warehouse floor. "You call that country? Phil, got any Johnny Cash?"

"Pop, Johnny Cash? Really? Hey Phil, how about some Florida-Georgia Line?"

Phillip smiled as he dangled a half-dozen CDs on his right forefinger. "I got ya covered." He looked up as Arnie, Nick, Joe and I grabbed sodas from the cooler. "Any requests?"

Nick glanced at his brother and shouted back to Phillip. "I'm partial to Rascal Flatts myself."

Joe put his arm on Nick's shoulder and glanced at Arnie. "Ever since their concert in Savannah last year, Nick believes their song 'Wake Me Up' was written to help him move on from losing Tammy."

Arnie looked at Zeb. "Where's John, Sam and Andy?"

Zeb moved closer as the music grew louder. He checked his pocket watch. "Sam and Andy should be here any minute. Not sure about John."

Headlights flickered out front. "Sorry guys," John shouted as he entered. "I had to drop Marie off first. Looks as though they've got quite a fancy party started over there." John turned to Joe. "Missy had the twins with her. Thought your momma agreed to watch them tonight."

Joe shrugged his shoulders. "Thought so too, but she couldn't leave the summer house until almost noon. She promised Missy she'd swing by as soon as she got into town."

Another set of headlights flashed out front. Sam walked in carrying a projector and a laptop. Andy followed with his hands tucked into his pants pockets. We watched DVDs of the Shiloh Saint's championship games for the next couple of hours. John added his ego-busting two-cents whenever Pete and Andy got carried away reminiscing their glory days.

Not long after Sam switched off the projector, Joe suggested we drive downtown and crash the girls' party. Zeb laughed. "It's getting too quiet around here anyway."

I parked next to Zeb and Sam across the street from the Butcher Shoppe. Arnie laughed as we climbed out. "Check it out. They're doing the Boot-Scootin' Boogie."

We held back across the street from the Butcher Shoppe contemplating whether we should just watch or go on in when the door swung open. Megan followed Jeannie onto the sidewalk laughing and giggling as they waved for us to join them. Liddy, Judy and Susanna gawked at us out the restaurant's front window. Lightning followed by a loud clap of thunder chased us across Main Street. Pete grabbed the door as we gathered beneath the awning. His laughter came to an abrupt halt when a sheriff's deputy pulled up.

Mitch, the sheriff's deputy I had gotten to know in recent months, stepped out of his patrol car. "Sorry to interrupt your fun this evening. Joe, Nick, I need to talk to you."

Joe and Nick stepped around the patrol car to speak with Mitch. A moment later Joe turned stone-faced while Nick shook his head as tears appeared. Joe walked into the Butcher Shoppe and embraced Missy and the twins. Missy pulled Lizzy and Lucy next to her as they began to cry. Joe walked back to Mitch and Nick. "We'll follow you," Joe told Mitch.

John walked to the driver's side window of Mitch's patrol car. A minute later, flickering blue lights danced off the buildings along Shiloh's downtown area. John said, "There's been an accident out on River Road. I'm afraid it's Missus Arians."

CHAPTER NINE

Larry's call woke both of us.

"Theo, Lucinda Arians passed early this morning."

"Momma Arians?"

"She never regained consciousness after the accident."

I sat speechless, allowing the words to sink in.

Liddy sat up and placed her hand on my shoulder. I turned and told her the grim news.

"What happened?" I asked Larry.

Larry sounded weary and agitated. "I just left the hospital, but from all accounts, seems she lost control and rolled her Lincoln into a drainage ditch. She wasn't wearing her seatbelt and suffered a severe head injury. A witness at the scene stated he didn't see the accident happen but came upon her right after. He said she moaned when he found her slumped across the front seat. He reached in and turned the ignition off in her car before he ran back to his car to call 911. By the time he returned to check on her, she had become unresponsive. The witness said a heavy downpour produced poor visibility on the road just minutes before the accident. He added that a dark-colored sports car passed him and nearly forced him off the road moments before he found Missus Arians."

"That's awful. I pray she didn't suffer."

I lowered the phone and eyed Liddy. "She evidently never regained consciousness."

Liddy squeezed my shoulder. "What about Missy and the twins?"

"Larry didn't mention them."

"Find out what we can do," Liddy said as she climbed out of bed but froze, her eyes and mouth wide-open. "Oh my goodness. Andy and Megan's wedding."

After I hung up, I embraced Liddy and said, "I doubt this will keep them from getting married as planned, but it might put a damper on the wedding ceremony and reception."

An hour later, we found Arnie sitting in silence beside Nick and Joe in the hospital waiting area. Arnie lifted his head with more of a grimace than a grin.

"Larry called to tell us," I said as Joe and Nick looked up. "We're truly sorry."

Liddy added, "Joe, is there anything I can do? How are Missy and the girls?"

"Thanks, Liddy." Joe sighed as he added, "When I hung up with Missy a few minutes ago, the girls were still asleep. She's dreading telling them about their grandma." Joe's red eyes pleaded before the words came out. "Miss Liddy, I didn't know what to say to Missy to comfort her either."

Liddy straightened Joe's dark hair with her fingers. "Would you like me to go over there and sit with her?"

Arnie rested his hand on Joe's shoulder and looked at Liddy. "I think that'd be an excellent idea. I'm afraid Judy's stuck at Marie's helping Susanna with the wedding preparations."

Joe squeezed Liddy's hand. "Would you mind? Missy could use some company."

Arnie looked up at me standing beside Liddy. "There's not much more anyone can do here. Why don't you take Liddy on ahead? Joe and Nick shouldn't be too much longer. I'll see you at Marie's."

Nick exhaled, regained his composure and tried his best to smile. "Will you please explain why we won't be there this afternoon? Joe and I don't want to take anything away from Andy and Megan's happy day."

"They'll understand, but we'll be sure to say something." I grinned and took Liddy's hand.

———

"Do you think Missy and the girls will be okay?" Liddy asked as we left for Marie's place right after lunch.

"Missy and the twins seemed to accept the news better than Nick or Joe. They all acknowledged Momma Arians led a wonderful, full life and will be sorely missed."

Clear skies brought smiles to our faces while our vehicle splashed through puddles along our drive to Marie's farmhouse. The usually sleepy Shiloh Creek roared beneath the narrow bridge's rain-soaked timbers, testifying all the more of the previous night's storm.

As we drove up, John pointed to vehicles already parked beyond the pasture gate beside the barn. Sam and the boys had set up chairs beneath a large, white tent. Sheets of plywood provided a mud-free walkway between the house, barn, and canopy while scattered hay hid most of the remaining muddy areas.

After we parked and headed toward the barn, I asked, "Aren't you glad you didn't wear these heels and this lovely dress?"

Liddy rolled her eyes. "I'm just glad Megan insisted we wait to change until we got here." She grabbed her shoes and dress and headed to the house to catch up with Marie and the rest of the bridesmaids.

Three o'clock sharp, Phoebe began playing a collection of wedding songs. I found a back row seat beside Larry and Zeb beneath the canopy while Martha floated about serving as the official photographer in Mary's stead. Ringo wandered out from the shadows of the barn, then sprawled behind John in a disinterested nap posture, only occasionally raising his head during the ceremony. John stood alongside the other best men.

At Andy and Megan's request, there were no fancy tuxedos or frilly gowns. The groom and best men wore jeans and long sleeve, white dress shirts. Andy also wore a leather vest on Susanna's insistence.

Megan's mother, Paula, a reserved, polite woman, sat prim and proper in the front row across the aisle from Susanna and Sam. She held a thin smile as Jeannie, Mary, Liddy, and Marie paraded down the aisle and took their places on the bride's side. Megan and her bridesmaids wore coordinating yellow, summer dresses. Arnie wore a navy blazer over an open-collared white oxford shirt and jeans. Megan's father strutted chest-swelled down the aisle in a drab, well-worn, charcoal wool suit and black tie with her clinging to his arm. Only Megan's rosy smile outshone her father's proud grin. Heads turned as Megan paraded past with white and yellow wildflowers adorning her blonde, braided hair, clutching a small bouquet of matching wildflowers in her free hand.

The ceremony lasted hardly twenty minutes. Right after Arnie pronounced them "man and wife," Andy kissed his bride, which cued Phoebe and she played "Just You and I" by Crystal Gayle and Eddie Rabbitt. Andy and Megan made their way to the back of the canopy where they greeted all the guests.

I took Liddy by the arm, and after congratulating the newlyweds, we pulled Susanna and Sam aside and shared the tragic news about Momma Arians.

Zeb stepped beside Sam and asked, "Either of you heard from Hal or Phillip? Thought they'd be here for Megan."

As Arnie walked past, I tapped his shoulder and whispered, "Do you have any idea why Hal and Phillip aren't here?"

Arnie panned the guests before he answered. "I expected them to be here too. I hope Harold's okay. Would you check on them later and let me know if everything's okay? My hands are full at the moment. In fact, I need to scoot out in a few minutes to spend time with the Arians family this evening."

I nodded with an obliging smile. "You did a great job with Megan and Andy today." I glanced over my shoulder and took in the smiles and giggles surrounding the newlyweds.

Arnie said, "I pray God will bless both of them with ample reasons to experience even more laughter and smiles in the days ahead."

Zeb laughed. "Gotta tell ya, looks like Paula and Carl certainly have found a reason to smile again. It's good to see them sharing in Megan's happiness."

Sam slapped Zeb on his back. "I think they know Andy'll do right by their daughter and take good care of her."

Bernie Thrope stepped beside us and yelled with her hands on her hips, "Please, excuse me, everyone! We have a special dinner prepared for you. Please help yourself."

Liddy and I followed behind Megan's parents as they inspected the selection of food items before choosing some rice and kabobs. We joined them and enjoyed sharing stories about Megan and Andy.

After a quiet pause in our conversation, Paula looked at her husband and said to Liddy and me, "Mister and Missus Phillips, Carl and I want to thank you so much for the compassion and kindness you extended our daughter. We feel as though we let her down when her marriage with Hank Archer fell apart."

"Paula, we did little more than listen. God did the rest, and today marks a beautiful new beginning for both you and your daughter." Liddy rested her hand on Paula's as she spoke.

Carl's quiet, misty gaze, which remained focused upon Megan and Andy enjoying themselves with their friends, spoke volumes. After a moment, he looked at me and mouthed, "Thank you."

"When's your book going to be out, Mister Phillips?" Paula asked with a friendly, curious smile.

Liddy giggled as she answered for me. "I'll personally make certain you get a copy. The Sentinel's sponsoring Theo's book launch the weekend before Thanksgiving. I hope you'll be there."

Carl stared at me, and I sensed what he feared to ask.

"Please plan to be there. I want you to rest assured, Megan's secret is safe, and I avoided any mention of her abusive relationship with Hank. I mentioned her in the book because of her fond memories of Coach Masterson." I locked eyes with Carl. His dimples deepened while his furrowed brow ebbed.

Our attention shifted to Andy and Megan cutting their cake. Everyone chuckled when Andy got called to remove the garter from Megan's leg. Megan made it easy for him by sliding it to her ankle. More laughter ensued when Pete leaped over the other bachelors and grabbed the garter after Andy flung it over his shoulder. Phoebe added to the merriment when she wrestled with Mary over Megan's bouquet. They playfully decided to each take half. Shortly before six, Andy and Megan drove off in Megan's red convertible Mustang, cans clanging behind them.

Liddy dozed off long before we arrived back into town. I stared at the brightly lit bronze dome atop the Masterson Administration Building. It reminded me that Hal and Phillip missed the wedding and renewed my concerns that something happened to Harold.

———

AT CHURCH ON Sunday, the usual chatter and lighthearted laughter was displaced by a muted, somber atmosphere. The older women, typically abuzz with gossip and murmurs, held hankies and shared tears of disbelief.

Martha shook her head as she and Larry greeted us in the foyer. "Momma Arians' loss to this community is being felt most by those who remember her feistier, more active days. They looked to Lucy, as her friends knew her back then, to spearhead many of the church and community activities, especially during Nick's and Joe's school years. During that time, her husband, Barnie, stormed in and out of the office where Joe now practices law. They both fought to safeguard Shiloh from the encroaching Twenty-First Century craziness that still threatens to change our blissful community. Everything changed though when Barnie died ten years ago. Lucinda retreated from the spotlight and began spending more time in their family's vacation home on Saint Simons Island. If it wasn't for the twins, she might have left Shiloh altogether."

"I never heard that about her. She was always so unassuming and gracious around us, and I know the twins idolized her." Liddy sighed, and we walked into the sanctuary.

Arnie concluded his sermon on the importance of the church and community. He then brought a brief smile to Sam's and Susanna's faces when he reported on the wedding before his light-hearted mood made a marked change.

"I'd be remiss not to share how sad we all feel about the unexpected passing of Momma Arians. We should all take solace in the notion that she and Barnie are together again. Her funeral will be here Wednesday morning, and we'll not hold our usual evening service, so we can take the time to share memories after the funeral."

As Liddy and I prepared to leave, Zeb and John pulled me aside. "Have you heard anything about Harold or his sons?"

"No, but I plan to call this afternoon."

———

LIDDY FIXED DINNER while I dialed Harold's home number. Maddie answered and suggested I speak with Hal.

"Hal, we missed you guys at the wedding yesterday and at church this morning. Is everything okay?"

"We had an unexpected guest Friday night. My mother."

I paused to absorb the news. "Your mother? After all these years?"

"We're all trying to make sense of her visit too. Dad stayed up into the wee hours with her after we went to bed. When we awoke yesterday morning, he was fast asleep on the sofa, and she was gone. Dad awoke confused after he realized she had left without saying a word. He's been rummaging through old family albums in his study ever since."

"I can only imagine how unsettling such a visit would be."

Liddy's ears perked up, and she nestled closer to catch Hal's response.

"Phil and I thought it best to stay with dad. For some reason, he believes she's coming back."

"If there's anything Liddy and I can do, please call. Do you mind if I let Arnie and some of the others know? They've been asking."

"I guess not, but until we understand why Dixie has returned, let's keep a lid on it.

CHAPTER TEN

THOUGH LIDDY ENJOYED TEACHING FOR MANY YEARS, SCHOOL BOARD infighting and bureaucratic intrusion sapped her enthusiasm seven years ago. Then Kay Abernathy, with the help of John and Phoebe, persuaded her teaching in Shiloh would be different.

Liddy scurried out the door before I poured my first cup of coffee, exchanging an untouched bowlful of cereal for a piece of my toast and a quick kiss. After I read the morning paper and munched on Liddy's bowl of granola, I called Arnie.

"Glad I caught you. You'll never guess why the Archers didn't show up this weekend."

"Dixie." Arnie's bluntness dumbfounded me.

"How'd you know?" I stammered.

"Hillary called not long after she got to work this morning."

"Did Hillary say anything about how Hal felt about her visit? When I talked to him last night, he struck me as being unsettled, facing a quandary, especially in light of how she departed as mysteriously as she arrived."

"How would you react if your estranged mother popped in unannounced after twenty years, then vanished again without a word?"

"Unsettled, I'm sure. Did Hal say anything more to Hillary about Dixie's visit?"

"No, but Hillary shared Hal's concern for his dad."

"What do you think?" I asked.

"In light of Harold's recent state of mind and health, I'm not sure what to think." Arnie paused. "Let's keep a lid on this for the time being. Lord only knows the sordid gossip this news might stir up."

"What about Larry, Zeb, and Sam? They might ask what I heard?"

"I don't expect you to lie. Just don't volunteer specifics for the time being."

———

NEARLY EVERY BUSINESS and the schools shut down at noon Wednesday. The pews swelled at Shiloh Baptist Church as carloads of family and friends arrived for Lucinda Arians' memorial service. Liddy and I managed to find seats in the back of the sanctuary after we paid our respects to the Arians family. Arnie opened the service at two o'clock and first thing allowed Nick and Joe to share memories of their mother while Missy consoled Lucy and Lizzie looking on from the front row. Arnie followed with a brief message before he exited behind the pallbearers as they carried Momma Arians' casket from the sanctuary. Fifteen minutes later, the motorcade pulled away and proceeded beyond the center of town, driving past the Arians' landmark homes and back through our neighborhood before moving on to Shiloh Cemetery.

Vehicles pulled off the road giving way to Mitch's cruiser, flashing its blue lights just ahead of the motorcade. As the endless serpentine string of cars and trucks with their lights on passed, folks bowed their heads along the shoulder of the road to offer their respects. Neighbors not at the service stood in somber silence on their porches.

A maroon canopy marked where Momma Arians' body would rest in peace alongside her husband Barnabas who passed ten years earlier. Liddy and I worked our way beside familiar faces, standing in the mid-afternoon sunshine to support the Arians family who sat beneath the canopy. Hal and Phillip escorted Harold to a chair reserved for him at the end of the first row. While Arnie offered some final words of solace, Harold fixated upon Momma Arians' casket. Only after Hal nudged him as everyone stood to leave did Harold break his contemplative gaze.

I wondered what went through his mind. Was he reminiscing about Momma Arians and her husband or conjuring thoughts about his own mortality?

On our way back to our vehicle, Liddy tugged on my arm. "Who's that beside that red convertible?"

A sober-faced woman wearing a sleeveless, navy dress and sunglasses stood in the shade of a moss-laden oak, hands folded in front of her. By the time I turned and shrugged in response to Liddy's inquiry, the woman had slid behind her steering wheel and drove off.

Susanna stopped before getting into Sam's pickup. "Y'all headed back to the church?"

Liddy said, "Right behind you. Susanna, did you see that woman under the oak tree?"

"The one who just drove off?"

"Do you know who she is?"

"I've never seen a fancy sports car like that around here either."

"It's too hot for idle chit-chat in this sunshine. Can we talk back at church?" I asked, looking at Liddy but plenty loud for Susanna to hear. Sam smirked, stepping into his truck.

———

THE FELLOWSHIP HALL overflowed with family and friends milling about while others filled their plates and headed to the tables to reminisce about Momma Arians. Judy, Mary, and Hillary made certain all the donated food and drinks found their proper place on the serving tables.

Liddy and I brought our plates and drinks to a table next to the Arians family where Zeb, Sam, Susanna, Larry, and Martha had saved us a couple of seats. While we ate, Liddy and I enjoyed listening to stories about Momma Arians and her husband.

Before too long, Arnie plopped in the chair beside me and let out a long sigh. "Momma sure left behind a lot of memories. I just heard some stories about her and old Barnie that I'd never heard before."

Zeb chuckled. "I bet there are even more stories you're not likely to hear about them as well. We'll just leave it at that if'n you know what I mean."

Sam looked at Liddy's curious stare. "He ain't talkin' about any sordid stories, mind you. Barnie and Miss Lucy instigated more good around these parts than most folks will ever know, but that's the way they preferred it."

Arnie sank back clinging to a smug smile, sipping on sweet tea.

A few minutes passed before Phillip walked up beside Arnie and whispered in his ear. Arnie nodded. Phillip turned and walked to the front entrance to the fellowship hall.

Arnie leaned in and said, "Dixie's here."

Before Arnie's words registered, the sound of the chatter fell like toppled dominoes as Hal and Phillip entered the fellowship hall ahead of Harold beside the woman we saw at the cemetery. Zeb, Sam and Susanna glared at each other before all three also noticed Arnie's affirming nod. Larry mouthed, "Is that who I think it is?"

Joe and Nick left their table and walked straight to Harold and Dixie. Hal and Phillip stepped aside and watched what appeared to be a friendly exchange. I couldn't make out their brief conversation, but Hal shared an animated shrug with Joe and Nick before they returned to their table.

Judy yanked off her apron and walked up to Arnie. Arnie took Judy's outreached hand, and they went to greet Harold and Dixie. Arnie shook hands with Harold while Judy and Dixie exchanged a hug.

Sam looked at us. "Do you know who that is with Harold?"

I nodded. "Dixie, I suppose."

Zeb said in a strained whisper, "It's been twenty years. What's she doing here?"

Liddy leaned close. "Susanna doesn't appear too thrilled to see Dixie."

Hal walked over to our table. "We had no idea she'd be here today. Hope it won't spoil the rest of the afternoon. Today's supposed to be Momma Arians' day of remembrance."

Zeb smiled at Hal. "Don't fret about it. Besides, I haven't seen your dad hold a smile like that in weeks."

"Let's just hope he's still smiling after she leaves," Hal muttered with a forlorn look directed at his mother.

———

BEFORE DAWN, I toasted a couple of bagels and poured coffee while Liddy got dressed for school. The morning paper provided Mary's perspective on Momma Arians' funeral along with a photo of the motorcade as it pulled away from the church. I enjoyed reading Mary's knack for choosing the right words to convey a story. Larry revealed his old-school newspaper background in his articles, whereas Mary provided the same succinctness the newspaper demanded but with a flair for words even her father admired.

Liddy scurried into the kitchen and checked the clock. "I've only got a couple of minutes. Can you put some cream cheese on my bagel and wrap it up while I drink a cup of coffee with you before I gotta run."

"You sure are enjoying being back in the classroom again aren't you?"

"The kids are like a breath of fresh air. They may not all be artists, but they're engaged and so far are eager to learn."

"I'm proud of you. You'll make a difference with these kids."

"Before I run, what do you think about Dixie and Harold?"

I paused and sipped my coffee. "Harold appeared happier than I've seen him in quite a while. But —"

"But what?"

"Hal and Phillip both seem uneasy about her presence. I haven't heard either refer to her as his mother."

"What do you expect? Phillip would have no memory of her, and Hal's gotta be festering all kinds of pent-up emotions that'll make it hard for him to accept her as his mother again."

"I agree, but did you notice how young she looked? From what Harold told me, she was much younger than him, but from a distance, she looks more like Hal and Hank's older sister."

Liddy glanced up and gave me a look that resonated loud and clear, the next words I said were critical.

"What I'm trying to say, in a roundabout manner, is she reminds me a lot of Megan. Although, I'm pretty confident Dixie's frosted hair isn't natural."

Liddy giggled. "The thought crossed my mind too. I wonder what she's been up to all these years. She looks amazing if you don't look too closely."

"Hun, the only face I enjoy inspecting up close is yours. But all the same, I think I'll see what more Larry can tell me about Dixie. In the meantime, I hope Harold's still smiling for several more days."

———

I WALKED INTO Larry's office shortly before ten. He stood from his desk chair and invited me to join him in the break room for a cup of coffee.

As I poured a cup for myself, I said, "Before I ask you something, I've gotta tell you how impressed I am with you letting Mary write more of the articles in the paper. She's got a real talent."

Larry took a swig of his coffee. "You trying to tell me she's a better writer than her ol' man?"

"Well, kinda." I peered at Larry's squint-eyed look.

"She may not be a better newspaperman yet, but let's face it, she's by far a better news writer." Relief came as a glint of appreciation appeared in Larry's eyes.

"I know you're right. That's what makes her such a crackerjack editor too. Now, what did you want to ask me?"

I put my coffee cup on the counter. "What can you tell me about Dixie? Before yesterday, I only heard her name mentioned a handful of times. I'm struggling to make sense of her reappearance after all these years."

Larry hesitated and took another gulp of coffee. "Dixie left Harold and the boys not too long after we arrived in Shiloh. Martha and I hardly know more than what others have told us since then. If you want to know more about her, see Sam and Zeb? They've known her the longest."

"Interesting you mentioned Sam."

"Why's that?"

"Liddy and I both noticed that Susanna didn't seem happy that Dixie showed up at the fellowship hall yesterday. Is there a history there too?"

"Go talk to Sam."

"I'll take that as a yes. Now you've piqued my curiosity even more."

Larry returned to his office as I walked toward the front and tapped Mary on the shoulder. When she looked up, I said, "I just wanted to see what a real news writer and editor looks like."

Mary looked puzzled but smiled all the same.

———

THE PHONE WOKE me Friday morning just before sunrise. I fumbled for the receiver and sat up on the edge of the bed, perching my glasses on my nose. Liddy sat up next to me.

"Theo, it's Arnie. Harold's back in the hospital. This time they think he might've suffered a heart attack. They're running more tests this morning. He's in ICU."

"Hal and Phillip with you?"

"Maddie's here too. She found him and called 911."

"Where's Dixie? Is she there?"

"No. Dixie left last night before all this happened. We don't know how to reach her."

"We'll be there shortly."

CHAPTER ELEVEN

"MADDIE," LIDDY CALLED OUT AS WE WALKED INTO THE MEDICAL CENTER'S waiting area.

"Oh, Miss Liddy, I'm so glad you're here. I'm right scared for Mister Harold."

Liddy occupied the seat beside Maddie while I stepped across the room where Arnie engaged Hal in conversation with one hand resting on Phillip's shoulder.

"How's your dad?" I looked squarely at Hal after a quick glance at Phillip's preoccupied stare and slumped shoulders.

"He's been taken for further tests. Doc Lucas called in his cardiologist and a neurologist. Both arrived not long ago." Hal's detached matter-of-factness revealed his disbelief.

"What do they think's wrong?" I glanced at Arnie and Hal.

Arnie said, "They're afraid he might've suffered a stroke."

I looked at Hal and tapped Phillip's arm to get him to make eye contact. "Sounds as though your dad's in good hands now. What happened?"

Phillip's swollen red eyes rolled toward Hal.

"Maddie said a loud thud upstairs woke her up. She found dad curled in a ball beside his bed. When she couldn't get more than an incoherent moan out of him, she woke us up. Dad opened his eyes but only mumbled a bunch of nonsense. The panic look on his face scared the living daylights out of me. I've never seen dad so scared in all my life. When Phillip and I struggled to get him back onto the bed, we realized he couldn't use his left arm. That's when Maddie called 911."

I peeked over my shoulder and noticed Maddie gripping a scrunched hankie, lost in conversation with Liddy. Arnie seemed to see the same helplessness I recognized on Liddy's face and excused himself. A moment later, the three huddled with heads bowed.

"Guys, I suggest we do likewise," I whispered. I then rested an arm on Hal's and Phillip's shoulders and lowered my head. While I sought God's hand to be upon the doctors and staff, Phillip muttered personal pleas to God. Hal pulled Phillip close and echoed my "Amen."

Phillip wiped his eyes. "Thanks, Mister P."

"You're welcome. By the way, where's your mother?"

Hal shot a cold look at me. "Dixie left last night."

Phillip nodded. "Dad urged her to stay because of the weather, but she claimed she had pressing business to attend to. She even tossed me her car keys and asked me to pull her car out front." Phillip's slight grin disappeared as fast as it arrived. "That was the only time she paid any attention to me while she was here."

"She didn't give me the time of day any better," Hal interjected. "She focused all her syrupy smiles on dad until she slipped her raincoat on and lifted the hood to protect her hairdo. I watched dad grow less steady by the minute as he held onto the open door."

"Come to think of it, dad did look washed out by the time she pulled away," Phillip said.

"I'm sure he just felt bad because she had to leave," I said. "From what I saw, he seemed to enjoy her visit. Besides, didn't she say that she'd be back?"

Deep in thought, Hal nodded. "Still, you should've seen the agonizing look that came over him as she climbed into her driver's seat looking like Little Red Riding Hood. After she pulled away, he eased the door shut and then went straight upstairs."

Arnie walked up with Maddie. He handed me the keys to my Expedition. "Liddy had Phoebe stop by to take her to school."

I slid the keys into my pocket and looked at Maddie. "Are you okay?"

"Yes, sir. But I'll feel a whole lots better if'n we hear somethin' soon from them doctors."

Arnie chuckled. "Don't you fret none, Miss Maddie. Harold's in good hands thanks to you."

Maddie bowed her head. "But Mister Harold—"

"Miss Maddie, I think he'll be okay after a day or two of rest," Doc Lucas said as he joined us.

Hal asked, "When can we see him?"

"It'll be another few minutes before we can get him situated in his room. They just finished examining him and running a couple of tests. He's still pretty disorientated, but he's regaining some use of his left side."

"Did he have a stroke?" Hal asked, but both of them gave wide-eyed looks as they waited for the answer.

"They feel he suffered a mini-stroke, what we call a transient ischemic attack. Don't mistake the term mini-stroke though. Luck sided with him this time. A TIA stroke often is the body's warning sign of a potentially more serious stroke or heart problem. He needs a couple of days of rest and further tests, but he's going to require significant changes in his daily routine to minimize the future risk of a stroke or heart failure. We can discuss all that later. In the meantime, I instructed the nurse to allow Hal and Phillip, along with Miss Maddie of course, to see him for a couple of minutes after he gets settled." Doc eyed Arnie. "He requires lots of rest, that's why we have him sedated."

Phillip sighed. "Thanks, Doc."

———

AFTER HAL AND Phillip checked on their father, they both headed to work. The doctor assured them Harold would be asleep the rest of the day. Arnie likewise excused himself when I promised to drive Maddie home after we stopped for some breakfast.

Cora squealed right after Maddie and I entered. "Oh my, Maddie. What's you up to with Mister Phillips?"

Maddie tried her best to greet Cora with a smile, but it collapsed right away. "Mister Harold's back in the hospital."

"What for this time? Is he okay?"

Maddie looked at me.

"He had a relatively minor stroke during the night. Thank God Maddie found him, and they got him to the hospital when they did. The doctor believes he'll be better after a couple of days of bed rest." I waved at Cecil.

Cora's pearly grin faded too, but her optimism shined through the concern on her face. "Maddie dear, if the doctors say Mister Harold's gonna get better, then you oughtn't to fret anymore." Cora pointed upward and added, "Besides, I don't believe God's ready for Mister Harold quite yet."

Maddie cracked a grin. "Thank ya, Cora. I knew you'd know what to say."

Cora escorted us to a table near the front counter. She got us coffee as Cecil walked over.

"Mister Phillips, you agree?"

"Yes, I do." I kept my real concerns about Harold to myself. "Is it too late to get one of your country breakfast specials?"

"For you, no sir. How about you, Maddie?"

"I'm not too hungry. This coffee suits me just fine."

Cecil returned to his grill as Cora settled into the chair beside Maddie. "You think Miss Dixie's visit had anything to do with causing this?"

"Can't say, but Mister Harold sure got reeled in by all the sweet talk Miss Dixie dished out. You'd have thought what happened all them years ago never happened. It didn't take long before they laughed and giggled about the ol' days," Maddie said with a scowl.

Cora gave Maddie a confused look before Maddie continued. "She disappears, walks out on him, two teenage boys and their baby brother, and returns twenty years later as if nothing happened. Fiddlesticks!"

I patted Maddie's arm to get her attention. "I'm confused too. Harold never shared a word about Dixie to me. All the same, it seems to make more sense if she had popped in to see her sons, but Hal and Phillip indicated she said little to them during her recent whimsical, abracadabra in-and-out visits."

"Mister Phillips, that woman's as phony as her bosoms and hair."

"What made you say somethin' so terrible?" Cora chided.

Maddie dropped her head toward Cora. "You're right, but anytime Mister Harold left her alone, she'd begin to snooping. When I asked if I could help her find anythin', in particular, she gave me the most dreadful stare until I went about my own business."

"Did you say anything?" Cora asked.

"I mentioned it to Hal."

I asked, "What'd he say?"

"Weren't no time to say much anything' before she left."

"Here ya go, Mister Phillips. Can I get ya anything' else?" Cecil slid my breakfast in front of me as he flashed a playful sneer across the table directed at Cora. "My wife's too busy socializing to take care of ya."

Cora barked, "You ol' fool. Can't you see I'm helping Maddie?"

Cecil dismissed Cora with his hand, grinned and retreated to the kitchen.

Maddie talked about Dixie's uppity reputation and how Dixie used to leave the boys under Maddie's care while she strutted about town or drove her fancy sports car like a crazy woman. According to Maddie, Dixie's exploits always gave the ladies in the church plenty to fuss about every Sunday. After her stress-filled pregnancy with Phillip, Maddie said Dixie got depressed. Either Maddie or Harold changed most of Phillip's diapers and got out of bed in the middle of the night to feed him.

On our way back to the Archer's home, I asked Maddie, "After all that you told me about Dixie, I'm still curious about something. How did Harold cope when she left him and the boys?"

"He never saw it comin'. For the longest time, he hardly slept and spent many nights trying to comfort Phillip when he'd awake, screaming for his momma. Mister Harold would rock him while whispering, 'Shush. Don't cry. Momma's coming back soon.' But she never came back. Mister Harold eventually turned his full attention to caring for his boys."

"He sure was lucky to have you around. Thanks for sharing Maddie. Call us if you need anything."

———

Early Sunday morning, I climbed out of bed and enjoyed the quiet of our living room. I dove into my daily devotion based on Malachi 2:15-16. God reminded me why he hates divorce. In God's eyes, marriage unites a man and a wife to rear godly offspring. As I meditated upon the message, Harold's muted comments about Dixie's estrangement began to make more sense and also hinted why Harold possibly never married after she left him.

"What's got ya in such deep thought?" Liddy's soft voice broke the silence as she curled up in her armchair across from me.

"Ever since Maddie told me more about Harold's inexplicable reaction to Dixie's return, I've tried to understand his absence of any ill feelings."

"What'd you figure out?"

"Maybe I sold Harold short, or should I say, I sold God short."

Liddy scrunched her eyebrows.

"Why didn't Harold ever remarry?" I pondered out loud but looked out the window. "Why did he choose to raise his boys on his own?"

"What are you getting at?"

"It dawned on me this morning that he had decided to remain faithful to the covenant promise he made to God for the sake of his sons. Harold didn't leave Dixie. She left him."

"Interesting thought. I suggest you discuss your supposition with Arnie. Speaking of which, how about breakfast before church?"

———

Phillip parked his Jeep Wrangler in Harold's usual spot across from the church. He waved as he exited his vehicle and saw us crossing Main Street.

"Where's Hal?" I asked as we approached and extended my hand.

Phillip glanced at Liddy with a boyish smile. "Hal stayed home with dad."

"They let him come home already?"

"Last evening. Doc got tired of dad's insistence that he preferred to risk a relapse rather than suffer another minute in his infernal hospital bed. Doc agreed to release him after we assured him that dad's bed would be downstairs before he came home. For good measure, Maddie promised she'd make sure he stayed in bed for the first couple of days." Phillip's grin widened as he shared the good news.

Liddy said, "That's terrific news."

"Yes, ma'am. Hal thought it a good idea for me to share the latest about dad."

The news about Harold circulated through the pews. After the service, Arnie vacated his usual place by the door and huddled privately with Phillip before Phillip hurried out the door and down the steps.

Liddy and I caught up with Larry and Martha in the foyer.

"Do you think Harold's going to have a full recovery?" Larry asked.

"Doc Lucas said he should, but the next few days will make a more confident prognosis possible," I said.

"We'll keep praying then. How are you coming with your first article about John and the team?"

"Nearly done. I'll have it for you Wednesday. I'm focusing on young Timmy Thompson and Ray Abernathy. I think you'll like their unique perspectives."

"See you Wednesday morning then."

"Hey Mister P, Miss Liddy," Pete said as he and Mary walked up beside us.

Liddy quipped, "And where are you two off to today?"

"Pete promised to take me horseback riding at Miss Marie's this afternoon," Mary said smiling, clutching Pete's hand.

"Y'all going to be home in time for dinner?" Martha asked, looking at Pete.

"Yes, ma'am. We'll be back before it gets too late this afternoon. What's for dinner?"

Larry and I chuckled as Martha said, "Butt roast, mashed potatoes and a green bean casserole." She then smiled at Mary. "And someone promised to whip up a cobbler for dessert."

Pete tugged on Mary's hand. "We better git. Marie and John already left. Wouldn't want to be late for dinner because we dilly-dallied around here too long."

Larry chuckled as Pete and Mary waved at Arnie and Judy after greeting them on the way out the door. "I hate to admit it, but that boy's growing on me." Larry's smile then became a smirk as he looked at me. "Just don't let on that I said that. You hear?"

CHAPTER TWELVE

"Don't forget about me this afternoon," Liddy said as she got out of our vehicle and closed the door.

I rolled down the passenger window. "Come to think of it, why don't you walk over and meet me at the stadium after school lets out? I've got to visit with John before practice this afternoon." I blew a kiss and drove off.

First and foremost this Wednesday morning entailed catching up with Ray at the Post Office. Although he had nodded his approval to being referenced in my article, he deserved to see it before it landed in the Sentinel's Friday edition. Since the Post Office wouldn't be open until after eight-thirty, I stopped at Bubba's for a cup of coffee and to chat with Cora.

"Good morn, Mister Phillips." Barb stood behind the counter with one of Bubba's monogrammed bib aprons protecting her blue and white floral dress.

"What a pleasant surprise to see you this mornin' Barb. Where's Cora?"

"She borrowed Cecil to help Maddie wrangle one of those highfalu-tin newfangled beds into Mister Harold's house. Kinda like them in the hospital but twice as big and a sight more comfortable."

"That's mighty nice of them and for you fillin' in. I can attest to Harold's cantankerous disdain around most hospital beds."

Barb giggled. "If'n Mister Harold ain't comfortable, then nobody's gonna be comfortable in that big ol' house."

"Speaking of Mister Harold's discomfort, have you heard about his ex-wife?"

"Mister Phillips, you know I'm not one to gossip, but Maddie's gotten herself all riled up over Miss Dixie's out-of-the-blue coming and going. If you ask me, and of course it's just my opinion, Maddie ain't been herself since that woman's stuck her nose inside that house again. And I'm afraid she ain't left for good either."

"What makes you say that?"

"Maddie told Cora that Mister Harold keeps asking if Dixie's come back yet."

"Hal and Phillip will keep an eye on Maddie and Mister Harold. How about a large coffee to go?"

As Barb poured my coffee, Bob carried in an armful of logs to feed his smoker's fire pit. He waved and greeted me before tossing in two pieces and stoking the flames.

"Here ya go, Mister Phillips. Be careful. It's hot."

"Thanks, Barb. Please tell Cecil and Cora I stopped." I laid two dollars on the counter, shouted greetings to Bob and left.

———

MY VISIT WITH Ray lasted only a few minutes. He read my article and looked up with an easy smile. "Looks fine to me. See you at practice?"

"Count on it."

I walked across Washington Street toward the main parking lot behind City Hall, stopping by my vehicle to toss my article inside before heading to the mayor's office. Hillary shoved a filing cabinet drawer shut as I entered, but her all-business demeanor relaxed long enough for a polite smile.

"Good morning. Is he in?" I pointed to Hal's closed door.

Hillary glanced at the phone on her desk. "He's on the phone. They're juggling his dad's furnishings around to make room for some new bed they ordered."

"I heard."

Hillary raised a brow. "How's that?"

I raised my to-go cup. "Barb told me about Cora and Cecil helping Maddie this morning."

Hillary stepped behind her desk. "Looks like he's hung up." She grabbed the receiver and, after a brief exchange, nodded. "Go on in."

"How's your apartment?"

Her eyes lit up. "Love it. After the sun sets, downtown becomes downright peaceful." She added with a grin. "Of course, I can't beat the commute to work. Hardly drive anywhere most days."

"How are you getting along with the mayor?" I pointed toward the door with an inquisitive smirk.

"He's a peach as long as I keep him organized and on-time."

"Then I better be short and sweet." I rapped twice, then entered.

"Come on in Mister P. What can I do for you this morning?"

"Sorry to barge in, but with all that's been going on since Momma Arian's funeral and your dad's situation, I wanted to check on you."

"I appreciate your concern. Reckon I'm doing okay. Besides, thanks to you, I've got Hilly out there keeping me straight." Hal rocked back in his chair.

I sat in an armchair in front of his desk. "Phillip filled us in a little, but how's your dad's recovery going?"

Hal sighed. "For certain, his speech is much better, but he's still not very stable and can't stand or walk without wobbling. He gets this dread-filled look whenever he attempts to do too much."

"It's gonna take time for him to recover."

"I'm not so sure about that. While we were getting the new bed set up today, dad demanded that we also order him a wheelchair. When we suggested a walker, he communicated loud and clear that he'd prefer the indignity of a wheelchair to the humiliation of a walker."

I paused to ponder Harold's reasoning.

"Know what bothers me the most?" Hal asked.

"What?"

"Those crazy dreams have convinced him he's dying. I'm afraid he's given up."

"That seems so far from the Harold I first met."

"As much as I hate admitting it, if Dixie does come back, at least dad perks up around her for some inexplicable reason."

"Have you made an effort to talk with her?"

Hal flinched. "She might've been my mother, but I don't know her, and she most assuredly doesn't know Phillip or me anymore either."

"Twenty years is a long time. Aren't you the least bit curious about what your mother has been doing the last two decades and why she's back? Dragging up the past may not help, but making an effort to reach out to her might benefit your dad."

His head drooped. "You're right. If she comes back, I'll try."

I stopped at the door on the way out. "If you need anything at all, just get hold of Liddy or me."

After I had shut the door behind me, Hillary looked up from her desk. "That bad?"

"What do you mean?"

"If it'll perk you up, I just let John know the Priestly Community Center will be available for Sanctuary's first meeting after Labor Day."

"That's great news, thanks."

———

"GLAD I CAUGHT you before you left for lunch. Here's my first article on John and the Shiloh Saints." I slid the clipped pages across the counter.

Mary skimmed the first page. "I'll let dad know you dropped this off when he gets back." She flipped through the handwritten pages. "I like the angle you took, contrasting Timmy's optimism and Mister Abernathy's down-to-earth expectations regarding Coach Priestly's first season back." She looked up with a stamp of approval across her face.

"Tell him also that I'm meeting with Sam this afternoon."

Mary lost her approving grin and stammered, "I'll pass the message along. Is everything okay?"

"Don't worry. It's nothing earth-shattering. Pete's dad should be able to provide some historical insight on a subject matter your father and me discussed."

"You two working on another special interest story?"

"I'm just curious about some of Shiloh's past. Catch you tonight at church kiddo. I gotta skedaddle." I felt awkward leaving Mary to second-guess, but my purpose for meeting Sam about Dixie's past remained solely personal.

———

PETE STOOD BEHIND Sam's pickup with one arm through a coil of electrical conduit balanced on his shoulder. He scooped up a coil of electrical wiring with the other arm and shouted as he dumped his load into their other work truck. "Pop! Mister P's here."

Sam's voice echoed from inside the shop. "Theo, come on in. I'll be right with you."

Pete wiped his hands and greeted me. "Dad said you'd be by today. I can't stay. Phillip wants some additional outdoor lighting installed at the community center."

"Hillary told me it'd be ready by Labor Day in time for Sanctuary's first meeting."

"They're landscaping this afternoon. That's why I need to hightail it and finish running the wiring for the lighting fixtures."

"That's good news. See you later this afternoon at practice."

Pete waved and drove off as Sam pulled the overhead garage door shut. "Susanna's got lunch for us in the house. Let's go wash up."

We walked across the driveway separating their home from their shop and entered through the screened back porch of the restored Victorian two-story Susanna's parents lived in before them. Susanna busied herself in the kitchen. "The two of you go wash up. Just fried up some bacon and sliced a couple of tomatoes for some BLTs. How does that sound to you, Theo?"

"The smell of the bacon already has my mouth watering."

Over the sound of the water running in the sink, Sam said, "Sweetie, if you wrap a couple of sandwiches for Pete, I'll take them over to him after we finish our lunch."

Susanna tossed Sam a hand towel. "You worry about you and Theo. I'll run his lunch to him. Joe's in court today, and I gotta hurry back to cover the office." She grabbed her car keys and a brown sack and headed out the way we came in.

"Grab a seat. Looks as though Suz put everything out on the table already."

After Sam blessed our lunch, we talked football before I shared Larry's comment about Pete. That led Sam to share how pleased he and Susanna felt about Mary's decision to stay in town.

"Is Pete getting serious about Mary?" I used a napkin to wipe some mayonnaise off the smirk on my face.

Sam paused. "Guess time'll tell." The glint in his eye said the rest.

"Have you heard from Andy and Megan?"

"Andy's been getting ready for their first game at South Carolina next week, and Megan's traveling with the cheerleaders."

"Sounds terrific for them. Does Megan know about Harold?"

Sam's easygoing grin dissipated. "Susanna keeps them updated but tries to filter what they hear."

"About Dixie?"

"As far as I know, Megan only knows of Dixie from the stories she heard when she lived there. Susanna feels it best not to make a big deal about Dixie's recent visits." Sam stared beyond the back porch.

I rocked back in my chair and intercepted his distant glare. "Why has Dixie's return caused a lot of folks to act out of sorts?"

Sam cleared his throat and wiped his mouth. "I guess this is why you wanted to have lunch today?"

I nodded. "Larry thought you'd be the best person to talk with about her."

"Remind me to thank Larry later." He ran his hand over his face as he took a deep breath and exhaled slowly. "Dixie grew up on a small farm not far from Marie's place, but her folks had her in their later years."

"Does she still have any family around here?"

"Not anymore. Her parents sold the farm some time after she left Shiloh. Her older brother died in Viet Nam when we were in middle school. Right after, her folks became recluses, and Dixie began to change too."

"How so?"

"Everyone knew Bobby Lee. He loved souped-up cars and scoring touchdowns on Friday nights. Everyone thought he'd make it big in college, but the Army drafted him right after graduation. He never made it back to Shiloh."

"How did Dixie respond to her brother's death?"

"Six years separated Bobby Lee and Dixie. His death caused her parents to become overprotective, but Dixie rebelled. By the time we both got to high school, she knew she had the looks and athletic talents that made others jealous. She also picked up where her brother left off and loved racing her car up and down the highway. Her parents tried to bribe her with everything but affection, and Dixie took advantage of it."

"What happened between Susanna and Dixie?"

"Why do you ask?" Sam looked directly at me.

"After Momma Arians' funeral, Susanna had an indignant look on her face when Dixie entered the fellowship hall. Liddy and I both noticed. When I asked Larry about it, he directed me to you."

Sam sighed and looked away. "By our senior year, Susanna and I dated pretty regularly until Dixie swooped in and began flirting with me. I enjoyed the attention." Sam's face reddened. "Heck, I wasn't a star player back in those days."

"So Dixie's advances made you feel special, and you dropped Susanna?"

Sam chuckled. "Drop Susanna? Hardly! When Susanna got wind of Dixie's flirting, she got suspended for fighting with Dixie during school."

I joined in on the humor of the image. "So Susanna didn't give up on you, I guess?"

"When I learned about their catfight, I realized right then and there who I'd spend my life with. Besides, Dixie soon revealed her real intentions and began braggin' about her college graduate beau and his fancy black truck."

"Harold?"

"Turns out she used me to taunt Harold. She played ol' Harold like a drum, and he married her a year after she graduated."

"Susanna's reaction the other day stemmed from that fight over you all those years ago?"

"Not exactly. Years later, right after Phillip was born, I guess Dixie wanted a distraction in her life. I often got called to the Archer home to resolve various plumbing issues, and Maddie usually greeted me at the door. That is until my last visit out there twenty years ago. Dixie called, and when I arrived at the door, she greeted me wearing a towel on her head and a pink satin robe." Sam's eyes widened, and his face paled.

"I'm almost afraid to ask, but what happened?"

"After she invited me in, I asked, 'Where's the problem?' She confessed that she needed my opinion as an old friend but figured I might not have come unless she claimed there was a plumbing issue. When I inquired about Maddie and the baby, she said Maddie had taken Phillip shopping with her. Dixie began telling me how she regretted how she used me back in high school. That's when I excused myself and made a hasty retreat."

"And Susanna found out?"

"Harold was the mayor by then, and I sure didn't want any misunderstandings or rumors floating about, so I told Susanna that afternoon."

I felt a huge grin come over me. "How did Susanna take the news?"

Sam laughed. "I had to hug her real tight because she had grabbed the keys to our truck after I told her. I finally convinced her that I thought Dixie felt embarrassed enough by me walking out on her and assured her I wouldn't accept another house call to the Archer home again. Soon after that, Dixie disappeared from Shiloh until last week."

We continued to small talk until I excused myself after Pete called and asked Sam to help him finish up in time to make the afternoon practice.

I RAPPED ON the doorframe of John's office at three-thirty. The rattling of lockers and clicking of football cleats competed with our conversation as I showed him a copy of the article that I handed Mary earlier that day.

"Timmy and Ray are both going to be pleased. All we have to do now is live up to their vision." John smiled as he leaned back in his swivel chair.

"I kinda believe they shared a good prospectus for the upcoming season."

John pointed to the door. "Come on. We've got a lot of work left to get ready for our first game against Pelham High School. They were the regional runner-up last year."

Liddy found me a short while later sitting beside Ray in the stands, and we watched practice for the next hour. When we got up to leave, Ray reached out his hand and winked.

"Thanks again. See you around."

On the drive home, I shared Sam's story about Dixie, which earned a startled look from Liddy.

CHAPTER THIRTEEN

A RAP ON THE FRONT DOOR PULLED ME AWAY FROM CLIPPING OUT FRIDAY'S article right after I savored my first sip of coffee at the kitchen table.

"Here ya go, Mister P." Timmy cradled six extra copies of yesterday's paper along with the Saturday morning edition.

"Why thank you, Timmy."

"Missus Scribner gave me a dozen extra copies, but my mom insisted I didn't need all of them, so I figured you'd like a few for yourself."

"That's mighty thoughtful. What did your mom and dad think about the article?"

"They made a fuss at dinner last night and asked if I actually said everything you wrote."

A huge smile emerged. "What'd you say?"

Timmy's freckled dimples grew. "I told 'em that you'd never write anything that wasn't true."

"You're right Timmy. The truth is always easier to write about than lies. Your unique prognostication about the upcoming season reinforced Mister Abernathy's comments on the subject."

Timmy arched his brows as he scratched his blonde scalp. "Pro-whatcha-cation?"

I chuckled, patting down his mussed hair. "Predicting future events."

"But I didn't predict anything. If you just know somethin's a fact, then it ain't like predicting, which in my mind is guessing." He made a fist and pounded it into the palm of his other hand.

"Know what Timmy? I stand corrected. Coach Priestly oughta be glad he's got you on his team."

Timmy puffed his chest. "You'll see Mister P. Shiloh's gonna have a shot at the playoffs this year."

"Can I quote you in my article next week too?"

"Sure! I gotta run, though. Got a few more papers to deliver."

Liddy walked up behind me as I stood at the front door while Timmy leaped onto his bike and then disappeared around the corner. She wrapped her arms around my waist and whispered, "Why did Timmy stop by this morning?"

I pointed to the six copies of yesterday's paper sitting on top of the table by the door.

"That was thoughtful. Guess he liked your article."

After breakfast, Liddy folded the morning paper. "Would you consider handling a little project for us?"

"Depends on what you mean by a little project."

Liddy grabbed my hand and led me down the hallway to our bedroom. She leaned down and peeled back the carpeting. "I've been thinking." She brushed the dust and dirt from the wood floor underneath. "That old carpet's just hiding all this beautiful southern pine. I bet if you ripped up the carpet, we might be able to restore the original floor."

I stooped down and inspected the flooring beneath the carpet. Liddy's bated breath hovered over my shoulder. "Why not? It'll take more than a couple of days. We'll have to sleep upstairs."

Liddy giggled. "Sounds like fun. When can we start?"

"Let me talk with Zeb first about what I'll need. Refinishing the original floor won't be easy, but I think it's a project worth tackling. In the meantime, how about helping with some of the yard work? The grass needs mowing, sidewalks need edging, and shrubs need trimming."

"I'll join you as soon as I finish cleaning the floors, dusting, washing clothes and emptying the dishwasher. Oh, and go grocery shopping too."

I smiled. "I'll take that as a no."

I spent the rest of the morning in the yard. An extended shower and several glasses of sweet tea during lunch helped cool me off. While Liddy double-checked her shopping list, I asked, "Would you mind dropping me off at Zeb's?"

Liddy raised her eyes. "I thought you wanted to take it easy for the rest of the afternoon."

"I did, but I've gotta look into buying a riding lawnmower."

Liddy smirked. "It's about time. You're not as young as you used to be."

BY TWO O'CLOCK, Adams Feed and Hardware's usual busy Saturday crowd had dwindled to a trickle. Zeb tossed a peanut into his mouth and stood up from his stool behind the counter when I entered.

"Hello, stranger." He offered some peanuts.

I scooped a handful and cracked one open. "Mind if I get a cold drink? I'm a paying customer today."

"In that case, what's your fancy?" Zeb pointed to the red barrel filled with ice and an assortment of flavors.

After I chugged half the can and swallowed, Zeb inquired still chuckling, "Looks like you've been working on your lawn again?" Zeb walked around the counter and grabbed himself an orange drink.

"That's why I'm here. How about showing me which riding mower would be best suited for me?"

"I've been wondering how long you'd continue pushing that mower across that great big yard. You're used to smaller lawns and that sissy grass that wilts in the heat of summer. The Bermuda turf most folks around here have in their yards, and that covers your lawn, thrives in the summer heat. The hotter the better, but it does require regular mowing."

"That's why I'm here. As much as I like the exercise, it takes me two days to cut my lawn with my push mower."

We walked to the rear of the warehouse. Zeb pointed to a mower under a gray tarp. "You interested in saving a couple of dollars?"

"Talk to me."

"This Massey ain't five years old. It used to belong to Ol' man Edwards."

"Wiley Edwards, the barber?" I peeked under the tarp at the like-new mower.

"Same one."

"For a man in his eighties, he's still spry and loves to gab." I removed my safari hat and ran my hands through my hair. "In fact, I gotta see him this week."

"Maybe around his shop, but Missus Edwards put her foot down and hired a couple of local boys to handle their yard work." Zeb pulled the tarp off and pointed to the ignition. "Sit down and start her up. Jim checked her out and gave her a tune up."

The engine started right up. "Sounds great. Liddy'll be pleased I saved some money too."

Zeb grabbed his suspenders. "Tell ya what I'll do. Take it for a couple of days. We'll settle up after you decide if it's right for you."

We shook hands. "Can you deliver it to the house?"

"I can do you one better. How about I have Jim run you and the mower by your house?"

"One more thing. Liddy wants me to yank up the carpet in our bedroom and refinish the wood floors to match the rest of the house. Can you give me any advice as to what I'll need and how long it'll take?"

Zeb rocked back and forth and chuckled. "You'll be with the floor expert around here. Jim can take a peek and answer your questions."

———

I HELPED JIM offload the mower from his truck. He pointed out the levers and pedals before I gave it a quick spin around the side yard as Liddy pulled in from the grocery store.

She stopped at the stoop, clutching two bags of groceries. "I see you got yourself a new toy."

"It'll do the trick. It used to belong to Mister Edwards and runs like new."

Liddy glanced at Jim. "Can this old fool operate it okay?"

Jim chuckled. "Yes, ma'am. Mister P can handle it just fine."

"If you help me with the rest of the groceries, I'll pour both of you some sweet tea."

Liddy went inside while Jim helped me with the last of the groceries. Two large glasses sat on the counter by the time we got inside.

"Hun, while Jim's here, he's gonna take a peek at the floor in the bedroom. Zeb swears Jim's the flooring expert."

Jim lifted the carpet in each corner of the room and even checked the closet floor. "Without being able to see the entire floor underneath, I'd say that old carpet's been hiding the original wood flooring. From what I can see, the floor's in pretty good shape too."

Liddy stood, arms crossed. "What about the squeaking?"

Jim ran his hand over the exposed planks. "I can show Mister P how to pull any bad nails without damaging the wood and refasten any loose boards properly." He then looked at me. "If you find any damaged ones, I've got some matching planks at the mill."

"I assume you have everything else I might need?"

"Absolutely, and it ain't hard to do either. Just don't rush it, and this ol' floor will look as good as the rest of the flooring in this ol' house."

Liddy asked, "How long should we plan on this taking?"

Jim scanned the four corners of the room. "Start to finish, about a week. In fact, if you can wait until next month, I'll lend you a hand."

Liddy smiled. "I can wait until you're free."

I nodded in agreement, and we went back into the kitchen to finish our sweet tea. Jim explained the steps we needed to take once we removed the furniture and ripped up the old carpet.

Jim stopped at the kitchen door before leaving. "Mister P, your article sure has gotten a lot of folks talking about the opening game next week. And I never knew Mister Abernathy played at Georgia. That was fascinating to read about."

"Ray's a quiet, unassuming fella, but he sure thinks a lot of Coach Priestly and loves his Shiloh football. By the way, glad to see you and Jay helping Coach Priestly. Do you believe we'll beat Pelham?"

"We'll see, but they better be ready for a dogfight."

———

SUNDAY ARRIVED WITH threatening clouds overhead, so we drove to church. We caught up with Zeb and his two sons in the foyer. Liddy thanked him for suggesting the mower and confirmed that I'd swing by to finalize the purchase tomorrow.

Jeannie approached Liddy, all excited. "I got to see the new Priestly Community Center yesterday. It's huge!"

Liddy asked, "What's it like?"

"Oh Miss Liddy, it's got this all-purpose flooring that'll allow us to play basketball or volleyball if we want. They were installing those basketball backboards that you can hoist out of the way with the press of a button. There's an exercise room with all kinds of equipment and a walking track on the second floor with meeting rooms off of it. And there's a full kitchen in the back."

Zeb roared, "Harold promised it'd be nice."

"Yes, sir," Jeannie said. "Mayor Archer, I mean Mister Archer, sure should be proud."

"Wonder if any of the Archers will be here this morning?" I scanned the foyer, then looked at Jeannie. "Where's your mom and dad?"

"Nick pulled in next to us. They got to talking with Joe and Missy when they piled out with the twins. I just dropped the twins off in the children's area for Missy."

Zeb craned his neck. " They're coming in with Sam and Susanna now. It's sure nice to see happy faces on Nick and Joe again."

Jeannie eyed Nick before she turned to Zeb. "He's been pretty much back to his usual self the last few days. He even asked me to help him hang a picture of his mom and dad on his office wall."

Sam and Susanna walked up with Missy.

Liddy greeted them. "Joe and Nick headed to the choir room?"

"The choir boys saw John and Marie. All four took off as usual." Missy pretended to pout, but her rosy cheeks and twinkling eyes showed that joy had returned to the Arians family.

I asked Sam, "Where's Pete?"

"You have to ask?" Sam turned his head toward the Sanctuary.

The chatter all around us fell to a whisper as heads turned to the main entrances. Judy stepped beside Phillip and Hal as Harold entered in his new wheelchair with Dixie helping him over the threshold. Harold's washed-out cheeks cracked a smile. Dixie wore the same dress from the funeral service, except she had added gold hoop earrings with an equally gaudy necklace and bracelets. Phillip and Hal in their sports jackets followed their dad and Dixie at a safe distance. Many of the older church members looked lost for words, but I couldn't determine whether their speechlessness stemmed from Harold arriving in a wheelchair or from Dixie being there.

Harold grabbed the wheels of his chair. "As you can see for yourselves, I've got a new set of wheels to get around on." He spun his wheelchair toward a group of blue-haired ladies staring, mouths and eyes agape. "Missus Edwards, I wanna thank you and all the ladies for your heartfelt wishes for my family and me," Harold shared loud enough for most in the room to hear. He then smiled as he said, "Please, y'all look like you've seen a ghost. Most assuredly, as you can plainly see, I ain't dead yet."

Giggles and chuckles crescendoed across the foyer. Missus Edwards and others then greeted Harold while Dixie stepped beside Judy, and they shared a smile as Dixie eyed the room.

Susanna grabbed Sam's arm. "Y'all ready to find our seats?"

A moment later, Mary began playing a prelude. Pete waited at the end of the pew in front of us. Jay and Jim slid in beside him. Phillip sat beside Jeannie on the other side of Pete.

Once the center aisle cleared sufficiently, Hal helped Harold down the aisle with Dixie by his side. Harold remained in his wheelchair, and Dixie sat at the end of the pew beside him. Hal sat behind his dad.

Arnie stepped up to the pulpit and shared a message on how we can best demonstrate our love for God through our attitudes and actions toward others. At the conclusion, Arnie said, "When you doubt if your attitudes or actions are right, look into a mirror and ask yourself a simple question. Do I love myself differently than the love I claim to hold for God or others?"

Several heads sank as Arnie closed in prayer. Before dismissing the congregation, Arnie asked, "How many of you have swung by Priestly Park the last couple of days? The new community center is nearly complete and is a beautiful testament to one man's magnanimous gesture." Arnie stepped off the dais, walked up the aisle, and stood beside Harold. The usual solemn decorum relented to a round of applause for Harold who rose from his chair and waved.

Harold then looked at Arnie and said, "I hope many of you will join the preacher and me at the opening game Friday night." Harold patted Arnie on the back before returning to his wheelchair with Hal's assistance. The aisles filled with well-wishers gathering near a beaming Harold. Susanna and Sam inched their way toward Harold. Susanna stopped to greet Dixie with a warm smile while Sam focused his attention on Hal and Harold.

CHAPTER FOURTEEN

FRIDAY MORNING BROUGHT RAIN SHOWERS FORECASTED TO BE LONG GONE before noon. I scrambled a couple of eggs for Liddy while she took longer than usual to get dressed. To celebrate John's return as head coach, the players voted to allow teachers and staff to wear game jerseys for good luck on game day. Quentin "Q" Higginbotham, the team's starting sophomore quarterback and one of Liddy's more talented students, gave his number eleven jersey to Liddy. Fretting last night over what to wear beneath Q's green and gold jersey, she broke down and called Phoebe. When the lights went out, her new gold Shiloh Saint polo and a pair of khakis lay folded on the seat and the jersey draped over the back of the chair beside our bed.

"Breakfast is served!" I hollered as I poured coffee into her SHS travel mug.

Liddy appeared cinching her belt. "How do I look?" She fussed with how the jersey looked tucked in.

I signaled her to walk closer, adjusted her collar, and swept an unruly lock of gray-streaked hair from her brow. "Quentin's jersey never looked better."

"Should I wear it tucked in or out?"

"Other than your belt covers the lower portion of the eleven, tucked works." I pointed to her chair. "Now sit down and eat your breakfast before it gets cold." I handed the morning paper to her. "Check it out. My article made today's front page."

Liddy sipped her coffee as she scrutinized the photo. "Mary captured John in the midst of one of his trademark grins, dangling his whistle between his fingers."

"What do you think?"

"Think he misses Jessie by his side?" Her eyes left the print and queried mine.

"John assured me that Jessie would make his presence felt tonight."

Liddy's head tilted to accentuate her confused expression.

"John's busing the team to Town Square right after school today and plans to give the players some quiet time at Jessie's memorial."

Liddy nodded with an approving twinkle in her eyes.

"Finish your breakfast. Let's just hope Jessie inspires those youngsters because Pelham's predicted to win by three touchdowns."

Liddy topped off her coffee and slipped on her rain parka. "Let's pray Pelham arrives a little too cocksure tonight." She hugged and kissed me before reaching for the kitchen door. "I'll be home as quickly as I can after school. How about we eat dinner at the game tonight?"

I smiled and nodded. "If you get hung up at school, Arnie and Judy will bring me to the stadium." I stood on the kitchen stoop and admired the peach-painted horizon dispelling the last of the gray mist that had replaced the earlier rain. Our Expedition sloshed through the rain's runoff as Liddy pulled out of the driveway and headed off to school.

———

THE SKIES BRIGHTENED by the time I headed for a haircut. Wiley Edward's barbershop had become a regular stop, though he offered nothing beyond basic haircuts. His throwback establishment adjacent City Hall also lived up to its reputation for harvesting the latest scuttle-butt and tall tales in town, exactly why Larry steered me to him shortly after I began writing for the paper. Of course, the aroma of hair tonic and the feel of a steamy towel on my face along with that of a straight razor skillfully gliding around my ears and neck made my regular visits nostalgic adventures.

Wiley slid out of his barber chair and set the morning paper aside when I entered. "Well, if it ain't the writer. Mus' be time to get your ears lowered again." He swatted the barber chair with a hand towel.

Once I settled into the well-worn leather seat, he adjusted the height and swiveled it just right, so we could watch each other in the mirror while he wet and combed my hair.

"Where are Hub and Marcellus today?"

His shop held three chairs usually maintained by two barbers chatting away while cutting and shaving with only brief breaks between customers. Everyone always seemed to know who would go next or if anyone needed to bump ahead because of a lunch break or other time constraint.

"It's game night. Hubbell and Marcellus will be in shortly. Our regulars on game day start piling in around eleven, and we stay busy until we lock up at five. Been like that for fifty years. Also, if the boys win tonight, they get free haircuts tomorrow, and that'll keep us neck deep in gators."

"You always offer free haircuts after they win?"

"Ever since Coach Priestly started coaching. Nearly twenty years, I reckon. 'Sides, their dads and brothers usually come along too." Wiley shot a sly grin and winked. "It makes for a busy Saturday, but old Hub and Marcellus enjoy handling the paying customers while I knock out buzz cuts for the players."

"I noticed the players all looked alike up top."

"Coach tells the boys each year that until the season's over if he can grab a lock of their hair, it's too long."

"If you don't mind, I'll pass on the player's cut. My usual trim will suit me just fine."

Wiley snipped and combed without impacting his dominance over our conversation. "Read your piece about Coach this morning. You sure have gotten to know him pretty good since you and your missus arrived in town. Everyone knows if it weren't for you he'd still be stuck in prison for a crime he didn't commit."

I eyed Wiley in the mirror. "I suspect I've been fortunate enough to lend a hand in helping John, but credit goes to Joe Arians once we figured out what happened. Since then, John and I have become close friends. We spent a lot of time together this summer too."

"Seeing you've got an in with Coach, how's it look tonight? I'd sure like to stay busy on Saturdays again if you know what I mean."

I chuckled as Wiley shifted sides. "I've got it from a very reliable source that if Pelham struts into our stadium cocksure of themselves, anything's possible."

"Sounds like a lot of maybes and ifs to me. From what I've seen, we're mighty thin on experience and size."

"It ain't the size of the dog in the fight but the size of the fight in the dog that determines the outcome."

"My great-grandson Keith is on the team this year, and he told me the same thing. Shucks! He ain't but a buck and a half sopping wet wearing all his football gear, but he can surely outrun a jackrabbit when he has a mind to, just like his great-granddad used to do."

I put my hand up causing Wiley to lower his scissors and comb. "You played football for Shiloh?"

Wiley pointed his scissors toward the wall plastered with Shiloh Saint memorabilia. He walked over and snatched a faded black and white photo and boasted, "Class of '48," as he handed it to me.

At the bottom of the picture a faded autograph identified the chiseled ballplayer as Wiley 'Woogie' Edwards. I glanced between the stillness of the gritty young athlete and the proud eighty-four-year-old barber standing behind me.

Wiley laughed. "Check out the nose. It got busted my junior year." He pointed to the bridge of his nose that heavily favored his left side.

"So where did the name Woogie come from?"

"I wiggled and waggled around defenders so well that Coach Black came up with it. He used to say if I'd forget about the boogie and just woogie, nobody could catch me."

I joined in Wiley's laughter as he recollected his heydays. "Now I understand where Keith got his nickname. You gonna be at the game tonight?"

"You betcha. Ain't missed a home game in seventy years."

Wiley ran his straight razor over my neck and around my ears while sharing more memories of his glory days. He finally tilted my seat back and lowered a hot, moist towel over my face as he bragged about how rough and tough players used to be. While Wiley patted my face with tonic, we both turned our heads in time to watch a red convertible drive past as it downshifted. I joined Wiley at the front window, and we recognized the back of Dixie's head as she roared north on Main Street.

Wiley turned from the window shaking his head. "Bless my soul. That gal's gonna get someone killed if not herself one of these days. She ain't changed a bit, even after all these years."

"So I guess you knew Dixie back then pretty well?"

"I knew her daddy and her brother before he traipsed off to Viet Nam and got killed. I don't know how long she'll be around, but the sooner she gets back to where she came from, the better if you ask me." Wiley shook his head again as he took my five dollar bill. "Here's your fifty-cents, Mister Phillips."

"Keep it. The history lesson was worth more than that. See you tonight."

CHAPTER FIFTEEN

LIDDY CALLED A LITTLE AFTER FOUR O'CLOCK TO SAY KAY ASKED HER AND a couple of other teachers to lend a hand with ticket sales. I told her I'd find her after I got to the stadium. Before she hung up, she suggested arriving early to beat the anticipated large crowd.

Arnie and Judy pulled up at five-thirty sporting their Shiloh colors. He had on a green and gold monogrammed polo, and she a gold booster v-neck top.

Arnie gawked at me as I climbed into the backseat. "Son, we need to swing you by the boosters concession before the game."

I tugged on my white golf shirt and smiled. "Liddy already bought me a shirt this morning."

Judy's SHS football earrings sparkled as she turned and giggled. "Welcome to Shiloh football."

After all I had written and heard about it, I was now witnessing Shiloh's Friday night mania firsthand. If my respected pastor and his wife dressed like this, I wondered what awaited me at the stadium.

We picked up Hillary along the way. She slid into the back seat with green and gold ribbons in her hair and wearing a well-worn green SHS t-shirt. "Hal told me they're expecting a huge crowd tonight. Glad you have your reserved parking spot."

The late afternoon sun kept the heat and humidity cranked, but any evidence from the morning rains had long disappeared. Though the stadium lights were already on, they would have little effect until the second half of the game. By the time we arrived, cars and trucks flowed into the stadium parking lot from all directions.

Arnie pulled into the reserved parking section near the pass gate. Liddy stood near the main entrance engaged with Phoebe and Kay. Arnie and Judy greeted Kay while Hillary and I caught up with Phoebe and Liddy. Liddy handed me a green and gold polo and matching visor along with the car keys and then pointed to our vehicle along the fence.

After my quick change, we headed to the concessions. Zeb's roaring laughter revealed his presence long before we saw him working the deep fryers. Silas shuttled trays of fries and onion rings to Bernie and Barb handling the counter along with Susanna. Bob pulled sausages and burgers off the grill while Sam slapped them onto buns and wrapped them as fast as they disappeared.

While we waited in line, I took in the sounds of high school football. Band members warmed up behind the locker room as cheerleaders laughed and giggled, rustling their green and gold pompoms nearby. On the field, footballs sailed back and forth as players went through pregame routines. I grinned when I recognized young Woogie shagging punts. John watched at mid-field as Pete, Jay, and Jim directed players through warm-up exercises. Timmy scrambled between the long-snappers and kickers feeding them footballs as they needed.

Pelham's strong contingent of parents and fans arrived showing support for their highly touted team. The black and gold uniformed players took up the far end of the field for their pregame regime.

"Theo, what would you like?" Liddy tugged on my arm.

"A sausage and fries."

Liddy handed me a bottle of coke and a brown sack containing my dinner. "Let's find some seats."

As soon as I turned to follow Liddy I heard, "Comin' through. Excuse us."

Harold wheeled his way through the crowd, aided by Dixie, as Hal cleared a path.

"Hello, Harold." I glanced at Hal before turning my puzzled gaze toward Harold and Dixie. Both Harold and Hal wore their apropos

SHS attire. Of course, Dixie stood out from the crowd dressed in a gold-sequined designer black top with tight black capris and high heels.

"I didn't expect to see you tonight. You must be feeling okay," I said.

"Theo, I wouldn't miss this opening game for anything. Besides, I'm feelin' much better thanks to Dixie." He reached back and tapped her hand.

Liddy managed to hold her bag and bottle of coke in one hand and greeted Dixie with the other. "I'm Liddy, Theo's wife."

Dixie cracked an awkward grin. "I've heard so much about both of you. Glad to finally meet you."

Hal stood, arms folded. "Dad, what would you and Dixie like?"

Dixie said, "Would you be a doll and get us both a burger and a coke, but no fries for your father." She looked at Liddy and me. "Please excuse us. It's just too crowded here." She pushed Harold beyond the railing and onto the painted asphalt track circling the field.

Hal's arms dropped to his side. "Don't take it personally. She's become overly protective of dad and pitched a fit when he insisted on coming tonight."

Hillary, Arnie, and Judy joined us with their dinners in hand. "You gonna hang with your dad or join us crazy fans in the stands Mister Mayor?" Hillary quipped.

"Let me fetch them some dinner and help them get situated, and then I'll come join you." Hal glanced at me and then at Hillary.

Liddy asked, "Are they gonna watch the game from there?"

"He's used to watching the games from the sidelines and insisted he'll be quite okay. I arranged for a folding chair for Dixie. Y'all work your way on up. I'll be along in a few minutes."

The stands overflowed by kickoff, and folks stood elbow to elbow along the sideline fence. Zeb, Susanna, and Sam joined us on the top row. Larry, Martha, and Mary squeezed in as the names of the starting players echoed across the stadium. We could hear Jay and Jim in the coach's box talking to Pete and John stalking the sidelines as the captains ran off the field. Pelham won the toss and opted to receive. A couple of minutes later, the ref's whistle blew, and the crescendoing sound of

Phoebe's trombone players spurred the crowd onto their feet as Colin Franklin, Shiloh's kicker approached the ball to start John's first season back after a three-year forced hiatus.

A Pelham player tried to field the line-drive kickoff but bobbled it. Before he could tuck the ball away, two Shiloh players slammed him to the ground. Woogie swooped up the loose ball and waltzed into the end zone. The home crowd roared as if Shiloh won the game on that opening play, but then Pelham blocked the extra point.

While John huddled his kickoff team before sending them back onto the field again, I overheard Jay shout into his headset, "John, Pelham's coach is furious and screaming at his players and coaches."

Pelham's offense pushed the ball down the field, but Shiloh's defensive schemes stymied their drives until late in the second quarter. The half ended with Pelham up, 10-6. Shiloh's home crowd gave the players a standing ovation as they exited the field. Even Harold stood and gave John a high five as John jogged by. Dixie yanked Harold back into his chair after John passed. They bickered as Phoebe led her motley band of musicians onto the field, the band's street attire forgotten as their musical talent stole the show.

After the second half kickoff, Shiloh managed a long drive to Pelham's thirty-yard line before facing a fourth and long decision. Shiloh broke its huddle, and as the others got set to run the play, quarterback Quentin Higginbotham, everyone called him Q, started walking toward John on the sidelines. Pelham's defense relaxed. Shiloh's center snapped the ball directly to Hunter, the senior tailback. Q turned upfield and raced up the sidelines as the Pelham defense stood frozen with their coach running down the sidelines screaming and pointing. Hunter launched the ball, and Shiloh went up 13-10 late in the third quarter after Q danced into the end zone, and we kicked the extra point.

The celebration lasted only until the next play when Pelham's return man fielded the kickoff and scampered eighty-five yards to Shiloh's five-yard line before being run out of bounds. Three downs later, Pelham went back up 18-13 after an errant snap turned into a two-point conversion.

Pete rallied his defense to come up with several big plays to thwart Pelham from scoring again, but the clock ticked into the final minute with Pelham still ahead. John's offense got stuffed on a critical third down deep in Shiloh's territory. After a timeout, Shiloh punted while the fans held their breath. The ball rolled out of bounds on Pelham's twenty-eight-yard line with fifty-five seconds remaining.

With only two timeouts left, Shiloh's fate seemed inevitable. On first down, Pelham's running back attempted to run wide but stayed in bounds as he got dragged down by three Shiloh defenders. The clock ticked off ten precious seconds by the time Shiloh called timeout. On the next play, the Pelham quarterback took a knee forcing John to call Shiloh's last time-out. Forty-one seconds remained as Pelham's quarterback faked taking a knee, and their lone wideout bolted past our cornerback. Pete raced down the sidelines, pointing and yelling. Q, in at safety, tracked down the receiver as their quarterback heaved the ball down the far sideline. The Pelham receiver juggled the ball on his fingertips as Q launched himself and dislodged the ball from the receiver's outstretched grasp.

Shiloh fans gave Q a standing ovation as he and the Pelham receiver both got escorted off the field after their violent collision. The Pelham coach called his last timeout with twenty-eight seconds remaining on fourth down. Pete grabbed Woogie and lifted his face mask to look eye to eye with his diminutive speedster. After a few words and a swift pat on his butt, Woogie replaced Q and ran onto the field to return the punt. Pelham lined up expecting Shiloh to go all out to block the punt. On the snap, only one Shiloh player rushed the punter, the rest peeled back and formed a wall of blockers along the near sideline. Woogie waited for the high spiraling punt at the twenty-nine-yard line. Hunter provided a crushing block that sprung Woogie who raced untouched toward his wall of blockers. All but one Pelham player got hammered by the wall of Shiloh blockers as Woogie sprinted down the sidelines. At the ten yard line, Pelham's safety forced Woogie between himself and the sidelines, but Woogie wiggled and waggled out of the Pelham player's arms. Once he pulled himself free, Woogie stumbled but managed to stay on his feet long enough to lunge across the goal line.

The fans in the stadium went hysterical, along with all the Shiloh players and coaches. Even Harold pushed Dixie aside and climbed out of his wheelchair to shuffle toward the goal line, hollering with hands waving. Hal and Phillip raced onto the field and helped Harold back into his wheelchair.

Sixteen-seconds remained. John took no chances. Colin squib-kicked the ball, and Pelham fumbled on its twenty-yard line. Shiloh recovered to end the game with a 19-18 upset victory. Shiloh fans poured onto the field as the horn sounded.

Arnie, Judy, Liddy and I worked our way onto the field. Doc Lucas stood with his hands on his hips beside Harold. "Unless you want these young players and the fans in the stands to witness you having a massive stroke, no more games! Do you hear me?"

Harold lifted his sweat-drenched head and nodded with a wry grin.

Hal glared at his dad. "I agree. No more games until Doc says otherwise. I'll make sure you get a copy of the game films for the rest of the season."

Dixie squeezed Harold's shoulders. Harold glanced at Hal and Phillip and then looked up to Dixie. "Deal. Take me home. I'm exhausted."

Phillip had maneuvered their truck onto the track, and Hal helped Dixie get Harold buckled into the front seat. The post-game bedlam sub-sided right after they drove away, leaving Liddy and me on the sidelines standing with Arnie, Judy and Hillary.

Nick walked between Liddy and me and squeezed our shoulders with his outstretched arms. "Welcome to Friday night football in Shiloh."

We all looked at each other and broke into laughter as we walked toward the concession stand. Kay and Ray stood talking with Zeb, Larry, Martha, Mary and Phoebe. Kay smiled and looked at Liddy. "Thanks for the help today. We've not had a crowd like this in quite a few years." Ray winked with a modest grin, grabbed Kay's arm, and they headed toward the parking lot.

CHAPTER SIXTEEN

THE INCESSANT CHATTER THROUGHOUT TOWN THAT WEEKEND ABOUT THE Saint's upset victory inspired me to consider another article. My gait felt somewhat faster than usual as I walked to the Sentinel Monday morning. I entered Larry's office, plopped down in front of his desk and waited for him to end his phone call.

"I've got an intriguing angle for my next article," I spouted as he hung up his phone.

Larry scratched his chin while he walked around his desk.

"Who would you say was the most unlikely MVP Friday night?" I clasped my hands behind my head and leaned back in my chair.

"A host of players made key plays."

"That's true, but one stood head and shoulders above all the others, at least figuratively."

Larry's grin grew ear-to-ear. "I reckon you mean that new kid, Keith Edwards."

"My friend, that young man was David making the most of his Goliath moment."

Larry continued his self-admiring grin. "You should write about him using that exact David and Goliath analogy. Folks around here would eat that up."

"Now hold on one sec. There's more to the story. What if I told you this new kid on the team is related to someone who played for Shiloh over sixty-five years ago?"

Larry's eyes popped. "Are you referring to Old Wiley Edwards?"

I bobbed my head before I added, "How much bigger did this story just get for you?"

Larry sat down and rested his elbows on his knees. "I didn't even know Wiley and his wife had any family left in town."

"Well, it's a fact he has a great-grandson playing for Shiloh High School."

"Sounds like a perfect story for you to wrap your arms around." Larry ran his fingers through his receding hairline, lost in thought. "I'll even see what the morgue might have about Wiley for you."

"I'd appreciate whatever you can dig up. I'll run this by Wiley before I talk to Keith though."

Larry shook my hand. "I'll bring Mary up to speed when she gets back into the office later today."

———

FIFTEEN MINUTES LATER, I popped into Mister Edwards' barbershop. Hub worked on the only customer while Wiley perused the morning paper, legs crossed and propped on the footrest of his barber's chair. He folded the newspaper and began to stand.

I motioned for him to remain seated. "This won't take long. I want to run something by you."

Wiley relaxed and rested his hands on the newspaper in his lap.

"I'm interested in writing a story about you and your great-grandson Keith. He played a whale of a game Friday night."

Wiley's weathered brow and cheeks perked up. "I told ya he'd live up to his nickname."

"Breaking that tackle to win the game was nothing short of special."

Wiley smiled and straightened his back. "What kinda story you thinkin' about?"

"I'd like to link him with the original Woogie Edwards if it'd be alright with you?"

Hub paused from cutting his customer's hair and glanced at Wiley and then at me.

Wiley's smile diminished as he hesitated. "What do ya mean link us? He's my spitting image and carries my nickname. What more do you want to know?"

I eyed Hub's growing interest in our conversation. "Well, I'd like to talk a little bit about y'all's family connection."

"What if there's a couple rotten branches in our family tree?"

I chuckled. "The article will remain about you and your great-grandson's relationship."

"I reckon that'd be okay. Mind ya, Keith's only been in Shiloh a couple of months."

"Where does he live?"

He lowered his voice and glanced at Hub peering in our direction. "He don't live with his parents anymore. His daddy's still on parole, and his momma ain't fit to care for herself much less a teenage boy. The State placed Keith under our care."

"What about the other family?"

Hub cleared his throat as he and his customer walked to the front of the shop. Wiley extended a polite smile and waved. As soon as his customer left, Hub grabbed a push broom and swept around his chair.

Wiley scratched his stubbly cheeks. "We're his family, and he stays with Hub's son, Marcellus, and his family. Marcellus' son, Byron, although everyone calls him Bobo, is Keith's age."

I gave Wiley a dumbfounded look. I peeked at Hub leaning on his broom before I turned back to look at Wiley.

Hub walked over. "Mister Phillips, you've never met Keith have you?"

"No, not properly."

"He's very light skinned, but his momma's black." Hub looked out the front window and sighed. "There are still some folks around these parts who cling to old ways of thinkin'."

Wiley hopped off his chair and put his arm on Hub's shoulder. "Ever since you and your wife moved into town, you've not run away from any of Shiloh's secrets and scandals, and folks' lives have been changed because of it. I reckon we can trust you'll write the article the right way."

"In my way of thinking, prejudice is the worst form of arrogance any person can let influence their thinking. This article won't deviate from its intended purpose and risk harming anyone, especially Keith. You've got my word."

———

I WALKED AROUND Town Square and headed for the Butcher Shoppe. The lunch crowd was backed up to just inside the door. Alex looked up as he cleared a nearby table. "Mister P, I saw you and Miss Liddy at the game Friday night."

"Why didn't you come over and say hello?"

"I sat with Phillip, Jeannie, and some other Sanctuary friends."

"Speaking of Sanctuary, you looking forward to helping when it starts back up next Wednesday?"

Alex tossed his damp towel over his shoulder and grabbed a tray of dirty dishes and trash. "Yes, sir, I plan to be there. I want to see the new community center. Jeannie told me all about it. Sorry, I gotta run." He balanced the tray on his shoulder and spun away.

My attention turned to the menu specials on the board above the counter.

"May we join you for lunch?"

Joe and Nick stood in the doorway behind me. "I've been looking to catch up to the two of you anyway."

Nick looked at Joe. "Theo and Liddy have become gen-u-ine Shiloh Saints fans. Liddy got them signed up as boosters after the game."

Joe laughed. "You mean Zeb and Sam bamboozled them into joining the boosters?"

"We're glad to join. There are a lot of fine folks we can get to know that way. Heck, I think Liddy likes this school social thing."

Silas greeted us at the counter. "My good friends! What can I get for you today?"

Nick and Joe ordered the chicken pita and fries lunch special, while I opted for the vegetarian feta wrap. Before we found a table, I asked Silas, "How long have you been helping with the sideline crew at the games?"

Silas moaned and reached for the back of his leg. "This was my first time. Coach stopped by last week and asked if I'd be interested."

Nick chuckled. "You got to see that little Edwards boy race down the sidelines though."

"He runs real fast. When that other player grabbed him, I thought for sure he'd be wrestled to the ground, but he just wiggled himself free like a scared piggy. He's going to be quite a player when he grows up." Silas raised his hand to his chest to mark Keith's height. "A tough boy, though. Maybe he will sprout up like Alex at about the same age."

I joined in the chuckling and looked at Silas. "Would you mind if I mention you in my next article? I'm writing about the Edwards boy."

Silas blushed as he shrugged and nodded.

"Old man, quit your silliness. Don't you see there are more customers behind our good friends waiting to eat?" Bernie stepped from the other end of the counter with our lunches.

Nick grabbed the tray and led us to the back booth. Nick and Joe sat across from me, and we exchanged small talk about the game between bites of our lunches. Both enjoyed the idea of my article and shared stories about Wiley Edwards from their school days. They remembered him as a fixture at football, basketball, and baseball games when they grew up.

"I was with Wiley last Friday getting a haircut and a history lesson about Shiloh football when Harold's ex-wife flew through town. Did either of you see her?" I asked and then took a sip of sweet tea.

Nick looked up from his pita and swallowed. "Jeannie ran back to my office and tried to get me to check it out. But by the time I got to the front window, it was too late."

"However, I got a birds-eye view from my office," Joe said after swallowing. "I heard her downshift before pulling out onto Main Street." Joe's smile widened. "A fancy European sports car in Shiloh is pretty hard to miss. We'll hear pickups roar through town once in a while, but none whine like Dixie's high-dollar Jaguar convertible. It brought flashbacks to the days when she raced around town with reckless abandon. Guess she hasn't slowed down much over the years. I just hope no one gets hurt before she leaves town."

"Funny, Mister Edwards said the same thing," I said with a broad grin.

Nick smirked. "And did you see that floozy's outfit Friday night?"

Joe blurted, "Years ago, we whispered about her when she wore similar provocative outfits to the games, but now we're whispering about her for a whole different reason. Gotta feel a little badly about someone begging for attention like that."

"I feel for Hal and Phillip. Harold may enjoy her flaunting, but Hal and Phillip must feel mortified."

"I've spoken to Hal, and he's trying his best to tolerate her pretentious behavior, but he won't acknowledge her as his mother. She's Dixie to him." Joe checked his watch. "Hate to cut this short, but I've got to run."

A moment later, I headed back to the house thinking more about the article. I had a lot to consider regarding how to address Wiley and Keith's relationship.

CHAPTER SEVENTEEN

BACK-TO-BACK ROAD VICTORIES SEEMED TO BRING OUT THE WHOLE TOWN for the Albany Christian Academy matchup. In the waning minutes of the game, Shiloh forced a crucial turnover as ACA looked to tie the game. The horn sounded, Q took a knee, and the Saints celebrated a four-game winning streak.

Media reporters clamored for John's attention after the teams dispersed following an impromptu post-game prayer huddle at midfield. Liddy and I ran down to the booster's concession stand and prepared sausage dogs, hamburgers and drinks for the players and coaches.

After the prayer, Woogie raced to the concession counter with a sweat-laced smile. "Mister Phillips sir, that last punt return was for you."

I stared at this five-foot-four giant killer. "I'm honored, Woogie, but why didn't you score?"

"Shucks, Mister Phillips, there was three of them. We did score right after that though."

I mussed his hair and laughed. "Great game, son. Proud of you and the whole team."

He grabbed a sausage dog and coke. "Wanna thank you for writing about my great grandpa. If it weren't for him, I just don't know where I'd be right now."

"He's pretty proud of you too."

"Oh yeah!" Woogie stepped aside. "This is Bobo Davis."

"Glad to meet you, Bobo. Your grandad told me about you. You helping Woogie get situated at school and showing him around town?"

"Yes, sir. Is she your wife?" He pointed to Liddy helping other players at the counter.

"Sure is."

"I'm in her second-period art class. She's my favorite teacher."

"She's my favorite teacher too. Now, y'all eat your sandwiches before they get cold." The two ran to where Wiley, Hub, and Marcellus stood near the locker room.

"Hey, Mister P! Don't us coaches count?" Pete wiped his face with a towel as Jay and Jim chased the last of the players toward the locker room.

Liddy packed a cardboard box with the remaining sausage dogs and burgers. They each grabbed a coke and put four more in with their sandwiches.

"Will that be enough for you? Don't forget to save some for Coach. I suspect he'll appreciate it once those reporters set him free."

Pete smirked and grabbed the box. "We'll save him a bite or two."

Zeb growled from the back of the concession stand. "Boys! Set aside a couple of those sandwiches and a coke for Coach as soon as you get inside. Hear me?"

"We hear ya!" Jay shouted as he and Jim bolted toward the locker room to catch up to Pete.

Susanna and Sam joined us as we closed down the concession stand. Jeannie, Phillip, and Mary stood nearby talking.

"Sounds like Pete's gonna be a few more minutes," Liddy jested as we joined them.

Sam patted my shoulder just before he and Susanna headed toward the parking lot. "You and Phillip planning on staying out late Jeannie?"

Jeannie looked at Phillip. "We won't be too late. We're just gonna hang a little bit with Pete and Mary."

Sam waved as he and Susanna walked beyond the main gate.

"Before we leave, what'd you think about the new community center after Sanctuary's first meeting last week?" I looked at Jeannie and Phillip.

Phillip said, "It's going to take some getting used to, but we love the added space. The middle schoolers had an area to mingle apart from the older kids who hung out together."

"How many showed up?" Liddy asked.

Jeannie looked at Mary. "I calculated sixty-five altogether. It helped that a lot of the players attended," Mary said.

"My dad enjoyed handing out those Sanctuary t-shirts you two bought for the group," Phillip said.

"Do we need to order more shirts? We weren't quite sure about the right assortment of sizes, but we saw quite a few wearing their shirts tonight."

Phillip smiled. "We'll check what's left and let you know. Thanks."

The door to the locker room flung open, and all the players piled out. The coaches followed soon after as the lights in the stadium went out.

"Be home by midnight! No exceptions, gentlemen. See you Monday." John locked the locker room door, pulled an aluminum foil-wrapped burger from his coat pocket and took a bite. He stood absorbing the empty stands and stillness as he inspected the field.

Before Pete joined Mary in his truck, he barked at the last of the players milling around by the gate, "Y'all better be gone before Coach locks up."

Hunter grinned and yelled back, "We're leaving now. I'm taking them all home. Good night, Coach."

Jay and Jim jogged over to Zeb waiting in his Bronco. Phillip and Jeannie jumped into Phillip's red Jeep, and they all followed Pete out of the parking lot. Only two vehicles remained.

Liddy tugged my arm. "Let's go. John doesn't need us bothering him. It appears his mind is somewhere else."

———

"THEO, WOULD YOU mind stopping off at the post office this morning? I forgot to mail Sissy's birthday present. Send it priority mail please."

"The one sitting by the front door?"

"Yes, dear. You're a sweetie pie."

I slipped the package into my jacket pocket. "I'll be back shortly."

"Remember the post office closes at noon on Saturdays."

"I'll head straight there before I run by Zeb's to see if Jim's free to help with our bedroom floor project."

When I pulled into to the post office parking lot, Dixie's Jaguar sat beside three pickups. Inside, Ray accepted an envelope from Dixie before she turned and headed toward the door. She appeared distracted until I said, "Morning Dixie," as she walked past me.

Dixie took a moment to realize who greeted her. "Hello, Theo." She lowered her oversized sunglasses onto her nose. "Sorry, I have to hurry off." She headed toward the door.

"How's Harold this morning? I reckon he heard about the victory last night."

She paused mid-stride and raised her glasses. "The boys are watching the game at the house. I'm sorry, but I simply have got to run. Say hello to your darlin' wife." She waved as she turned her back and walked out the door.

"Theo, would you hand these to Miz Arnaquer?" Ray held out a manila envelope and a mail-order newspaper.

"Huh? Miss Arnaquer?"

Ray interrupted his customer and pleaded in an undertone voice. "Theo, Dixie. Catch her before she drives off."

I grabbed her mail from Ray and bolted out the door. "Dixie! Wait a minute."

Her brake lights lit up.

"Didn't mean to startle you. Mister Abernathy gave this to me to give to you. You musta left them at the counter."

"Why thank ya, Theo." She reached out, but I let go too soon.

"Oops, I'm sorry." I knelt down and recognized the mail-order paper as a copy of the Shiloh Sentinel addressed to Delilah Arnaquer, 132 Lake Drive, Picayune, LA and forwarded to a Shiloh post office box. The manila envelope from Samuel G. Appleton, Attorney at Law, Shiloh, GA was hand addressed to Delilah D. Arnaquer at the Shiloh post office box.

"You okay sugar?" Dixie raised her glasses as I hesitated before standing up.

"Here you go. I'm sorry that I was so clumsy."

She flipped her mail face down on the passenger seat and lowered her glasses again. "Don't think anything about it. Why don't you and the Missus stop by and visit us at the house soon?"

"We need to do that. I'll talk to Liddy. Say hey to Harold for me."

She sped away in her shiny convertible, and I returned to the counter inside, pulled Sissy's package from my jacket and handed it to Ray. "Priority mail, please. My granddaughter's turning nine this week."

"No problem Theo." Ray placed the package on the scale and calculated the postage.

"Would I be out of line asking you a question about Dixie?"

Ray looked up. "It depends. What do you want to know?"

"You called her Miss Arnaquer."

"That's her last name."

"I didn't know that, but it makes sense she doesn't go by Archer anymore. What do I owe you for the package?"

Ray handed me my change and receipt. "You and Liddy going to the game over in Ocilla?"

"Probably not. We're doing some remodeling next weekend."

———

Jim climbed into his truck just as I pulled up to the front of Adams Feed and Hardware. He rolled down his window after I caught his attention.

"Glad I caught you. Are you still available to give me a hand with my floor?"

"Of course. Are you ready to get started?"

"I thought we could start on it next Saturday if that's okay with you?"

Jim squinted. "Will late morning suit you? We won't get back until late from Ocilla. Can you and Liddy move everything out of the bedroom and yank out the old carpet? That'll free you and me to jump right in on fixing the floor. I'll bring what tools we'll need and a few replacement boards just in case. Oh yeah, and check with Pete's dad. He's got a floor sander. We'll need that. My dad has everything else in the store."

"We're not going to the game this week, so we can finish clearing out the room and dispose of the old carpet by Saturday morning."

Jim's eyes widened. "Mister P, you and Miss Liddy can't miss the game."

"I think you guys can manage one game without us in the stands. We can use Friday night to get ready."

Jim slipped his truck into reverse but held his foot on the brake. "Guess that makes sense. All I can say is we better not lose, or y'all will never hear the end of it."

We both chuckled as he slowly backed out and left.

"What were you two jabber-jawing about?" Zeb leaned against the door and waved as Jim pulled away.

"He's coming over to our house Saturday to help with that flooring project I mentioned to you. Jim said you'd have everything we need."

"Did he tell you to see Sam about a floor sander?"

"Intend to swing by and ask him on my way home."

Zeb took me inside and found all the supplies I'd need to restore the floor. I slid the box into the back of my vehicle as Zeb watched from the store's platform.

"Sorry to hear y'all will be staying home Friday night. Should be a good game, but it looks like you two will have plenty to keep yourselves busy. You tell Liddy that Jim'll have your bedroom floor looking as good as the rest of that old house in no time."

———

MARTHA CALLED THE following Monday morning. "I checked our subscription records. Delilah Arnaquer has been a mail-order customer for the past sixteen years. She paid her last annual subscription in full back in March. Why is this so hush-hush? Who is she?"

"I'll tell you later. Can I talk to Larry?"

"I'll get him to pick up." Martha didn't bother putting me on hold before she yelled, "Larry, Theo's on line one."

"What's up?"

"Martha followed up on that note I gave you after church. You might find this particular mail-order customer's history of some interest."

"Why? Who is this Delilah person?"

"Delilah D. Arnaquer is none other than Dixie, Harold's estranged ex-wife. She's been getting your paper mailed to her for the last sixteen years."

A long pause came at Larry's end. "What do you make of it?"

"Larry, I'm trying to figure that out. I discovered the connection Saturday when I ran into her at the post office. She received a copy of the paper addressed to her Louisiana address but forwarded to a post office box she rented here. I also noticed she had an envelope from Gus Appleton's law office."

"What do you think we should do with this information?"

"I'm not sure what to think yet, but can you make a few calls?"

"Come to think about it. I've got a friend of mine at the New Orleans Picayune Times who might be able to help us out. In the meantime, think you can arrange to talk to Dixie and Harold? Maybe she'll let her guard down enough to reveal something about her past and the real reason why she came back."

"I hope my gut's wrong, but I sense she's up to something. I'll take Liddy with me to see her and Harold. I'll also swing by City Hall and have a sit-down with Hal too. He's not been comfortable with her since she first popped in on them."

CHAPTER EIGHTEEN

"Mister Phillips, may I have a word with you." Missus Edwards stepped away from Judy and the other ladies gathered near the main door of the church when we entered Wednesday evening.

"Yes, ma'am. How may I help you? Is Wiley okay?"

Missus Edwards fidgeted with her pocketbook's clasp. "Mercy sakes. He's better than fine. What I wanted to confess to you is that ever since your article, Keith's been stopping by almost daily, and the two of them sit and laugh on the front porch for hours. The more they laugh and carry on, the more I realize what Wiley must've been like at the same age." She pulled a tissue from her pocketbook and dabbed the corners of her eyes.

"I appreciate you telling me that Missus Edwards."

She rested her hand on my arm. "Please, call me Malvinia."

Judy stepped from the other ladies and nonchalantly pointed. "I believe Liddy's trying to catch your attention over there."

Liddy's eyes sent a loud signal as soon as I saw her locked in conversation with Harold while Dixie listened by his side.

"Sorry Miss Malvinia, but it appears my wife needs me."

As soon as I joined Liddy and slid my hand into hers, Harold interrupted himself. "Oh, there you are Theo. It seems as though you've turned Missus Edwards usual scowl into a rosy smile."

"She just shared a little story about Wiley. How are you doing?"

"Now that you've joined your wife, Dixie wanted me to ask the two of you to come have dinner with us at the house." Harold patted Dixie's hand resting on his shoulder.

Dixie's cold smile dispelled any notion of sincerity. "I've heard so much about you."

Liddy peeked at me. "We'd be glad to, but we'll have to make it one evening next week. We've got our hands full at the house this weekend."

"Why don't you call as soon as you get free?" Harold's charming smile looked up at Liddy.

Liddy squeezed my hand.

"We look forward to it but insist on bringing dessert," I said, trying to be cordial while staring at Dixie's equally commendable lipstick framed smile.

Harold looked over his shoulder. "Dixie my dear, Liddy makes the best peach cobbler."

Liddy giggled. "Sounds fine to me."

The sound of Zeb's voice turned our heads. "Come on y'all. Service is about to begin."

The church had more than the usual number of empty seats with most of the younger members attending Sanctuary. Arnie shared the story of Jezebel using her conniving influence over Ahab to execute an innocent man and gain property she and Ahab coveted. After reading the text from the platform, Arnie stepped onto the main floor and from the center aisle attempted to elicit responses about the relevance of the story. He only managed to garner silence from the long faces in the pews until Harold blurted, "Guess back in those days they didn't have the right of eminent domain." Snickers and giggles followed.

After church, Liddy wrapped her arm around my waist as we walked across Main Street. "Interesting take on that story tonight."

"Arnie's comments reminded me how severe God's warning is about covetousness since it resides at the heart of most sins. I just hope God'll forgive me for coveting after my wife's heart." I drew Liddy to my side.

"It's not coveting if you already possess it." She wiggled free and jogged across the street and onto the sidewalk. "But tonight you'll have to hurry up to catch it." She turned and screamed as soon as I began to chase after her. Her playful laughter raced upstairs when I reached the front door.

———

OUR BEDROOM FURNITURE occupied much of the hallway and dining room by the time we went to bed Friday. The following morning, I walked downstairs from our temporary accommodations and made coffee. I then walked outside and grabbed the paper and opened it on the porch to read Larry's commentary on Shiloh's 17 to 7 loss to Ocilla. Larry's bare-bones article reported that Quentin scored the lone touchdown but fumbled trying to score the go-ahead score late in the game. An opposing defender grabbed the loose ball and ran untouched the length of the field to lock up Ocilla's victory.

Liddy had poured herself a cup of coffee by the time I returned to the kitchen to tell her about the game. "You know Jim's going to blame us for them losing," she said with a straight face.

"Guess that means we can't miss any more games."

Liddy cracked a smile. "Guess not. What time do you think Jim will be here?"

"Your guess is as good as mine. Let's haul that carpet to the alley and sweep the floor after breakfast."

Jim knocked on the storm door shortly after ten-thirty. Liddy yelled from the hallway. "Come on in Jim, but I don't want to hear a peep about us not being at the game last night."

"Yes, ma'am. Coach told the players on the way home we all got careless and handed them the game, but we still have another five games left in the regular season."

"I feel just awful for those boys. They've played so hard. You coaches too," Liddy said as she accompanied Jim to our barren bedroom.

"Maybe this little project will help get your mind off that game. The fact remains, you guys are still in the hunt for the playoffs," I said as I knelt in the corner by the closet. "Jim, would you look at this." I pointed to three adjoining floorboards, apparently a patch-job in the otherwise remarkable original floor.

Jim knelt down, pulled a putty knife from his toolbox, and eased the blade into the joint of the first board. The board popped loose after a couple of jiggles. Jim quickly removed the two other boards, inspected them and shrugged. "Doesn't look like there's any damage to the other boards or the floor joists underneath." He reached into the black cavity and removed an old flour sack.

"Anything else in there? By the looks of this old sackcloth, it looks like it's been there a long time." I knelt over Jim's shoulder and peeked into the hole.

Liddy grabbed a flashlight from Jim's toolbox. "Will this help?"

I shined the light as Jim wiped his fingers across a dust-covered leather pouch. He laid it next to him then ran his fingers all around the hole. "I think that's it."

Liddy leaned over and wiped the dust from the leather pouch. She unsnapped the flap and pulled out a sealed envelope and a handwritten letter.

"What's the letter say?" I asked. Jim appeared as intrigued as me.

Liddy stared for a moment. "It's dated January 16, 1923 and addressed to Zeke."

"Who's it from?" I asked.

Liddy glanced at the bottom of the letter. "Poppa."

The three of us looked equally clueless. I figured the letter had something to do with the Priestly family and the house's construction.

Liddy stepped closer to the window. "Dear Zeke, The enclosed envelope contains a copy of an agreement between Mister Archer, Sr. and myself. I helped his company a few years ago, which saved many jobs for our town. As long as he or his company continue to act in good faith for the good of Shiloh, I do not wish the terms of this agreement executed. I trust you will accept the responsibility my request carries for you as my heir. If you need advice, Mister Arians knows about the agreement. May God guide and keep you. Poppa" Liddy's eyes remained glued to the page.

I looked at Jim. "Does this mean anything to you?"

Jim shook his head. "Can I see that Miss Liddy?"

Liddy handed him the letter and the sealed envelope. He glanced at the handwritten page and then turned his attention to the envelope. He held it up to the light and ran his fingers over the flap. "This is embossed above the seal." He held it to light once again. "H. H. Archer Holdings Company, Shiloh, Georgia"

"John may know something about this." I put my hand out to Jim, and then slid the envelope and letter back into the leather pouch. "I've got a feeling this never found its way to Zeke after it got stashed for safekeeping. Maybe old Ezra decided against giving it to him." I looked up to Liddy and handed her the pouch. "Put this away for now, and we'll call John later."

Jim and I had reinserted the three floorboards before we went to work restoring the floor. We spent the rest of morning on our knees inspecting and repairing the floor before we began sanding after lunch. By dinnertime, we applied a topcoat of spar varnish over the old pine floor.

Liddy came down the hall as we were cleaning up. "Looks fabulous Jim. I'm impressed."

"Jim assured me that the refinished wood would dry by tomorrow night and match the rest of the flooring in the house pretty well." I patted Jim on the back, and we shared smiles.

Liddy said, "I've got dinner almost done. I assume you're staying Jim. I cooked up plenty of fried chicken, mashed potatoes, green beans, and just pulled out a tray of biscuits. We can turn on the Georgia game while we eat."

"That'll suit me just fine, and I'll consider it as payment in full." Jim looked at me. "Remember to stay off the floor for twenty-four hours, and don't put the furniture back until Monday afternoon to be on the safe side."

We enjoyed watching the second half of the Georgia versus Georgia Christian game while we ate dinner. GCU lost in a dogfight, but we caught glimpses of Andy on the sidelines. I called John right after Jim left and arranged to meet after church.

JOHN AND MARIE followed Liddy and me back to the house after church on Sunday. Liddy showed Marie the bedroom floor while John and I sat in the rockers on the front porch. I handed him the leather pouch, and he examined the contents while I shared how we stumbled across it.

"Looks like this came from my great-grandpa Ezra all right."

"What do you think? How's Zeke related to you?"

"I'm pretty sure that was my Grandpa Ezekiel's nickname."

"Do you know what this might be all about?"

"I suspect it's just some old, outdated agreement. It doesn't mean anything to me." He put the letter and envelope back into the pouch and handed it to me. "They belong to the house. You and Liddy keep 'em."

"Would you mind if I looked into this before dismissing them as just some historical memorabilia with no value? Aren't you the least bit interested in the agreement in the envelope?"

John shook his head. "Nothing involving some business deal with the Archers interest me."

"I understand, but I'll show this to Joe and see what he has to say since it does mention one of his ancestors too."

John chuckled. "You just can't help yourself, can you? Go ahead and check it out. You have my blessing."

Liddy and Marie walked onto the porch. Liddy asked, "You two solve the mystery?"

John grinned. "I'll let your investigative reporter here figure it out. Means nothing to me." He glanced at Marie. "You don't recall any secret agreement between my great-grandpa Ezra and the Archers do you?"

Marie laughed. "That's well before my time. I'm sure Theo will have some fun looking into it. How about you and Liddy join us for dinner at Bubba's? My treat."

"Beats smelling varnish all afternoon. We'll follow you over."

CHAPTER NINETEEN

AFTER LIDDY HEADED OFF TO SCHOOL ON TUESDAY MORNING, I SAVORED another cup of coffee on our porch. I needed time with God before sorting out how best to wrangle my growing curiosity about Dixie's open-ended return, which on the surface seemed only to benefit Harold. Had my instincts steered me wrong? Harold's well-being mattered, but both Hal and Phillip expressed ill feelings over their mother's cold, capricious behavior.

I got a chuckle out of my devotional reading when it dawned on me, Samson's blindness began when he fell in love with Delilah. After recording this revelation and its relevance in my journal, I called Harold and agreed to have dinner at his house Friday night since Shiloh had a bye week. The mysterious leather pouch on the kitchen table served as a reminder to also call Joe's office.

"Susanna, is Joe in this morning?"

"Sorry, Theo. He'll be in court until Friday. Can I help you?"

"Joe may be able to assist us with some papers we found in the house. Can you check his schedule for Friday?"

Susanna mumbled to herself and then said, "He'll be busy most of the morning. How about 11:30? Maybe you can take him off my hands for lunch."

"That'll work. By the way, did you hear from Andy this weekend?"

"He called Sunday night. The boys razzed each other about their respective team's losses."

After I had hung up, I reached Hillary and confirmed Hal was free after lunch. I got dressed and headed off to the library to snoop into the history of H. H. Archer Holdings Company before meeting Hal.

ATTACHÉ IN HAND, I waltzed into City Hall feeling a little more confident about Shiloh's early twentieth-century history. Hillary's head remained glued to the newspaper spread out on her desk. "What's got your attention?"

"Hey, Theo. Just killing time while I finish my lunch break."

I looked toward the closed office door. "Hal hasn't got back yet?"

"He just ran across the street for a quick sandwich. Have a seat." She removed remnants of her lunch from the chair beside her desk and crumpled the bag before dropping it into the trash. "We didn't see you two at the game Friday night."

"Jim told us about the game Saturday afternoon after ragging on Liddy and me for jinxing the team."

Hillary smiled. "They played great until one itsy-bitsy oops turned the game around and made the long drive home seem a lot longer."

"That's pretty near how Jim described what happened. Maybe the boys learned a lesson that'll make them tougher for the rest of the season. Everyone forgets how young the team is. Mistakes were bound to happen."

The sound of rapid steps turned Hillary's focus to the hallway. She folded the paper and set it aside.

"Any calls, Hilly?" Hal's voice made it around the corner before he did. "Hey, Theo. Please go on in." He pointed to his office door and lagged behind to consult with Hillary.

"I'm not interrupting your lunch am I?"

Hal sat behind his desk, unwrapped the foil from his sandwich, slid the paper off his straw and dropped it into his drink. "Only if eating my lunch while we talk bothers you. Did you eat?"

"I'm good. Go right ahead."

A knock preceded Hillary poking her head into the office. "Theo, I got you a coke from the fridge. I figured Hal would be eating his lunch in front of you."

"That's mighty considerate of you." I popped the tab and took a sip as I returned to my seat.

Hal relaxed into his swivel chair. "Give Theo and me about thirty minutes to chat a bit while I finish my lunch."

Hal took a long draw on his drink as Hillary pulled the door shut. "I heard that you and Liddy plan to be at the house Friday evening."

"News travels fast. I just spoke with your dad this morning."

Hal leaned forward and offered me half of his sandwich, which I waved off.

"Maddie and I touch base two or three times a day to keep me informed about dad, and . . ." He took a bite of his sandwich.

"How's it going with Dixie? From my vantage, she's becoming attached to your dad."

Hal swallowed. "Maddie informed me that she found Dixie's empty suitcase in the closet and her things in the chiffonier in dad's old bedroom."

"She's sleeping in his old bedroom?"

Hal nodded as he sipped his drink. "His old bed too."

"Is your mother's first name Delilah?"

Hal rolled his eyes. "Yeah, why?"

"I helped her when we crossed paths at the post office recently, and she had a package addressed to Delilah D. Arnaquer."

His attention focused on where to take the next bite of his sandwich, but he paused to mutter, "The D is for Dixon, a.k.a. Dixie. The Arnaquer is her new married name."

"I'm confused. What happened? Where's her husband?"

"He passed away."

"Do you know anything about him?"

"I think she said his name was Beau. All I know is she made some inference to him being her Rhett Butler."

"So why did she decide to visit you guys after all these years of no contact?"

Hal glanced at his dad's photograph. "I asked her that exact question, but she only gave a lame response about how miserable she's felt all these years for abandoning us and wanting to reconnect." Hal's eyes remained distant.

"Do you feel that she's making more of an effort to reach out to you and Phillip since she's decided to stay to help with your dad?"

"If she is, I don't feel it." Hal took one last bite and wiped his face with a napkin.

I fidgeted with my coke can. "What's been said about Hank?"

"She and dad talk quite a bit about him."

"Does she try to sit with you or Phillip and just talk?"

"I've tried to start a conversation a couple of times, but as soon as I inquire about her past, she makes an excuse and diverts the conversation to something about us or the town."

"I'm guessing she didn't tell you that she's been receiving a copy of the local paper for nearly fifteen years. That might explain why she seems more comfortable talking about you."

"She's not said a word, but that explains why she knows so much about Shiloh. Just the other night at dinner she asked me about what happened the night the courthouse burned down. Her eyes stay glued to me and made me feel quite uncomfortable as I regurgitated the events of how Jessie saved Hank and me that night."

"I hope she'll soon be comfortable talking about her recent past. Have you talked to your dad to see if she's shared anything with him?"

"Nah. He's so infatuated with her I doubt he cares to know right now."

I inched to the edge of my seat. "Maybe when Liddy and I come over we can steer the conversation a little bit, if you don't mind."

"That'd be great. I look forward to Friday night." He slurped the last of his drink.

I stood as he cleared his desk of his lunch trash. "Thanks for the time Hal. There was another question I wanted to ask you about some research I'm doing for another project."

"Shoot. What do you need?"

"I'm looking into the history of the Shiloh Lumber Mill. Does the name H. H. Archer Holdings Company mean anything to you?"

A grin appeared. "It's the official corporate name for Archer Construction. Why?"

"Didn't your family start the mill?"

"Yep, but they sold it to Zeb's family during the Depression."

"It's a little ironic that your family agreed to sell your raw timber to the mill to get it back on its feet. This town is pretty lucky to have formidable families like yours and Zeb's to protect the community's interests over such a long history."

Hal's smile and handshake offered a fitting end to our meeting.

———

AFTER I HAD left City Hall, I diverted from heading straight home and ventured across the street for a haircut. Wiley stood over Sam, while Marcellus took care of another customer at the other end of the shop. As soon as I stepped inside, Wiley stopped snipping Sam's hair long enough to say, "Mister Phillips, take a seat. I'll be with you in a few minutes."

Marcellus smiled and turned on his clippers. His customer's hair landed at his feet.

"What are you up to today?" Sam looked at me in the mirror.

Wiley nudged Sam's head. "Quit fidgeting and hold still. When I get done, you can chat with your buddy over there."

"How's Keith been since Friday night? Sorry I missed the game."

Wiley continued trimming around Sam's ears. "Pretty upset, but I reckon he'll be just fine. I told him losing from time to time makes ya appreciate the hard work it takes to be a winner."

"Sounds like Keith's got a wise great-granddad to coach him up."

Wiley looked up with a grin and peered at Marcellus who offered me a sly wink.

I grabbed a two-month-old Georgia Farming sitting atop a stack of well-read periodicals and flipped through the pictures until I heard Wiley snap his towel, and Sam hopped down.

"Does Liddy like how your bedroom floor turned out?"

"She's thrilled with it. She's picking up a couple of runners, so our bare feet don't start each morning on unforgiving wood floors."

Sam chuckled. "Pete told me y'all found some old papers tucked away under the floor."

"Not sure they mean much, but they appeared to have been written by John's great-granddad Ezra. John gave everything back to me, so I could check into their historical significance."

Wiley listened in as Sam said, "That's right up your alley. Anything special about 'em?"

"I'm not sure yet, but they may have something to do with John's family and its ties to the Archers about the time Ezra built the house we're living in."

"Let me know what you find out."

Wiley wiped off the chair, and I climbed into the seat. We talked about the game while he snipped until I asked, "This may be even before your time Wiley, but do you know anything about why the Archers sold their lumber mill to Zeb's grandfather?"

"That's going way back. The Depression hit here pretty hard right after I was born. In those days, Shiloh was a busy place and still the county seat, but it wasn't exempt from hard times. My daddy worked at the mill like a lot of the men then. I remember momma skimped, so we could get by after daddy lost a lot of his hours. Old man Archer did everything he could to avoid closing, but even cutting everyone's hours didn't help. Mister Archer just couldn't pay the workers. Not sure what exactly happened, but Mister Adams, I think Zeb's grandfather, bought the business and kept it running. I remember how busy the mill got right after that. The government began needing lots of lumber for FDR's rebuilding projects."

"Sounds like old man Adams not only saved all those jobs, but the business prospered too."

Wiley raised a wry grin. "You might say there were some ill feelings between the Adams and Archers after that, but old man Archer didn't go belly up. His construction business boomed then too."

While Wiley finished trimming my hair, I heard more of his boyhood stories about the Depression and the war. His recollections helped fill in some of the gaps that the library failed to provide.

CHAPTER TWENTY

CLAPS OF THUNDER WOKE ME EARLY FRIDAY MORNING. I CHECKED THE TIME, but my bedside clock failed to offer any assistance. Liddy remained motionless, oblivious to all the racket. I grabbed my robe and fumbled down the dark hallway to the kitchen where I found a flashlight. Protected by the storm door, I watched my hammock sway as windswept rain soaked our porch. No lights flickered on Calvary Street except periodic lightning flashes.

My flip phone told me it was almost five-thirty. In the kitchen, I pulled down Liddy's mother's old coffee pot, rinsed and filled it with water, replaced the percolator basket and added coffee grounds before lighting the gas burner. While the coffee perked, I grabbed a lighter, and then lit candles to illuminate the kitchen and living rooms. Minutes later, I peered out the window from the comfort of my recliner, savoring my first cup of coffee. My thoughts traced what I learned from the library and in talking with Hal and Wiley. I contemplated the historical connections between the Priestly, Adams and Archer families, as well as Dixie's present, inexplicable behavior and cloistered past. My thoughts helped me sympathize with Hal's and Phillip's awkward feelings towards Dixie's coddling of their dad. She seemed to be wedging herself into their lives again, but why? Of course, Dixie's doting provided Harold with a timely spark that yanked him out of his health-related, woe-is-me doldrums.

"How'd you make coffee?" Liddy muttered behind a long yawn.

"Your momma's old coffee pot came in handy. I'm proud of myself for remembering how to use it."

Liddy shuffled into the kitchen and a moment later curled up in her comfortable chair opposite me. "How long has the power been off?"

"I'm not sure, but I imagine Hal and his utility crews are working on getting us back up."

Liddy set her coffee aside, grabbed her pocketbook and turned on her phone. While she listened, she looked at me and mouthed, "Kay." After she set her phone down, she said, "School's starting an hour later this morning because of the power. . ."

Lights flickered throughout the house.

"You were saying. . ."

With a silly grin, Liddy turned on the lamp beside her and snuffed the candle.

The sound of a car splashing slowly up the street turned both our heads. Timmy tossed papers from the passenger window of his dad's sedan. I went onto the porch, umbrella in hand, intending to rescue my copy before it got drenched. Mister Thompson slowed to a crawl and waved as Timmy launched the morning paper onto the walkway. I raised my hand in response as I dashed out into the rain.

Liddy cooked eggs and toast while I shared my plans to visit Joe for lunch. "The most interesting fact I discovered at the library dealt with Ezra Priestly's death in the fall of 1924, the year after he built this house."

"How'd he die?"

"According to his obituary, a farm accident. He was but forty-five at the time. He and his wife Ethaline had only one son, Ezekiel, who was eleven at the time, the same age as our oldest grandsons."

"Such a tragic story. Does John know what you found?"

"I want to see what Joe can tell me about the papers we found first."

STORMY SKIES GAVE way to a more promising partly cloudy day by the time I left my umbrella beside Joe's main office entrance. I recalled the mention of a Mister Arians in Ezra's letter to his son as I ran my fingers across the painted letters identifying this as the office of Joseph P. Arians, Attorney-at-Law.

Susanna knelt in front of a file cabinet. "Good morning, Theo. Joe has Gus Appleton in his office. It'll be a couple of minutes yet." She clutched a stack of files to her chest as she struggled to stand up.

"Do you need help?"

She grabbed my hand and pulled herself upright. "Thanks, Theo. I hear you found some old papers in your house."

"That's why I'm here." I pulled the leather pouch from my attaché.

"My granddaddy had one just like it. I think he and Granny kept valuable family papers and certificates in theirs."

"Susanna, I reckon you may have the right idea. How long have the Arians practiced law in Shiloh?"

Susanna laid her files down on her desk. "Good question. I have only worked for Joe and his dad." She snickered. "Without double-checking, since about 1890 or so. I know for certain at one time Nick's home housed the family's law office until they moved into this office building seventy-five years ago."

The door to Joe's private office swung open, and the two attorneys appeared laughing and patting each other on the back.

Susanna grabbed an envelope from her desk. "Here you go Mister Appleton. Let me know if you need anything else."

Gus Appleton took the envelope and greeted me. "Mister Phillips, I hear your book is due out soon. I look forward to reading it."

Joe tapped Gus on his shoulder, and they shook hands. "We'll talk more in a few days." After Gus left, Joe looked at me. "Come on back. Let's talk for a few minutes before we go get some lunch."

We sat at his conference table. I removed the handwritten letter and the sealed envelope before I handed the pouch to Joe to examine. "This sure has not seen the light of day for a long time. Still looks almost new."

"We found it tucked under an old flour sack underneath the floor in our bedroom."

"Who's we?"

"Jim Adams, Liddy and me."

"Interesting. Gus asked about it already."

"Heck, you know this town. Nothing stays secret for long."

Joe placed the pouch back on the table and looked over the hand-written letter. "This is dated 1923. Isn't that the same year they built the house?"

I nodded as he continued examining the letter. He added, "Looks legit. We've got files stored away dating back to that time. Won't be too hard comparing them with similar documents. Did John identify who Poppa and Zeke might be?"

"John knows his grandfather's name was Ezekiel and thinks Zeke refers to him."

"I agree, but I don't know much about Mister Archer, Sr. off the top of my head. But the Mister Arians in the letter likely refers to my great-granddad, Joseph N. Arians, Sr." He paused, raising a nostalgic grin. "Why didn't you or John open the envelope with the agreement?"

"John dismissed it as irrelevant and gave it back to me to do as I wished. However, when I found Ezra Priestly's obituary notice, I decided to wait until we sat down to open it."

"What did it say that caused you to be so curious?"

"His death certificate recorded that he died on November 11, 1924 as a result of a farm accident. However, his obituary reported his wife and son had found his body inside the barn at their farm after he failed to come home for dinner. It may be nothing, but I've learned since we moved here last year, anything involving the Priestly and Archer families deserves careful handling."

Joe examined the envelope. "It's got H. H. Archer Holdings embossed on it all right, but look closely at the wax seal."

"It looks like a fancy old English P."

"I'd say that indicates Ezra most likely sealed this envelope for safe keeping. But that's about to change." Joe pulled a penknife from his pants pocket, slit one end without disturbing the seal, and carefully unfolded the two typewritten pages between us.

"What do you make of this?" My finger pointed to the date in the upper corner of the first page.

"December 24, 1914." Joe counted using his fingers. "Just over eight years before the date of the handwritten letter."

"The date of Ezra's letter to Zeke makes sense since it follows just after the construction of the house, but this loan agreement between Ezra and Mister Archer doesn't. What happened leading up to Christmas Eve 1914 that would've led Ezra to lend $10,000 to Mister Archer? That was a lot of money back then."

Joe read the agreement without saying a word before he gently folded and slid it back into the envelope. "I need to do some digging in the county records and look into our old office files too. How about you give me a couple of weeks to research this further?"

I slipped Ezra's letter into the leather pouch and handed it to Joe. "Keep these too for the time being."

Before we walked out of his office, Joe said, "Let's keep this between you and me until we know more about the facts surrounding this agreement. Your instincts about any dealings between the Archer and Priestly families are well-founded my friend."

———

MADDIE'S VOICE CAME over the intercom at the gated entrance to the Archer estate. A moment later the black gate swung open, and we drove toward the house. A light drizzle began right after the last sunlight got swallowed by the storm clouds.

"Let's try to enjoy ourselves for Harold's sake, but if you get a chance to talk to Dixie, it'd be nice to explore more about her time in Louisiana. Remember, Hal told me about Beau Arnaquer and his death. Please don't bring that up unless she volunteers to talk about it."

Liddy squeezed my hand. "You remember why we're here too. I'll be on my best behavior if you promise to be as well."

Maddie stepped off the porch and met us with an umbrella as we exited our vehicle. Inside, she pointed to the great room in the back of the house. "Mister Hal and Mister Phillip are waiting for you by the fireplace."

Hal and Phillip stood and greeted us before we sat across from each other on the twin sofas by their fireplace. Hal said, "Dad will be right out. Dixie went to let him know you're here."

Maddie reappeared. "As soon as y'all are ready, I've put out some finger foods for ya."

Phillip stood. "Miss Liddy, would you and Mister P like a little wine before dinner? Dad asked me to get out a couple of bottles for tonight."

Liddy looked at me. "I'm not much of a wine drinker, but I'll try a small glass."

I stood up. "A small glass will be good for me too. Show me what you selected."

Hal and Liddy chatted while Phillip accompanied me to the buffet table in the dining area of their great room. Phillip poured some Pinot Noir for each of us.

The sliding door to Harold's downstairs bedroom opened. "Liddy, you look exceptional this evening. What'd you do with your husband?" Harold wheeled himself into the room. He had on a blue blazer with an open-collared, starched dress shirt and his longer-than-usual graying locks tucked behind his ears.

I handed a glass of wine to Liddy and set my glass down before I grabbed Harold's hand. "Did I hear you making a pass at my wife?"

Harold chuckled and looked at Liddy. "Should we tell him our secret?"

Liddy blushed as she put a forefinger to her lips. "Shush. Being as Dixie and Theo are here, we better keep it our secret."

Before I released Harold's hand, I rotated our grip. "You're wearing your rings again. Expecting to add another, I suspect."

Harold's face beamed as he stared at his fingers. He slid the largest one off his right ring finger and handed it to me. "They don't fit as tight as they used to. That one I bought to commemorate Shiloh's last state championship." He let out a sigh as I handed it back. "I hope I'll be around for at least one more of these."

Dixie sat beside him on the arm of the sofa. She patted him on his back. "Don't you fret none darlin'. If them boys don't win you another championship, we'll jus' go get you another one of those gaudy diamond rings."

Harold turned with a sad stare. "Dix . . ." He held out both hands to show Dixie all three of his rings. "These have more value to me than just what they cost."

"Dad, don't be too hard on her. Let's enjoy this evening," Hal said as he raised his wine glass.

Harold's otherwise cheerful demeanor rebounded. "Why don't you get your mother and me a drink so we can enjoy this evening with our dear friends?"

Liddy got up. "Come on Dixie, let's get you and Harold a glass of wine."

Phillip looked at his dad. "Want some of Maddie's hors-d'oeuvres? I'm hungry."

"Thanks, son."

"How about you Mister P?" Phillip asked.

Hal stood and said, "We'll get something for you too. You and dad stay here and chat."

"Harold, you're looking much better. How are you feeling?" I asked.

"Better lately, but I still have some days when it's hard to get out of bed."

"It appears having your family around helps."

"The boys and Maddie are often worse than Doc Lucas and those nurses, but I know they care."

"What about Dixie?"

Harold stared at Liddy and Dixie talking by the buffet table. "Don't get me wrong; she's been a godsend. We've rekindled some good memories and shared some laughs, but between you and me, I think she needs me more than I need her. I kinda feel sorry for her."

"What do you mean, if I can ask?"

"She's lost more than her husband in recent months. She confided that she lost her house and had no family left but us." Harold's eyes remained glued to Dixie as he spoke.

"So, is she going to be staying?"

"Good question. She hasn't warmed up to Hal and Phillip as a mother should, and that's got me worried. But she does ask a lot of questions about Hank."

"Here you go, Dad." Hal gave him a small glass of wine, which Harold eyed as if he was a young child at an adult party.

"Don't give me that look. You're not supposed to have any alcohol on top of those meds Doc prescribed for you."

Harold's scowl received some relief when Phillip slid a small plate of food onto his lap.

The evening revolved around Harold and Dixie sharing embarrassing stories of their three sons as young children, but no one broached what happened in the years after Dixie walked away from the family.

After dinner, we enjoyed Maddie's peach pie and Cajun chicory coffee on the veranda. The chilly, damp air felt good as our conversation shifted to recent events. In the midst of Harold discussing the remaining season for Shiloh, Liddy placed her hand on my arm to get my attention. "Dixie asked about your book."

Dixie turned her eyes toward mine. "I've heard a lot of folks talking about your book. What's it called?"

"Jessie's Story."

Dixie offered a coy grin. "I hear it expands upon those articles you wrote about Jessie and how he saved my sons from that terrible accidental fire that burned down that beautiful old courthouse. Shame he lost his life."

"That's part of his story in the book," I said matter-of-factly, feeling uneasy with the nature of her inquiry.

Dixie glanced at Harold, Hal and Phillip glued to her next words. "Will you make sure I get an autographed copy? I'd love to read it, so when my oldest son gets out of jail, I'll understand better about what happened." A series of sidelong glances followed.

"I'll be sure you and Harold get a copy."

Liddy stood and grabbed my hand. "It's getting late. We should call it a night."

Harold cleared his throat. "I'm pretty tired myself. I wanna thank y'all for joining us tonight." He stared at Dixie as he wheeled himself toward the veranda door.

"Thank you for sharing this evening with us. It was my pleasure to get to know you better," Dixie said.

Liddy said, "Our pleasure, and we'll need to get some of that coffee. I liked it very much."

Hal and Phillip walked us to our vehicle. Before Hal closed my driver side door, he said, "I can't explain why she said what she did at the end of this evening, but you got a taste of what I meant when we talked."

CHAPTER TWENTY-ONE

I CRANKED MY MOWER SATURDAY MORNING AFTER THE UNOBSTRUCTED SUN-shine dried up the standing water left over from the previous evening's persistent drizzle. By the time I reached the last couple of swaths of scraggly grass in the backyard, Liddy had motioned me to cut the engine. She handed me a glass of ice water after I had removed my straw hat and sunglasses and wiped my face with the towel draped around my neck.

"We're about to have visitors."

"Who?"

"Maddie and Cora."

I put my glasses and hat back on. "Their church selling something?"

"No, silly. Cora said Maddie asked to visit with us."

I looked at the uncut lawn. "I'll be five minutes at the most."

"They'll be here any minute." Her stern look watched me restart the engine and drop it back into gear. She didn't take a step toward the house until grass clippings spewed into the mower's bagger. By the time I swung around for the final pass, Liddy had disappeared inside.

———

LIDDY STEPPED ONTO the front porch carrying glasses of sweet tea and a plate of molasses cookies as I strode around the side of the house. Cora and Maddie sat side by side with polite smiles. While Liddy placed the tray on the table, I tucked my sunglasses into my shirt pocket and made one last swipe with my sweat-soaked towel. I put both my hat and towel on the hammock before joining the ladies.

"Miss Maddie, Miss Cora, please forgive how I look. If I'd known you were coming, I'd have waited to do my mowing later." I inspected and then brushed my pants off just before I reached for a glass of sweet tea and sat down beside Liddy and across from Cora and Maddie.

Cora's polite smile grew broader and whiter. "Mister Phillips, don't fuss on our account."

Maddie looked at Liddy after taking a small taste of a cookie. "These are mighty fine Miss Liddy. They's still warm too."

"Thank you, Miss Maddie. That means a lot coming from you."

I set my glass aside and leaned forward, propping my elbows on my knees. "What brought the two of you this morning?"

Cora glanced at Maddie who held her glass with both hands and stared at the ice floating in her glass as if they would conjure up her next words. "Mister and Missus Phillips, I wanted to thank you for sharing the evening with the family last night. Mister Harold, sure enough, looked forward to your visit. But I gots to tell ya how sorry I felt after Miss Dixie spoke that way to you. That woman ain't got the sense the good Lord gave her. She had no good reason for inferring you was somehow responsible for her grown boy being in jail."

"I took no offense to her comment. She just prefers to believe that her oldest son couldn't have done anything so heinous to wind up in jail, so she vented her feelings upon me. I imagine she doesn't know or want to know the truth of the matter."

"Mister Phillips, Lord, forgive me for sharing my mind, but that woman's got a cold, selfish heart in her. I just feel in these ol' bones that she's just trying to sink her claws into Harold and take advantage of him."

Liddy placed her hand on Maddie's arm. "Dixie seemed pleasant enough when I spoke to her. Besides, Harold sure appears perkier around her."

Maddie bowed her head. "Miss Liddy, even a she-devil knows how to use honey to lure her prey, and I'm not at all sure that Mister Harold's all that blind to her wiles, but he chooses to keep his eyes and mouth closed all the same."

Cora leaned toward Maddie and whispered, "Tell 'em what you said to me."

"When Mister Harold takes his late morning and afternoon naps, Miss Dixie goes into his study and snoops around while she talks on the phone. Whenever I stick my head in to check on her, she shoos me away and closes the door."

"Any reason to think she's up to no good?"

"Only that she acts mighty peculiar whenever she realizes I'm around, especially when she sits at Mister Harold's desk and is on the phone."

"Peculiar?"

"Yes, sir. When she sees me in the next room, she'll tell whoever is on the phone to hold a second. Then she'll give me a nasty look and close the door tight."

"Have you said something to Harold or the boys?" Liddy asked.

"Yes, ma'am, but she turns on her syrupy charm, and if that don't work, she whines about me sticking my nose in her personal business." Maddie sighed briefly. "The other day, Mister Harold told Miss Dixie in front of me to not fret so much over my foolish notions and asked me to apologize."

Liddy's eyes popped. "Did you?"

"Like to have bit my tongue clean through, but I did to keep the peace. That's why I acted a bit cold around her last night I reckon."

"What about Hal or Phillip?" I asked.

"Mister Hal told me to keep my eyes and ears tuned to Mister Harold. He confessed that he's hoping Miss Dixie will leave before too long."

I reached my hand out to Maddie's. "Hal's advice sounds good to me. If she's making calls to friends, she may be missing their company and planning on leaving as Hal suggests."

Cora smiled at Maddie. "I told ya. You're simply making too much of that crazy lady . . ." Cora covered her lips with her fingers. Her cheeks glowed with embarrassment. "I'm sorry, I mean Miss Dixie."

"Maybe I am, and maybe I'm not, but until that woman leaves in her fancy automobile, I'll be as polite as I can to her, but she'll know I've got an eye on her."

Liddy giggled. "Probably a wise thing as long as you feel as you do."

Cora grabbed Maddie's hand. "Come on, woman. We've got errands to tend to, and these lovely folks got things to do also."

As Cora pulled away from the front curb in her van, we waved from the bottom of the porch steps. Liddy squeezed my hand. "What do think about Maddie's concerns?"

"I believe God blessed Miss Maddie with the gift of discernment." A contented look stared back at Liddy. I felt unsure of the extent of Maddie's concerns, but I believed her wary eye would keep a check on Dixie for the remaining days she chose to tend to Harold at their estate.

Liddy wrinkled her nose as a cute, crooked smile appeared. "Speaking of the gift of discernment, you need to go get a shower while I put lunch together. The Dawgs kickoff against Kentucky in less than an hour."

———

MONDAY MORNING WHILE I cleaned up breakfast dishes after Liddy had left for school, the phone rang.

"Morning, Barry. How's life as the Editor-in-Chief at Cornerstone?"

"Getting geared up for several projects to hit the streets in the next few weeks before the Christmas season. You remember the juggling act?" Barry tried to be silly, but his business-like tone stifled his humorous effort.

"So what's up? You need an extra hand?"

"What I need is for you to drive up here for a couple of days to discuss the marketing plans for your book and to run some cover design ideas by you. We want to go to print in the next couple of weeks. Think you can break away?"

"I'll need to touch base with Liddy, and she's at work, but I suspect I can be up there by tomorrow afternoon."

At noon, Liddy got my message to call.

"Barry needs me to run up to Peachtree for a couple of days. Think you can work out getting a ride to school with Phoebe until I get back probably on Friday?"

"I'm sure I can. Either way, you deserve a couple of days away."

I called Mary at the Sentinel office and gave her the good news about the book. I promised to bring her back an advance copy of Jessie's Story Friday afternoon.

———

AFTER THREE NIGHTS away, I retraced the scenic route we took eleven months ago when we first moved to Shiloh. Peachtree held onto its unique charm for those who clamored for suburban life outside of Atlanta, but I checked out of the hotel right after a quick breakfast and drove nonstop until I parked at Bubba's. Most of the folks had shuffled away from their tables and lined up to pay their tabs by the time I walked in.

Bob closed the smoker's fire pit door and then walked over. "You're a wee bit late for lunch." He pointed at the line of customers waiting to pay Cecil at the register. "Looks like there's going to be a big crowd at tonight's game."

I looked at all the Edison Red Raider crimson shirts and smiled. "They're an eager bunch, aren't they?"

One of the Red Raiders fans overheard Bob and me. "You just wait until the rest of our folks show up for the game tonight. We drove over with the team on the booster club's charter bus."

"Welcome to Shiloh." I exchanged handshakes with a couple of the Raider faithful before Bob cleared the table and offered me a seat.

"I'm plumb out of ribs and brisket," Bob said as he wiped the top of the table. "But I've got some mighty fine Brunswick stew left."

I nodded. "Sounds great. How about a large sweet tea with that?"

Bob turned to Cora cleaning tables. "Cora, can you get a bowl of stew for Theo and pour him some tea? It's on me."

Cora rendered her trademark ear-to-ear, pearly smile framed with bright red lips. "Mister Theo, I'll be right with you."

I watched the Red Raider fans piling into their bus parked in the motel's parking lot while I flipped open my phone and left a message for Liddy.

"Here you go." Cora slid a heaping bowl in front of me along with a dish of cornbread.

The delicious stew invited a quick taste. "Mmm, mmm! Thank you, Miss Cora."

After she filled my glass, Cora sat down beside me and peeked over her shoulder before giving me a sober look. "I'm so glad you stopped by. Maddie called this morning all upset. Miss Dixie demanded that Mister Harold fire her."

I froze with another spoonful headed to my mouth. "No way! She'd have to burn the house down before Harold would contemplate firing Maddie. What happened?"

"She told me she walked in on Miss Dixie at Mister Harold's desk with her back to the door and phone to her ear. Miss Dixie plainly called Hank by name and mentioned something about Mister Appleton handling whatever they were discussing. Miss Dixie turned in her chair and caught Maddie backpedaling from the room. After she hung up, she scolded Maddie and demanded to know what she heard."

"What'd Maddie say?"

"She tried to apologize but claimed that crazy woman only got madder until Mister Harold intervened. Maddie said Miss Dixie went straight into Mister Harold's bedroom and slammed the door behind her. Maddie said she could hear Miss Dixie demand Harold fire her."

"Maddie didn't get fired though."

"She said Miss Dixie opened the door all red in the face when Mister Harold asked Maddie into the room. Maddie apologized, hell-bent to not upset Mister Harold any further. When he asked what she might've overheard, Maddie felt Miss Dixie glaring and lied."

"How did Harold leave it?"

"Mister Harold gave her an earful, but Maddie felt he did that for Miss Dixie's benefit. Mister Harold tried to calm Miss Dixie down after Maddie left the room."

"Is Maddie okay?"

"Yes, sir. But she won't be herself again until that woman leaves once and for all." Cora looked up. "Lord, forgive me for the ill-feelings I'm holding for that woman."

"It's a good idea to leave this in the Lord's hands for the time being. Kinda believe Maddie can handle herself around Miss Dixie, but she mentioned both Hank and Mister Appleton by name?"

"Yes, sir." Cora's smile returned.

"Will you let Mister Theo eat his lunch before it gets cold?" Cecil walked up and slung a towel over his shoulder.

Cora's cheeks glowed as she glared at her husband. "I'm coming you ol' coot."

———

By HALFTIME, THE obnoxious, rowdy visitors across the field had sobered after Shiloh's lead grew to 24-0. I took advantage of the lopsided game and updated Liddy and our friends on my visit with Barry and the Cornerstone staff.

While the others ventured to the concession stand, I grabbed an advanced copy of my book with its final cover from my vehicle and handed it to Mary. "Take care of this. We still have six weeks before the book launch, but check out the title and acknowledgment page."

She ran her hand across the book cover, then looked inside. Her curious smile widened as she read my note and saw her name in print. "I'll make sure this one stays tucked away. What did Barry say about it?"

"He loves the book but sure fussed at me for letting you turn down his offer. He said his staff bragged how little they needed to do to get the manuscript ready, and he knew who deserved the credit."

Larry nudged Mary and smiled.

By late in the fourth quarter Shiloh had played everyone but Timmy, the equipment manager. I leaned toward Larry. "Before I forget, have you heard anything from your contact in New Orleans?"

Larry continued to look at the action on the field but shook his head back and forth. "I'll follow up with him next week. Why?"

"It may be nothing, but Maddie overheard Dixie talking with Hank on the phone and mentioned Gus Appleton in one of their conversations."

Larry turned his head. "Well, she's his momma."

"I know, but she's been doing some running around, and I'm wondering if she's doing more than talking to him on the phone."

"You think she's been to the jail to visit him?"

"It's crossed my mind. Can you possibly use your connections and check into it?"

Larry snickered, "Sure."

When the scoreboard horn sounded, the Shiloh fans stood and applauded as the opposing players shook hands.

CHAPTER TWENTY-TWO

THE FOLLOWING SATURDAY, LIDDY AND I DROVE TO ADAMS FEED AND Hardware. She'd had her eye on their abundant display of pumpkins and gourds since last week. Liddy dragged me through the store until we found Zeb in the warehouse loading a customer's truck.

"You two looking for me?" Zeb removed his work gloves, slapped the dust off and laid them on a storage shelf.

"I've got a win-win proposal to bat around with you," Liddy said as I greeted Zeb.

"What kinda proposition do you have in mind?"

"I've been looking at your inventory of pumpkins and gourds out front. How would you like to sell more at a higher price?"

Zeb crossed his arms. "And how would that work exactly?"

I sensed Liddy had plotted her strategy long before she asked me to bring her this morning. She had put on washed-out work jeans and a tattered flannel shirt, sleeves rolled up, and her hair pulled back into a ponytail. Zeb didn't stand a chance.

Liddy stepped closer and playfully smacked Zeb's arm. "Glad you asked. Let's say I scheduled some art students to decorate some of your ordinary pumpkins and gourds, and they spruced up your display with signs, hay bales and corn stalks too. You could then charge more for the decorated pumpkins and gourds, which of course you'd donate to our art class."

Zeb stroked his beard as he contemplated Liddy's shrewd, win-win proposal. "How soon are you thinkin' you'd get started?"

Without taking a breath, Liddy spouted. "Load the back of my vehicle with a bunch, and I'll have them back here by Wednesday. I'll get approval for some of my students to be here during school hours on Tuesday to fix up the display."

Zeb peered at me. "You got a smart lady here." He extended his hand. "Deal. I'll get one of the boys to pick out, let's say, two dozen of each to get started."

While Zeb held the front door for Liddy, he turned and pointed to the Old Country Store. "Theo, why don't you go say hello to our new assistant manager."

I walked beyond the archway and saw Marie fiddling with a display of cane syrup jars.

"Hello, Marie. What're you doing here today?"

Marie adjusted a jar. "Working."

"You getting lonely out on your farm?"

"John's barely around this time of the year. Ringo can only offer so much company. And let's face it, Pete doesn't stop by as much as he used to." A wry grin surfaced across her tan cheeks. "So I got it in my head to ask Zeb if he'd let me sell my syrup in the store. One thing led to another, and I agreed to spend a few hours each week until Christmas. He told me how Jim and Jay are splitting more of their time between the store and the mill, so he bribed me with the title of assistant store manager." Her familiar, good-natured grin followed.

"Good for you. I've been worried about you out on the farm by yourself. Any chance you'll consider coming to watch John and the boys at one of their games? They're now six and one after beating Adelphi last night."

Marie's expression fell. "I'm working on it. John keeps asking too. Part of me wants to be there, but . . . ." Her distant, blank stare disrupted her words.

"When you're ready, you'll know it. I know John understands. If it'll help, Bob's making some super sausage dogs this season, and you know how good Zeb's fries are. Our last road game is against Beckley this Friday.

So, if you change your mind, we'll save you a seat for the following two home games. Only the Lord knows for sure, but there's a chance the boys can get into the playoffs if they win their last three games."

"That would be special, and Jessie would've been proud. I promise to try and make a game," Marie said stiffening her upper lip.

"Marie! Zeb told me you're his new assistant manager," Liddy shared, engaging her in a warm embrace.

Liddy filled Marie in on her deal with Zeb. Without any hesitation, Marie volunteered to help Liddy and offered to bring some hay bales and bundles of cornstalks from her barn Tuesday morning.

———

I WALKED TO the Sentinel office Wednesday morning before checking out Liddy's decorated pumpkin and gourd display at Zeb's. The foliage on the trees in Shiloh showed only promises of oranges, reds and yellows, whereas further north, rich autumnal colors dominated the rolling hills around Atlanta by this time in October.

Martha offered a warm smile when I entered. "Mary showed me your book. You thinking of writing one about John too?"

I smiled and surveyed the office. "Kinda enjoying the peace and tranquility, which makes me almost feel retired now."

Mary peered around her computer screen and held up her copy of the book. "I couldn't say no to mom, but I did to Pete when he found out. Told him he'd have to wait like everyone else."

"Is your dad around?"

"Yeah, but he's been distracted this morning about something. Thought I oughta forewarn you," Mary said.

Martha blurted, "Mary, what do you think about Theo writing another book?"

Mary's eyes lit up as she snickered. "I'll be happier right now if I can get him to write an article on John and the Saints as they wrap up their miracle season." Her wide eyes turned to catch my response.

"I'll give it some thought. There are three more games left."

"Theo! Come on back. I need to talk to you." Larry's serious voice filled the front office.

After I took my usual seat in front of his desk, Larry turned the chair beside me so he could face me. He sat down but scooted to the front edge of the seat. "Your suspicions about Dixie were well-founded. Hank's not only been calling her, but she's been visiting him every week since earlier this summer."

"You sure?"

"My contact at the jail checked the visitor registry, and Hank's had three visitors in recent weeks, Arnie Wright, Gus Appleton, and Delilah Arnaquer. He's checking back for me but says he and a couple of the other officers know for a fact that Missus Delilah Arnaquer has been a regular visitor since June."

"How so?"

"Her accent and the way she dresses as if she's on the prowl left a memorable trail."

"I bet Hank enjoyed his mother prancing into the jail."

"No one there knows she is his mother." Larry looked like the cat that just ate the canary.

"Wait a minute. Did you say she's been visiting since June?"

"He's double-checking the visitor records, but he felt confident that she'd been showing up since June."

"But she didn't show up in Shiloh until just before Megan and Andy's wedding in early August."

"Maybe she visited someone else in the area before she stuck her nose into Harold's life again." Larry looked as baffled as I felt.

"I think I'll talk to Arnie and see what he might know from his pastoral visits with Hank."

Larry slapped his knees. "I'll let you know what the jail tells me about the dates. In the meantime, Mary wants me to get you to write another article to wrap up John's fantasy season."

"She just hinted at it. I guess it makes good sense. John and the entire team deserve a little more press whether they win out or not."

"What do you mean whether they win or not? Them boys are going to the playoffs. I can feel it in these old bones of mine." Larry chuckled as if willing himself to believe the fantasy season would not come to an end short of another championship.

"Before we order tickets to Atlanta, let's thank God for the excitement this town is feeling again. But if it'll help, I've already begun gathering some thoughts about another article. Just need to wait for the proper ending."

"Winning it all in Atlanta will suit me just fine, but I hear you."

"Before I forget, I've got a story you should talk to Mary about." I proceeded to tell him about Liddy's art students decorating pumpkins and gourds at Zeb's store and about Marie's new position there.

———

Arnie and Judy picked us up Friday evening, and we met up with other Shiloh Saints' faithful at the stadium before the wagon train of decked-out vehicles followed a packed charter bus out of town. The trek to Beckley took an hour to drive the thirty-six miles as the sun set behind us. Judy and Liddy chatted in the back about Liddy's latest promotional idea at Zeb's and asked if she had seen the advertisement in the paper that Zeb placed mentioning SHS art students being on hand Saturday to personalize pumpkins. Liddy bragged about the two-hundred dollars they've raised so far and how her students delivered more decorated pumpkins and gourds to the store.

Upfront, Arnie maintained his focus on keeping pace with the train of vehicles following the charter bus. He appeared deep in thought whenever I glanced over.

"Everything alright, Arnie?"

He tightened his ten-and-two grip on the steering wheel and kept his focus on the taillights ahead of us. "Huh?"

"You haven't said a word since we left Shiloh?"

"Been thinking about what Liddy said about Marie working at Zeb's. I offered to pick her up tonight, but she begged off again."

"I think she's come a long way since Jessie's death, but sitting in the stands overlooking the sidelines that he and John once shared may be the last hurdle for her to overcome."

Arnie sighed. "I know you're right. Her decision to get off the farm more and mingle with the folks at the store may stir her to take that last leap."

I nodded as Arnie glanced out the corner of his eyes. "Where's Hillary tonight?"

"Behind us, riding in Nick's truck along with Hal and Phillip. Think she feels more comfortable rekindling old friendships rather than being a tag along with her parents."

"I think Hal enjoys her as his assistant in City Hall."

"If it weren't for all the drama going on with the Archer's, I'd agree more."

"Why do you say that?"

"Hillary told me that Dixie doesn't like her and makes little effort to hide that fact whenever she pops in on Hal at City Hall."

"What did Hal say about that to Hillary?"

Arnie turned his head with a cocky grin. "To ignore her."

"Since we've brought Dixie's name up, you aware she's been in contact with Hank since early this summer?"

"Wouldn't surprise me. I've been wondering why Hank's attitude in my last couple of monthly visits has appeared far less gloom and doom. How do you know about her visits?"

"Larry."

"That figures."

"His contact at the jail joked that she'd been there enough to have made a reputation for herself without revealing that she's Hank's mother."

"That explains a lot. Last month I bumped into Gus Appleton leaving the jail and Hank sure appeared in good spirits during our visit. When I asked about Gus' visit, Hank bragged how Gus is trying to get him released early for good behavior."

A few minutes later, Arnie followed the other vehicles into the Beckley's parking lot. Zeb and some of the boosters were tailgating by the time we all arrived.

By the sound of the referee's whistle to end the game, more Shiloh fans sat on the visitor side of the field than home fans on the home side. The score earned Shiloh its seventh victory for John and his team.

When we began to pile back into our vehicles to return home, Joe stepped away from Missy and his twins in matching cheerleader outfits. "Theo, I meant to say something earlier tonight. Would you mind stopping by my office Monday night about seven?"

"Why? What's up?" I said leaning against the passenger door of Arnie's Tahoe.

"John will be there too. I've got some answers about those papers you found."

"Like what?"

"Monday night." Joe waved as he corralled his family toward their SUV.

CHAPTER TWENTY-THREE

"Phoebe approached me after school today," Liddy blurted during dinner Monday evening. "Are you listening to me?" She rested her hand on mine.

"What about Phoebe?" All I had heard was Phoebe's name. Decades-old facts about Ezra Priestly and his untimely death occupied my mind.

Liddy slumped in her chair with arms crossed. "Thought you'd be interested in what Phoebe asked me when she slipped into my room after her students disappeared."

"What did she ask my wise wife?"

"If she was too old to get married and start a family."

"Why would she ask you this?"

"If I had to venture a guess, because she celebrated her fortieth birth-day last week."

"Why do you think she never married?"

"When I asked her that question earlier this summer, she told me her love for teaching and music always got in the way."

"What's changed?"

"I think her biological clock is approaching the eleventh hour, and she fears time's about to expire on her."

"What's preventing her from actively looking? She's certainly attractive and talented enough."

"I'm guessing it's not about her finding someone, but someone hasn't recognized she's been waiting for him."

I felt my eyes widen. "You mean . . ." Liddy began nodding before I said, "John."

"Did she mention him?"

"No, silly. It's so obvious that even you figured it out."

"How did you leave it with her?"

"That she needs to find the right time and words to let him know how she feels before it's too late."

"You realize I'm about to see John tonight?"

Liddy squeezed my hands and glared, leaning closer. "Don't you dare say a word to him!"

———

JOE LOUNGED ON the sofa in his office across from John. John stood and pointed to the empty armchair when I walked in.

I checked my watch as I sat down. "How long have you two been here?"

John said, "I came straight over after practice. We've been just talking about these last two remaining games for a few minutes."

"Coach seems a little concerned. The boys might, in fact, find a way to win these last two games and wind up in the playoffs," Joe said with a sly grin as he sat up. "Want anything to drink before we get started?"

"No thanks. I'm all right."

Joe opened a folder on the coffee table. "John, I asked you to be here because, quite simply, you're Ezra Priestly's sole remaining heir. As such, you have the option of making these papers more than historical artifacts from your family's past."

John scooted to the edge of his seat. "But these were found in the house Theo and Liddy legally now own. I appreciate the fact that they offered them to me, but they're part of the home's heritage."

Joe spread his arms along the back of the sofa. "That's your prerogative of course, but this agreement," Joe leaned forward and handed it to John, "is only a historical document in Theo's hands."

John read over the agreement creating an extended silent pause before he laid it back on the table. "What are you trying to tell me?"

Joe eyed me before continuing his exchange with John. "What if I said this agreement between your great-grandfather and the H. H. Archer Holdings Company remains binding and enforceable?"

John and I exchanged glances.

Joe added, "Before we let our imaginations and emotions run wild, let me tell you what I found out."

I caught John preparing to speak. "Before you say another word, as a friend, I'm asking that you hear Joe out. I asked him to investigate the legitimacy of these documents, and I know you had no idea about the agreement we found in the sealed envelope."

John slouched back and pulled one leg over the other knee.

"John, Theo is right. I also know how you feel about any further legal dealings involving the Archer family. I'm not suggesting you do anything, but you have a right to hear what I found."

John waved his hand just before he tucked it beneath his crossed arms. "I can't imagine how this may change my mind on the matter, but go ahead."

Joe filled John in on the findings that detailed the agreement's creation a century ago and how his grandfather Ezekiel more than likely never knew anything about his father's note and the envelope because of Ezra's untimely death in 1924.

John dropped both feet to the floor and sat tall. "So you're telling me that even after my great-grandfather Ezra died, the Archers never repaid the loan to my great-grandmother?"

Joe stretched both arms across the back of the sofa again. "I took this to Gus Appleton. He admitted that H. H. Archer Holdings Company, a.k.a. Archer Construction, has maintained a twenty-five percent reserve on the company's stock on account of this agreement. Had the loan been repaid it would have freed up the set-aside shares."

I interjected, "Who in the Archer family knows of this agreement?"

Joe looked at John. "As far as Gus knew, only Harold. He showed me a copy of the original agreement locked away in a file cabinet in his office along with other H. H. Archer Holdings Company legal documents."

John's head fell as his elbows rested on his knees. "Thanks for laying this albatross in my lap." He grabbed the agreement and read it over again. "What if I decide to let it remain unclaimed?"

Joe stared at John until they made eye contact. "As of midnight Christmas Eve, the terms of the agreement dissolve. By default, H. H. Archer Holdings Company will then become absolved of the debt."

John swayed his head back and forth as he gathered the agreement, folded it neatly and exchanged it for the handwritten letter to Zeke. "God had his reasons for letting this lay hidden all these years. I'm not interested at this point in making a fuss over some century-old agreement. I don't need or want whatever it'd be worth. Besides, I don't know how this would impact Harold. It's not worth it." John pointed to the pouch and agreement. "Theo, you found it. You keep it, and don't say anything until well after its value expires."

Joe nodded. "That settles it then." He tucked the agreement back into its envelope and slid it back into the leather pouch. "Here you go, Theo. At least it might carry some historical significance and offer quite a tale to share with friends and family."

I looked reluctantly at John. "You sure about this?"

John nodded and placed the handwritten letter into his jacket pocket.

I turned to Joe as he stood. "What're you going to tell Gus?"

"Good question."

John rested a hand on each of our shoulders as we prepared to leave. "Thanks for going through all this trouble. If nothing else, I learned more about where my love for this town comes from."

———

IN THE CHURCH foyer, before the Sunday service began, Larry asked Liddy, "How'd it feel to see Shiloh pull off a come-from-behind victory over your old high school?"

Liddy laughed. "Larry, how'd you know I went to Lake City High School?"

Larry shrugged with a smug grin.

"Never mind. Forget I even asked such a silly question." Liddy blushed.

Martha giggled and patted Liddy's shoulder. "Now you know what Mary and I have to put up with every day with this man."

I winked at Larry. "To answer your question, after Q hit Woogie over the middle, and he zigzagged sixty yards through all those Lion defenders into the end zone, Liddy hooped and hollered louder than she had all season. I think she's a bona fide member of the Shiloh Saints now."

A few moments later, Phillip pushed Harold over the threshold into the foyer. Harold's voice rose above the muddled conversations in the room. "Good morning! Did everyone notice God's handiwork with all those colors announcing this glorious new day?"

Liddy looked at him. "You seem unusually chipper this morning? Where's Dixie?"

Harold glanced at Phillip before answering Liddy. "She decided to go off for the day, so Phillip volunteered to help me come to church this morning, just like the good ol' days."

Judy walked over. "Good morning, Harold. You look good today."

"Why thank you, Judy. I feel rather well today. If it weren't for Phillip, I'd have tried to walk into church all by myself today."

"What sparked you this morning?"

"Hal, Phillip and I watched the Lake City game films yesterday, and I've convinced the boys that I'm going to be at the Alexandria City game Friday night."

I gave Phillip a puzzled look.

"Dad's been doing much better lately, and, well, it's the last game. It can't be any worse at the game than how he carries on watching the film of the game the day after." Phillip shrugged with a quirky smile.

"What did Dixie say?" Liddy asked.

Harold huffed. "Guess that's why she decided a drive in the country-side would be a good idea."

Phillip tried to hide his smile.

I asked, "What did Hal have to say?"

"I had to agree to stay in my seat during the game," Harold said with a great big smirk.

"I'll be down there during the game with him too," Phillip added.

"Enough fussing about me, I'm fine. I promise. Besides, this game is for the playoffs if we can squeeze in a win against the Argonauts. There's no way I'd miss being there." Harold fiddled with his three championship rings as he spoke.

"Where's Hal anyway?" I asked.

Phillip pointed to the doorway where Hal and Hillary talked on the landing.

Zeb, Sam, and Susanna joined us and heard about Harold's intentions.

Zeb laughed. "I bet ol' Dixie's fit to be tied and is headed over to Alexandria this afternoon to warn 'em."

Harold's and Zeb's laughter became infectious.

During the service, Arnie appeared to enjoy having Harold seated near the front row again. Hal sat directly behind his father with Hillary and Phillip by his father's side.

Arnie addressed the congregation about passing the mantle from one generation to the next. He used the story of Bathsheba pleading with David at the end of his life to anoint Solomon as his heir even though Solomon's older brother, Adonijah, deserved the crown by tradition. Arnie emphasized how our traditions and rituals never limit God. During the closing hymn, Harold glanced over his shoulder at Hal and Phillip. I wondered what Harold thought about his oldest son, Hank, as he listened to the message.

Just before Arnie dismissed the congregation, he asked, "Who will be joining Harold at the pep rally and bonfire Thursday night at Priestly Park?"

Harold muscled himself out of his wheelchair and faced the congregation to see the many hands up and waving before Phillip tugged him back down.

CHAPTER TWENTY-FOUR

I savored Bernie's frothy Greek brew between bites of her fresh Bougatsa pastry while leafing through the Thursday morning paper. Alex swept around the tables and chairs while Bernie and Silas cleaned up after the breakfast customers had left to start their work days.

"Mister Theo, may I sit with you?" Silas anticipated my response with one hand on the back of the chair.

I folded the paper. "Please Silas, have a seat."

"Thank you very much. It's been far too long for you and me just to sit and talk."

Alex appeared beside his father. "Papa, you want coffee too?"

Silas nodded. "And you want a refill Mister Theo?"

"Sure, and please tell your mother her Bougatsa tasted awesome."

Alex took my empty plate and demitasse cup.

I leaned back in my chair. "Are you and Bernie going to the pep rally tonight? I imagine Alex plans to attend."

His scruffy chin jutted. "You betcha. Coach Priestly deserves everyone in this town coming out. But. . ." He sighed, his eyes glazing over. "It still hurts to think about him this time last year." A smile crept back across his sad face. "But Mister Theo, you helped him to come back home."

"Silas my good friend, I did very little. He already had others who never gave up hope and helped overturn the injustice done to him."

"Here you go, Mister P." Alex brought two steaming cups of froth-filled coffee.

Silas took a sip but continued to eye Alex until he left. "How is Mister Archer?"

"Mentally, much better, but physically, I imagine Doc Lucas isn't too pleased about Harold's decision to attend tonight's pep rally and the game tomorrow night. Why'd you ask?"

Silas groomed his long dark mustache with his fingertips. "Bernie thinks I'm sticking my nose where I shouldn't . . ." He looked around the empty restaurant. "While at the bank Monday, I recognized Mister Appleton talking with Mister Archer's ex-wife."

"Mister Appleton is the Archer's attorney."

Silas cleared his throat. His dark eyes strained to validate what they witnessed. "The two of them didn't look like they were discussing business, if you know what I mean."

"What are you trying to tell me?"

"Mister Theo, I know you and Mister Archer are friends, but she hugged him after she leaned close and whispered in his ear."

"How do you know it was more than just a friendly exchange?"

"The look on Mister Appleton." Silas nodded, his eyes affirming his conclusion.

I stared at Silas. "Where were you to be able to see this?"

"Outside the bank, about to pull away in my truck. Her fancy red convertible had caught my attention before I recognized them standing behind the rear door to Mister Appleton's office."

I slumped further back into my chair trying to picture what he saw. "I wouldn't give it another thought. I'm sure Gus felt flattered by Dixie's flirtatious nature, that's all." My words defied the puzzling emotions Silas stirred in me.

His wrinkled brow and grin mirrored my skeptical look. "You are probably right. I'll just leave it alone just like Bernie told me to do."

I got up to leave and reached for my wallet. "See you tonight my dear friend."

Silas tugged my arm. "No, no! See you and Miss Liddy tonight."

A BANK OF clouds on the horizon swallowed the last daylight as we arrived at the Priestly Park entrance. Students with flashlights directed the bottleneck of vehicles at the main gate toward the roped-off parking area.

I carried a blanket in one hand and held Liddy's hand with the other. "Looks like Silas got his wish."

Liddy looked up. "What do you mean?"

"He hoped the whole town would turn out tonight to honor John for all he has overcome to make this even possible."

We weaved our way through the rows of cars until we came to the ceremonial, stacked wood pyramid. Concrete blocks provided a safe perimeter around it with plenty of folks settling in to enjoy the bonfire. Hillary found us and escorted us to where Joe and Missy sat talking with Nick while the twins played with other children at the playground.

Missy said, "Glad Hillary found you. Better lay claim to a spot before you have to wade in the creek to watch the pep rally. I don't believe Hal or Missus Abernathy dreamed this many would show up tonight."

"Who else have y'all seen so far?" I asked.

Hillary pointed. "Mom and dad just pulled up."

"Zeb's over there by the pavilion with Hal, John and the Abernathys," Nick said, craning his neck. "And Sam and Susanna are talking with Jeannie and Phillip beside Harold's truck. I can't tell from here, but I think Harold's in the truck."

"There's Mary," Liddy shouted as she stood on her tippy-toes to see over the growing crowd.

"Where?" I asked.

The flash of Mary's camera answered my question. Larry looked out of place still wearing his three-piece suit with his tie loosely knotted and dangling beneath his open shirt collar. Martha clung to Larry's arm as she maneuvered in heels through the grass and sand.

Liddy giggled as she held her hand out to Martha.

Martha growled. "If someone had listened to me, we'd have left the office in time to change."

Larry coughed and glared at Mary. "Our zealous editor wanted to adjust the layout for tomorrow's paper to make room for a last-minute picture from tonight's pep rally."

Mary turned the camera on her parents and snapped a picture capturing their frazzled looks. "Y'all quit your fussing. I'm the one who'll have to race back to the office tonight to load the photo so the presses can run the morning edition."

Martha giggled along with Liddy as Hillary and Missy joined in.

I pointed to our blanket. "Take a load off, Larry. It'll be a few more minutes before they get started and light the bonfire."

"Well, I wish they'd get it started soon. The temp's gonna drop as the night sets in." Larry grumbled.

Phoebe marched the band to the front of the pavilion with drums striking the cadence. Cheerleaders led the players to the roped-off area surrounding the microphone stand. A moment later, Hal appeared from the crowd with John and Kay behind him. A spotlight flicked on and illuminated the flag flying in front of the Priestly Community Center. Everyone stood as the band played the National Anthem.

"What an impressive turnout!" Hal shouted into the mic after the music stopped. "It's been four years since our town held a pep rally like this, and this new park facility offers the perfect setting for it."

Applause rang out as more people continued to arrive. I glanced toward Harold's truck and saw him in his wheelchair atop the hill alongside Phillip, Jeannie and her parents.

The band played "When the Saints Go Marching In" while the cheerleaders led the players as they all danced around the perimeter, and the crowd clapped and sang along. Pete, Jay and Jim joined the players and seemed to enjoy being in the center of all the attention.

"Thank you Mayor Archer," Kay said before turning and pointing up the hill toward Harold. "And a special thank you to our former Mayor, the Honorable Harold Archer, for his support over the many years."

Harold pushed himself up and stood with help from Phillip and Jeannie at his sides. He waved and blew kisses to the crowd.

"Now, I know you didn't come here to listen to me. Please welcome our very own Coach John Priestly." Kay handed the mic to John as a roar came over the crowd, and everyone took to their feet.

John stood flush-faced as the crowd settled down. "Tonight is not about me but about my coaches and these outstanding young men who have endured and overcome challenge after challenge this season. They stand before you tonight before their final regular season game having suffered just one, hard-fought loss." John then introduced each player as they entered the marked off perimeter surrounding the ceremonial pyre.

John then looked at the players and whistled. Quentin and Hunter ran to where Ray Abernathy stood, while Woogie and his cousin Bobo hustled to Wiley's side. "We would not be here tonight if it weren't for all our faithful fans cheering us on each week."

The crowd burst into applause as the cheerleaders and players encouraged them until John raised both hands.

"With that in mind, I'd like to recognize two unsung fans at this time. First, often seen but seldom heard unless you visit the Post Office on a regular basis, he graduated from the University of Georgia where he played for the great Vince Dooley before a career-ending injury changed the trajectory of his life. He met his charming wife on campus forty years ago, and the two of them have graced our community for the last twenty-five years. He has endured countless blazing hot practices and sat through many miserable, chilly games over the past two-plus decades. Please recognize, Mister Ray Abernathy."

Ray towered over Quentin and Hunter as he stepped forward and joined the team inside the perimeter.

"Our next special fan, as far as I am aware, has the distinction of being the oldest living former player from Shiloh's notable football past. He lettered as a running back from 1945 through 1947—Mister Wiley, the first Woogie Edwards." Woogie and Bobo steadied Wiley as he strutted up to Ray and the others.

"Before I ask Ray and Wiley to ignite our bonfire, they should be appropriately recognized as our honorary team captains this week." John reached into a bag and pulled out two game jerseys. Wiley broke into tears as Ray helped him pull on his number 47 jersey. Kay struggled with her emotions as well as she assisted Ray with his jersey.

The players and cheerleaders exited the inner perimeter as the drummers played a series of drum rolls. Zeb brought two lit torches and handed them to Wiley and Ray. In no time, the stacked lumber shot embers into the night sky.

Hal took back the mic after the cheerleaders performed for the crowd. "Folks, please enjoy mingling with the players and coaches before they leave to get a good night's sleep. Remember, tomorrow night is Halloween, and the churches are sponsoring a Trunk or Treat tailgate party before the game in the stadium parking lot from four until six o'clock. See everyone at the game."

Hal wandered to where we mingled, while Mary snapped last-minute photos of Ray and Wiley before she left for a late night at the Sentinel's office.

I pulled Hal aside. "Glad to see your dad tonight. He appeared energized by the amazing turnout."

Hal turned to see Phillip climb into the driver's seat and wave. "Tonight helped him get over whatever was eating at him this evening at dinner."

"What do you mean?"

"Dixie excused herself from the table complaining of a headache, and dad brooded for the remainder of supper. He almost backed out on coming tonight until Maddie fussed at him and promised to keep an eye on Miss Dixie."

"Tomorrow's another day. I'm confident they'll resolve whatever went on between the two of them."

"Theo, I agree. Dixie promised to accompany Dad tomorrow night, and even Maddie asked to come along when I shared that I arranged for chairs."

I patted his back as we turned our attention to Nick and Joe laughing and sharing stories about their Shiloh Saints glory days.

—

LIDDY STAYED AFTER school Friday to help Judy and Hillary with Shiloh Baptist's Trunk or Treat table in the stadium parking lot. A little before six, Arnie pulled up in Hillary's Camry and honked. As I got in, he said, "Don't ask."

By the time we pulled into the stadium, discarded candy wrappers had provided the only evidence of the Halloween tailgating event. Liddy, Judy and Hillary stood beside our Expedition and Arnie's Tahoe. As soon as Arnie climbed out of Hillary's sedan, he tossed her the keys.

We entered the stadium and climbed into the stands to claim our seats beneath the press box. Marie shared a blanket with Martha and Larry.

Larry looked up as we covered our legs with our blanket. "I told you the weather was going to change. It's dropped ten degrees since sundown, and with this damp air fog should roll in before the game's over."

Liddy zipped her parka while I wished I had more than my flimsy windbreaker. Just before kickoff, Joe and Missy arrived with the twins bundled in coats and hats with their cheerleader outfits underneath. Uncle Nick followed behind with Zeb, Sam and Susanna as the ref's whistle sounded to start the game.

The Argonaut faithful from Alexandria swelled their side of the stadium with their black and gold colors. Both cheerleading squads rallied their fans to scream back and forth trying to out-spirit one another. The crowd's noise swamped the game announcer's voice on the loudspeakers.

As promised, Hal had Harold driven onto the infield track before the game started. Harold remained in his wheelchair with Hal on one side and Dixie, Maddie, Phillip, Jeannie, Ray and Kay joining them.

I tapped Larry on his shoulder and pointed. "I doubt they will see most of the game from their vantage point, but at least Harold got his wish."

Harold wore a Shiloh ball cap and athletic jacket. Dixie wore a dark red gabardine cloak and held Harold's hand most of the game with Maddie, bundled in a wool topcoat and hat, beside them.

The game quickly became a defensive matchup. Pete's defense kept the Argonauts out of the end zone, but John's offense struggled as well. By the time Phoebe's band marched on the field for its halftime show, the scoreboard reflected a scoreless tie. The moist, chilly air had given way to a growing fog. Even the stadium lights failed to penetrate the gray cloud settling across the field by the start of the second half.

In the fourth quarter, an Argonaut cornerback intercepted one of Q's sideline passes and raced untouched to break the tie. Q got even after the kickoff and pump-faked the same cornerback as Quentin's brother, Zack, ran past the cornerback and caught the ball along the sidelines for a Shiloh touchdown. With Shiloh's failed extra point try, the Argonauts clung to a one-point lead going into the final minutes. The fog worsened, making visibility tough for everyone. Pete's defense stuffed the Argonauts with their backs to their end zone and forced a punt. Woogie circled beneath the high punt, but the ball ricocheted off his shoulder pads. The Argonauts recovered at midfield, and Pete's defenders buckled down after giving up two first downs. On fourth down, the Argonauts kicked a forty-one-yard field goal that only the two officials beneath the uprights could see sail between the goal posts.

Woogie scooped up the squibbed kickoff and escaped two would-be tacklers before running out of bounds at midfield. Q avoided a sack on the first play, tucked the ball, and finally got wrestled down at the twenty-five with only thirty-five seconds left on the clock.

Liddy clutched my arm. "We have to score a touchdown, don't we?"

I pried her hand off my arm and hugged her. We heard Jay from the coach's box above us screaming at John to call a timeout.

Through the dense haze, we strained to watch as Q took the snap and flipped the ball to Woogie on a reverse. The defense converged on Woogie, but he planted his feet before he crossed the line of scrimmage and threw the ball across the field where the Argonaut coaches stood screaming and jumping up and down with their arms in the air. The wounded-duck pass landed in Q's arms at the twenty-yard line, but the Argonaut safety chased Quentin down at the eight.

As the excitement on the field unfolded, Harold struggled to stand. Dixie tried to pull him back, but he swatted her hand away as Hal stood beside him with his arm around his father's shoulders.

Eight seconds remained on the scoreboard after Q threw a quick pass out of bounds. After John called his final timeout, Hunter, the senior running back and team captain, lined up beside Q as Woogie went wide with Zach in the slot.

On the snap, one of the Argonauts linebackers raced up the middle untouched. Q spun away at the last second. Zach improvised and stopped at the three-yard line. Q fired the ball as two Argonaut defenders swarmed him. As soon as Zach hauled in the pass, two Argonauts slammed into him before he could turn and cross the goal line. Hunter arrived in the nick of time and buried his shoulder into Zach to drive them both the last two yards into the end zone, but the ball squirted from Zach's hands. Woogie grabbed the loose ball and twisted free from one defender. He ran parallel to the end zone, then found a crease between defenders.

John raced down the sidelines waving and screaming. Both sides of the stadium stood and hollered. Woogie planted his foot, turned his shoulders to the goal line, and wedged himself between two Argonauts as he approached the near sideline. Woogie disappeared into a mass of opposing bodies.

Whistles blew as the referees converged on the pile and pulled players off one another. Bobo stood over the pile with his hands raised until he saw the official mark the ball inches short of the goal line. The stadium fell silent as the head official blew his whistle and hoisted the ball above his head as the scoreboard clock ticked off the final second.

Shiloh players consoled one another, and the coaches walked onto the field while the Argonauts celebrated. Wiley hobbled onto the field and embraced Woogie.

In the midst of the excitement, we failed to notice that Harold had collapsed beside his wheelchair. Hal hovered over him while Phillip waved the ambulance through the gates. The flashing lights drew everyone's attention.

Doc Lucas joined the EMTs and strapped Harold onto a stretcher. Maddie held Harold's hand as they loaded him into the ambulance. Hal and Phillip kept Dixie back as the doors closed, and the flashing lights exited the stadium.

CHAPTER TWENTY-FIVE

HOSPITALS IN THE WEE HOURS ACCENTUATE EVERY NOISE, AND SATURDAY'S pre-dawn vigil in the waiting room proved no exception. Liddy sat with Maddie and Hillary sipping the same tepid, watered-down coffee as the rest of us, more to occupy our time than to stimulate our weary minds. Phillip nibbled on a vending machine bear claw, occasionally dipping a chunk of it into his coffee.

Hal paced the hallway, hands deep in his pockets, hair mussed and his green Shiloh polo shirttail untucked. His lips moved, but his voice remained inaudible to Arnie and me as we leaned against opposite walls facing each other. Between sips of coffee, we shared predictions on Harold's prognosis. Doc Lucas had long disappeared, and none of the on-duty nurses offered any updates, just weary faces.

The opening and closing of the entrance door turned heads. John walked straight to Hal. The two drifted further down the hallway until Cindy, the same nurse from Harold's previous hospital visit, stepped beyond the nursing station and motioned for Hal and Phillip.

"Doc Lucas wanted me to tell you that your father suffered a major stroke and remains unresponsive. But, he's receiving the best of care while we're waiting for more test results." Cindy's empathetic eyes connected with Hal and Phillip.

"Thank you, Cindy," Hal said. "I know everyone is doing their absolute best. Will you at least notify us as soon as we can go back and see him?"

Cindy smiled. "Of course, but I suggest all y'all go get some rest for now. It'll likely be several hours before the doctor will allow anyone to visit him or have any further updates."

Phillip's eyes widened. "But—"

"Phillip, we know how to reach you and your brother if anything changes before then." Cindy signaled for us to assist in getting Hal and Phillip some needed rest.

Liddy clutched Maddie's hand and stood. "I've got an idea. We've got plenty of room at our house. We'll leave our telephone number with Cindy."

Maddie squeezed Liddy's hand as she stared at Hal. "We're not goin' to be doin' your father any good mopin' around here, and I, sure enough, don't wanna go all the way back out to the house. Besides, I suspect Miss Dixie's still upset about not being able to ride to the hospital with Mister Harold."

"You're right as usual." Hal glanced at me and then Liddy. "We appreciate your offer, Miss Liddy. I should at least leave a message for Dixie at the house."

Hillary put her arm around Liddy's shoulder. "How about I lend a hand in the kitchen? I bet they'll get more rest with some real food in their stomachs."

Liddy said, "I'd appreciate that Hilly."

Arnie leaned closer and whispered, "I'll stick around here and inform you if anything changes. Should Harold wake, I can offer a friendly face until the family gets here."

John nodded. "Guess I'll hang with the preacher and keep him company. I got nothing better to do this early in the morning."

Arnie patted John on the back. "No thanks, John. You've got to be bushed and hungry too. Why don't you keep Theo company?"

I motioned for John. "Come on. I'll drive."

———

AN HOUR LATER, Hillary cleaned up the last of the dishes in the kitchen while Liddy took Phillip, Hal and Maddie upstairs to lie down.

"Why don't you go lie down as well?" I suggested to Liddy when she came back downstairs. "Hillary can sack out on the sofa while John and I sit on the porch and watch the sunrise. We'll wake y'all up if we hear anything."

Liddy grabbed her patchwork quilt and laid it on the sofa for Hillary. "Will you be okay out here?"

"Liddy, I'll be quite comfortable." Hillary flicked the light switch beside the sofa, slid under the quilt and rolled onto her side.

"John, by the way, I'm proud of you and those boys. Y'all made this whole town proud. Next year you can fuss about the playoffs," Liddy said.

"Thank ya, Liddy. I'm pretty proud of those youngsters too. Now, go on and get some rest. I'll keep Theo company."

John and I scooted our rockers closer to the porch rail and propped our feet up to watch the emerging orange glow encroach upon the gray clouds overhead. John tucked his hands into the front pockets of his sweatshirt, while mine warmed inside my jacket's lined pockets. Our breath puffed visibly in front of us while we talked about the game and reflected on the season.

John paused, then suddenly sat up. "I just don't get it. Why exactly wasn't Dixie with the rest of the family at the hospital?"

I continued rocking using my propped feet on the rail. "I'm not sure, but she sure threw a hissy fit after Maddie got into the ambulance with Harold, and Hal and Phillip kept her from interfering."

"So she couldn't have just driven over herself?"

A smile rose on my face as I continued staring into the distance. "You've been too busy to notice, but Dixie's got an agenda that best suits her. Whenever things don't go her way, she can be pretty vicious. I guess she drove home not wanting to be around all the family. I bet she'll show up this morning bright-eyed and bushy-tailed."

John chuckled as he repositioned his feet on the rail. "Once a spoiled brat, always a spoiled brat, I reckon."

The rattle of Timmy's bike and the yips and yaps of the dogs down the street caught our attention. A moment later, Timmy's brakes squealed. His freckled face held a curious stare. "Coach, is that you?" He dismounted with my morning paper in hand.

"Morning hot shot," John said loud enough for Timmy to hear but with care not to disturb Hillary or those upstairs.

Timmy bounded up the steps and handed me the paper. "Mister Scribner wrote a pretty fair assessment of last night's game in his article." He unfolded the paper and pointed to the picture of John on the sidelines taken when Woogie failed to score at the end of the game.

I showed John. He stared at the photo as if he had never seen himself in the paper before. "Who is this with his hands raised right behind me," John said looking at Timmy.

"Gosh Coach, I thought we had scored," Timmy muttered, quite embarrassed.

John reached up, yanked Timmy's baseball cap off his head and mussed his hair. "Timmy, I did too, but I'm not disappointed. We gave our all, just like those boys on the other side. The only score that matters is right here." John tapped his heart. "Do you think we played as hard as we could?"

"Yes, sir." Timmy fiddled with his cap in his hands.

John looked at me. "Mister P, what do you think? Did the boys give their all last night?"

"Absolutely."

Timmy rolled his eyes upward. "Is this what you meant when you said we could win even though we might lose a game?"

John's smile grew. "Life never guarantees that we'll never experience defeat along the way, but if we always give our best and never quit, we'll discover the secret to winning in life. All the scoreboard signifies is that time ran out on us."

Timmy's mouth hung open for a moment before his lips came back together and formed a broad grin. He returned his cap to his head. "Thanks, Coach. See you Monday morning. We need to start thinking about next year."

"We sure do Timmy. Enjoy your weekend."

I waved as Timmy jumped onto his bike and pedaled away.

Not a minute later, I jumped to my feet as soon as I heard the first ring of the phone and answered it during the second.

John looked up as I returned to the porch with a puzzled look. "Was it the hospital?"

"No. Arnie."

"What's the matter then?"

"Dixie arrived with Gus Appleton a few minutes ago, just before Cindy checked to see who was still there. She saw Dixie and invited her back to look in on Harold. Arnie suggested Hal and Phillip might want to head back over."

———

ARNIE AND GUS Appleton stood talking just outside the hospital's main entrance when we pulled into the parking lot. Hal, Phillip and Maddie parked next to us. Hillary pulled beside her father's Tahoe.

"Where's Dixie?" I asked as we greeted Gus and Arnie.

"She's not gotten back from checking on Harold," Arnie muttered as he eyed Gus.

Liddy asked, "Any word yet on Harold's condition?"

Gus looked up. "None yet."

Arnie held the door as we all returned to the waiting room. Hal went straight to the nurse's station. A minute later, Phillip and Hal followed a nurse down the hall.

Maddie looked at Arnie. "Preacher, would you sit with me a minute?"

Arnie pointed down the hall to a small room that served as a chapel. "Please, after you." He left the door open, but they sat down off to one side.

John looked at Hillary, Liddy and myself. "Might as well take a seat folks." He slid an extra chair in front of the chair he sat in and propped his feet up, hands clasped behind his head. Hillary sat beside John with Gus taking a seat on the opposite side of the room, looking a little uncomfortable. I grabbed two chairs, and we sat across from Hillary and John.

Not thirty minutes later, Doc Lucas walked down the hallway with Dixie, Hal and Phillip. They spoke in a huddle for a couple of minutes before the doctor disappeared, and Dixie and her two sons walked toward us with long faces. Hillary stepped over to the chapel and retrieved Arnie and Maddie to hear the latest news about Harold.

Dixie's tear-soaked mascara ran onto her cheeks as she swayed her head back and forth. Gus tried to comfort her. Hal rested his arm on Phillip's shoulder and said, "Dad suffered a cerebrovascular attack, or CVA stroke, caused by a ruptured brain aneurysm. Doc says the next few hours will determine whether he will pull through or not because it's far too dangerous to operate in his current condition."

Liddy squeezed my upper arm and buried her head in my chest.

Hillary embraced Hal and Phillip. "Your dad's an old war horse. If anyone can survive this, he can." Hillary peeked at her father.

Arnie kept his arm wrapped around Maddie. She maintained a vacant stare before looking upward. "Lord, we knows you are with Mister Harold. We knows your perfect will and purpose will prevail, but I beseech you, my sweet Lord, pour out your Spirit on this family to defeat the terrible fears we're feelin' right now. We needs to feel the comfort of those still waters and green pastures for the challenges that may lie ahead. May your grace, your loving kindness, and your mercy touch each heart here in this circle. Amen." Maddie continued to mutter inaudibly with her eyes squeezed tight before she lowered her head and glanced at each of us with a reassuring pursed-lip grin.

Arnie smiled as he stepped into the middle of our circle in the waiting room. "Now that we have decided to trust God over the next few hours, I suggest we do not need to wear ourselves out hanging around."

Hal adjusted his shirt. "I'll stay here for a while yet. Preacher, you've gotta be tuckered out. Hillary, please take your father home. We'll inform you the minute we hear anything."

"Phillip, would you take the truck and bring Dixie, I mean mother, and Maddie back to the house?" Hal glared at Phillip until he nodded back. "Gus, would you mind staying with me for a bit?"

Gus eyed Dixie before answering. "Sounds fine to me Hal."

Liddy tugged on Hal's arm. "How about I run and get some lunch for you guys before we head home?"

"Thank you. I'd appreciate that." Hal replied as the group dispersed.

"I'll wait here with you and Gus until Liddy gets back," I said to Hal, handing Liddy the keys.

John got up from his chair. "Where're you going for lunch?"

"Bubba's, I reckon." Liddy turned to Hal and Gus. "Is that okay with you two?"

Gus said, "A large sweet tea with a pork sandwich and fries will work for me. How about you Hal?"

Hal nodded and reached for his wallet.

John said. "I got it." Then he looked at Liddy and me. "Y'all want the same?"

"Sounds good," I said eying Liddy.

"Great. Y'all head home. I'll drop yours off after I swing back here."

"Are you going to check on Marie?" Liddy asked as we headed toward the door.

"I'll call her from Bubba's and will bring us both home some dinner. Might even see if Bob's got some leftover bones for Ringo. I ain't seen either of them since yesterday morning."

CHAPTER TWENTY-SIX

LONG BEFORE DAWN SUNDAY MORNING I FELT COMPELLED TO VISIT THE hospital. Barry at Cornerstone Publishing had sent me a hardback copy of Jessie's Story with a note: Fresh off the press. See you in three weeks. I recalled promising Harold a copy of my book and felt the pressing need to make good on that promise.

Hal raised his head when I entered Harold's ICU room, interrupting the cadence of beeps and rhythm of Harold's assisted breathing. Phillip lay awkwardly but fast asleep between two chairs on the far side of Harold's bed.

I whispered, "The nurse told me you were here. Any change?"

Hal wiped his eyes and ran his hands through his hair. "Outside of a couple of twitches, nothing." He stared at the monitor. "They're concerned that his temperature remains abnormally high. What are you doing here so early?"

"I promised a copy of my book to your dad, and this showed up yesterday in the mail."

Hal stared at the front cover and then the back before leafing through the pages. "I'll read some of this to him later. Thanks."

"How about a cup of coffee?"

Hal appeared reluctant to leave his dad's side but agreed to join me for a cup of vending machine coffee. At the door to the room, I asked, "How's Phillip doing?"

"He's been a trooper. He brought me some of Maddie's home cooking for dinner last night and told me that Dixie opened a bottle of wine right after they got home. She spent the afternoon watching television before falling asleep on the sofa. Maddie kept preoccupied in the kitchen until she went to bed right after dinner."

I glanced back at Phillip. "I'm not sure who had the more uncomfortable vigil, you or him."

Hal snickered. "No doubt he got about as much conversation out of Maddie and Dixie as I managed with dad, but we talked quite a bit last night before we dozed off."

"Does Hank know about your dad's condition?"

Hal took a long sip of his coffee. "Can't see how it'll help him worrying about dad. It's not like he can come running over here, but I should try to reach him later this morning."

"When did Gus leave?"

"Not long after y'all left but not until he told me that dad had recently added Dixie to his will. He said, in light of the situation, I should know."

"It's none of my business, but . . ."

"I'd rather not talk about that right now." Hal examined the remains in the bottom of his coffee cup. "You know, you'd think by now someone would come up with a better way to filter the coffee grinds."

I mustered a curious grin and nodded, inspecting the coffee residue in my cup. "Know why I think your dad and I got along?"

Hal wrinkled his brow.

"We have a lot in common."

"Such as?"

"Besides the fact that we're the same age, my two sons are about the same age as you and Hank. Also, from our uniquely different perspectives, we cherish the timeless values that make Shiloh our home."

"Funny, you and Miss Liddy escaped Atlanta to come here while my dad sought to leave here to move to Atlanta for the longest time."

"Well, as odd as it may sound, what gravitated Liddy and me here is the same attraction that allowed your father to recognize why he could never leave Shiloh in spite of his aspirations."

"Theo, you left me with a lot to mull over. I appreciate you checking in on us, and I'll call if there's any change in dad's condition. Please let everyone know why we're not in church this morning."

"I will. I'm sure Arnie will swing by a little later this morning anyway."

———

BUNDLED IN HER blue terry robe and slippers, Liddy waved as I exited our vehicle. "I've got plenty of coffee left in the pot. Want some?"

"Yes, ma'am. I'd love some real coffee about now."

"Come and sit down. The paper's on the table."

The street lights flickered off as I walked onto our porch and sat down.

"Here ya go, hun. Do you want some grits and biscuits? I cooked enough figuring you'd be hungry when you got home."

After a quick taste of my coffee, I nodded. "Please."

I grabbed the paper and scanned the front page. Mary had written an excellent tribute to Harold and positioned it beside a stock photo of him from his better days. She researched enough to mention that he was third of four consecutive Archers who served as mayor stretching back to 1924. The rest of the article spoke of his collapse Friday night, demonstrating his indomitable support for the team and the town by his ill-advised presence at the game. Mary's piece concluded by noting he remained in the vigilant care of the Shiloh Medical Center staff.

I found Zeb on the center page grinning from ear to ear with Marie by his side inside the Old Country Store at Adams Feed and Hardware. The article announced Marie's position as assistant manager along with information about the arrival of their expanded Christmas inventory.

Liddy backed out of the glass storm door carrying a bowl of grits and a dish of biscuits. As she set them down, she said, "Now tell me about your visit. How's Harold?"

"Still non-responsive but well taken care of."

Liddy looked at the paper folded to Zeb's photo. "We've both been far too busy to notice that Thanksgiving is right around the corner, and Christmas ain't far behind. We're going to need to start shopping for the kids again. Between my school schedule and your book launch, we might be a little pressed again this year."

"Tell you what. Let's stay in town for Thanksgiving and plan to brave the stores while you're on break for the holiday weekend. The boys will be here soon enough for Christmas with their families, just like last year."

Liddy paused. "You promise to go shopping with me on Thanksgiving weekend?" Her eyes scrutinized mine.

I crossed my heart and raised three fingers. "I promise."

"Eat your breakfast before it gets cold. I'll get you another fresh cup of coffee." As she leaned over to snatch my cup, I pulled her onto my lap and hugged her. "You're right. We've been far too busy and need some uninterrupted 'us' time. How about dinner out while we're in Alexandria shopping?"

"You asking me on a date?"

"I guess I am. What do you say?"

Liddy leaned close and kissed me. "Only if you get me home before curfew."

I returned her kiss. "I'll try my best."

Liddy grabbed my coffee cup and headed for the kitchen. "Finish eating. We need to start thinking about showering and getting dressed for church."

———

CHURCH BUZZED WITH competing conversations regarding Harold. Zeb and Sam motioned for Liddy and me as soon as we entered. Susanna greeted Liddy while I caught up with Zeb and Sam.

Zeb asked, "Heard y'all were at the hospital this morn. How's Harold and the boys doing?"

"Harold's not out of danger but getting great care from Doc Lucas and his staff. Hal and Phillip seem tired but fine otherwise."

"Arnie just left us a few minutes ago. He looked a little worried and asked if I'd be prepared to close the service if a call comes in from the hospital." Zeb's wide-eyed, forlorn stare made me a little uncomfortable.

Sam tapped my arm. "Zeb's afraid he'll have to stand up front in church."

"Why don't you volunteer? You're a deacon too?" I joked.

Sam eyed Zeb. "We thought you'd be willing to stand in should Arnie need to leave early."

Larry and Martha joined us.

Sam smiled at Larry as they shook hands. "Settle something for us. Which of the three of us . . ." Sam pointed to Zeb, me, and then himself, "is best suited to speak in front of the congregation if Arnie needed someone to fill in for him?"

Without a second thought, he blurted, "Theo, of course."

Zeb exhaled as Sam patted my back. "It's settled then. Thanks, Theo. I'll let Arnie know." Sam and Zeb hustled off before I could utter any objection.

We found our seats a few minutes later. The congregation continued incessant murmuring until Mary began the processional for the choir's entrance. Marie led the rest of the choir down the center aisle. Bringing up the rear, John, Nick and Joe guided Pete to his place beside them on the last row. Mary beamed more than usual as the choir sang "Majesty" and "What a Mighty God We Serve." Jay and Jim covered their broad grins with their hymnals raised higher than usual. Susanna clung to Sam's arm as they sang with equally proud smiles.

Arnie motioned the congregation to sit once the music stopped. "Before we continue this morning, I would be remiss if I didn't share an update regarding Harold Archer." He cleared his throat. "Hal and Phillip are at his bedside hoping Harold will show signs of recovery from the acute stroke he suffered. We prayed together with Doc Lucas and the nurses on duty before I left Harold's room not long ago. Doc Lucas told me that Harold is in the Great Physician's care now. There's nothing more anyone can do except pray for Harold and his family." Arnie stepped off the dais and stood with his hands raised. "Please bow your heads with me, and as you feel led, share your heart with God on Harold's behalf during this time of silent prayer."

Arnie's message came from Paul's plea in Second Corinthians for God to remove the thorn in his side. Arnie said before closing, "No one knows with any degree of certainty the nature of Paul's malady, but there's little doubt it caused enough sufficient pain and discomfort that he begged God for relief from the torment three times. Then Paul realized that God's grace—or as I like to think of grace, God's presence with us—is more than sufficient to comfort us in times of suffering. And the weaker we feel, the more humble our circumstances, the more God's loving-kindness and mercy becomes evident and impacts our lives. It's hard for anyone to know what's going through Harold Archer's mind in his comatose state, but I sense God is by his side. There are no signs of pain or distress. He appears peacefully asleep at this moment. Each of us should take heart that God's grace is sufficient for whatever ails or haunts our lives."

Arnie interrupted his closing and stared at the side door to his office. "Folks, I apologize, but I'm going to ask Mister Theo Phillips to close us in prayer. My presence is needed urgently at the hospital."

Arnie whispered in my ear as I arrived beside him. "Just a simple closing prayer will be sufficient, and then nod to Mary. She'll do the rest. And then, remain up front until the choir exits and follow them as you have seen me do it each week. You'll do fine. Thanks. I'll call you later once I know anything."

———

Just after four o'clock, the phone rang. Liddy answered and then held the phone out for me. "It's Arnie."

"Harold's hanging in there, but Doc told me he almost lost him before I got here. They have him stabilized for now, but after Hal and Phillip spoke with Doc Lucas and me, the family has agreed to honor Harold's living will request. Hal and especially Phillip struggled over the decision, but Harold did not want to be kept alive only to forestall death. As Doc Lucas said, it's now up to God when Harold goes home."

Liddy listened and rested her head on my chest as I responded. "I'm glad you're there Arnie. Has anyone notified Hank?"

"Hal's headed to the jail shortly. Phillip just got off the phone with Maddie."

"What about Dixie?"

"Phillip said she went off. She might be headed here for all I know."

"Call us if you need anything."

The dreaded call came from Arnie just before dawn.

CHAPTER TWENTY-SEVEN

Right after lunch Wednesday, I visited City Hall. Arnie said Harold's death weighed upon the entire Archer household and suggested I check in on Hal. I sensed something amiss when Hillary raised her eyebrows and glanced at Hal's office door as I approached.

"Is this a bad time?"

Before Hillary could utter a syllable, Dixie's anger reverberated through the wall behind Hillary. "What do you mean you don't know if Hank will attend his father's funeral? You're his brother and the mayor. Do something!"

The silence that followed swallowed the noise throughout the main floor. A moment later, Hal's office door flew open. Dixie stomped out, flashed a fiery stare at me, then glared at Hillary. "I want a call from you as soon as the mayor makes arrangements for Hank to attend Harold's funeral." Her request crescendoed and left no doubt she wanted Hal to hear.

Hillary listened, her clasped hands resting on the desk, then responded, "Yes, ma'am. As soon as I hear anything, I most certainly will give you a call." Dixie paraded down the hallway toward the rear exit without uttering another word.

Hillary rolled her eyes and snarled as Hal appeared in his office doorway and shook his head. "Don't fret about her. I'll make sure she's informed when she needs to know anything."

"As you wish, Mister Mayor." Hillary's cheesy coy look made Hal and me break out laughing.

A moment later, Hal sat across from me in his office slouched in his chair with his hands clasped behind his head, legs extended and feet crossed. "Sorry you had to witness Dixie's surly temper. She's already got everyone at the house walking on eggshells."

"Maybe she's struggling to cope with Harold's funeral, and that has her all out of sorts."

"Phillip and I would like to think so, but I suspect she's going to be strutting her stuff for quite a while longer."

"What do ya mean?" I crossed my arms over my chest.

"Dad told Phillip and me if anything happened to him, he wanted Dixie to stay at the house as long as she wanted." Hal's drawn out words and long-faced expression reflected the conflict he faced adhering to his father's wishes.

"Maybe she'll move on again after the funeral. That may sound awful since she's your mother, but it appears she cut the umbilical cord a long time ago."

"Hope you're right, but I have no doubt she'll stick around until the reading of Dad's final testament. Gus wouldn't tell me the specific changes Dad made, but Dixie made it abundantly clear she knows she's getting something."

"No sense in fretting about it. Whatever your dad did is done. What's going on with Hank and the funeral?"

Hal stared at the ceiling fan. "When I spoke with him about dad, he confessed he already knew and asked for my help to attend the funeral. He also seemed cocksure Gus' pending appeal for an early release coupled with dad's death would allow him to not only attend the funeral, but he joked about the family setting a place for him at Thanksgiving dinner."

"Have you confirmed this?"

"Mitch called this morning to tell me that he'd been selected to escort Hank to the funeral and return him that night to jail."

"What about the early release?"

"Joe confirmed that even John offered no objections but said Judge Fitzgerald possessed the last word on the matter."

"So why didn't you tell Dixie?"

Hal smirked. "The way she asked, I guess. I'll handle it tonight."

"Do you mind if I share this with Larry?"

Hal shook his head. "I'd be shocked if he didn't already know something was cooking about Hank's release."

———

FILLED WITH THE latest news about Hank, I walked straight to the Sentinel. Mary and Martha hovered side-by-side at the layout table as I entered the front door.

Mary smiled as she looked up. "Hey, Theo. I was about to call you."

"About what?"

"Dad suggested you be the one to write the article on Harold for this Saturday's edition."

"Why me?"

"Because you knew Harold the best in recent months," Larry chimed in as he appeared from his office.

Martha revealed a silly smile. "No one is better qualified."

Larry patted my back. "Come on back. Let's talk."

I sat in my usual chair while Larry sifted through the files on his desk before selecting a folder and sitting down. He opened the folder, leaned forward and extended two photos to me. "Mary dug through our files and suggested we use these to frame your article."

One photo was a dated snapshot of Harold standing with Dixie and their two oldest sons on the day his father swore him in as mayor. The other picture depicted Harold swearing in Hal earlier this year.

"When do you want my article?"

"How about Friday morning? That'll give Mary more time to type it up and complete the center pullout layout."

"I better jump on this then. But first, can you dig into what Hal shared about Hank?"

"About him getting released early?" Larry asked with a know-it-all grin.

"How'd you know already?"

"Lucky guess I reckon." Larry's smile confirmed the uncanny reliability of his sources.

"So I guess you know he'll likely be out by Thanksgiving?"

"I do now. And, I assume Hank will attend Saturday's funeral too?"

I nodded. "Before I get out of your hair, any word from your contact in New Orleans?"

"Not yet."

On my way out carrying the folder of photos and Mary's notes, I stopped before opening the door and raised the folder for Mary to see. "Thanks for your help. I promise to have my article to you first thing Friday morning."

———

THOUGH WE ARRIVED minutes before the start of Wednesday's service, turnout appeared lighter than normal even factoring that Sanctuary diverted the youth and some of our young adults to the meeting at Priestly Community Center.

Hillary stood beside the foyer entrance. "Hal wanted me to explain why he couldn't make it tonight. It seems Dixie didn't appreciate him not being straight with her today regarding Hank."

"I wonder how she found out." I tried not to smile.

Liddy looked puzzled. "What are y'all talking about?"

"Miss Dixie made a huge scene this afternoon in Hal's office when he played dumb when she asked if Hank would be able to attend the funeral." Hillary's coy grin only added to Liddy's confusion.

Liddy's eyes darted between Hillary and me. "Why can't the two of them get along with each other?"

I hugged Liddy's shoulders. "I think there's a lot more going on that we don't know. Hal's got his reasons I'm sure."

"I gotta agree with Theo. But more importantly, did you hear that Megan and Andy are coming into town for the funeral?"

Liddy relaxed her wrinkled brow. "No, we didn't."

"GCU has a bye week, and they'll arrive late Friday night."

"That's good news, but we need to find our seats. Mary's about to start." I grasped Liddy's hand, and we headed into the sanctuary while Hillary dashed off to help her mother in the children's department.

After the service had ended, Arnie and Judy greeted us. He leaned close and whispered, "What do you think about Hank?"

"About the funeral or getting out of jail early?" I whispered back.

"Both. On my way to visit him yesterday, Gus passed me in the visitor parking lot headed for his car. He waved without stopping. When I met with Hank, he acted like the cat who had just swallowed the canary."

"I hope it's a well-deserved turn of events for him, and he's ready to move on with his life. We don't need him carrying any grudges back to Shiloh."

———

"THE BODY SOWN perishable shall be raised imperishable. The body sown in dishonor shall be raised in glory. Even if sown in weakness, it too shall be raised in power. Though sown a natural body, it shall be raised a spiritual body. The Apostle Paul teaches us, flesh and blood shall not inherit the kingdom of God because the perishable can never inherit the imperishable. Harold knew his weaknesses and the frailty of his life but answered the trumpet call that woke him from his deep sleep and grabbed his Lord's hand, exchanging his perishable body for an imperishable one, mortality for immortality. At that moment, the sting of death that continues to haunt us lost its grip on Harold." Arnie's words rose above the sniffles and sobs filling the sanctuary Saturday morning.

The standing-room-only crowd overflowed along the back wall. We were fortunate to arrive on time and find seats amidst our friends in our customary pews. Dixie sat in the front row wearing her scarlet hooded cloak over the same dark blue dress she wore for Momma Arians' funeral. Phillip, with Jeannie by his side, sat nearest the aisle while Hank, Hal and Maddie sat on the other side of Dixie. A uniformed Mitch, holding his wide brim sheriff's hat by his side, stood at ease near the side door to Arnie's office.

Arnie stepped aside as Hal walked onto the dais and pulled his notes from his sports jacket. "I want to thank Doctor Wright for his heartfelt words." He then glared at the closed casket beneath him and the abundance of flower arrangements cluttering the front of the church. "My whole family wants to thank all of you for braving such a dreary morning to honor my dad. The outpouring of well wishes and sharing of fond memories reflects the twenty-five years my father faithfully served as mayor of Shiloh. Dad would be the first to tell each of you that he only regrets that he could not have done more for the town he loved."

Hal's anecdotes about Harold brought chuckles to many in attendance. He then pointed to Dixie. "I would be remiss if I neglected to share how much my brothers and I appreciate our mother's return to Shiloh at a time when my dad needed her the most. Thank you for tending to Dad's care these last couple of months. Welcome home."

I couldn't see Dixie's face, but Phillip handed her a handkerchief just before Hal invited him up to offer a closing prayer.

Arnie stepped to the head of the aisle after Phillip finished. Hal, Hank, Phillip, Gus, Zeb and John walked down the aisle to escort the casket from the sanctuary with Arnie following. After Mary finished playing a recessional, the pews slowly emptied.

The motorcade proceeded from the church and wound through the streets of Shiloh past the school and stadium and then out of town to the Archer estate. The parade of vehicles followed the driveway past the Archer mansion onto a gravel road leading to their family's cemetery. An open grave waited beside Harold's father's and mother's tombstones beneath a majestic oak. The funeral home attendants directed all but the family to remain in their vehicles. We watched as Arnie held an umbrella over Maddie and a hooded Dixie until they reached the green canopy. After a brief graveside ceremony, all but Hank riding in the sheriff's cruiser returned to the church for a lunch reception. Mitch drove Hank straight back to the county jail.

—

LIDDY WENT TO help Susanna, Judy and Hillary in the kitchen as soon as we arrived back at the church. Zeb and I greeted everyone at the door and took care of the rain-soaked jackets as the fellowship hall filled up. Hal and Phillip escorted Maddie and Dixie into the crowded hall. Maddie joined a table occupied by Cecil, Cora, Bob and Barb, as well as Wiley and his wife, Malvinia. Dixie settled into a seat across from Gus while Hal and Phillip walked around the room and stopped a few moments at each table.

While almost everyone had dessert in front of them, Zeb and I scurried up to the buffet line and found Arnie scrounging to fill his plate. I looked at Liddy, but she only smiled and shrugged.

Out of the corner of my eye, I spotted Phillip helping Dixie with her cloak before he zipped his jacket and they exited. Hal maintained his twisted grimace even while Hillary appeared to be consoling him, and Maddie rested her hands on his shoulder.

I walked over to Hal's table. He motioned for me to lean closer and said, "Dixie expressed her frustration about Hank not being at the reception by taking exception to your article about Dad. When she voiced a snide comment directed at you, she and Nick got into a heated exchange. I didn't hear all they said, but you might want to talk to Nick. He got rather hot under the collar before Dixie stood and demanded Phillip take her home."

I stepped to the opposite end of the table, and Joe looked up at me. "I don't know what got into Nick. He accused Dixie of being responsible for Momma's accident."

Nick frowned as he looked up. "I just defended you and your article. She copped an attitude and got her nose out of joint before she made some high and mighty wisecrack about wishing she'd drove so she could leave. That's when I said, 'So you can race around town scaring folks off the road in your fancy sports car?'"

Missy interrupted. "Nick shouldn't have said what he did, but Dixie felt Nick accused her of having had something to do with his momma's accident."

Joe added, "Before anyone could smooth things over, Dixie got up and demanded Phillip take her home."

Hal walked over and joined the conversation. "I'm sorry Nick. She had no right to fly off the handle like that."

"I shouldn't have said what I did. It was my fault for being a smart aleck and commenting about her reckless driving," Nick said.

Hal grinned. "Don't think twice about it. She'll get over it. Besides, she does drive like a bat out of you know where."

CHAPTER TWENTY-EIGHT

Zeb called right after Liddy left for school Tuesday morning. "With all that's happened the last couple weeks, I'd like to invite you to join me and a couple of others on an overnight fishing trip."

"Zeb, I haven't been fishing since my boys were in high school, but it sounds like fun. Who else is going?"

"My cabin on the river will sleep six, so I also invited John, Hal, Phillip and Nick."

"When?"

"I can pick you up Friday about four o'clock, and you can tell Liddy we'll be back about sundown Saturday."

"What do I need to bring?"

"Just a change of clothes and your toothbrush. It'll be pretty damp and cold on the river, so be sure to dress warm and bring rain gear just in case."

I shared Zeb's invitation when Liddy arrived home after school.

"I'm glad you agreed to go, but when was the last time you roughed it on an overnight fishing trip?" Liddy giggled.

My mind churned but drew a blank. "Never, but I've always wanted to. Does that count?"

"Whatever fish you bring home best be cleaned and ready for the frying pan."

———

At dusk Friday, Zeb turned off River Road thirty minutes out of Shiloh and maneuvered his Bronco along the muddy back road. Nick grabbed the back of my seat several times as Zeb revved his vehicle to maneuver over and out of the deep ruts in the road. Behind us, Hal and Phillip experienced the same bumpy ride in John's dually.

Zeb's headlamps illuminated the front door to his rustic, green cabin while we carried our stuff inside. Zeb lit two kerosene lanterns, and the rest of us staked out the bunk beds.

John patted me on the back and said, "If you don't mind, I'll take the top. You'll be more comfortable below."

My smile made my preference clear as I tossed my bag onto the lower mattress. Phillip and Hal grabbed the middle set of bunks. Zeb sat on the remaining lower bunk and grinned at Nick who hoisted his overnight bag on top of the only unclaimed mattress.

Minutes later, Zeb brewed a pot of coffee on top the cast iron wood stove, which also removed the damp chill inside the cabin. The rear porch jutted out and over the river and cast the only flickers of light onto the water after the sun retired for the evening. The river licked the pilings beneath the porch as the current slipped downstream. The indigenous critters along the banks of the lazy Flint River voiced their annoyance to our invasion of their habitat.

John and Hal joined me on the porch. "What do you think we'll catch tomorrow?" I asked, entirely unaware of what lurked below the surface of the river.

"Some of us can fish right off the porch for some bream and catfish, and three can fit into Zeb's johnboat and try their luck hooking a couple stripers or largemouth bass," John shared as he stared at the river's surface.

Hal looked at me. "Which do you fancy, Mister P?"

"I'll be quite content casting some worms out from right here."

"If it'll make you feel any better, Zeb asked me to take his boat out. He prefers to fish for the bream that hang out around the pilings." John eyed Hal. "You think Phillip will be okay staying behind with Mister P and Zeb? I'd like you, me and Nick to go out in the boat together."

"I'll talk to him, but I suspect he'll not make a fuss about it."

I laughed. "Tell Phillip he can sleep in like I hope to do. Besides, we'll have the advantage of hot coffee on the stove all day."

Just before dawn, I awoke when I felt John slide out of the top bunk. Though I tried to roll over and go back to sleep, the shuffling of feet, a stoking of the fire and whispering kept me awake. I sat up and watched Hal toss another log into the stove's belly. Nick and John loaded the johnboat secured along the porch rail.

"Hal, can I help you with anything?" I whispered as I pulled my sweatshirt on and covered my bare feet with my wool socks.

"You can grab one of those Krispy Kreme boxes and hand it to them," Hal whispered as he pointed to the cardboard box sitting beside the table.

On the porch, I stopped and stared at the thick mist blanketing the river's dark surface. John stood in the boat checking the motor. Nick looked at me, arms extended. "Those for us?"

Hal backed out the door with two thermoses of coffee and set them on the rail before zipping his parka and flipping the hood over his head. "Y'all about ready?"

Nick stowed the last of the fishing gear. Hal handed the thermoses to Nick and turned toward John. "Captain John, permission to come on board."

John chuckled. "What do you think this is, the Queen Mary? Get your butt in here."

The motor sputtered before John adjusted the throttle. "Theo, would you mind untying us once they settle their fannies into their seats?"

I untied the boat's tether and tossed it to Nick. He shoved the bow free as John throttled the motor, and they headed downriver. Once the mist completely swallowed them, I checked my watch. Instead of crawling back into my bunk, I grabbed a donut and more coffee and sat on the porch, contemplating the grand fish fry Zeb promised later that afternoon.

The screen door squealed and promptly slammed shut, snapping me out of my distant thoughts. Phillip rubbed his eyes after he zipped his jacket and sat down beside me. "How long ago did they push off?"

"About an hour. Is Zeb up?"

"He turned his nose at the donuts and is busy whipping up some grits."

"Some hot grits sound good to me."

Phillip stared through the stubborn mist to the far bank. "Hal and I want you to know that we appreciate your article about Dad. It amazes me that you only knew him for a year, but you seem to have understood him better than most anyone else in Shiloh."

"I appreciate you sharing that." I paused to recollect. "Remember when you and your dad first visited Liddy and me at the house?"

Phillip's ruddy dimples deepened as his fingers ran through his hair. "How could I forget? Seems so long ago, though. A lot of water has flowed under the bridge since then."

"How's Maddie been?"

A sigh followed. "Still grieving, though she tries her darnedest to hide it. Of course, Mom isn't making it easy for her either."

"What do ya mean?"

"Dixie hollers when Maddie doesn't answer her right away and cusses at her when Maddie sticks her nose in to check in on her. It seems Maddie can't please Mom."

"Could they both be grieving in different ways?"

"If this is grieving, then I feel sorry for both of them. Mom locks herself in either Dad's study or bedroom for hours on end when she's not drinking and watching television in the den. Make no mistake. Maddie still sets a plate for her at the table, but Mom makes it abundantly clear she'll eat when it suits her."

I scratched my stubble. "Do you have any idea what's gnawing at your mom? Sounds like more than grieving going on."

Phillip sipped his coffee. "I'm not sure. I just wish I knew what she's doing in the study and Dad's bedroom when she locks the door. Hal walked into the study Sunday evening as she rummaged through some of Dad's drawers. When he asked if he could help her find something, she claimed to be just straightening up and filing away papers left out on his desk. But I could tell Hal didn't believe her."

"What does Hal think?"

"She's looking for a copy of his revised will."

"Not that I need to know the specifics, but do either of you know what changes he made?"

"I think only Mister Appleton knows, and he hasn't told us anything."

I popped the last of my donut into my mouth. Before swallowing completely, I muttered, "I imagine whatever all of you need to know you'll know soon enough."

"How's that?"

"Unless there's a problem with your dad's final testament, Gus will let you know when and where the reading will take place in a few days."

Phillip sighed. "Think Mom will leave after that?"

"Don't know how to answer that. It appears to me that your mother has a mind of her own."

The screen door sprung open and then slammed shut as Zeb walked out. "Who's got a mind of their own?"

I grinned and patted Phillip's shoulder. "Dixie."

"I'd have to agree with y'all's assessment of that woman." Zeb raised his bowl. "There's plenty more on the stove."

Shortly after one o'clock, the three of us had used up all our worms, and a dozen acceptable-sized panfish found themselves attached to the stringer dangling over the porch rail in the water below. The hum of the boat motor drew our attention as John steered upstream. Nick and Hal smiled as they lifted two large stripers and a channel cat.

I had forgotten the fun of scaling and gutting fresh-caught fish and the smell that clung to one's clothes. John made short work of their catch, while Phillip and I gutted and cleaned the dozen bream we caught. Zeb deep-fried all the fish along with plenty of mouthwatering hushpuppies in a large cast iron cauldron filled with peanut oil. By four o'clock, our bellies begged for mercy as we packed up and headed home. Phillip and Hal voiced how much they enjoyed the diversion while they joked with John as we loaded our vehicles. John waved as he drove off first.

On our return to town in Zeb's Bronco, Nick leaned forward from the back seat and whispered, "Why do you think Dixie got so upset when I joked about her crazy driving?"

Half-asleep, I muttered, "Because she's Dixie, I reckon."

"But why did she think I accused her of running momma off the road? Dixie wasn't even in town when that happened was she?"

Zeb laughed. "I wouldn't give too much more thought about what Dixie says or does. It won't change anything anyhow."

"That's what John said too." Nick sank into the back seat and stared out the window as we drove into town.

CHAPTER TWENTY-NINE

Shortly after Liddy got home from school Tuesday, she put on her apron, rolled up her sleeves and hurried about the kitchen peeling potatoes to boil and mash. Collards and stewed okra already simmered in crockpots, the result of Liddy's earlier-than-usual morning. We expected Larry, Martha, Mary and Pete at six.

At five-thirty, I pulled on my windbreaker and placed two seasoned pork tenderloins on the grill. Refreshed by the mid-November evening air, I stayed outside as the neighborhood lights came on up and down the street while the meat cooked. A couple of minutes before six, I headed inside with the tenderloins just as headlights indicated the arrival of our guests.

By the time I got to the kitchen and set the pork on the counter, Liddy had already greeted Larry and Martha at the front door.

Larry noticed my puzzled look. "Don't fret, Mary's bringing Pete. He had truck problems."

The sound of stomping feet announced Pete and Mary's arrival before I took off my windbreaker. Liddy grinned at me as Pete followed Mary through the door wearing pressed khaki slacks and a blue oxford dress shirt beneath an autumn-colored argyle sweater. "Mary, you certainly are having a mighty fine impact on Pete."

Pete's eyes widened as he turned his head toward Liddy.

I said, "I think my sweet wife is trying to say that you look quite handsome this evening."

Mary squeezed Pete's hand. "I think so too."

Larry and Martha exchanged smiles before Larry said to me, "So tell me a little about this fishing trip I heard about after the fact."

I raised my hands. "Hey, take that up with Zeb, but I don't think your gabardine britches and wingtip shoes would've fit in at Zeb's cabin, which didn't have running hot water or electricity. His bunk beds also brought the concept of roughing it to whole new dimension, even for just a one-night outing."

"Martha, I've washed Theo's clothes twice and hung them outside to get the fish smell out of them," Liddy said smiling at Martha and Larry.

Pete roared. "That's how ya know they caught any fish." Pete looked at me. "What all did y'all catch?"

"A stringer of bream, couple stripers and a channel cat, but we ate our fill before we came home."

Larry asked, "Who all went beside you and Zeb?"

"Phillip, Hal, John and Nick. It turned out to be therapeutic for Hal and Phillip after what they've had to deal with the last couple of weeks. John also looked as relaxed as I've seen him since early summer."

"Coach deserved a Friday night off," Pete said.

After dinner, Larry stood next to me by the coffee pot and said, "Can we go out on the porch for a few minutes?"

I looked at him and nodded before I caught Liddy's attention. "Hun, Larry and I are going out on the porch with our coffee."

Liddy asked Pete to stoke the fireplace while Martha and Mary sat down in the living room.

———

WE ROCKED AND sipped our coffee for a moment before Larry blurted, "I heard back from my friend at the Picayune."

"What'd you find out?"

"Her so-called husband, Mister Beauregard Arnaquer, died a year ago."

"What do you mean 'so-called husband'?" I leaned closer, my elbows resting on my knees.

"There's no record of them ever getting married, although she received a Louisiana driver's license identifying her as Delilah Dixon Arnaquer, and her name appeared on the deed to their house, which they paid cash for fourteen years ago."

"How'd she get a driver's license under that name if they weren't married?"

"I asked the same question. My friend replied, 'That's Louisiana for you.'"

"What else did he tell you?"

"The reason he took so long to get back with me is that her dear Beauregard's drowning, though reported as an accident, remains under investigation. Evidently, Mister Arnaquer was a person of interest in an investment fraud scheme. Though they cleared Dixie of any criminal complicity months ago, half-million dollars remains missing, and the Louisiana Bureau of Investigation still wants to interview her."

"What'd you tell your friend?"

"They don't know she's here if that's what you're asking." Larry leaned back in deep thought. "But, you also need to know she sold their house to pay off mounting debts after Beauregard's death. She left Louisiana with her belongings squeezed into her fancy Jaguar convertible."

I stretched my legs and crossed my feet. "What do you make of all this?"

"Part of me hopes she's just trying to make a fresh start, but then there's a side of me that believes she might be up to no good."

"What should we do with this information?"

Larry swallowed the last of his coffee. "Give her the benefit of the doubt for the time being, at least until I can talk with her. If there's any smoke from her past tailing her, we sure don't want it to pollute Shiloh or Harold's legacy either."

"Did you call her?"

"Wanted to see what you thought first. Only you and I know what I just told you."

I sat upright and scooted to the edge of my seat. "I'd sit down privately with ol' Dixie. Her sons don't need to know anything for the moment."

Larry stood. "She's already agreed to meet me at the office Friday afternoon."

"What excuse did you use?"

"Our interest in writing a piece about her return to Shiloh. And for the time being, neither Mary nor Martha need to know anything more than that either. I want one of them to be out front but not too curious while I meet with Dixie in my office."

"That's a good idea. Let me know how it goes."

"In the meantime, you and Mary have enough on your plates with your book launch on Saturday."

My wrinkled look revealed my trepidation about both pending matters. "I confess, I'm pretty nervous but no more than how you oughta feel about your upcoming tête-à-tête with Dixie."

The storm glass door opened, and Mary poked her head outside. "Dad, you ready to leave? It's getting late."

"We were about to check on y'all."

Liddy and I watched from our porch until both vehicles drove off.

"You talk to Larry about the book launch?" Liddy asked.

"As a matter-of-fact we did. By the way, are you getting as anxious as me about it?"

Liddy giggled. "Of course silly."

———

"THE WOMAN THREATENED to sue you, me and the paper if we didn't stop meddling," Larry whispered in the Sentinel's break room.

"What did you say?" I asked as I poured two cups of coffee and handed one to Larry.

"Our meeting started fine enough. Dixie seemed to warm up to the idea she'd be in the local paper. That is until I asked a few questions about her days in Picayune. Her friendly smile evaporated, and an icy stare appeared."

"Did you ask her about anything you learned?"

"I told her if there's anything she'd rather not discuss right now, I'd understand. With guarded reluctance, she gave her okay. I began by asking about her relationship with Beauregard. She promptly told me to refer to him as Beau."

"What about her claim to be married?"

"She told me she met Beau in New Orleans, and they married in 1998."

"Did you ask when her divorce went through from Harold?"

"Funny you should ask. She stuttered before claiming she couldn't recall the exact date, but she pulled a gaudy diamond ring and matching wedding band from her purse. They were attached to her keychain, and she bragged that Beau bought them right afterward."

"What did she say about him?"

"She kept that simple. Rich, handsome and loved to spoil her. She said he was a successful investment adviser and traveled quite a bit for his clients whom she said she never met."

"So what happened that she blew up at you?"

"After she teared up recounting how she learned of Beau's death from two detectives with the Louisiana Bureau of Investigation, I asked why they were the ones to notify her. Her teary-eyes turned cold as she emphasized that he drowned, and that's all she knew. When I asked whether it had been accidental or not, she snapped back and questioned why I needed to ask that. I tried to apologize, but she waggled her finger at me and demanded that I tell her why I needed to know about her past."

"You must have said something else. What happened?" I asked.

"I slid her a copy of the article I received from the Picayune Press about Beauregard's death. It featured a photo of her wealthy, handsome Beau. In the article, the LBI stated that Beau's business dealings connected him to parties of interest in an ongoing investment fraud case. The LBI was also reevaluating the coroner's findings of an accidental drowning. Dixie turned white at first, but then her neck veins turned scarlet before she went on her tirade of threats as she headed out the door."

"How did my name come up?" I shook my head fearing the worst.

"I mentioned you'd be writing the article about her."

"Here we go again, partner. What now?"

Larry relaxed into his swivel chair. "Let's just allow this to simmer awhile and see what she does next. In the meantime, folks will start showing up here in another hour for your book launch. Get with Mary and enjoy being a celebrity for the rest of the afternoon."

———

THE SENTINEL'S FRONT door remained wide open until nearly five o'clock with folks flowing in to talk with me and to get their copy of Jessie's Story. Barry from Cornerstone arrived with two boxes of marketing handouts and spent the day doling them out to everyone as he asked them to tell their friends about the book.

Liddy charmed each person who patiently waited while I scribbled a personalized note above my signature on more books than I dared count. Mary answered questions as she kept the supply of books filled on the counter. Martha gladly received either cash, check or a credit card.

Timmy brought his mom and dad by after lunch, and they purchased two copies. Pete poked his head in with Jeannie, Jay and Jim in tow as Timmy and his family prepared to leave. Timmy opened his signed copy and showed Pete. "Mister P even noted the page where he mentioned me in the story."

Pete grinned and patted Timmy on his back. "Mister P, will you show me where we're in your book?"

I looked up from signing another book. "Who said I mentioned you guys by name?"

Jay barked and pointed. "Mary did."

Mary turned to me with an oops kind of grin.

The boys bought extra copies for Andy and Megan, Pete's mom and dad, Zeb and John. Pete said John felt uncomfortable picking up his copy I promised him. He'd stop by later to get it signed.

When Joe and Nick stopped in, Joe asked me to call him about having lunch in the next couple of days.

Just before five o'clock, Hal pulled up in his dad's black dually. Phillip exited the passenger side. "Mister P, got at least four more copies?" Phillip walked through the door ahead of his brother.

I looked at Mary. "Hand me four of them, please."

"These are on me fellas." I looked up as I opened the first book. "Who's getting this one?"

Hal looked at Phillip and said, "The first one's for Maddie."

"What about this one?" I said after signing Hal and Phillip's copies and opening the fourth.

Hal whispered, "Would you sign this one for Hank?"

"I'd be honored since there were two brothers saved by Jessie at the end of the story."

Hank, Remember what your dad once told me—God graces Shiloh as a sanctuary for the challenges in the present, a testament to the cherished memories of the past, and a sentinel guarding against unwarranted changes that the future promises.

Barry leaned over my shoulder. "I gotta write that down. It belongs on the book cover."

"Harold Archer gets the credit, not me." I handed the last book to Hal. "Where's your mother?"

Hal gave Larry a serious look before he said, "She stayed home."

———

Right after Liddy and I got home, Liddy said, "How about a sandwich for dinner? I'm too tired to cook. Besides, it's already after seven."

"I'll turn on the Georgia game. It will be in the fourth quarter I imagine."

While Liddy rummaged through the refrigerator, she asked, "Ham okay?"

"Sure, but hurry. We just kicked off after tying the score with Tennessee. There're eight and a half minutes to go."

We managed to stay awake long enough to watch Georgia kick a field goal in overtime to win, but not long after we climbed into bed the phone rang.

"Theo, this is Mary. Sorry to wake you, but dad wanted me to tell you that we're at the office. Someone smashed the front window, and the sheriff's deputies are with dad now."

"Did anything else get damaged? Anything missing?"

"Outside of broken glass everywhere, everything seems fine."

"Do you need me to come over there?"

"Don't think so, but dad insisted I call you. Pete's already securing some plywood over the broken window."

After I hung up the phone, Liddy rolled over. "What got broken? Anyone hurt?"

I squeezed her hand and whispered, "Nothing to worry about. Go back to sleep," but I tossed and turned until near dawn.

CHAPTER THIRTY

ARNIE ENDED SUNDAY'S SERVICE WITH A REMINDER ABOUT THE FAMILY SERVICE Wednesday evening. He promised to announce the latest about this year's Christmas in Shiloh pageant plans.

Larry and I veered away from our wives in the foyer and corralled Hal. He stood alone checking his phone with his back turned to those around him.

"Anything wrong? Where's Phillip?" I asked.

"Dixie upset Maddie shortly after breakfast this morning. Phillip opted to accompany Maddie and attend Mount Zion with her. I think Phillip heard Maddie bragging about her congregation's Sunday fellowship meals."

Larry said, "Makes me hungry just thinking about it. How about joining us over at Bubba's for a bite to eat?" Larry peered at my surprised look. "It'll be just you, me, Theo, our wives and maybe Arnie and Judy."

"Why not? I gotta make a quick stop at City Hall first." Hal said as he headed for the rear exit door before he added. "Sorry to hear about the vandalism last night."

Larry sneered. "A hazard of being in the paper business, I guess. Pete got us boarded up in no time. No real harm done. Nothing damaged or stolen."

"That's good news. I won't be long. See you there." Hal disappeared out the door.

Larry lingered until the door shut.

"I guess we better let our wives know." I scanned the foyer and tugged on Larry's jacket sleeve.

Larry turned baring a contrived grin. "Sorry for the short notice. I'm curious if you-know-who stayed home last night."

My eyebrows arched, but I knew who he meant. "I'll break the news to our wives. You go talk to Arnie."

Liddy and Martha stood across the room chatting with Malvinia.

"Wiley not feeling good this morning?" I asked with a polite smile directed at Malvinia.

She extended her white-gloved hand. "Mister Phillips, good morning. As a matter of fact, our grandson dropped by last evening and spent the night."

"Woogie's daddy?" I asked as I accepted her hand.

"Wiley's cooking breakfast for both of them this morning."

Liddy asked, "Did Woogie come over too?"

"He spent the night as well. We were thrilled to hear that Wilson, that's our grandson's name, landed a job in the area."

Liddy said, "That should allow Wilson to spend more time with Woogie."

"We sure hope so." Malvinia's warm smile became reserved as she spoke about Wilson.

"Missus Edwards, sorry to interrupt, but I need to talk to my wife and Missus Scribner." I squeezed Liddy's waist a bit tighter, and she glanced up.

"Please excuse us, Missus Edwards," Liddy quickly added.

Malvinia excused herself and headed for the door. I watched her stop to speak with Judy and Arnie before I turned back toward Liddy and Martha, both glared at me. "Larry and I invited Hal to meet us in a few minutes at Bubba's."

Martha peeked over at Larry conversing with Arnie and Judy. "Are they joining us too?" Martha furrowed her brow. "This isn't entirely social then?"

I shrugged and offered a sidelong grin to appease their curiosity.

Larry arrived in the nick of time. "They'll meet us there. I'll drive."

———

A FLUSTERED CECIL greeted us as we entered Bubba's. Cora had decided to remain after church so she could eat with Maddie and Phillip at Mount Zion's fellowship dinner. Barb had to fill in for Cora. By the time Cecil seated us, Barb already hovered over my shoulders, pen in hand.

"What's your pleasure this afternoon, folks?" she asked in her familiar high-pitch voice.

"Hold on, Miss Barb," Arnie spouted, approaching with Judy and Hillary right behind him. "Hal's on the phone and will be right in."

"I reckon I'll just get y'all some more sweet tea." With a cheery smile, Barb tucked her pad and pen into her apron pocket.

Hal sat down a minute later across from me. Barb filled his glass and took our orders.

As soon as Barb walked away, Hillary said, "Before I plumb forget, Susanna asked me to confirm that all y'all are coming to their house for Thanksgiving." Everyone except Hal nodded.

Hillary stared at him. "I thought we already discussed this. If she doesn't want to come, it's her loss."

"It's not Dixie. Hank's coming home Wednesday."

Arnie rested his hand on Hal's. "It'll do him good to come too. You know he's welcome." Arnie looked around the table as we all shared our affirmations with Hal.

Hal sank into his seat. "I'm just worried how he'll feel about it and more importantly what he might say."

Liddy let out a light chuckle. "Silly, you just get him and your mother there. We'll do our best to make sure they both feel welcome."

A reluctant head bob followed. "I'll do my best. Maddie's already talking up a storm about helping Susanna in the kitchen."

Larry chuckled, adding to Liddy's contagious giggles. "I'm glad to hear Maddie's going to help with the cooking."

I eyed Larry and Hal. "What about Phillip? Does he feel any better since Maddie and Dixie butted heads again?"

He broke into laughter. "Whatever went on between the two of them this morning started as a spat last night. Of course, most of their squabbling started and finished pretty much one-sided, if you catch my drift."

Larry stared at Hal. "So, you had your hands pretty full with both of them last night and this morning."

Hal restrained his laughter to respond. "Into the wee hours, thank you very much. Once Dixie gets riled up, she takes a long time to simmer back down."

Judy laughed. "You shouldn't be so hard on your mother. I think she's just jealous of Maddie."

"Here ya go, folks!" Barb and Cecil leaned over our shoulders and handed out platters of ribs to everyone.

My crumpled napkin lay beside my dish of bare bones by the time Pete arrived with Mary. "Did y'all save us any of them ribs?"

Barb cackled as she directed them to the table beside ours. "Child, you and Miss Mary sit down over here. I'll take good care of ya."

Pete winked as he helped Mary with her jacket. "So, everyone coming Thursday?"

Hillary blurted, "Tell your momma to count on a full house."

———

SEVERAL UNFAMILIAR FACES filled the sanctuary pews Wednesday evening. Only the Arians were absent among our circle of friends. They left town earlier that day headed to their family's home on Saint Simons Island. Nick and Joe said they wanted their family to enjoy the house for a few days before deciding whether or not to sell Momma Arians beloved vacation home. Fortunately, Megan and Andy's arrival overshadowed the absence of the Arians family.

Before the service began, Andy, Pete, Jay and Jim cracked jokes with one another just like when we first moved to Shiloh a year earlier. Hal helped Hillary and Judy tend to the young children filling the front two rows. Phillip settled in between Megan and Jeannie.

Silence filled the sanctuary when Arnie rose from his chair, gripped the edges of the podium and smiled. "I look out at all the familiar and new faces and stand before you humbled. This service marks the twenty-sixth Thanksgiving Eve service I've shared with you or at least those old enough to remember back that far." He stared at Judy and Hillary. "In another three weeks, Judy, Hillary and I will also witness our twenty-sixth Christmas in Shiloh pageant as well. Sadly, this will be the first one without the Honorable Harold Archer presiding. This year, our new mayor, the Honorable Henry 'Hal' Archer, will preside in his place." Arnie motioned to Hal to join him on the platform.

"Thank you, Doctor Wright. I'm quite nervous about filling my father's large shoes this year and will certainly miss his supportive smile the few times I had the privilege of speaking on behalf of the city. This edition of Christmas in Shiloh will kickoff the seventeenth, the Wednesday preceding Christmas Eve. All the decorations on Main Street and Town Square are ready to welcome the arrival of another magnificent Christmas tree to be lit that first night. We have a special night of music planned, and I received confirmation from the North Pole this morning that Santa will once again be with us." Hal focused on the young faces smiling up at him. "I hope to see all of you and lots of your friends there."

Arnie's message spoke about how thankful we should feel this year because of God's greatness. He stood over his open Bible, read the 145th Psalm and then shared, "This timeless passage speaks of God's goodness, greatness and graciousness. Over this past year, God manifested himself right here in our community, changing many lives forever. Maybe we got a bit sidetracked in recent years by tragic events, but that didn't mean God stopped working in our hearts." Arnie panned the room as he stepped away from the pulpit.

"There are two related questions I'd like to offer this Thanksgiving Eve. How have you over the course of this past year testified to the Lord's goodness, greatness and graciousness in your daily life and the lives of your family members? How have you offered him the praise of thanks he deserves? Please bow your heads and allow your hearts to speak privately with God as you feel led."

A minute later, Arnie's pastoral voice broke the silence. "The apostle Paul wrote: 'Is there injustice with God? Of course not! He shows mercy to those whom he wants to show mercy and offers compassion to whomever he chooses to show compassion. God's mercy and compassion do not depend upon our will or effort, but on God alone.' May we all find a reason to give thanks to God this Thanksgiving. Amen."

I raised my head as Liddy squeezed my hand and smiled. Beside Liddy, John and Marie shared tears. In front of us, Sam, Susanna, Megan and Andy hugged one another as smiles erupted. Jeannie leaned close to her mother to exchange whispers. Jeannie beamed and immediately turned and embraced Megan.

Liddy nudged me and asked, "What's going on with them?"

"Beats me. I haven't seen Sam smile like that before."

Liddy scooted from our pew first and pulled Susanna aside. They whispered back and forth. Liddy walked back with a smug grin and whispered, "It's a secret until tomorrow at their house, but Megan's pregnant."

"But how? Doc Lucas told her last year she couldn't." I stuttered.

"That's why doctors practice medicine, and God is God, I guess. Now don't say a word. They're not going to tell Pete until later tonight. They're afraid he'll blurt it to the whole world before Andy and Megan can announce the news at their house."

Hal stood beside Phillip, Hillary and Judy near the main entrance door while Arnie greeted the last few members and their guests as they left.

I approached Hal. "Didn't get a chance to talk to you before the service. Hank get home okay?"

"I picked him up this afternoon. He's been spending most his time talking with Dixie since he got settled. We left them laughing and talking on the veranda. Guess he's become her new center of attention."

"Did you ask them about tomorrow?"

"They'll be there." Hal's hands-in-pocket pose and wrinkled grin reminded me of when I first met him in church standing in the shadow of his dominant, older brother.

CHAPTER THIRTY-ONE

THE KITCHEN WINDOW OFFERED AN UNOBSTRUCTED VIEW OF THE ORANGE-red glow beneath a bank of dark clouds on the horizon while I waited for my first cup of coffee. I mumbled, "Red sky at night, sailor's delight. Red sky in the morning, sailor's warning."

"You talking to yourself?" Liddy asked at the tail-end of a suppressed yawn.

"Thinking about this afternoon and hoping the weather cooperates." I adjusted her robe's fleece collar and freed her ponytail. "Coffee?"

"Yes, please." She looked out the kitchen window after I stepped aside to pour two cups. "No matter what a red sky foretells, it sure is mighty beautiful to look at."

We walked into the living room. Liddy climbed into her armchair, unfolded her patchwork quilt and covered her legs stretched across the ottoman.

I rocked back in my recliner and examined the weather forecast below the front fold of the morning paper. "Looks like we'll have partly cloudy skies with temperatures in the low seventies this afternoon, but a cold front is bringing rain after sunset."

"I'd put my money on what the Almanac had to say versus last night's news broadcast," Liddy said as she stretched her hand out. "Let me see the paper. I wanna check some of the Black Friday ads."

I laid the paper on my lap instead of in her hand. "I've been thinking. How about we drive up to Albany first thing tomorrow? We'll make a long weekend of it. Barry mentioned a couple of bookstores that ordered my books. I'd like to squeeze in a visit to one or both between our stops at the malls."

"Sounds terrific. I'm flattered you thought of this all by yourself." Her eyes sparkled. "When was the last time we took a long weekend for ourselves?" She tapped her chin with her finger.

"Albany's got plenty of stores and a variety of places to choose from," I added as she pondered my offer.

"Should I pack a fancy dress for a Saturday night date?" She flitted her eyelids and flashed a coy smile to earn my broad grin.

"While you're cogitating about our weekend, how about more coffee and some toast? We best save room for the feast Susanna's cooking up."

———

JOHN ARRIVED RIGHT behind us with Marie and Phoebe in his truck. Zeb stepped off the front porch as we exited our vehicles. "Sure glad y'all showed up. Maddie's done shooed me out of the kitchen twice. Sam and the boys are busy setting up tables and chairs out back."

"Where's Arnie and Judy?" John pointed to their Red Tahoe next to our Expedition.

"They got here a couple of minutes before y'all did. Reckon Arnie's getting thrown out of the kitchen about now too." Zeb's contagious belly laugh served as an invitation for John and me to head around back while the women went inside.

Zeb snapped his suspenders and announced, "I better wait here. Others should be pulling up shortly."

Susanna directed Sam and the boys with the setup of the tables and chairs beneath twin century-old shade oaks in the backyard. John and I stood out of the way with Arnie until Sam finished and joined us. Shortly after, Larry and Martha showed up with Hal and Phillip right behind.

Arnie greeted Hal, "Where's Hank and Dixie?"

"They'll be along shortly. Hank insisted on testing out Dixie's fancy Jag-U-ar." Hal's contorted face indicated his unabated second thoughts about inviting Hank and Dixie.

Susanna's well-planned Thanksgiving feast cluttered two tables with a conga line of bowls, dishes, and platters brimming with mouthwatering delights right out of the kitchen. Megan and Jeannie laughed and giggled as they filled glasses with tea.

Maddie hollered from the back porch. "Zeb! Sam! I need y'all to tote these birds for me." Maddie's beckoning stirred Zeb and Sam to excuse themselves mid-conversation.

Susanna mustered everyone to take their seats at the tables. Sam stood at the head with Zeb at the opposite end. Maddie hesitated and stood off to the side by the buffet tables until Susanna helped Maddie untie her apron. Zeb pointed to the empty chair between Hal and Phillip. "Here you go Miss Maddie."

Once we all settled into our seats, Sam announced, "I'd like to thank all y'all for joining our family this Thanksgiving." He pointed to the buffet feast that tantalized our senses. "As you can see, there's plenty of turkey and fixings, so don't be bashful. Before I ask Arnie to say grace, I'd first like to express my thanks to Maddie for helping Susanna in the kitchen the last couple of days."

Susanna shouted, "Amen!" spurring applause and whistles as Maddie's ebony cheeks blushed, and her reserved, pearly smile widened.

Sam waited until the ruckus directed toward Maddie subsided. "Susanna also asked me to say a little something, so please bear with me." He eyed Andy and Megan, and a relaxed smile emerged across his face. "Thanksgiving is an annual tradition that brings families and friends together to celebrate the blessings of the past year." Sam paused and panned our affirming faces. "This year we lost a couple of dear friends who we'll sorely miss, but God also blessed us with new friends and family members. Thank you, Hal, Phillip, Maddie and of course, Miss Phoebe, for celebrating with us this year. We're also pleased Hillary decided to call Shiloh home again."

Sam glanced at Arnie and Judy. Just then, the sound of car doors slamming diverted our attention. Sam said, "Sounds like Dixie and Hank have arrived—"

"Why, Sam Simmons, thank you kindly for such an eloquent introduction."

Dixie's syrupy Nawlins twang matched her la-di-da red stilettos and black skinny-leg jeans as she sashayed into view clinging to Hank's arm. Zeb stood and pointed to empty chairs across from Hal, Maddie and Phillip.

"Sorry we're a teensy bit late, but Hank couldn't resist testing out my little convertible on the way over," Dixie shared sporting an unrestrained smirk.

Hank grumbled inaudibly and tried to hide his scowl by dropping his eyes to the back of his chair. Their windblown hairdos provided indisputable evidence of their top-down adventure in Dixie's car. Hank's appearance reflected little change after almost a year in the county jail until he removed his aviator jacket. His tight-tucked, black t-shirt stretched like a second skin across his thick chest. Its snug, short sleeves accentuated his carved biceps.

Hank helped Dixie out of her crimson leather jacket. While he draped it behind her chair, she propped her oversized sunglasses atop her mussed hairdo and inspected her designer jeans and white satin blouse. Her pretentious antics received our undivided attention until she settled into her chair.

Once Hank sat down, Dixie flashed a practiced smile. "Sam, forgive us for disrupting your most gracious oration. Please continue."

Sam stood speechless until Pete nudged him. Sam blinked a couple of times and stammered, "Like I was saying, we're glad everyone could make it. Arnie, would you bless this bounty before us. I guess we're all pretty hungry about now."

After Arnie's "Amen," everyone filled their plates and began eating. Liddy bragged to Judy about our plans for a long weekend away and asked Arnie to excuse our absence from church Sunday morning.

I talked with Hank, Hal and Phillip while Dixie and Zeb shared memories of Harold. I learned Hank was in no hurry to return to the family business, which didn't seem to bother Phillip at all. When Hank joined in Dixie and Zeb's conversation, he confessed how much he missed his father, but it appeared he relished his mother's newfound attention toward him.

Hal spent most of the dinner disengaged. After Phillip abandoned him and joined Jeannie, Pete, Andy and Megan, Hal appeared content to engage Maddie in conversation.

Dixie brought a plate to where Larry and Liddy sat talking. Larry looked over his shoulder with deep furrows growing across his forehead. Dixie smiled, put one hand on his shoulder, and leaned over to set a piece of pumpkin pie in front of him. She paused long enough to see everyone focused upon her draped awkwardly over Larry's shoulder. She then stood and rolled her shoulders and eyes.

"I know y'all don't like me very much. In fact, I know I'm not quite the ideal mother image y'all expect around here, but I'd like to convince all y'all that I'm not as wicked as y'all believe I am. Since I've been back, I've gotten to get to know my boys again and got to see another side of Harold before he passed away. He even promised to make it possible for me to remain in Shiloh as long as my boys will have me."

Dixie eyed Larry's flustered face uncomfortably staring at the pie plate in front of him. She then eyed Maddie swaying her head and then glanced over at me.

"I guess what I'm trying to say is I wanna thank all y'all for sharing your Thanksgiving with my sons and me."

Judy stood and embraced Dixie. Susanna edged around the table and whispered to Dixie, resulting in an odd smile from Dixie. Hal grabbed Phillip and patted Maddie on the back after he whispered something to her. Whatever Hal shared, his words failed to ease Maddie's worried look. Hal then tapped Hank on the shoulder as he and Phillip approached Dixie now engaged with Susanna, Judy and Liddy behind me. Hank stood off to the side while Hal and Phillip assured Dixie she'd be allowed to stay as long as she wanted.

Sam let out a shrill whistle. "Dixie, we're all glad you came today, but those clouds are hinting that we should start cleaning up in a few minutes. But first, Andy's got something he'd like to share."

Andy arose and looked at Megan. "I'm not sure how to say this without either crying or laughing, but Megan and I have some great news."

The commotion around Dixie settled as everyone turned their attention to Andy.

"Some of you heard our good news last night, and I wanna thank those who kept it a secret until now." Andy glared at Pete's puzzled look. "We just learned last week that Pete's gonna be an uncle. Don't know if it'll be a boy or girl yet, but whichever God decides, this child will be nothing short of a miracle."

Pete jumped up and bear hugged his brother and Megan. He then looked at Mary with a crooked grin. "Did you know?" Mary nodded with a smile and shrugged her shoulders.

Hal and Phillip left Dixie and came around the tables to where Andy and Megan greeted everyone. Hank's scowl returned, and Dixie comforted him as they wandered off while everyone else huddled around the glee-filled couple.

Hank barked at Dixie, "We wanted to give dad a grandchild, but the doctor told us she couldn't have kids. I just don't get it! Does God hate me that much?" Dixie pulled him close and attempted to console him as tears ran down his gritted jaw.

Maddie edged her way to Megan. "Child, may I?" Maddie's wrinkled hands gently rested on Megan's abdomen. "Father God, thank ya for answering this dear woman's prayers. Watch over this child, Miss Megan, and Mister Andy in the coming days as they care for this miracle baby."

Marie muttered, "Amen" as she hugged Maddie and looked at Megan.

I looked over my shoulder for Dixie and Hank, but they had disappeared. I walked toward the side yard, but the sound of screeching tires and the whine of Dixie's vehicle abruptly ended my search.

Hal walked up. "Don't think Hank was quite ready to handle their good news like the rest of us. He'll get over it though."

"I hope so." I stared in the direction of the screaming engine racing through town.

Hal patted my shoulder. "I don't think either of them will be around Shiloh much longer either way."

I looked at Hal's forlorn gaze and asked, "Why would you say that? Dixie just—"

"Don't believe it for a second. Dixie's just waiting for Gus to read dad's will and see if he left her what he promised."

"What's that?"

"His shares in the family business. Dad told me a few weeks back he placed all our property and the home into a family trust but decided she deserved a source of income. So, he left her his shares of H. H. Archer Holding Company stock. That should give her enough income to help her until she gets back on her feet."

I asked, "But what if she sells her shares?"

"She can't. She'd need to have majority consent, and I doubt that'll happen." Hal smirked. "How about one last piece of pie before they carry it all back into the kitchen?"

———

THE ALMANAC'S UNCANNY accuracy brought the promised rain showers as we drove home. Liddy broke the silence. "Maddie said something to me before we left that concerns me."

I glanced over at Liddy staring out the passenger side window. "What'd she say to you?"

"She didn't know who to tell because she didn't want any more problems between her and Dixie, but she felt she needed to confide in someone."

"About what? It's not a secret they don't get along very well, but Hal seems to think Dixie will be leaving in a couple of weeks anyway."

Liddy turned with a fearful stare on her face. "Maddie told me Dixie's got a gun."

"How does she know?"

"Maddie said she was cleaning Dixie's bedroom like she's been doing since she moved into Harold's old room. She didn't see Dixie's handbag lying on the bed, and when she yanked the blankets to make the bed, the purse tumbled onto the floor. Maddie didn't want any reason for Dixie to get angry, so Maddie bent down to put everything back into the handbag and saw the pistol beside the purse. She said she was afraid to touch it, but she didn't want Dixie to find out that the contents of her bag had spilled out onto the floor. She used her apron to grab the pistol and slide it back into the handbag along with some makeup that spilled. Dixie walked in before she could place it on the dresser."

"What did Dixie say?"

"Dixie accused her of snooping, but Maddie told her it fell harmlessly on the floor when she was making the bed. Funny, Maddie felt bad and confessed she might not of have been all that forthcoming with Dixie, but she didn't lie either."

I gripped the steering wheel even tighter. "Dixie may have had a reason to carry a pistol back in Louisiana, but I doubt she has any reason for it here. All the same, that's another reason I hope she decides to leave soon."

Liddy sighed. "You're right, but would you let Hal or Phillip know?"

I nodded. "For now, let's focus on our weekend away. Okay?"

Liddy forced a dimple-filled smile and nodded, but her hazel eyes revealed her lingering concern.

CHAPTER THIRTY-TWO

ALTHOUGH LIDDY DRAGGED ME AROUND TWO MALLS OVER THE WEEKEND, I didn't put up much of a fuss. We also visited the Book Nook, a cozy downtown bookstore Barry told me about, before we began shopping. The courtesy stop lasted a wee bit longer than the quick few minutes I had assured Liddy.

Carolyn, the owner of the store, enjoyed showing us where she displayed her inventory of Jessie's Story. She asked me to sign a couple of copies for herself and her daughter, which instigated several customers to inquire about the book. An hour later, Carolyn thanked me for stopping and assisting in the sale of a dozen copies. I left amazed how those I spoke with recollected the news of Jessie's horrific tragedy four years ago.

At the second bookstore, the manager, Gregory, showed off his display of my books along with his recent order for two more cases. Liddy breathed a sigh of relief after I said goodbye to Gregory and handed him my business card. She clutched my arm and took control throughout the rest of the weekend.

Our headlights illuminated the stoop while I maneuvered our luggage through the kitchen door and flipped on the lights. I set our luggage aside and nearly collided into Liddy as she carried some of our many shopping bags through the doorway.

"I'll get the rest while you adjust the thermostat and turn on more lights."

As I lowered the tailgate, Liddy ran onto the stoop and screamed. "Theo! Theo! Somebody's broken into our home."

"What do you mean? How do you know?"

She grabbed my arm and pulled me into the kitchen. "Set those bags down and come see for yourself."

The drawer of my reading table hung halfway out with my journal and notes strewn all over the floor. Liddy then muttered and pointed, "Look!"

The unlatched hall closet door caught my eye. "Let me check the rest of the house. You stay here."

But, Liddy followed me into hallway and whispered, "I'll look upstairs while you check the back rooms."

I glared back at Liddy and barked, "No! Stay put!"

I first poked my head into her craft room. Her easel laid toppled on the floor with her work table shoved aside from its usual location beneath the window. The closet stood wide open, much of her supplies dumped out onto the floor.

Liddy's unrestrained whisper filled the hallway, "Theo. Did you find anything?"

"Just more things out of place. Stay there. I still gotta check our bedroom."

I grabbed the door handle, took a deep breath, and opened it enough to reach in and flip the light switch before opening the door further. Dresser and bedside table drawers hung open with some contents scattered on the floor and other garments precariously hanging from other open drawers. A quick peek into our bathroom revealed nothing disturbed except the raised toilet seat. In our walk-in closet, boxes, shoes and clothes appeared hastily shoved willy-nilly. My eyes then darted to the far corner of the closet. Only a shadow filled the void where my Pop's old office safe should have sat.

I stepped back out of the closet and looked toward the hallway with my hands on my hips. "Liddy! Call the sheriff's office. We've been robbed."

Liddy stepped from the shadows of the hallway. "I'm right here. What's missing?"

"Pop's old safe."

Mitch arrived thirty minutes later. He followed me through the house until I pointed to the empty closet corner and described my Pop's antiquated, steel safe. He scribbled more notes before he called to report the break-in and then walked the perimeter of the house.

Liddy remained in the bedroom resisting her urge to straighten the drawers and return clothes where they belonged. She tucked her hands beneath her crossed arms, fighting back her tears. The sudden sound of Liddy's craft room window being shoved open startled me.

"Mister Phillips, I've got something to show you." Mitch's smile looked in the open window. "Is this your safe?" His flashlight lit the ground beneath the window.

I stuck my head out and saw Pop's safe laying upside down, wedged askew in the sod. "I'll be right there."

I said to Liddy, hotfooting it down the hallway, "Mitch found the safe."

By the time I reached Mitch, Liddy was leaning her head out the window. "Has it been opened?" she asked.

Mitch smiled. "No ma'am, and whoever tried to steal this thing must have realized how heavy it is and how hard it would be to open."

I knelt down to inspect it.

"Don't touch it Mister Phillips." Mitch blocked my hands. "A detective is on his way. We need to look for fingerprints and take photos."

"Can I borrow your flashlight?"

I squatted down and examined the lock on the safe. Outside a couple of scratches and paint residue from the window sill, it had thwarted the tenacious thief's intentions. I sighed and looked up at Liddy. "We got lucky."

"What's going on, Mister P?"

Mitch shined his flashlight on Pete's face. "Hey, Pete. Looks as if someone tried to rob the Phillips."

Pete offered me a hand as I stood. "I had a funny feeling last night, so Mary and I stopped by on the way to her house. I jiggled the doors and walked around the house, but everything seemed fine." Pete pointed. "I can tell both of ya that darn thing wasn't here last night when I checked."

Mitch grabbed his pad and pen. "What time did ya stop by?"

Pete thought a second. "About ten-thirty."

I eyed Mitch. "That means whoever did this likely came after Pete stopped by."

Mitch grinned. "Or, by what I see, Pete probably scared whoever was in the house. The burglar panicked and ran off when he couldn't handle the safe, which also indicates he worked alone."

"Nothing got stolen?" Pete asked.

"Doesn't seem to be." I scratched my scalp. "I don't get it. Why didn't he steal the TV or Liddy's jewelry? Why rifle through drawers and closets and only take this old thing?"

Mitch slid his pen into the top of his pad. "As a calculated guess, I'd say this is what he came after." He shined his flashlight on the safe once again.

Liddy leaned out the window further. "How would anyone know about this old thing? It's not like we've got a lot of valuables or cash stashed inside, just mostly personal documents and house papers."

"I don't know Miss Phillips. If we catch this guy, maybe you can ask him."

Two hours later we sat in our living room. Mitch entered with his detective carrying a black bag. "We took photos and dusted for fingerprints. Miss Phillips, you can put everything back if you want." He looked at me and raised a plastic bag. "Look familiar?"

I stared at the broken brown button and a torn swatch of green and brown cloth. "Not at all. Where did you find them?"

"Under the safe." Mitch eyed his detective and then looked back at our tired faces. "I can't be sure, but I'd speculate your thief got his jacket snagged when he muscled the safe out the window. If this button and the patch of material are what I believe, it's likely he got his arm snagged trying to muscle the safe out the window, which further leads me to speculate why he abandoned the safe and fled."

"That makes sense. Where's our safe?"

"Pete volunteered to clean it up for you."

Pete grunted, grappling with the safe through the open kitchen door. "Where do ya want this thing?"

———

"DID YOU SLEEP okay?" Liddy asked as I walked into the kitchen squinting.

"What time is it anyway?"

"Seven-fifteen, and I gotta leave in a few minutes. I'm glad you finally got up. I climbed out of bed before dawn and made sure everything's back in its proper place." Liddy swayed her head back and forth as she poured a cup coffee for me.

"There's a lot about last night that kept me from getting a good night's sleep. The most haunting question I can't answer is why after rifling through the house did the thief focus on that safe only to abandon it after muscling it out the window? Seemed pretty industrious to believe one person could've walked away with that thing." My fingertips massaged my warm coffee cup while my sleep-deprived eyes focused upon Liddy.

Liddy slipped the car keys into her jacket pocket, slung her carry-all bag over her shoulder and grabbed her umbrella. She leaned over and kissed my furrowed forehead.

"Whoever did this is long gone by now. Why us and what our perpetrator was after will just have to remain a mystery."

She pointed her folded umbrella toward the living room. "Outside of minor repairs to the window sill in my craft room, everything seems fine." She stroked my hair with her fingers and stared at me until I looked into her hazel eyes.

"You're probably right," I smirked. "Our burglar probably sized up Pete and figured he selected the wrong home to break into, just like Mitch suggested. I've little doubt my Pop's old safe bit him pretty good too. That blasted thing weighs at least a hundred and fifty pounds."

Liddy giggled, jiggling her keys. "Let's just say we got the last laugh on that poor fella. I'll see you this afternoon. I shouldn't be too late."

The phone rang after she left. "Theo, this is Hal. The sheriff called me first thing this morning. Sure hated to hear about the break-in. It must'a put a damper on your weekend."

"It certainly caught our attention last night, but to tell you the truth, we feel we had the last laugh on whoever it was."

"How's that?"

I gave Hal a few details but figured he already knew most of them from Mitch's report.

"I'm certainly glad nothing got stolen and more importantly that you two weren't hurt. If it's okay with you, I'd like Larry to print a story about the break-in and mention I've asked City Council to approve my request to restore the city police department."

"Isn't the sheriff department policing Shiloh and the surrounding community?"

Hal sighed. "Yeah and doing an admirable job too, but they only dispatch one patrol car from Alexandria. We could use what we pay the county to reinstate our local police force. We may not have a huge crime problem, but we could do a better job controlling city traffic and discourage further thefts and vandalism."

"You think you can get City Council to go along with your proposal?"

"If you and Larry nudge them a little with a timely article."

"I'll see what I can do. Before you go, everything okay with Dixie and Hank?"

"I haven't talked much with Hank, but Dixie says he told her what happened between him and Megan. She made it sound as though Hank's considering leaving Shiloh to get a fresh start."

"What do you and Phillip think about that?"

"Whatever Hank decides, I'm okay with it. So is Phillip. Hank's still working out his demons, and without dad around, he probably would be better off away from the constant reminders in Shiloh."

Three loud raps on the front door disrupted our call. I looked out the kitchen window and saw John's truck. I gave Hal a quick goodbye and hung up just before I opened the door.

John stomped his feet on the doormat and followed me into the kitchen.

"What brought you here this morn? Aren't you supposed to be at school?"

"They can get along without me for a bit. Pete told me about your break-in," John said with a relaxed grin.

"The house is okay, but it sure gave us a scare when we first got home."

"Pete joked about your father's old safe when he told me how he struggled to tote it back into the house," John said with a reflective smile. "And we both know how pigheaded strong ol' Pete can be too."

"Whoever it was, we suspect Pete's responsible for scaring him off when he stopped by Saturday night, though I don't think Pete realized it at the time," I said.

"Funny you should mention that." John paused to run his hand through his hair. "Early Saturday evening, Ringo followed me over to Marie's for dinner. About the time she set a large piece of spice cake in front of me, Ringo began growling and barking. When I stepped outside to check, I saw a light shining around my cabin. I immediately took off with Ringo two steps ahead. When I got about a football field from my place, I saw someone shine a flashlight out of one of my windows. Before I could grab his collar, Ringo bolted ahead of me barking up a storm. I caught up to him at the far corner of the house. His barks had subsided into angry snarls, but whoever it was had hightailed it into the woods."

"And?" I asked as my eyes also urged him to continue.

John wiped his cheeks as his eyes connected with mine. "I checked inside and discovered an open window in the front room. Muddy prints marked the floor. After a quick walk-through, I secured the windows and door and left Ringo inside to discourage a return visit. When I told Marie what I found, she said drifters wander onto the property once in awhile, but she'd never had any problems. Of course, she pointed to her double barrel hanging on the wall. She persuaded me to not worry about it, especially with Ringo on duty."

I paused to consider John's raised brow and sideward grin. "Hold on a second. Your place is five miles from town. I seriously doubt there's any connection. Just a coincidence if you ask me."

John shook his head. "I tend not to believe something happens by chance. I left a bunch of tools out on my porch and in my truck bed that afternoon. This person had no interest in stealing them nor anything else as far as I can tell. Guess I'm just thankful I don't have an old safe too."

My eyes widened. "What are you trying to say?"

He turned his head and pointed toward the television and some of Liddy's nicer knick-knacks displayed around the living room. "Your thief evidently had something specific in mind, but it sure had nothing to do with pawning your tv or Liddy's valuables."

"So tell me why in Sam Hill would anyone break into my house and not steal the obvious? And, if by some strange coincidence, the same person just mighta snuck into your place earlier that evening, what was he looking for?"

John shrugged. "That's why I stopped. Wanted to see what you might think."

I sank into my chair. "The only thing I can think of that is that leather pouch and its dated contents, but what value would any of it have to someone else?"

"Where'd you put it?"

"With the rest of our house papers, in the safe." I found John's curious smile staring back at me. "But who'd risk breaking into a home for that? How'd they know what to look for?"

John folded his arms over his chest. "I imagine, whoever it might've been, knew what might've been inside the leather pouch. When he didn't find it in my spartan cabin or rifling through your drawers and closets, your safe made logical sense to him. I reckon he figured it contained something of value."

"But why?" I stammered, trying to spit out my racing thoughts. "If you're right, the only person, or persons, who might know the value would be the Archers." I shook my head, doubting my conclusion.

"Don't rule the possibility out. Something's brewing with that family, but we can't jump to conclusions. Besides, I don't believe any of the Archers had the opportunity or gumption to break into our homes. I'll wager whoever did is still in the area though."

"Can Liddy and I borrow Ringo for a few days?" I said, trying to laugh.

"I doubt you'll have another intrusion, but keep your doors and windows locked. Besides, Ringo keeps Marie company during the day. She might not like him not being around."

After John left, I called Larry. I said nothing about John's visit. I felt keeping that under wraps might prove beneficial in the investigation. If the thief was still around town, we didn't need Larry juxtaposing John's and our break-in in print. Larry liked Hal's suggestion to tie our break-in with Hal's proposal to reactivate Shiloh's police department, especially in light of the recent vandalism the Sentinel suffered.

CHAPTER THIRTY-THREE

"Is Woogie going to Sanctuary's Christmas Social tonight?" I asked Wiley as he slathered the back of my neck.

Wiley slid his razor up and down the leather strop attached to the barber chair. "Sure enough. Hub's locking up tonight, so I can leave a bit early and drop Woogie off at the community center." Wiley adjusted my head as he slid the razor down the back of my neck. "Gotta tell ya. Malvinia and me both are sure proud of that boy. Thanks to Coach Priestly and those Sanctuary meetings, the changes we've seen in both Bobo and Woogie are nothing short of a miracle. Their grades have shot up, and they're now both talking about going to college." Wiley glanced at Hub's wide grin as he trimmed a customer's sideburns.

Hub pointed his scissors at Wiley and me. "Yes, sir! Bobo's gonna be the first in our family to get a bona fide college degree, and that's a fact, Mister Phillips." Hub returned to snipping around his customer's ears while he bragged away about both Bobo and Woogie.

Wiley wiped the back of my neck with a warm, moist towel. I asked as he adjusted the collar of my shirt, "How's it going with Wilson, Woogie's daddy?"

Wiley snapped the damp towel over his shoulder. "Hadn't seen hide nor hair of him since before church Sunday. Reckon he'll be back when he gets a mind to or when he needs something." He splashed Clubman lotion on his hands and rubbed my neck and cheeks. "Your missus just pulled up."

I waved at Liddy and pulled out my wallet. "You tell Woogie and Bobo that we've got some goodies for tonight."

After I buckled up, Liddy wrinkled her nose. "You know I can't stand that tonic Wiley puts on you."

"Me neither, but I'm not about to tell him so."

"Bernie mentioned that Alex wanted to come tonight too. Hope you don't mind, but I promised that we'd pick him up along with the pastries we ordered."

"That's fine with me, but let's swing by the house first. I want to change my clothes while you put on my favorite aftershave," Liddy said with a wink and pursed lips.

———

WE PULLED INTO Priestly Park a little after six and parked across from the vehicles already parked out front for Sanctuary's last gathering before Christmas. Alex and I grabbed Bernie's dessert delights with their Greek names written on each box. Without Alex's help, though, none of us knew which was what inside the boxes. We just knew they're all good.

John greeted us as we walked in. "The kids are going to appreciate the fact that you and Liddy showed up for our Christmas social. Why don't you put those in the kitchen?"

By the time of the party's advertised six-thirty start time, the main floor of the community center brimmed with teenagers under the watchful eye of a handful of adults. Even after Pete caught everyone's attention and John announced the start of the night's activities, more kids wandered inside.

Woogie and Bobo straggled in a few minutes late, but Wiley's old truck rarely left second gear whenever he drove around town anyway. Malvinia often joked about how it was a good thing they lived across the alley from the barbershop; otherwise, he'd always be late for work and dinner.

Liddy helped Jeannie greet students by the door. John and I stood off to the side and admired the young adults who had taken over leadership of the group.

John whispered, "Jessie would've been pretty proud to see how Sanctuary's turned out."

"At least as proud as you, I imagine." I stood shoulder to shoulder with John sharing the same stoic, arms-crossed pose. Sharing an occasional wisecrack, we watched the interaction between the students and their young leaders, the original members of Sanctuary.

After everyone had grabbed a pastry and a coke and filled the tables lining the community center's main floor, John embarrassed Liddy and me by recognizing us for providing the food and drinks. He then asked how many students had a copy of Jessie's Story at home. More than half raised their hands, earning a smile on my face.

"For all the others, I'd like to remind you how Mister Phillips dedicated the proceeds of his book to Sanctuary." He then looked at me. "By any chance, do you have a few of your books with you?"

Liddy nodded and disappeared out the door.

"I think my wife's getting them right now."

John laughed. "Would you mind autographing some tonight?"

Liddy handed me a half-empty box and sat down at a table near the door. Mary joined her and processed a few credit card purchases with her cellphone. I gripped the technology I was most familiar with, my pen.

At eight-thirty, Mary moved to the piano, and we all sang Christmas carols. "Silent Night" ended the evening. By nine o'clock, Liddy and I stood outside by the front door zipping our jackets. Pete, Mary, Jeannie, Jay and Jim straightened up inside and began to turn off the lights. All the students had left except for Woogie and Bobo, who laughed and swung at the playground across from the parking lot. Liddy and I walked over and found out Marcellus was on his way.

Liddy sat in one of the swings and joined the boys. I walked in place as the dampness penetrated the soles of my shoes. I shivered in the cold air, exacerbated by Shiloh Creek a stone's throw away, as I listened to Liddy cutting up with the boys.

"Y'all going to stay with them?" John asked poking his head out of his truck window.

"Bobo's dad is on the way. Go ahead. We got it."

While Pete locked the doors, Alex ran over to tell us he was riding home with Pete and Mary.

Bobo jumped off his swing as Marcellus drove up. "Thanks Mister and Missus Phillips."

Woogie yelled, "Geronimo," a moment before he kicked hard and launched himself off the swing, landing a couple of steps in front of me. He wiped his hands on his jacket and stretched out his right hand. "That goes for me too. I think it's great what you're doing for Sanctuary."

I shook his hand, but his torn, buttonless jacket sleeve captured my attention. "Thanks, Woogie." The other sleeve had a brown button similar to the one Mitch had found. "I like your camo jacket, Woogie. Are you warm enough?"

Liddy paused, her arm resting on his shoulder.

Bobo shouted from the back seat of his dad's car. "You coming?"

"Is this your jacket, Woogie?"

He gave me an odd look before stepping toward the car. "No, sir. It belongs to my dad. He left it at PawPaw's house."

"You're almost as big as your dad now. Have a good evening."

After Marcellus drove off, Liddy clutched my arm. "Do you think?"

I walked toward our vehicle with my arm around Liddy. "Not sure what to think, but I'm beginning to believe John when he said there're no such thing as coincidences."

———

EARLY THE FOLLOWING morning, I stoked the lingering embers from the previous night's fire and added two pieces of split oak. I sat down in my recliner with a cup of coffee. Thoughts about the likelihood of Woogie's dad as the one who broke into our house had deprived me of restful sleep. I needed to mull over the possibilities. If in fact, Wilson Edwards turned out to be our burglar, how would Wiley, Woogie and Malvinia react?

My journal's daily passage referred me to John's Gospel where Jesus declared, "The man who does not enter the sheep pen by the gate but climbs in some other way is a thief and a robber. The man who enters by the gate is the shepherd of his sheep. He knows his sheep by name, and they respond to his voice."

After a few minutes of rereading the passage, I unscrewed the cap on my pen and wrote, "A thief breaks into a house at night with intentions to steal what is not his to possess. A thief is willing to harm, even destroy, if necessary. Only those who enter another's home the proper way demonstrate the abundant life God blesses upon his children. Our thief showed signs of compassion by not needlessly wrecking our home until he discovered what he came to steal. But then, our thief abandoned what he intended to steal when he felt it wasn't worth the effort any longer. Lord, how should I respond if our thief proves to be Woogie's father?"

I stared into the gray dawn until the reflection of the fireplace dancing on the window had caught my attention. At that moment, I realized the best person to confide in was Joe. I felt he alone would understand what John and I shared with one another about our break-ins. Joe certainly could help me decide how to handle what Woogie's jacket indicated.

During breakfast, Liddy affirmed my decision to seek Joe's advice, though she had no idea what John and I had discussed as the likely motive behind the theft attempt. I kept wondering what possible interest Wilson Edwards would have in an old document that had value only to John.

———

SUSANNA GREETED ME when I entered Joe's office. "Joe's running a few minutes late. Would you like some coffee?"

I nodded with a smile but motioned her to stay seated. After I poured a cup for myself, I turned holding the pot. "Need a refill?"

Susanna smiled and held up her cup. While topping it off, I asked, "So how's it feel to be an expectant grandmother?"

She sipped her black coffee and smirked, "Old."

"You're not old. God's just making it possible for you to spoil your first grandchild while you're young enough to enjoy doing so." I returned the coffee pot and sat on the sofa in the waiting area. "Remember, Liddy and I have been at this grandparent racket for almost a dozen years. We felt the same way when Tommy and Kari first told us their good news too."

"When Andy announced he wanted to marry Megan, I accepted the fact that my hopes for grandchildren rested with Pete and Jeannie. But he certainly appears to be in no hurry, and Jeannie boasts about her career in real estate and property management."

I chuckled. "What our grown children wind up doing with their lives isn't always for us to have a handle on. Love, marriage and babies happen as God's blessings and in his timing, not theirs nor ours."

Susanna gave me a skeptical raised brow.

"You want proof? Remember when you and Sam first started dating? What plans got changed after the two of you fell in love and decided to get married? How did Pete's birth change y'all's lives?"

"Sorry I'm late Theo. I stopped home for lunch and enjoyed a few extra minutes with Missy after a full morning in court." He removed his overcoat and motioned for me to follow him into his office. "Any messages Susanna?"

Susanna handed Joe a pink note, then looked at me and mouthed. "Thanks."

"So what's this about your break-in you need to talk to me about?" Joe grabbed the phone on his desk and dialed.

I started to reply, but Joe put a finger up as he raised the receiver to his ear. "Gus, this is Joe returning your call. What's up?" After a flurry of muttered "got-its," Joe jotted on the back of the pink note and said, "Next Thursday, two o'clock, your office. Thanks, Gus. See you then." He hung up his phone and gazed out his window toward city hall for a frozen moment.

"Everything all right?"

"Hal stopped by yesterday. He asked me to represent him and Phillip at the reading of Harold's final testament."

"Are they expecting issues?"

"All I can say is an Arians has never represented an Archer before yesterday." Joe broke his distant look and turned to me with a friendly smile. "Now, what do you have for me?"

"Mitch showed Liddy and me some of the evidence retrieved from our home—a large broken brown button and a swatch of torn cloth—he suggested whoever was in the house snagged his jacket when he muscled our safe out of the window before he ran off."

Joe nodded. "And?"

"And we think we know whose jacket the button and swatch came from."

Joe folded his hands in front of him on his desk. "Pray tell? Who?"

I took a deep breath. "Wilson Edwards."

Joe's eyes opened wide. "What made you conclude that?"

"Woogie had on his dad's jacket last night at Sanctuary's Christmas social, and its torn right sleeve had a button missing. When I asked Woogie about the jacket, he said his dad had left it at his Paw-paw's house."

"Wiley and Malvinia's house?"

I nodded. "When I spoke with Wiley yesterday at the barbershop, he told me Wilson disappeared Sunday morning, and they haven't heard from him since."

Joe paused a moment to scribble some notes. "Have you told anyone about this?"

"Just you."

"Let me get ahold of Mitch and see what he thinks. If Wilson is the one who broke into your house, why?"

I told Joe all I could about the state of the house when Liddy and I came home Sunday evening and what Mitch and his detective suggested about the break-in based on the evidence. Joe wrote down some more notes as he prodded me for details.

"Here's what Mitch doesn't know. John visited me Monday morning and told me someone broke into his cabin Saturday evening, but his prowler vanished by the time he and Ringo showed up. Just like our house, nothing ended up stolen."

"What did the two of you conclude?"

"John suggested, for some strange reason, it appears this burglar might have been after the agreement we showed you a few weeks ago. I questioned his logic since it only has value to him."

Joe rocked back in his chair. "That's not entirely accurate. It's true it only has monetary value if John chooses to exercise it, but the Archers could've been willing to pay for its retrieval as insurance against John changing his mind."

"Are you insinuating that someone in the Archer family offered to pay Wilson to get their hands on it?"

Joe smirked and slowly rocked back and forth.

"Only you, me and John knew where the agreement ended up after John declined to exercise the legal claim on it."

"It's very possible someone else could have speculated where it wound up."

"Who?"

"Let me deal with that possibility for the time being. Where's the agreement now?"

I said with some reassurance, "Still safe and secure inside my father's old safe."

"I'll make some calls and see if we can get Mitch and his detectives to follow up on your lead about Wilson." Joe leaned forward. "You do realize that we won't be able to keep Woogie and Wiley out of this. The sheriff's department will want to get their hands on that jacket."

"I wish there were another way, but Wiley can help Woogie get over their shared disappointment that Wilson may have done this and may face more prison time."

"Let's take this one step at a time. If Mitch agrees to pursue this and they arrest Wilson, maybe we'll find out whether John's theory is right or not."

———

SATURDAY AFTERNOON WHILE I was raking leaves in the front yard, Mitch pulled up.

"Wanted you to know we arrested Wilson Edwards this morning."

"Where was he?"

"We found him holed up in the old abandoned mansion north of town."

"Liddy and I know that place. We ventured out there not long after we moved here."

"It was his flashlight that tipped us off. A patrol car noticed a light shining in the old house. The officer spooked Wilson, and he tried to run but didn't get far. Thought you also oughta know that I just stopped by Mister Edward's house. He's going to break the news to Woogie."

"Thanks, Mitch. Has Wilson said anything yet?"

Mitch shook his head. "He lawyered up, and Gus Appleton got called."

Liddy arrived on the porch. "What's happened?"

Mitch tipped his hat. "I better run. Just thought you should know."

I turned to Liddy as Mitch pulled away. "They caught Wilson."

CHAPTER THIRTY-FOUR

LEAVES LITTERED THE SIDEWALK AS WE BRAVED THE COLD AND WALKED TO church. After scurrying across Main Street, John exited his truck and greeted us.

"I need to talk to you two." He tucked his hands deep into his pants pockets and headed inside.

John blew into his reddened hands as he scanned the faces of everyone wrapped up in conversations of their own. "I just stopped to check in on Wiley and Malvinia. Woogie's struggling over his father's arrest and wants to talk to you."

Liddy peered out the corner of her eye at me. "Of course. When?"

"Malvinia's making dinner for us and expects us right after church."

I felt Liddy squeeze my hand. "Are you going?"

"Marie and I will both be there. Who'd want to miss out on one of Malvinia's Sunday dinners?"

Arnie preached a heart-wrenching Advent message about God's love. When he reached his conclusion, he closed his Bible and gazed upon the congregation. His final comments struck a chord.

"Regarding God's admonition on the proper manifestation of his love, God desires us to demonstrate his love, not by merely reading about it, writing about it or even talking about it. In truth, we all tend to be pretty good at those things." Arnie paused with an affirming grin and gentle nod of his head. "However, God searches for evidence of his love in our deeds and attitudes as we respond to others. In just seventeen days, we will once again celebrate God's greatest love gift that mankind has ever known. Therefore, as we approach Christmas this year, please be mindful that the only gift God desires from each of us is to witness his love shared through our deeds and attitude."

After we filed out of the sanctuary, I waited for Joe and Nick to exit the choir room while Liddy occupied Missy and the twins.

"Joe, can I talk to you a moment?" I smiled at Nick but tugged on Joe's arm.

Joe looked at Nick. "I'll be right there." After Nick left, he turned to me. "What's up?"

"Wilson is in custody."

"I didn't hear anything, but that's good news."

"Kinda. Mitch stopped by and told me about his arrest but mentioned he lawyered up and called Gus."

"That's smart for any felon, especially one on parole. He stands to lose a lot if convicted." Joe stroked his chin. "He called Gus?"

"That's what Mitch told me, and now we've been invited to dinner with Wiley and Malvinia right after church. Evidently, Woogie's not handling the news well and asked to speak with us."

"I'll make some calls. Touch base with me tomorrow morning if you don't hear from me."

———

THE MOUTHWATERING AROMA of Malvinia's ham filled their home. Marie and Liddy ventured into the kitchen while John and I joined Wiley and a sullen Woogie in the living room.

"Liddy and I are pleased you invited us to dinner. We've heard so much about your home. It's the oldest house in the center of town, isn't it?" I inspected the decorated mantle after I sat in one of their fireside armchairs.

"That's a fact alright. Every creak and crack in this old home testifies to its old bones, just like me." Wiley chuckled as he admired the built-in bookcases lined with books and framed photos on either side of their red brick fireplace and hearth.

John leaned forward, elbows on his knees. "I remember mom and dad dragged me here for many Sunday dinners as a youngster. I didn't appreciate the smells coming out of the kitchen like I do today."

Wiley's eyes lit up. "You was no bigger than Woogie back then." He reached over and poked Woogie's propped up knee. "Look at Coach Priestly today. I bet you'll grow up to be just as big, thanks to your Maw-Maw's cooking. Ain't that right, John?"

John stared at Woogie's reluctant grin.

During their exchange, I tried to envision John at Woogie's age as well as Zack and Betty Priestly sharing a similar conversation with Wiley about John thirty years ago.

"It don't matter none," Woogie mumbled with a doleful pout.

I asked, "Why would you say such a thing?"

He examined his Paw-Paw and John. "I'm going to end up like my Pa anyway."

"What you become is up to you, unless you choose to believe your Pa's circumstances will hold you back." I clasped my hands against my chest and looked to John and Wiley.

"Mister P's right. Your Pa's made some mistakes affecting his life, but they're not your mistakes." John sat back in his armchair, eyes glued to Woogie.

"But—"

Wiley blurted, "Buts are for cowards and for those afraid to take control of their own life. Your Pa don't want you to fall into the same life he carved for himself. He loves you, boy! More than you'll ever understand."

Woogie buried his chin into his chest.

"Answer me this, Woogie. How did you always manage to break away from all those defenders when you ran with the ball?" John glared at Woogie.

"I didn't want to be dragged down without fighting my hardest because I'd let you and the team down."

"Exactly! It's the same choice you can make about life too." John's hard stare relaxed and his brow raised.

Woogie sat taller and stared at his Paw-Paw. "Hadn't thought about it like that before. How can I help my Pa wiggle out of this mess he's in now?"

I edged forward in my chair. "Do you want to talk to your Pa?" I glanced at Wiley and John. "I suspect you could get him to understand that his future rests in his decision to cooperate and fess up."

"We believe someone put him up to it," John added.

Woogie looked at his Paw-Paw. "Will you take me?"

Wiley patted Woogie's knee. "First thing in the morning."

"Okay menfolk. Dinner's on the table."

———

LIDDY BEGGED ME to drop her off at school Monday morning, so I could go by Zeb's and pick out a Christmas tree. We'd been so stymied by our weekend away and the events since that our Christmas decorations remained in storage.

"Promise me you'll trust Jim and Jay to pick out the right tree." Liddy leaned over and kissed me.

"Just as soon as I stop by the post office and check in on Hal. We'll spend tonight getting ready for Santa. I promise." I added a cheery smile as she got out and closed the passenger door.

I checked Liddy's note and walked into the Post Office to pick up the postage for her Christmas card mailing.

"Good morning, Ray. How are you staying busy on Friday nights lately?"

Ray fumbled through a drawer and counted ten books of stamps for me. "Basketball season started this week." He continued to smile as he handed me the stamps and my receipt.

"I'll try to bring my sons to a couple of games over the Christmas break. Thanks, Ray."

I walked toward the door, tucking the stamps into my jacket pocket when I got shoved aside. "Hey, watch where you're going please," I muttered as a knee-jerk response. I looked up and realized who barged past me.

"Hank, is everything alright?"

He looked over his shoulder from his place at the end of the line. "Yeah, just peachy. What's it to you anyway?"

"You just rammed into me without saying a word. I guessed you had something on your mind. That's all." Hank's disinterested glare lasted but a moment.

"Look Mister Phillips!" Hank grumbled. "Why don't you mind your own damn business? I'm getting sick and tired of you sticking your inquisitive nose into my family's business."

"Hank, let me remind you where you are," Ray barked.

Hank glared at Ray. "Do I look stupid or something?"

"No, but you sure are acting pretty stupid at the moment. I suggest you apologize and calm down or leave immediately," Ray snapped with a stern look at Hank.

Hank measured Ray and ground his jaw before he muttered. "Sorry, folks."

I winked at Ray and slipped out the door to avoid inciting Hank's hair-trigger anger any further.

———

"Need a hand Hilly?"

Hillary knelt by her desk retrieving some papers. She stood and extended her free hand toward me. "Thanks. Just straightening up from the whirlwind that blew through here a few minutes ago."

"What happened?"

"Hank stormed out of here after getting into an argument with Hal."

"What about?"

"I'm not sure. After they barked at each other, Hank stomped out of Hal's office, slammed the door behind him and stood beside my desk huffing with his jugular veins about to pop. I suggested he take a couple of deep breaths and calm down. That suggestion didn't communicate well. He responded by sweeping his hand across my desk, then blasted me with several off-color suggestions before he headed down the hallway toward the rear exit."

"What'd Hal say about it?"

"He poked his head out, saw the mess and asked if I was okay. He apologized while he helped pick up most of the mess."

"Glad you're here." A frazzled Hal stood in his office doorway. "We need to talk."

Hal waved me into his office, then peered at Hillary. "Again, I hope you know how sorry I am."

Hillary smiled. "I'll hold all your calls for a while."

I stood in front of Hal's desk. "What just happened?"

"With Hank?"

"Of course with Hank. He just darn near bowled me over in the post office lobby a minute ago and then launched into another tirade about me interfering again. Thankfully, Ray Abernathy intervened, and I scooted out the door."

Hal leaned up against his desk. "You won't believe what Hank and Dixie have dreamed up."

"Considering recent events, there's not much I won't believe."

Hal adjusted his rolled up shirt sleeves. "They want to sell their shares of H. H. Archer Holding Company. I reminded Hank that as far as I was concerned, Dad would have to rise out of his grave before I'd allow that to take place. Hank smirked and then asked if Phillip and I preferred that they both left Shiloh. When I told him I wouldn't stop either of them, he insisted, in no uncertain terms, that we needed to buy them out. Otherwise, they'd sell their shares to another interested party."

"What'd you say?"

Hal snickered. "Phillip nor I have that kind of money. Since Hank and Dixie both want to sell their shares, Phillip and I can't stop them. They will hold the majority of outstanding shares in the company as of Thursday."

"What're you going to do?"

"I don't rightly know. Threats obviously won't work. And, confidentially, I'm pretty sure Gus Appleton is in cahoots with Dixie and Hank, which is why I asked Joe Arians to represent Phillip and me."

"Joe will think of something."

Hal shook his head. "They've got us over a barrel unless Phillip and I can scrounge enough money to keep the shares in the family like my dad, his father, and his father before him, desired. Plain and simple, we need a miracle by Thursday."

I placed my hand on Hal's shoulder. "Just remember, God's in control."

"No matter what happens, we'll at least have our home. Just hope it'll be enough of a consolation if they sell the family business out from under us."

LATER THAT AFTERNOON, I waited for Liddy outside the school with the Christmas tree Marie and Jay helped me select. After we got home, she pulled out boxes of Christmas decorations while I secured the tree onto its stand in the living room.

"Where do you want it?" I asked.

Liddy paused and pointed. "How about the same as last year but a little further from the window this time. We darn near ran out of space behind the tree for all the presents last year."

After Liddy approved the right spot, I strung the lights while she got the step ladder and placed the star on top. Stepping down, she asked, "Did you get my stamps?"

I walked over to my jacket hanging beside the door. "They're right here. Oh yeah, meant to tell you earlier, I quite literally ran into Hank at the post office."

Liddy's head popped up as she hung an ornament on the tree. "What do you mean by literally?"

I told her about Hank's behavior in the post office and before that at City Hall.

"Poor Hilly," she sighed. "She should've called the sheriff." Liddy's hazel eyes grew dark and distant as we spoke about Hank.

"Hal told me he and Phillip asked Joe to represent them at the reading of Harold's last testament on Thursday."

Liddy picked up another ornament. "After all these years handling their family's affairs, why do you think Gus would cozy up to Dixie and Hank knowing it would create a rift within the Archers?"

I poked my head out from the far side of the tree. "Joe told me he planned to talk with Gus. Joe will get to the bottom of whatever's going on."

Liddy stared at the sparkling red and silver ornament she held. "Seems that Dixie's bamboozled Hank and seems willing to bust up the family all over some money."

I shook my head and shrugged. I couldn't help but wonder how much of Dixie's past might be goading her scheme.

CHAPTER THIRTY-FIVE

WEDNESDAY MORNING, WHILE BALANCED ATOP OUR STEP LADDER HANGING lights across the porch eaves, the phone rang. I managed to answer it during the third ring.

"Hey Joe, what's up?"

"Thought I missed you, Theo. Would you be available to stop by just before noon? I'll buy lunch."

I took an extended look out the window at our Nativity and Santa illuminated lawn ornaments and then the ladder on the porch beneath the strand of half-hung lights. "I should be free by then. Anything special going on?"

"Yeah, but I'd rather not discuss it over the phone."

———

QUARTER TO NOON I poked my head into Joe's office and interrupted Susanna's search through file folders on her desk only long enough for her to point toward the sofa. "I'll let Joe know you're here," she muttered as she grabbed the phone.

Joe stepped out of his office. "Come on back. We've been waiting for you."

"We? What's going on?"

Joe smirked as he gestured for me to go ahead of him into his office. John sat beside the conference table, feet perched on another chair and hands clasped behind his head. I slid a chair away from the table and faced John while Joe stepped behind his desk and flopped down into his swivel chair.

John looked over his shoulder and peered at Joe. "Now that Theo's here, what's this meeting about?"

I added. "And why the melodrama?"

Joe leaned back after he pulled a yellow legal pad into his lap. "What I need to discuss with you is to remain just among us for the time being." He paused to receive our curious nods. "Wilson Edwards confessed to breaking into both of your homes."

John shared my puzzled look and then said, "Sounds like Woogie got to talk to his dad."

I nodded toward John but kept focused on Joe who was busy checking his notes.

"He also admitted to shattering the Sentinel's front window," Joe added, marking his notes with a black felt tip pen.

John pulled his feet off the nearby chair and spun in his seat to face Joe. "Why would he go and do something as stupid and foolhardy as that and a few days later sneak into our homes? It doesn't add up."

"Unless he was put up to it," I said, spitting out what jumped into my head.

Joe's dimples deepened, though he didn't look up from his notes. "Gus Appleton."

I scooted onto the front of my chair. "Gus? That makes no sense. What's he got to do with our break-ins and Larry's smashed window?"

John turned with a raised brow. "I agree with Theo."

"Gus hasn't been exactly implicated yet, but he visited me last night." Joe scrawled something at the top of his legal pad. "Gus and I have never been bosom pals, but we've always shared a degree of mutual respect over the years. He confessed that he felt bad about Wilson facing a lot of hard prison time for crimes others coerced him into committing."

"What do you mean by coerced? By whom?" I asked.

"Three years ago, Wilson got caught red-handed pawning goods from a burglary he committed over in Alexandria. Wilson called Gus to be his lawyer, and Gus managed to get a deal cut with the DA's office. Wilson pleaded guilty to a reduced charge of home invasion and served only two years. Afterward, Wilson came back into the area to get his life back in order and make good on what he still owed Gus."

John glanced at me. "Does that mean that Gus leveraged Wilson's outstanding debt for some criminal favors?"

Joe leaned forward as he tossed his legal pad onto his desk. "This is the point where what I tell you must remain confidential."

We both nodded.

"Gus came to me for personal advice, not legal counsel, but still what I am about to tell you deserves our utmost discretion. First, Gus enlisted Judge Fitzgerald to stand in at the reading of Harold's final testament tomorrow. The judge moved the venue for the reading to a meeting room in City Hall." Joe looked at his watch. "By now, Gus is confessing to his role in putting Wilson up to committing the crimes."

"What's going to happen to Gus?" I asked.

Joe sighed. "Don't know at the moment, but he's done as a lawyer and faces some serious felony counts."

John propped his elbows on his knees and interlocked his fingers. "What about Wilson?"

"I'm looking into what I can do to help him, but for now I'm speaking with two of his victims." Joe's eyes bounced between us.

"What can we do?" I asked.

Joe clasped his hands together atop his desk. "Do either of you want Woogie to lose his dad again?"

John and I shook our heads.

"If the two of you contact the DA and ask that the charges be dropped, at worst Wilson may face a vandalism charge unless you can get Larry to cooperate."

John said with a glib grin, "He's your buddy, Theo."

"Don't worry about Larry. If I explain the facts, he'll cooperate. The worst he'll demand is that Wilson works off the cost of the window."

"Let me talk to the DA. In the meantime, would you like to know who's really behind this mess?"

John crossed his arms. "There's more?"

Joe let out a contrived laugh. "You don't think Gus stirred this mess up on his own do you?"

"Were we supposed to?" John huffed.

"Gus didn't want to say a whole lot, but in so many words he admitted that the break-ins resulted from a promise he made to Dixie. Gus said he feels like a fool. He allowed himself to believe Dixie wanted to rekindle their relationship from years ago. Since he knew about Theo's discovery of the hidden pouch, Gus decided to eliminate any chance that John would experience a change of heart once he got wind of Dixie's plan to liquidate her and Hank's shares."

John eyed me. "What's that old agreement got to do with the price of tea in China?"

My eyes popped as I rattled off what Hal told me. "She wants to secure majority control of H. H. Archer Holding's outstanding shares of stock. She already got Hank to use his shares to force Hal and Phillip to either buy them out, or she'll sell their combined shares out from under the family's control."

"What are you talking about?" John barked back.

My furrowed stare captured John's attention. "Don't you get it? That old agreement remains binding as a legal testament between your two families. Tucked away as if by fate all these decades, I believe God chose you to bear the auspicious right to exercise Ezra's instructions meant to protect Shiloh's future interests, not serve any one person's selfish motives. Once you allow Joe to make your legal claim, you'll get twenty-five percent ownership in H. H. Archer Holding Company. You'll be in the position of helping Hal and Phillip regain majority control and thwart Dixie and Hank from cashing in their shares. You'll protect Shiloh's best interests as your great-grandfather intended a century ago." My words crescendoed as I coupled all I understood with what I believed Harold would advise John to do.

John glared at Joe. "I don't want to own any part of that business."

"I figured you would say that, but there's another way. You can transfer your shares to Hal and Phillip, unless you'd prefer that Dixie and Hank destroy that company." Joe's eyes pled with John.

"I know you've got plenty of valid reasons to carry a grudge against Archer Construction, but consider the jobs and lives at risk. Think about Phillip who has restored some goodwill back into the company, and that's been no joyride after all Hank did to wreck its reputation."

John slouched in his seat with a long face and stared at Jessie's statue across the street.

I leaned closer and nudged his knee. "What would Jessie tell you to do?"

"Joe, I can't sit back and allow Hank and that woman to swindle the business away from Hal and Phillip. Can you make it legal for me to transfer those shares straight to Hal and Phillip?"

"That's why I suggested it." Joe tossed me his keys. "Can you drive to your house and meet us in, let's say, twenty minutes for lunch next door?"

———

I RETURNED JOE's Navigator to his parking space behind the Arians Building and walked around the corner to The Butcher Shoppe. Inside, Silas joked with Joe, John, Hal and Phillip in the back corner of the restaurant.

John looked up. "We took the liberty to order the special for all of us."

"Mistor Theo, today we have our Angus and feta pita, a side of roasted Greek potatoes, and lots of Bernie's fresh tzatziki sauce." Silas kissed his fingertips.

"That sounds delicious. I'll have a coffee with my meal too."

Silas looked at Alex clearing tables. "Please bring Mistor Theo a coffee please."

Joe leaned close and whispered. "Sorry, I forgot to mention Hal and Phillip would join us for lunch."

I handed him his keys with a conjured grin.

Alex reached over my shoulder and placed a cup of coffee in front of me. Silas arrived a minute later with our lunches.

While we ate, the five of us listened to Hal discuss the city's plan to hire a police chief and two officers after the first of the year. "Theo, you might like to know they'll operate right from City Hall. We've already got two attached offices set aside near the rear entrance. I'm sure Larry will be pleased with the news too."

I swallowed a sip of coffee and grinned. "If I know Larry, the minute I tell him and Mary, he'll ask me to write another article for the paper. Which means I reckon you'll let me know when you're ready to announce the naming of the new police chief?"

"Already sent out a feeler to someone I'd like to hear back from first. I'll let you know more soon."

Joe craned his neck and then said, "Looks like we can talk openly for a few minutes." He looked at me. "You got it?"

I reached inside my jacket and pulled out the leather pouch and handed it to Joe. He untied it, lifted the flap and checked inside. He then glanced at Hal and Philip across the table. "Your fears about Dixie and Hank liquidating their shares in your family's business are over. Inside this pouch is an agreement that made a serendipitous manifestation at Theo's house several weeks ago. John at first wanted no part of it, but in the light of recent events, this hundred-year-old testament between your great-grandfather and John's great-grandfather may well serve a fortuitous purpose. It just might, once again, save your family's business from being sold out of the family."

Hal and Phillip stared at the yellowed stationery and handed it to John. "This is yours, John."

John recoiled back into his chair. "Hal, you and Phillip have gone through enough. I've no desire to become a partner in your family's business, but Joe says he can legally transfer the shares referred to in this testament to whomever I designate, but to accomplish the desired outcome, I need to negotiate a fair selling price for the shares."

Hal and Phillip looked nervously at each other before Phillip asked, "How much did you have in mind?"

John peeked at Joe and me, "How about whatever the original par value amount is on each share?"

Hal laughed. "Are you kidding me?"

Phillip tugged his brother's sleeve. "How much would that be? Can we afford it?"

"Relax, little brother. We can't afford not to do it." Hal smirked and reached his hand across the table and shook John's hand. "It's a deal."

Our smiles fell as the rumble of Hank's old truck turned our heads. Hank parked out front, and a moment later Dixie climbed out the passenger's side.

"Well, Hilly was right. They're huddled up with three of my favorite friends in all the world." Hank unzipped his aviator jacket as Dixie stepped beyond him clutching a letter.

She glared at Hal, but Phillip did not turn around. "What do you know about why dear ol' Gus isn't handling the reading of your daddy's will tomorrow? Why are we meeting in City Hall rather than his office as initially arranged?"

Hal stood and faced Dixie. "It was Gus' decision. He requested Judge Fitzgerald oversee the reading of Dad's will in his place."

"Phillip! You want to add anything to what your brother just said?" Hank growled from behind Dixie.

Silas stepped around the counter. "Mistor Hank, I don't wanna any trouble."

Hank sneered. "Mind your own business, Silas. We'll be out of here in a moment. We just want some answers."

John rose from his chair. "Hank, why don't direct your attention over here and leave Silas alone."

Dixie turned and put her hand on Hank's chest. "Let me handle this. Wait right here." She then stepped toward Hal. "Thanks to Hank, I know you're aware that after tomorrow, our shares will be available to you and your brother for the price he told you. Otherwise, I will have no choice but to accept the offer from an old acquaintance of mine back in Louisiana. The choice is yours."

John folded the agreement, returned it to the pouch and handed it back to Joe.

Hal eyed Phillip. "What do you think?"

Phillip pushed his chair out and stood beside Hal. "You'll get our answer tomorrow."

"Tomorrow I expect a cashier's check in my hand for five-hundred-thousand dollars or else you can meet the new majority owners of the family business in a few days." She cackled as she turned to leave and follow Hank out the door.

John walked to Hal and Phillip. "Cool, very cool Phillip. Let's get this legal and proper, so you can give her your answer in the morning. I'll get a good night's sleep tonight knowing I'm selling my shares for only two-hundred-and-fifty dollars." John looked at Joe. "That's what you said par value was for those shares, right?"

Joe laughed and bobbed his head.

We apologized to Silas and Alex while Joe settled our lunch tab. I excused myself, and they went back to Joe's office to handle the paperwork.

I spent the afternoon getting our Nativity and Santa illuminated figurines in the front yard wired up before I called Larry. He agreed to cooperate after I told him about Gus and Wilson. We ended our conversation on a lighter note as I shared my inside scoop on the City's decision to reactivate the Shiloh Police Department. By the conclusion of our phone conversation, I faced the challenge of two news articles over the next few days.

CHAPTER THIRTY-SIX

LIDDY CHANGED INTO A PAIR OF JEANS AND A HOODED SWEATSHIRT BEFORE SHE joined me on the porch after she got home Thursday. She sat beside me revealing a cutesy grin as she secured her ponytail with a bright red scrunchie.

I reached over and clutched her hand. "You know how proud I am of you?"

She squeezed my fingers. "Why? What did I do?"

"You've made a difference in the lives of a lot of youngsters in town. How's it feel to have your first semester behind you?"

She gazed at the setting sun's beams reflecting off the belly of the cloud bank overhead. "I'm already looking forward to seeing my students right after New Years."

Her persistent, relaxed smile lessened my concerns regarding Wilson, Gus and the Archers. "Was John at school today?"

Liddy broke her gaze and shifted in her rocker. "He stopped by right after the bell rang and said hi before checking in on Phoebe. Why?"

"I haven't heard any news about Woogie's dad or how things went with Hal and Phillip. I just thought he might've said something."

"Not a word, but if it'll help, Woogie seemed in better spirits today."

"I'm sorry you have to go in for a half a day tomorrow, but how about I treat my sweetheart to lunch at Bubba's?"

Her cutesy, dimpled smile returned along with some giggles. "Of course silly. I'd enjoy that."

Phillip drove his Wrangler around the corner and came to a stop along the curb. Before he turned off the engine and headlights, Hal stepped out from the passenger side, headed up the walkway.

"Sorry to interrupt you two lovebirds."

Liddy waved. "You and your brother get yourselves on up here. We were just wondering about you two."

Hal pulled a rocker around to face both of us. Phillip remained standing but leaned against the porch railing at the exact moment our Christmas lights clicked on. Phillip jumped with his mouth and eyes wide open. Hal and I laughed as Phillip regained his composure and, after examining the colored lights, repositioned himself on the rail.

Liddy looked at Phillip. "Don't you mind those two clowns. How did it go today?"

Phillip unbuttoned his jacket and peered at Hal. "We're stuck with Hank and Dixie as part owners in the business if that's what you mean."

I inspected Hal's awkward grimace. "I take it they weren't exactly thrilled with your news that you two acquired the unissued twenty-five percent of the company."

Liddy tapped Phillip's foot with hers. "You called her Dixie."

Phillip's head dropped. "Yes, ma'am. After what she and Hank tried to pull, I can't imagine ever calling her mom again."

Hal winced as he added, "I don't know which of them cussed more when Joe told them about John claiming his shares and selling them to Phillip and me."

"What about when Joe told them that Gus and Wilson were due to appear before Judge Fitzgerald tomorrow morning?" Phillip chimed back.

"What happens now?" I asked.

Hal eyed Phillip. "We expect to face more fireworks when we get home. We already gave Maddie a heads up and advised her to lay low for the time being."

A long-faced look overtook Liddy's cheeriness. "Is Maddie going to be okay?"

"It's not Maddie I'm worried about," Phillip said.

"What do you mean?" I gave both a quick look.

Hal blurted, "Hank threatened to get even with John. Although he didn't express it quite that way."

"Does John know?" I asked.

"Called and left a message on his phone," Hal said as he scooted to the edge of his rocker. "We better head home. I'd rather deal with Hank and Dixie than Maddie if we don't show up soon."

As Hal and Phillip walked off the porch, I hollered, "Call if you need us."

We waved moments before they climbed back into Phillip's Jeep and drove away.

Liddy nuzzled close. "Think Hank and Dixie will cause any more trouble?"

"I sure hope not." I wrapped my arm around her shoulder and planted a kiss on her cheek.

———

Liddy called later the following morning to say she invited John and Phoebe to join us for lunch, and they would all meet me there. I capitalized on the extra few minutes and swung by the Sentinel to check with Larry. The city's giant Christmas tree dangled from the crane's extended boom as city workers secured it onto the wooden base on the same corner of Town Square like last year.

I parked next to Pete's truck outside the Sentinel. His sturdy frame extended over the counter, engaged in a private chat with Mary. Only Martha took notice of my arrival.

Mid-bite, Martha lowered her sandwich. She nodded toward Larry's open office door before she bit into her sandwich.

"Mister P! Didn't hear you come in. Did you hear about this nasty weather we might get tomorrow night?" Pete reached out his hand.

"I heard a front might bring some rain and cooler yet temperatures this weekend."

Mary leaned back in her chair. "The latest forecast doesn't look good.

Tornadoes touched down in southern Missouri and northern Arkansas last night. We'll likely be under a severe storm watch tomorrow."

"When was the last time a tornado hit this area so late in the year?"

Pete tendered a smug look. "Fifty years ago."

Mary swatted Pete's arm. "We just looked that up for my article in tomorrow's edition."

I waved and headed for Larry's office.

"Theo, stay tuned to the news," Mary urged.

Larry looked up from his desk. "Have you heard anything more about Wilson Edwards or Gus?"

"They both were scheduled to stand before Judge Fitzgerald today."

"And?"

"That's all I know at the moment, but Joe's negotiating with the DA's office."

"What about the Archers? I understand Judge Fitzgerald was in town for the reading of Harold's will."

"John exercised his great-grandfather's agreement and sold his shares to Hal and Phillip, which pretty much poured cold water all over Dixie and Hank's plans to liquidate their shares."

Larry huffed. "That must'a gone over like a ton of bricks."

"Dixie embarrassed herself, and Hank threatened to get even with John."

"Any concerns you might end up in the crosshairs of either of them?"

"Our names didn't come up in any of their threats, according to Hal and Phillip." I felt my collapsing grin betray the confidence I intended to display.

Larry opened the top drawer of his desk and removed a folder. "I've been sitting on this hoping Dixie wasn't serious about wanting to start anew in Shiloh."

I scanned Larry's notes and correspondence he'd received from Louisiana. "Give it a few more days. Unless something changes in their favor, Dixie and likely Hank too are about to leave Shiloh for good."

Larry tucked the file back into his drawer. His demeanor changed, and a grin appeared. "Your boys bringing their families again this year for Christmas?"

"They'll be here next Wednesday. The grandkids are excited about seeing another Christmas in Shiloh parade."

Larry stepped around his desk. "Don't think it'll be as grand as last year, but then again, every Christmas is a magical time in Shiloh."

———

CORA GREETED ME with a down-in-the-mouth scowl when I walked into Bubba's. "Miss Liddy and the others are waiting on you Mister Phillips."

"Where's your usual warm smile? You and Cecil get into a tussle or something?"

"No, sir. Maddie called. Them folks in that house just aren't right. She's fed up with the whole lot and asked if she could spend the weekend at our house."

I gave Cora a one-arm hug as she directed me to our table. "I'm sure the Lord's in control and all their fussing and feuding shall also pass."

"Maddie and I be praying exactly that for everyone's sake."

Liddy waved as Cora led me through the noisy lunch crowd. To my surprise, Jeannie and Nick also occupied our table.

John extended his hand as I sat down across from him. "Larry keep you with all his jabber-jawing?"

I greeted Nick seated next to John. "Wasn't all Larry's fault this time. Mary gave me the latest about some nasty weather headed our way. The National Weather Service has issued a severe storm watch for South Alabama, the Florida panhandle and South Georgia. It sounds as though Ol' Man Winter's going to make a grand entrance this year. There's a slight risk of hail and heavy winds accompanying his arrival."

Nick's happy-go-lucky look disappeared. "Let's hope Old Man Winter wears himself out long before he drags his frosty self upon us."

John nodded. "As soon as we get done here, I better head right out and help Marie batten down around the farm. She may want the animals in the barn tonight."

"I'll go with you," Phoebe said.

Nick looked at Jeannie with his calming, devil-may-care grin. "Enough of this doom and gloom talk. Jeannie and I have some great news to share."

"Thank God." Liddy smiled at Jeannie. "What kind of news do you two have?"

Jeannie looked at Nick. "Arians Realty and Property Management is opening an office on Saint Simon Island, and Jeannie has accepted her new title as vice president and general manager of the Shiloh office. She'll take over here in Shiloh while I get our new office up and running."

Liddy looked oddly disappointed by the news, but I understood Jeannie's simpatico, professional relationship with Nick.

Liddy turned to Nick after she hugged Jeannie. "I thought you were selling your family's Saint Simons home?"

"Joe and I decided to take it off the market. With Momma gone, I don't need to hang around Momma's old house across from my big brother and his family. It's time I moved on, and with Joe's help, we're going to remodel the vacation home and make part of the downstairs into an office."

John laughed. "You gonna still have a couple of guest rooms for your dear friends looking for a beach getaway?"

"Absolutely. Joe insisted the guest rooms remain for when he brings Missy and the girls to visit."

I leaned forward and peered toward Jeannie. "Sounds like your first house sale will be Momma's old house here in Shiloh."

"Already have a young couple interested in buying it." Jeannie's red dimples deepened.

"Anyone we know?" Phoebe asked.

"Can't say quite yet."

Cecil arrived balancing a tray in each hand. "Who ordered the brisket?"

We continued to talk until our crumpled napkins rested on the table. Cora appeared at the head of the table. "Separate checks?"

Nick reached out. "I got this today."

———

An ominous, coal-colored blanket rolled over Shiloh from the west and swallowed Saturday's partly sunny skies before noon. By mid-afternoon, wind gusts stripped the remaining leaves from the trees. I disconnected our front lawn Christmas decorations and stored them on the porch. Liddy kept busy cooking and baking as she fretted more about not being ready for our family's arrival in a few days. I tuned to the local news channel, and the red warning running across the bottom of the television screen confirmed my fears. The elevated severe storm warning included Adams County and the surrounding counties until midnight.

"Are we going to be okay?" Liddy asked as she swirled the batter in a mixing bowl. "Sure don't want to lose power before I'm done baking all these cookies."

"Hopefully just a lot of rain and wind." What I shared with Liddy did not reflect my concerns over tornadoes that touched down in Mississippi and Alabama that afternoon.

After dinner, I nibbled on a few of the less-than-perfect cookies Liddy set aside for me. I donned an apron and scrubbed away at the bowls and cooking trays as I munched. We listened to Christmas music on the radio to try and forget about the storm threat for a bit.

The phone rang about eight o'clock just before I switched off the light in the kitchen to join Liddy in the living room.

"Theo, it's Hal. Thought you deserved a heads up. Hank stormed out of here in dad's truck madder than a hornet trapped in an old coke can."

"Where's he headed?"

"Don't know. He left a packed duffle bag by the door, grabbed the truck keys and stormed out. He sprayed wet gravel everywhere when he hightailed it down the drive."

Liddy peeked over her shoulder just before she fixated on the wind-blown rain hitting the window.

"How's the weather at your place? The wind and rain sure are picking up over here," I said staring out the window.

"Not so good here either. Phillip just ran back inside and reported several tree limbs are now blocking our driveway."

"Where's Dixie?"

"As far as I know, upstairs packing. Just before Hank left, she came out of her room, leaned over the balcony rail, and screamed at him after he bounded down the stairs. She threatened to drive off without him if he didn't get back before she was ready to leave in the morning. She said something about needing to tie up some loose family matters in Louisiana. He tossed his duffel by the door and hollered, 'If I'm not back by then, you know where you can find me.' Dixie cussed the air and slammed her bedroom door."

Liddy jumped to her feet. "Theo, listen!"

The sound of sirens grew louder across town.

"Hal, I gotta go. Sirens are going off." I looked at Liddy. "Get in the master bathroom. I'll be right there."

I ran to kitchen stoop and looked into the black night. The wind began to wail moments before the hail started. A minute later, Liddy and I huddled behind the bathroom door praying. Don't know what rattled louder, my knees or the house's frame as the storm raged around it.

As fast as the storm swept into Shiloh, it dissipated. The power flickered, but the lights stayed lit. Liddy and I walked onto the porch and stared into the distant eery darkness on the far side of town. The storm with its cracks of lightning headed out of Shiloh following Old Mill Road.

I pointed to the large limb from one of our oaks that just missed landing on our vehicle and the house. "We'll deal with the mess in the morning."

Liddy wrapped her arm around my waist. "Looks like the storm's headed right for Marie's farm."

As soon as we got inside, Liddy dialed Marie and then John. "Neither are answering. I'm worried. We need to drive out there first thing in the morning."

CHAPTER THIRTY-SEVEN

AFTER A SLEEPLESS NIGHT, I SLIPPED ON JEANS AND A SWEATSHIRT AND GRABBED A flashlight. Outside, the only storm casualties appeared to be a couple of missing roof shingles and a strand of Christmas lights dangling from the porch eaves. A chainsaw also would be needed to dispatch the fallen oak branch taking up my front lawn, but overall our home weathered the storm well.

I uprighted our porch rockers, no worse for wear, and found our Christmas lawn ornaments wedged between the shrubs and the house. Except for a couple of repairable scratches, relief came when I plugged the ornaments and lights back on before I headed inside to brew a pot of coffee and reread yesterday's paper.

Our oldest son Junior called just before daybreak. "Dad, you guys okay?"

"We're just hunky-dory now, but I gotta admit we experienced a pretty good scare last night."

"Tommy called to check to see if I had heard from you and mom. Figured you'd be up."

"Mom's still asleep, but I'm glad you called. We were lucky. The worst of the storm barely bypassed Shiloh."

"That's good to hear. Stacie and the boys are looking forward to seeing you and mom Wednesday. I'll call Tommy."

As I turned from hanging up the phone, Liddy mumbled as she cinched her robe, "Which one called?"

I reached for another mug and poured her some coffee. "Junior, but Tommy had called him before he called us. I told them everything's fine, and we'll see them Wednesday."

"We were darn lucky weren't we?" Liddy asked, then took a sip.

"Not certain how the rest of the town fared, but I think the storm's worst skirted by Shiloh. Thanks to God, we only experienced minor damage."

Liddy's eyes sparkled as she nodded while I recounted how our home fared. That is until we both heard footsteps on the porch followed by three solid knocks on the front door. "Mister P, its Pete! You up?"

"Come on in, Pete." As soon as he stepped into the living room, his serious look made me ask, "Something wrong?"

"Miss Marie called. John spent the night at her house but went to check on his cabin before breakfast. When he didn't come straight back, she cut across the pasture to check on him. She discovered the meadow gate near John's cabin had been busted open and Mister Harold's black dually out front of John's place. When John noticed her approaching, he yelled for her to go back to the house. He said he'd be along shortly, but Ringo's growl made her sense something was wrong, so she called me to fetch you after she couldn't reach you on your phone."

"Did she say anything else?"

"Just that she's worried, and I should get you there lickety-split."

"Give me one minute. I'll come too." Liddy headed down the hall.

"No! I need you to call Hal and Phillip and then stay right here by the phone." I grabbed my jacket leading Pete out the door.

Pete peered at me as he cranked his truck. "Buckle up and hold on."

———

BROKEN TREE LIMBS littered River Road, but Pete raced over most of them. Twice he yelled, "Hang on," a second before he jerked his truck onto the shoulder barely slowing down. When we arrived at Marie's and John's mailboxes, Pete's truck skidded on the wet gravel as he slowed only enough to manage the hard turn onto the narrow road that carried us across Shiloh Creek on the rickety bridge. As soon as we cleared the tree line, I spotted the shattered remnants of the gate that allowed access to the pasture and John's cabin scattered on both sides of the well-worn tire tracks leading across the field. Before I uttered a word, Pete slammed on his brakes. He down-shifted as his tires spun on the wet gravel. He jerked his steering wheel hard and drove like a bat out of hell straight across the pasture, headed for John's place.

One hand kept me from slamming into Pete's metal dashboard. The other clamped onto the door frame. My head bounced side to side as we bounded through the meadow.

Pete whooped and hollered as if we were on some wild carnival ride, but his eyes stared straight ahead. As we neared the fence in front of John's place, we saw the shattered gate beneath Harold's truck out front but no sign of Hank nor John.

Pete slowed as we drove through the busted open gateway and pulled beside the dually. John lay lifeless across the porch deck. Ringo strained against his leash, snarling and baring his teeth. Hank stood beyond Ringo's reach, a bottle in one hand and an ax handle in the other. He ranted incoherently toward John, competing against Ringo's unrelenting growls.

Hank's jugular veins protruded on his swollen neck, and his glazed-over, red-eyes glared. In the midst of the disjointed ruckus, neither he nor Ringo paid any attention to our arrival.

The moment we exited Pete's truck, the distinct smell of gas filled the air, and then I saw a rag tucked in the bottle that Hank gripped. John moaned as Hank dug into his jacket pocket, pulled out a lighter and lit the gas-soaked rag. Hank raised the bottle, arm cocked.

Ringo lunged even harder toward Hank.

I stepped towards Hank with both hands raised high. "Hank! Stop!"

Hank spun around. "No, you stop! You and Pete better get back, or you're gonna get a taste of this." Hank swung the ax handle back and forth.

Pete continued to walk toward Hank. "Hank, stop and think about what you're doing."

"Shut up! Step back, or you'll join him." Hank retreated as John's moans increased.

"For the love of God, don't!" I hollered inching slowly closer, my hands now extended in front of me.

"God doesn't care about me. Now get back, dammit!"

"How will all this honor the love your father had for you?"

Hank's voice quivered as he cocked his arm higher. "His love for me died with him."

Ringo's leash finally snapped when he lunged once more at Hank's raised arm. Hank recoiled. Gas spilled onto his sleeve, immediately igniting it. He flailed wildly at the flames before flinging the bottle when Ringo spun and sank his teeth into his thigh.

Pete raced forward and buried his shoulder into Hank's ribs, causing both to tumble onto the ground. Ringo clamped onto Hank's ankle until Hank kicked Ringo skyward. I raced to Ringo and grabbed his collar with both hands. Pete reached for the ax handle, muscled it under Hank's chin and pinned him down. Hank then frantically pointed to his dad's truck. Flames and black smoke spewed out the open passenger and driver side windows.

"Theo! Hand Ringo to me." John had managed to prop himself against a porch post. Blood stained the back of his head and forehead.

Pete stepped off Hank's chest with the ax handle. "Now get up, so we can scoot back away from the truck. It's too late to save it."

Hank gasped as he got to his feet. Pete took a step behind him and pressed the ax handle under his chin again. Hank's hands fell to his sides as his father's truck smoldered.

I wrestled Ringo over to the porch. John wrapped the broken leash attached to Ringo's collar around his hand. He slipped his other hand under the dog's collar while I examined John's wounds.

"How do you feel?" I asked.

"Like someone used my head as a battering ram. What happened?" John blurted, staring at the charred truck.

"Mister P, Dixie's here!" Pete shouted as he backpedaled closer to the porch.

Dixie exited her convertible, raised a pistol into the air and fired. She lowered the hood of her scarlet cape. She eyed Pete and grinned, "You can let him go now, Sugar."

Hank slapped the ax handle away as Pete relaxed his grip.

"Put the gun down, Dixie." I walked beside Pete. My left arm pressed against his chest to separate him from Hank. "You do realize that at best you only have a couple more minutes before the sheriff arrives."

Dixie poised her gun at my chest. "What makes you think that?"

I pointed to the pillar of black smoke above Harold's burned-out truck cab. "If that doesn't draw enough attention, the sound of your gunshot cued Marie to call the sheriff. I wouldn't doubt that she's already headed this way toting her double barrel twelve-gauge."

"He's right mom. We need to get out of here." Hank surveyed the meadow and then the gravel road to Marie's house as he stepped beside Dixie.

Ringo snarled and tugged against John's firm grip.

"Shut that mutt up, or I will." Dixie shifted her aim towards John and Ringo.

John remained propped against the porch post but tightened his grip on Ringo. He looked at Dixie and Hank. "Hank's right. Y'all need to git while you still can. No one needs to do anything they'll regret the rest of their lives."

"Listen to John." I raised my free hand, took one small step forward, but still pushed my other hand against Pete's puffed out chest.

"Back off, Theo! I don't want a reason to have to hurt you. Liddy might not take kindly to me putting a bullet in you." Dixie pointed the gun at my chest and cocked the lever. "Hank, get in the car."

Hank stared at Pete and me before he turned toward her car. Then he froze. "Listen!"

The sheriff deputy's siren grew louder as it raced toward Marie's house with its blue lights flashing.

"Just get in the blasted car, Hank!"

Hank opened the passenger door, grabbed Dixie's satchel on the seat and stared inside. "Where'd all this money come from?"

"Don't you mind about that now. Toss it in the back seat and get in." Dixie backed away with her pink handled revolver still aimed at us.

Hank reached into the bag, then turned around clutching Harold's championship rings. "These were to have been buried with my father. You stole all this from him didn't you?"

"Shut up! That cruiser will be here any second." Dixie's eyes hardened as she backed toward her car.

Pete pushed my hand away as he stepped in front of me. "Lady, if you're gonna use that thing, you better start cause you ain't gonna git away with this. Hank, can't ya see? She's just been using you."

Hank glared at Dixie, but she screamed, "Don't listen to him! I'll explain later."

Ringo broke free from John's grip, raced between Pete and me, and snarled. She shrieked and aimed her cocked gun at Ringo. I reached for Ringo's collar.

"Dixie, no! Don't shoot," I pleaded. Hank's watery eyes stared at me.

The sound of spinning tires struggling to maintain traction on the gravel road along with the squeal of the sheriff's siren echoed across the meadow. Pete reached for Dixie's gun. She yanked it back and aimed at Pete. Hank stepped in front of Pete.

"If you wanna stay here, that's fine with me. I gave you a chance to come along, but I'm leaving."

Hank grabbed the gun. It discharged. His wide-eyed look froze his mother as he collapsed to his knees and clutched his stomach. His dad's rings fell onto the ground. "Mom?"

Dixie screamed and fired another round narrowly missing Pete and me. She knelt down, pocketed Harold's rings, and then ran to her car. Her Jag fishtailed as she spun around headed down the gravel road toward the oncoming sheriff's vehicle. At the last second, the cruiser ricocheted off the fence to avoid a head-on collision.

"Come on! We'll head her off." Pete grabbed my arm and yanked me toward his truck. Before I could buckle up, Pete popped the clutch. We sailed in reverse over the busted gate into the meadow. He jerked the steering wheel hard to spin us around. My head snapped back as he engaged the clutch, shifting from first to second to third in a matter of seconds.

The sheriff's vehicle stopped briefly at John's cabin before spinning around in hot pursuit of Dixie.

When we approached the far side of the meadow, I yelled, "There she is!" With her convertible top down, I couldn't see more than the top of her head. Pete's truck roared across the grass-filled pasture trying desperately to cut her off.

"We gotta catch her before she gets onto Old Mill Road. My truck will never keep up with her Jag-war on that road." Pete downshifted and revved the engine as we made a hard right onto the gravel road headed toward the bridge over Shiloh Creek.

As we approached the one lane, steel-framed bridge, Pete smacked his steering wheel. "We need a miracle now."

That's when we saw Phillip's red Jeep approaching the bridge from the opposite direction. Dixie slammed on her brakes. Her Jag spun out of control and caught the bridge's railing, sending her airborne.

Pete gripped his steering wheel with both hands and stomped his brakes as we skidded sideways. The truck came to rest just short of hitting the bridge's rail. Phillip and Hal jumped out of their vehicle and stumbled down the opposite embankment. Pete and I worked our way down the slippery slope on our side. We all reached Dixie's upside down car in the middle of the swollen creek at the same time. Dixie lay face down in the water a few feet from her car. Phillip trudged through the waist deep water and cried out when he realized she was dead.

Hal looked at Mitch looking down from the bridge when he reached his brother and shook his head.

"You guys okay? We need to free the bridge for the ambulance." Mitch pointed to the Jeep and Pete's truck blocking each end.

Hal looked at me. "Keys are in the Jeep."

Pete helped me up the muddy embankment. A few moments later, the first EMS vehicle rolled up. It stopped momentarily to talk with Mitch before speeding off toward John's cabin.

A second EMS crew retrieved Dixie's body. Pete and I helped Phillip climb up the slippery slope while Hal stayed behind and inspected Dixie's partially submerged vehicle. The three of us watched from the bridge as Hal bent over and reached into the water. He then stood and stared at Harold's championship rings before depositing them into his pants pocket.

CHAPTER THIRTY-EIGHT

AFTER I HAD FILLED LIDDY IN ON WHAT HAPPENED AT JOHN'S PLACE, SHE spent the rest of Sunday afternoon piddling in the kitchen quelling her 'what-if' fears. I needed time alone too since my own heart still shuddered as the morning's surreal images replayed in my head.

During a TV commercial break near the conclusion to the movie Sands of Iwo Jima I had lost myself in, I climbed off the sofa and added a couple more logs onto the fire. I turned and found Liddy sobbing with her arms extended. "Please hold me."

We embraced in front of the Christmas tree until Liddy raised her head from my shoulder and pointed to the television. "Even your beloved John Wayne found out it only takes one bullet."

When I tried to say I'm sorry again, she put her fingers to my lips. "Theo Phillips, if you ever leave me behind like that again, I'll kill you myself." She wiped her tears with her apron just before she held my cheeks between her hands and kissed me. She then pulled her head back and grinned. "Ready for some dinner?"

As we cleaned the dinner dishes, headlights shined in the window. "Arnie and Judy are here," Liddy said.

Arnie held onto my hand as he greeted me in our living room. "You okay? From what John told me, you were some hero this morning."

"How is he?" I directed Arnie toward Liddy's armchair across from my recliner. Judy put her arm around Liddy, and they disappeared into the kitchen.

"He ended up with several stitches, but Doc Lucas stopped in before I left his room and said his X-rays cleared him of any serious head injuries."

I shook my head and snickered. "Thank God John's got such a hard head. I thought for sure Hank cracked his skull wide open."

"That's what I said to John, but when he tried to laugh about it, he winced instead."

"I have little doubt he'll have quite a headache for a few days. Any word about Hank?"

Arnie leaned forward and lowered his voice. "Doc said he got lucky. The bullet exited his side and only caused superficial, internal damage. Though, he lost a lot of blood and will be pretty sore for a few days."

"But, what about —" I stuttered.

"There was a detective from the sheriff's department asking John a lot of questions when I got there."

"I can imagine. Mitch questioned Pete and me about what happened too."

Arnie stared at me. "What'd you say?"

"But you already heard John —"

"Humor me, Theo."

"That John appeared unconscious on the porch with Hank shouting incoherently and in an uncontrollable state of rage when we first arrived. We got Hank under control, thanks to Ringo and Pete, minutes before Dixie showed pointing a handgun at us."

"What did you tell them about how Hank got shot?"

"He refused to leave with Dixie and instead protected Pete. The gun discharged when he grabbed Dixie's hand. Why do you want to know if John already told you?"

"That's pretty near what John told the detective."

"Have they charged Hank with anything yet?"

"Not yet, but they stationed a deputy at the hospital." Arnie sat back and crossed a leg over his other knee. "Sounds to me like God had a reason for Marie requesting Pete to get you there."

"Why would you say that? I was way over my head."

"Yes, you were. But John made it clear to me that you connected with Hank as neither he nor Pete could."

"What about Dixie? How can I explain what happened to Hal and Phillip? They witnessed their mother's death?"

Arnie sighed. "Theo, I doubt you could've done anything to prevent what happened to her, but you kept Hank from getting in her car."

I sank into my recliner. "I haven't admitted this to anyone yet, but other than that first shot in the air, I don't remember hearing the others."

"That only verifies how God watched over you and led you to accomplish his will."

Before I could protest further, Liddy and Judy brought out coffee and cookies. The mood shifted as Arnie bragged about the Advent message we missed on God's desire to deliver peace on earth.

———

By Monday's dawn, no empirical evidence remained, bar the lone tree limb sprawled across my lawn, that a deadly storm had swept past Shiloh Saturday night. The sound of Timmy on his bike freed me from pondering over the debris in my yard. I acknowledged his exuberant wave as he heaved the morning paper onto the porch.

The town's Christmas tree appeared on the front page beside a story about its miraculous stand against the storm's fury. The article also included the city's commitment to have downtown ready for Wednesday's Christmas in Shiloh kickoff parade. Below the fold was a piece by Mary about Dixie's fatal accident. I finished the paper and pulled out a skillet to cook breakfast.

"Sausage smells good. What time did you climb out of bed?" Liddy poured a cup of coffee, plopped down at the table and slid the paper in front of her.

"Just before sunrise. Scrambled eggs okay?"

Liddy nodded, eyes glued to the front page. "That's excellent news about the city's tree and decorations. I know the grandkids are anxious about seeing the parade Wednesday night."

"That reminds me, we need to swing by Zeb's store today. That tree branch isn't going to disappear on its own."

Liddy looked up from the paper. "Right after we stop by the hospital this morning."

———

PHOEBE AND MARIE sat on either side of John's bed. He reclined atop the sheets, propped in an upright position, wearing jeans and a t-shirt. Sutures above his eye blended with his dark eyebrows, a far better sight than just a day ago.

"How are ya feeling? Arnie told me Doc joked about your thick skull protecting you from serious injury."

John sat more upright on the bed and turned his head. "Glad school's out for a couple more weeks. Doc darn near scalped me before he stitched me up back there."

Liddy edged closer and examined his wounds. "I would have thought you'd have a bigger knot. Does it still hurt?"

"Smarts a bit, especially when I lean over or laugh." An uneasy grin encroached upon John's stubbled cheeks.

"Have you heard anything about Hank?" Liddy asked, stroking John's upper arm.

Marie tapped Liddy on the arm and pointed. "They moved him from the ICU this morning to a room down the hall."

John added, "Doc Lucas said Hank got lucky. His wound should heal in no time, but psychologically he's gonna need a specialist to help him recover from what happened."

I stood at the foot of John's bed. "What do you think is going to happen to Hank?"

"Don't rightly know for sure, but let's go find out." John swung his sock feet onto the floor and hesitated on the side of the bed before standing. Phoebe rose from her chair to offer a hand, but John turned and said, "Please forgive me, but y'all stay here while Theo and I go see Hank for a few minutes."

Phoebe gave John a baffled look but sat back down. Marie smiled and patted the edge of John's bed, and Liddy sat down. John rested his hand on my shoulder as we walked toward Hank's room.

Mitch was talking with a deputy in the hall when we got to Hank's door. "Hal's in there."

I knocked and slowly opened the door. John entered before me.

"I'll have to call you back," Hal said as he slipped his phone into his pocket.

Splotches of black and blue covered Hank's face and neck. Wires and tubes remained attached to his arms and the back of his hands. His sunken, bloodshot eyes caught most of my attention.

Hal grimaced when he saw John's stitches. John smirked as he showed him the back of his head. "I'll live. I think. How's your brother?"

Hal glanced at Hank. "He's not talking a whole lot, but he should pull through okay."

I looked at Hal's tired face. "How are you doing?"

"I keep seeing her red Jaguar ricochet off the bridge if that's what you mean."

"Why'd she come back?" Hank mumbled.

"In my heart, I wanna believe she needed to see us again. Whatever the truth is, God brought her back to be at dad's side when he needed her most." Hal glanced over his shoulder at John and me.

John stepped nearer to Hank's bed. "I need to ask you a question."

Hank turned to John.

"What stopped you from leaving with her?"

Tears welled in the corners of Hank's eyes. "I wanted to believe that she cared for me and that her fairytale promises could help me leave Shiloh. By the time the rug got yanked out from under the scheme her and Gus cooked up, she'd convinced me that I'd been cheated out of what rightfully belonged to me. But seeing all that money and Dad's rings in her car brought me to my senses. It dawned on me that none of you were my enemy, I was. I chose not to disappoint Dad anymore."

I asked, "What made you stand in front of Pete?"

Hank began to laugh but moaned instead and grabbed his side. "I didn't think she'd pull the trigger. Apparently, I was wrong," he sighed with a crooked grin. "Besides, when I realized that Pete risked taking a bullet for you two, I couldn't allow her to hurt him. I just wanted her to leave." Tears trickled from the corner of Hank's eyes.

John squinted at Hal and then Hank. "I believe Theo will back me up on what took place. As far as I can best recollect, we just got into another one of our heated arguments. I stumbled and smacked my head against the porch rail. Before any of us could respond, Dixie arrived, threatening all of us. You got shot trying to take Dixie's gun away before she drove off." John winked at me. "Is that about right, Theo?"

I stuttered breaking my slack-jaw pose. "Umm, yeah that sounds about right."

Mitch knocked on the door. "May I come in?" He presented the satchel with the cash to Hal. "We recovered this after we hauled Dixie's car out of the creek."

Hal took the bag. "Theo, I might as well go ahead and introduce you to Shiloh's new Police Chief."

Mitch smiled as I shook his hand. "Congratulations! The city made a wise choice." I looked over at Hal.

John motioned to Mitch. "You and I need to talk."

After John had stepped out of the room with Mitch, I turned to Hank's wide-eyed stare. "I understand Doc Lucas has arranged for a specialist to come see you. I strongly suggest you take advantage of Doc's offer. It's high time you send your worst enemy packing for the last time."

"Mister Phillips, I plan to. I'm gonna need all the help I can get. Dixie sure riled up my demons with her empty promises." Hank turned away and glared at the ceiling before squeezing his eyes tight and returning his focus to me. "Of course, I'm curious why she insisted we needed to go back to Louisiana. She never explained what family matters were so pressing to risk going back there."

Hal nudged Hank's arm. "Enough of that! What only matters now is what Phillip, you and I do from here on out as our testament to Dad. You game?"

Hank reached up and grabbed Hal's arm. "Thank you, brother. I'm ready."

———

ON THE DRIVE over to Adams Feed and Hardware, I explained to Liddy what took place in Hank's room. She opened her mouth to ask a question but instead opted to squeeze my hand and tender a knowing smile.

We found Zeb behind the front counter. I filled him in on what happened at John's place and updated him on John's and Hank's conditions.

He scratched his scraggly whiskers. "I well remember a time when Hank and Hal were thick as thieves running all over town after Dixie abandoned them. Without a mom, those two took care of one another and kept an eye on their kid brother too. Heck, Phillip weren't but a toddler, but they took such good care of him. Harold never had to worry. Maybe they'll take care of one another like that again."

"What a fitting testament that would be to Harold," Liddy said, smiling.

CHAPTER THIRTY-NINE

LATE WEDNESDAY AFTERNOON, CONTINUOUS OUTBURSTS OF LAUGHTER AND chatter filled our home. Ten-year-old Sissy taunted our twelve-year-old grandsons, Bubba and Teddy. The four-year-olds, Buzz and Conrad, occupied themselves in front of the Christmas tree. They created a little town of their own using the miniature ceramic house and the tree and caroler figurines they gave us last Christmas. Their dads and moms refereed when needed, while Liddy and I shared our tempered version of recent events.

The temperature dropped as a cloud-free moonlit night fell upon Shiloh. We corralled the kids after dinner, and with my sons and I toting folding chairs and blankets we headed to Main Street. This year's Christmas in Shiloh kickoff offered no dedication ceremonies like last year but promised more entertainment before the lighting of the city's tree and the annual parade.

Bernie and Silas greeted us and then helped us remove the tables they used to reserve enough room for our family in front of their restaurant. The bundled kids sat perched on the curb in front of us with their parents. Holiday music played as carolers wearing turn-of-the-century costumes broke into smaller groups and encouraged the growing crowd lining Main Street to sing along to the Christmas music. Liddy and I laughed as we pointed to Marie, Missy, Joe and Nick with Lucy and Lizzy tagging along, all of them dressed in Victorian attire complete with top hats and colorful bonnets.

A few minutes later, Hal stepped into the center of Main Street and welcomed the swelling crowd. He introduced Arnie as the narrator of the Nativity reenactment on Town Square, which included Judy dressed as the heavenly angel. During the closing scene, the carolers led the crowd in singing "O Little Town of Bethlehem."

Hal stood with Hillary beside Jessie's statute until the music stopped. He stepped once again into the center of Main Street and yelled, "Are y'all ready to light your tree?" The crowd hollered a resounding "Yes!" Hal raised his hand high above his head, fingers spread. "Well, then, help me with the countdown."

Our grandkids stood with their hands cupped around their mouths. "Five, four, three, two, one!"

The lowest strands of lights illuminated the base first, then the strands above followed in succession until the entire tree lit up moments before the white star atop the tree shimmered. "O Christmas Tree" played over the speakers, and the crowd joined in with the carolers again. When the singing stopped, a brand new black and white police truck flashed its lights and sounded its siren drawing all heads to look toward Bubba's at the end of Main Street.

Mitch Johnson, wearing a navy blue ball cap with SPD stitched across the top, marshaled the cavalcade of floats and bands as the parade proceeded toward Town Square. Behind Mitch in his police truck, two bright red trucks from the Shiloh Fire Department and an Adams County EMS vehicle blared their horns as they crept forward.

SHS cheerleaders came next and marched ahead of the Shiloh Booster Club float towed behind Sam's silver truck with Susanna riding beside him in the cab. John crouched with his arm on Timmy's shoulder and the football team surrounding them. Woogie, Quentin, Hunter, Bobo and Zach jumped off the float and pulled candy from the pockets of their new green and gold letter jackets and handed it to the younger kids.

Bob and Barb pulled the Saint James AME Church sponsored trailer. Cora, Cecil, Maddie, Hub and Marcellus were among their robed choir singing, clapping and swaying to "Joy to the World."

Not far behind, Phoebe Thatcher led Shiloh High School's band out of the parking lot onto Main Street. They played "Here Comes Santa Claus" as Ray and Kay Abernathy trailed behind riding in a golf cart.

Zeb drove a red tractor that pulled Santa's sleigh atop one of his trailers. Jay, Jim, Jeannie, Phillip and Alex walked alongside and tossed candy to the kids while jolly old Saint Nick, with his curly red beard hidden beneath his white beard, bellowed, "Merry Christmas!" Missus Claus joined Santa as an unannounced addition this year. The float stopped when it reached Town Square. Bubba and Teddy grabbed Buzz's and Conrad's hands and along with Sissy joined the stream of kids pouring out from the crowd and surrounding Santa's float.

Santa stood, his hands outstretched. "How many of you were good this year?"

Hands waved high as all the children screamed.

Santa puffed his chest out and gripped his shiny black belt. "In that case, in just seven more nights, I'll be visiting each of your homes. And to make sure I don't fly past your town, your mayor has promised to keep that great big star atop your tree lit until I comeback Christmas Eve." The kids looked up to the shining star and cheered.

All the carolers and Nativity characters mustered behind Santa's float just before Zeb shifted his tractor into gear and inched his way toward the parking lot behind Shiloh Baptist Church.

Woogie raced across the street ahead of Wiley, Malvinia and his dad. "Mister Phillips, I hadn't had the chance to thank you and Missus Phillips."

Liddy hugged him as Wiley, Malvinia and Wilson caught up. "Whatever for?"

"For giving me the best Christmas gift I ever had." He grabbed his dad's jacket sleeve. "My Dad."

Wilson reached his hand out with a sheepish grin. "I don't know what to say. If it weren't for you and Coach Priestly, I—"

"Merry Christmas. Nothing more needs to be said." I shook his hand and shared smiles with Wiley and Malvinia.

Wilson clutched my hand with both of his. "If you need anything at all, let me know. Also, I wanted you to know that I've got me a job thanks to Mister Zeb."

Liddy embraced Wilson. "Just take care of your boy and your grand-parents too."

A ruckus of familiar voices approached from the church. Our sons recognized John and the other guys and greeted them while Liddy intro-duced Hillary and Phoebe to Kari and Stacie.

Nick stepped beside me. "Glad I caught you. I'm leaving first thing in the morning for Saint Simons. I would've felt awful if I didn't get the chance to wish you and Liddy a Merry Christmas before I left."

"I'm sure you'll be back to visit on a regular basis," I said as I turned to greet Joe and Missy with the twins.

"You'll hardly know he moved away from us." Joe laughed.

"Any news about Hank and Gus?"

"Spoke with DA Jared Hardman this afternoon. No charges are being filed against Hank. As for Gus, he'll likely receive probation but undoubt-edly face disbarment."

"How's Hank doing?" I asked.

Joe looked to his office window. A shadow looked down at our gather-ing of friends. "Doc agreed to let him attend tonight as long as Hal brings him straight back to the hospital afterward. He needs a couple more days of recovery before they will officially release him."

"That means he'll be home for Christmas this year."

"That's true, but he's agreed to Doc Lucas' recommendation and will head back to the VA Hospital in Bethesda, Maryland right after to help him with his recurring PTSD anger management issues."

Behind us, we heard the women "ooh and aah" at Megan and Andy. Megan's blushing cheeks gave me the impression the fuss had to do with her four-month baby bump until Liddy glared at me and pointed to Pete and Mary walking hand-in-hand, still in their costumes except for their hats and wigs.

Confused, I just shrugged.

Nick tapped my shoulder. "Pete proposed to Mary tonight."

After we congratulated them and waved goodnight, Liddy leaned close and whispered, "You didn't have a clue, did you?"

I grinned and shrugged.

———

THE FOLLOWING MORNING in pre-dawn solitude, I read God's promise to King David in Psalm 132. "If your sons will keep my covenant and my testimony, which I will teach them, their sons shall sit upon your throne forever." I thought immediately of Harold and his sons and inscribed in my journal: The testament of a man lies not in the magnitude of possessions and property left to his heirs, but the reach of his legacy long after his death.

ACKNOWLEDGEMENTS

WHAT BEGAN AS A JOURNEY TO PUBLISHING ONE NOVEL HAS BLOSSOMED into dimensions exceeding my wildest dreams since my pen first touched paper—figuratively speaking, of course. Thanks to you and so many others like you who have read (and reviewed) this second installment of my Shiloh mystery series, I am busy completing Purgatory, A Progeny's Quest which introduces a precocious, teenage girl from Natchitoches, Louisiana to little old Shiloh. All I will confess at this time is it follows the misadventures of a rag-tag band of teenagers during a summer of discovery.

Once again, my grandchildren, Noah, Brannon, Natalie, Eli and Dillon, have provided all the inspiration I have needed to invest the countless, sequestered hours required to put into words what my imagination conjured to write Testament.

My wife Connie continued to serve as my help-mate and confidante and endured countless miles of shared walks while we talked about various characters and plot twists. Without her unswerving encouragement and engagement I would have stopped writing after Sanctuary.

Kari Scare, signed on again as my writing coach and editor. I shall remain forever indebted to her patience, persistence, and at many times, perseverance. Without her tutelage, lil' ol' Shiloh's colorful setting and characters may have remained a menagerie of ideas and images bouncing around in my head. I am pleased to have witnessed how her coaching and editing aspirations have developed since we first partnered up years ago. To know more about her visit karilynnscare.com.

A special shout out goes to my friend G. Ray Sullivan, Jr. His abiding love for Bo, his former canine companion, was captured in Ray's photographic book tribute, Zen and the art of dog walking. The images and tales of Bo became the inspiration for Ringo, the unsung hero of *Testament*. For more info go to graysullivanjr.com.

There are unquestionably many more locales and towns from all my years of travel in the South that I relied upon to create Shiloh. But I would be remiss for not giving a special shout out to Sparta, Camilla, Pelham, Baxley, and of course, my own hometown of Newnan, Georgia for their specific inspiration and contributions to the story.

Finally, but not least of all, I thank God for planting the seed that sprouted into these stories—

Sanctuary, 2017—1st Edition

Sanctuary, A Legacy of Memories, 2018—2nd Edition

Testament, An Unexpected Return, 2018

Purgatory, A Progeny's Quest, 2020

zen
and the art of dog walking

G. Ray Sullivan, Jr.

ABOUT THE AUTHOR

T. M. BROWN, MIKE TO FRIENDS AND FAMILY, EMBRACES HIS GEORGIA HERITAGE, thanks to the paternal branches of his family tree. In Testament, you met Wiley Edwards, and his name was not chosen by chance. Mike's family tree records two patriarchs named Wiley Virgil Brown, his father and grandfather. Both bore enormous influence on Mike throughout his life. However, it wasn't until 2008 after his father passed did he and his siblings learn the full depth of the hard times and sacrifices the Brown family endured, which precipitated their grandfather leaving Georgia during the Depression to find work in Miami. As a child, Mike remembers many warm Sunday afternoons driving past Stone Mountain to visit his Great-Uncle's farm. However, it was not until his father passed away that Mike discovered why his father loved talking about his Uncle Kerry and Aunt Monk and that old farm. During the darkest days of the Depression, Mike's grandfather left the family behind to find work but not before the family got broken up and Mike's dad, the oldest son ended up living with his Uncle and Aunt until the family got relocated to Miami before World War II. Though Snellville's dust-filled red clay backroads have been widened and paved for decades, Mike recalls getting bitten by barb-wire pasture fences, sipping cool well-water from a ladle, and getting scrubbed in a washtub near the front stoop of Uncle Kerry's and Aunt Monk's old farmhouse.

Retired since 2014 from the 9-to-5 life, Mike and his wife Connie reside below Atlanta near Newnan, Georgia. When not writing or traveling for book events and such, Mike and Connie enjoy sharing time with their two sons and their families. Writing about Shiloh has conjured up many near-forgotten memories, and thanks to his Pop and Poppa, he cherishes this truth—"The testament of a man lies not in the magnitude of possessions and property left to his heirs, but the reach of his legacy long after his death."

To learn more visit TMBrownAuthor.com or send an email to info@ TMBrownAuthor.com.

Share Your Thoughts

Want to help make *Testament* a bestselling novel? Consider leaving an honest review of this advance reader copy on Goodreads, on your personal author website or blog, and anywhere else readers go for recommendations. It's our priority at Hearthstone Press to publish books for readers to enjoy, and our authors appreciate and value your feedback.

Our Southern Fried Guarantee

If you wouldn't enthusiastically recommend one of our books with a 4- or 5-star rating to a friend, then the next story is on us. We believe that much in the stories we're telling. Simply email us at pr@sfkmultimedia.com.

Also by Hearthstone Press

Sanctuary: A Legacy of Memories, T. M. Brown
Testament: An Unexpected Return, T. M. Brown
Purgatory: A Progeny's Quest, T. M. Brown
Ariel's Island, Pat McKee
Paper & Ink, Flesh & Blood, Rita May Walston